THREE LETTERS

Josephine Cox was born in Blackburn, one of ten children. At the age of sixteen, Josephine met and married her husband Ken, and had two sons. When the boys started school, she decided to go to college and eventually gained a place at Cambridge University. She was unable to take this up as it would have meant living away from home, but she went into teaching – and started to write her first full-length novel. She won the 'Superwoman of Great Britain' Award, for which her family had secretly entered her, at the same time as her first novel was accepted for publication.

Her strong, gritty stories are taken from the tapestry of life. Josephine says, 'I could never imagine a single day without writing. It's been that way since as far back as I can remember.'

Visit www.josephinecox.co.uk to read her exclusive serial, catch up with her online diary and to find out more information about Josephine.

JOSEPHINE COX

Three Letters

HARPER

Harper
An imprint of HarperCollins*Publishers*
77–85 Fulham Palace Road,
Hammersmith, London W6 8JB

www.harpercollins.co.uk

This paperback edition 2012
1

First published in Great Britain by
HarperCollins 2012

A catalogue record for this book is
available from the British Library

ISBN: 978-0-00-741999-9

Set in ITC New Baskerville by Palimpsest Book Production Limited
Falkirk, Stirlingshire

Printed and bound in Great Britain by
Clays Ltd, St Ives plc

To my darling Ken, as always.

Dear Reader,

It never ceases to amaze and touch me deeply, when I read your wonderful and very honest letters. I hope you can confide in me whenever you feel lonely or sad and, as ever, I will always reply as soon as I can.

For those of you going through a very difficult time, I hope things will be alright and I do understand and listen. For now, my thoughts are with you.

All my love,
Jo x

PART ONE

~

Blackburn – March 1958

Lies

Below is part of the letter that Casey receives from his father.

For Casey

My love will always be with you, son, and
if it's possible, I will be ever by your side,
watching and guiding you. When you're
worried and sad of heart, you might
hear the softest rush of sound about you.
It will be me, come to encourage and
help you.
Be brave, my son. Follow your heart,
and know always that I love you.

CHAPTER ONE

'**R**IGHT, LADS, TIME to finish up.' The foreman's voice echoed through the factory. 'We've all got better things to do than hang round 'ere, so come on, chop chop.'

Grateful to be at the end of another week, the men heard Bill Townsend's instructions and the machines were quickly switched off.

Tormented by his thoughts, Tom Denton had not heard the instructions and he continued to grade the metal parts, as they travelled along the conveyor belt.

'Wake up, lad!' the foreman shouted. 'It's time to go . . . unless yer want to spend the weekend 'ere?'

Tom acknowledged the order with a nod of the head. He switched off the machine, quickly stacked the graded tools into a packing case, then collected his bag.

Hurrying down the gangway, he fell in with the other men; their voices creating an eerie echo as they chattered amongst themselves. Marching towards the door, their heavy boots made a comforting rhythmic sound against the concrete floor.

'I can't wait to get home,' said one, 'I've a meaty hot-pot waiting for me.'

One of the men chuckled. 'A meaty hot-pot, eh? What's

JOSEPHINE COX

that, your wife or your dinner?' His cheeky comment created a roar of laughter amongst his workmates.

Waiting with the men's wage packets, Bill Townsend focused his attention on Tom; a quiet young man in his early thirties. From starting work as an apprentice at the age of fourteen, he had proved himself to be a hard worker, thoroughly reliable and greatly respected by his colleagues. He was also popular, with his kindly nature, and easy smile, even though for the sake of his son, he was made to tolerate a shameful situation at home. A situation which, unbeknown to Tom, was common gossip in the local community.

He had two great loves in his life. One was his music. The other was young Casey, the son he doted on.

He was more than willing to pass the time of day during the short break, especially with his mate, Len, who was the mechanic that kept the machines in top working order, though today, Len was off work having three of his teeth out.

Bill wondered about Tom, having noticed how quiet he had been of late. His smile was not so quick, and his shoulders were hunched, as though carrying the weight of the world.

Having heard the latest gossip in the neighbourhood, Bill had a good idea what was playing on Tom's mind, but it was not for him to interfere and, more importantly, Tom would not thank him for it. As far as he was concerned, any friction between a man and his wife was for them to deal with. Others could mind their own business.

Just then, sensing that he was being watched, Tom looked up to see Bill staring at him. Feeling uncomfortable at having been caught out, Bill gave him a quick smile, and hurriedly returned to his paperwork. 'No doubt that woman has been giving him grief again!' Like everyone else, Bill was aware of the gossip.

6

Tom guessed what was going through Bill's mind, as it must be going through the mind of every man jack on that factory floor. He had long suspected they were aware of his unhappy marital situation. In fact, he was sure the whole of Blackburn must know about his wife's sordid affairs by now.

Whenever he tackled her about seeing other men, she always denied it, but occasionally the evidence betrayed her. A trusted neighbour might tell him; or he might catch a glimpse of her in the street on the arm of some stranger, and once he came home to find a man's wallet lying on the floor of their bedroom.

Like a good and practised liar, she always had answers. After a while, for the sake of peace, Tom pretended to believe her lies, but he had so much bitterness and regret in him, so much pain. There was a time when he had adored her, but his love for Ruth had diminished in the face of her betrayals. For the sake of appearances, and the wellbeing of their son, he had stayed in the belief that it was better for young Casey to be part of a slightly damaged family than not be part of a family at all.

He made himself believe that he must be partly to blame, that somehow he had failed not only Ruth, but himself. In the end, seeing no way out of his impossible dilemma, and unable to right the situation, he left her to her own devices and devoted his life and energy to Casey.

If it hadn't been for his son, Tom would have left his cheating wife long ago, but Casey was the light of his life and at times, his only joy.

Now, though, ironically, his careful reasoning was undermined, because Fate had intervened, driving him in a different and unexpected direction.

As he queued for his wages with the other men, Tom silently dwelt on his life and the way things had turned out. Ruth had been the wrong woman for him, and because of her, he had never taken the chances when they came along. And there had been one or two, the most memorable being a certain occasion when his musical talent might have carried him into the big time. Now that was a dream long gone. His chances of becoming a serious musician were lost for ever. He would never know the joy of playing to audiences far and wide because, like a fool, he had listened to Ruth, and now it was all too late.

Pushing the bad thoughts from his mind, Tom thought of Casey, and a gentle, loving smile washed over his face. That cheeky, darling boy had appeared to inherit his daddy's passion for music, and a quenchless curiosity for knowledge. He wanted to know everything: about music, about life and the way of things in the world.

From the minute he could speak, Casey questioned everything, wanting to know where the sun came from in the morning and where it went at night. He spent hours watching the birds in the back yard, and when they sang he mimicked them and sang back.

In his odd little way, Casey had danced before he could walk, and whenever Tom brought out his guitar to play, Casey would sit on his knee to watch and listen, his face wreathed in amazement while the music filled his soul. Then his mammy would complain about the noise and the music was stopped.

Thinking about that now, Tom realised there were things he was powerless to change, and he was filled with a great sense of sorrow. Now, although it was too late for Tom himself, it was not too late for Casey.

'You all right, Tom?' Ernie Sutton, a workmate, sidled up to him. 'What's up with yer?'

Tom was instantly on his guard. 'Nothing. Why?'

Ernie gave a shrug. 'I were just wondering. I mean . . .

you've been quieter than usual, that's all.' Like the others, he had noticed how Tom had barely spoken a word today. 'A problem shared is a problem halved,' he ventured gently. 'I'm older than you, son, and I've seen a bit of life. I might be able to advise you . . . if you've a problem, that is?'

'I'm not saying I don't have problems,' Tom admitted wryly, '. . . because I do . . . like any other man, I expect. The thing is, Ernie, we all have to deal with them in our own way. Isn't that right?'

'Aye. That's right enough, I dare say.' Ernie thought it best to leave him be. 'Sorry if I overstepped the mark, son. I just wanted to let you know . . . I'm here if you need a friend.'

'You're always a good friend, Ernie, but I'm all right. Really.'

Stepping aside, Ernie felt unsettled. Over the years he had come to know Tom well, and he sensed that there was something playing on the younger fella's mind. Something more than usual, even more than money. None of the men was well off, but Tom was a grafter who provided well for the boy. He even sustained a shameless hussy who flaunted herself at any man who would give her the time of day.

Thinking of Ruth Denton made Ernie grateful for his own wife of twenty years, a fine woman, content with her man. It would never enter her head to go throwing herself about like some cheap tart.

Tom was anxious to collect his wages and get home now. He needed to talk with Ruth, and this time she must listen to what he had to say. Twice before he tried to discuss his concerns, but she was never interested. The last time he had broached the subject, she had just walked away. Tonight, though, because of the latest development, he was determined to say his piece.

He had borne the burden of his secret for too long. Time was running out and the truth must be faced.

'What about you, Tom?'

Tom was startled. 'Sorry, Bill, I wasn't listening. What did you say?'

'I were just saying, it's Friday, and I, for one, am off to the pub for a quick pint.' Bill Townsend was a mountain of a man, with an unhealthy liking for the booze. He was a good foreman and a straight-talking, likeable fellow, but when he got the booze inside him, he could be argumentative, itching to flatten anyone who got in his way. 'Come on, lads! Half an hour at the most,' he persisted. 'You'll not get the chance of a crafty pint, once the wife gets her hands on your wage packet!'

Dishing out the little brown envelopes containing their week's wages, he continued to coax them. 'Look, you can't send me in there on my own. There's no fun in that, is there, eh?'

'It's all right for you, Bill.' John Howard was older, sincere and loyal to his workmates, while good-naturedly grumbling about his wife of many years. 'You don't have a wife who would throw a sulk all weekend just because you had a drink with your mates. You don't know what she's like.'

'That's very true.' With no woman of his own and no responsibilities, big Bill had a twinkle in his eye, and a bigger twinkle in his pants. With his wages tucked safely away, he was looking forward to an hour or so in the pub, where he hoped to enjoy an eyeful of the barmaid's large and attractive assets and, if he was lucky enough, maybe even a romp in the back room afterwards, and not for the first time either.

'At least you've a woman of your own!' he told John. 'There are times when I'd kill for a feisty, jealous woman waiting for me at home. It's a lonely old life on your own.' He shifted his sorry gaze from one man to another. 'Come on, lads, just half an hour of your company, that's all I'm asking.'

John was adamant. 'Not me, Bill. Sorry, but I'm off home to put my feet up, and hopefully pick out a winner or two from the racing page.'

Bill shrugged. 'Suit yourself.' He turned back to Tom, still hoping there might be a possibility that he could help with whatever was troubling him. 'Won't you change your mind, Tom? Join me for a pint or two and a chat, eh?'

Tom was adamant. 'I'm sorry. I really can't . . . not tonight.'

'Why's that then?' Bill gently quizzed him. 'What's so desperate you can't come out with me and the lads for half an hour?'

Tom took a moment to consider his answer. The last thing he needed was a grilling. 'It's not that I'm "desperate" to get home,' he said. 'It's . . . my boy, Casey.' He hated lying. 'I promised I'd take him to the pictures tonight.'

'Oh, I see.' The older man was not fooled, but he went along with Tom's explanation. 'Well, that's reason enough for me, lad! You must keep your promise to the boy.'

Seeing the questioning look in the older man's eyes, Tom knew his lie was found out, and he felt ashamed. 'Another time maybe?'

'Yeah. Another time.' Bill Townsend felt a rush of sympathy. He suspected that Tom's cheating wife had been at her old game again. She made no secret of her liking for other men. And, as if that wasn't enough humiliation for Tom, she had a habit of belittling him in public when, rather than argue in the street, Tom would simply walk away.

'Right then!' Bill quickly shifted his attention to the other men. 'So, there's none of you up for it, eh? Fair enough, I'll go on my own, and sit in the corner like some poor lost soul.'

'Oh, go on then, you've talked me into it.' Will Drayton was a bit of a Jack-the-lad. A family man, at heart, he still believed he had a right to be single whenever it suited him. 'Count me in, boss.'

'Me too!' That was Arnie Sutton. Married with four children, he often rolled home, drunk and violent. Thankfully, his long-suffering wife was a match for him. An hour in the pub would cost him a week of nagging and deprivation in the bedroom. But did he care? Not one jot; because the making-up was well worth the aggravation.

'Count me in!' Jacob Tully was a quiet, unmarried young man, burdened with a dictatorial mother. She thought nothing of thrashing him with the poker, the scars of which he carried on his back. Usually he would not have accepted Townsend's invitation, but tonight he felt the need to fortify himself before walking into the usual war zone at home.

Jacob had long promised himself that one of these fine days he would pack his bag, and walk out of his mother's house for good. Deep down, though, he knew he could never abandon her. For good or bad, Mabel was his mother. Maybe her quick temper was his fault; maybe he wasn't earning enough, or looking after her well. Maybe she was lonely and frightened, needing to vent her frustrations on the only person left in her life since her husband died two years ago. If he left, how would she manage? She had little money, and whenever anyone mentioned her going to work, she panicked, claiming she was too ill, that no one realised how hard it was for her to get through each day.

Jacob was the breadwinner, solely responsible for the bills and upkeep of their home. Each day his mother seemed to lean on him more, and slowly but surely, he had allowed it to happen.

Even now, when he found himself the butt of her vicious temper and spiteful ways, he could not find the heart to desert her. But if he ever did summon up the courage to leave her, where would he go?

As a schoolboy, he had been discouraged from making friends, and later when he'd started dating, his mother always managed to get rid of any girl he brought home.

Now, without real friends or interests, Jacob felt life was passing him by. He deeply regretted that, but life under his mother's rule was impossible to change. He had no idea how he might regain his freedom.

He gave a deep, inward sigh. As Bill Townsend had implied just now, being all alone in the world was a frightening prospect. Sometimes, you were better off with the devil you knew.

Bill Townsend had been pleasantly surprised at Jacob's offer to join him. 'You're sure, are you, lad? I mean . . . as a rule, you're allus in a rush to get home.'

Jacob's uncomfortable existence was a secret from his workmates.

'There's no need for me to rush home. Not tonight anyway,' Jacob answered warily. 'Mum won't be home till late,' he lied. 'She's visiting some old friends in Darwen, and I'm to get my own dinner. To tell you the truth, I'm not much good at peeling spuds and all that, so I might as well enjoy a pint or two in the pub with all of you.' Taking matters into his own hands was a rare and exciting thing. It made him feel proud, like a man should.

Of course his mother would make him pay for this, but just for tonight he didn't care. He knew he would feel the weight of the poker across his back when he rolled home, all the merrier for a few pints, but his back was broad enough to take it, and his spirit all the stronger for having defied her.

'Right then!' Bill's gruff voice rattled across the factory

floor. 'Anybody else? And don't tell me you haven't got a thirst on, because I know better! Surely, the missus won't begrudge you one pint.'

He was greeted with a flurry of excuses.

'Huh! You don't know my missus.'

'I've promised to take mine down to the Lion's Head. There's a darts match on tonight.'

'An' I'm looking forward to my woman's fish pie and chips . . . best you've ever tasted.'

Bill decided they were all cowards of one sort or another. 'Go on then, clear off,' he taunted jokingly. 'Miserable buggers, the lot of you!'

The men collected their wage packets and left one by one, some for home, some to make their way down to the pub.

The last person to collect his wages was Tom Denton.

'What's bothering you, Tom lad?' Bill had promised himself that he wouldn't ask again, but he didn't like seeing Tom so troubled. 'You've not been yourself of late, and today you've been miles away in your thoughts. Is there anything I can do?'

Tom forced a smile. 'Like I said, I promised the boy. And . . . well, I've got things to do, you know how it is.'

That was no lie. And they were important things, too long neglected.

For what seemed an age, the older man studied Tom. He was saddened to see how Tom's ready smile never quite reached his eyes, and how he occasionally glanced towards the door like a man trapped. 'I'm concerned about you,' Bill admitted.

'You've no need to be.'

'Mebbe, mebbe not, but I want you to know . . . if you've got worries gnawing at you, I'd like to help if I can.'

Tom gave a weary little grin. 'Show me a man who

hasn't got worries gnawing at him, but I'm fine. Thanks for your concern.'

'Just remember then, lad, I'm here if you need to talk. You can trust me. I hope you know I'm not a man to blab about other folks' business.'

'I know. But like I say, I'm fine.'

In truth, Tom was desperate to confide in someone – his foreman, his own father – but it would not change the situation. Because they could not help him, however much they might want to.

Thanking Bill once again for his concern, he bade him good night.

When Bill heard the outer door bang shut, he went across to the window and looked out into the rainy street. 'Why, in God's name, do you put up with her, Tom, lad?' he muttered. 'She's a bad lot. You'd be better off without her . . . you and Casey both.' He gave a slow shake of his head. 'If you ask me, it's high time you took your boy, and cleared off out of it!'

He continued to watch as Tom pulled down his flat cap, turned up his coat collar and hurried away.

Bill's mind was still on Tom, as he carried out a tour of the factory, checking that everything was safe and secure. It's a pity he ever met that damned woman, he thought angrily. She's like a bitch on heat, and I for one would never put up with it . . . not for love nor money.'

He glanced out the window, but Tom was long gone. 'He's a decent sort,' he muttered to himself, as he turned off the many lights. 'The lad deserves better.'

Hurrying along the street, Tom was deep in thought. Having carefully examined the situation for the umpteenth time, he was convinced he had made the right decision for everyone concerned. Even so, he felt no satisfaction or joy; only guilt.

He hurried on. When the tears rolled down his face,

he brushed them away. Don't you falter now, Tom, he softly chided himself. You know in your heart there is no other way.

~

'MAM!'

Having run up the stairs, the boy was about to open the bedroom door when he heard his mother yell out, 'Casey, is that you?'

'Yes, Mam.' He tried to open the door but it wouldn't budge. 'The door's stuck.' He gave it another shove but it stayed fast.

'Stop pushing on it!' Ruth yelled back. 'I've locked it. I don't want folks bursting into my room when I'm changing.'

Buxom and shapely, with flowing brown hair, and dark eyes, Ruth Denton was an attractive woman, except for her narrow lips and whiney voice.

'Stop being a damned nuisance,' she warned, 'or you'll feel the back of my hand across yer arse!'

'You said we were having fish and chips tonight. If you give me some money, I'll go and get them.'

'I'll be down in a minute.'

'But it's ten past five. Dad'll be home soon.' He tried the door again, but it wouldn't budge.

'Get away from that door, and wait downstairs. I'll not be long.'

'That's what you always say, and you still take ages.' Putting his back to the door, Casey slid down into a crouched position. Slightly built, with thick brown hair and dark, striking eyes, he had his father's kindly nature. 'Mam?'

'I thought I told you to clear off.'

'Has the man gone?'

'What man?' Panic marbled her voice. 'What are yer talking about? There's no man 'ere!'

'No, I mean just before, when I came up the street, I saw a man at the door. I thought you'd let him in.'

She gave a nervous chuckle. 'Oh, *that* man? O' course I didn't let him in. I sent him packing.'

'Did you? But I never saw him go.' Casey's instincts told him she was lying, and it wouldn't be for the first time.

'Just do as yer told!' Ignoring his comment about 'the man', she softened her voice. 'Go down now, Casey. I'll be there directly with money for the fish an' chips.'

There followed a long pause, causing her to believe he'd gone.

'Little sod! He's eight years old, going on eighty!' Snuggling up to the man's naked body, Ruth ran her fingers down his neck. 'I were counting on the two of us having a good hour together, and now he's gone and ruined it.'

The man reached out and tweaked her erect nipple. 'Aw, well,' he sighed, 'next time, mebbe. When the brat's at school.'

'MAM!'

'For pity's sake, I told yer to go downstairs!'

'Who are you talking to?'

'Nobody!'

'I thought I heard somebody.'

'Well, that were probably me, talking to myself, like a crazy woman. It's *you* that sends me crazy, allus hanging about, spying on me at every turn. Do like I say and sod off downstairs.'

'There's nothing to do.'

'Well . . . *find* summat to do. Clean your dad's guitar, if you want. Just busy yerself till I come down.'

'But I need you to come down now. I need to get the fish and chips. Dad'll be hungry.'

'By, yer a persistent little git, aren't yer, eh?' Grabbing her shoe from the floor, she threw it at the door, where it landed with a thump. 'I'll not tell you again! Just get off out of it. D'you hear me?'

'Can I really clean Dad's guitar?'

She hesitated. 'Well, yeah . . . I expect so.' She knew how much that guitar meant to Tom. His own father had taught him to play it when he was even younger than Casey was now.

Some years ago, when his father contracted arthritis in his fingers and couldn't play it any more, he handed the guitar down to Tom.

'Take good care of it, lad,' Tom had told her many times of what his father had said, 'When you play, you must open your heart to its magic. Listen to what it tells you, and you'll be repaid tenfold.'

On teaching his own son how to play it, Tom told Casey of his grandfather's words, and Casey had never forgotten them.

He recalled them now. 'Mam, I'll go downstairs, but if I polish the guitar, can I play it afterwards . . . please?'

'YES! I don't give a bugger *what* you do with the thing. So long as yer don't keep botherin' me. It doesn't make money, and it doesn't put food on the table, and sometimes when your father's down there playing till all hours, we can none of us get any sleep. That blessed guitar is for neither use nor ornament. As far as I'm concerned, yer can tek it to the pop-shop. Tell old Foggarty he can have it for a few quid.'

The boy was shocked to his roots. 'You can't say that! It's Dad's guitar, not yours!'

When there was no response, he waited a moment, pressing his ear to the door. He thought he heard someone sniggering, and it didn't sound like his mam. Now, though, in the ensuing silence, he wasn't so sure.

'You won't be long before you come down, will you, Mam?'

He was greeted with silence.

'I'm going down now, Mam, but I need to go to the chip shop. All right?'

The silence thickened.

'MAM!' He couldn't get her suggestion out of his mind. 'You wouldn't really take Dad's guitar to Foggarty's, would you?'

'I bloody would! *I'll tek you, an' all, if you don't get away from that door!*' The impact of a second object being hurled at the door made Casey back off.

Concerned by her threat to sell his dad's guitar to old Foggarty, he kicked the door with the toe of his shoe, and ran off down the stairs. A smile crept across his face at the idea of playing his dad's guitar. Then he thought of his mother, and the smile fell away.

Deep down, he knew his mam had no love for his dad, and that was not fair, because he worked hard to give her everything; to give them *both* everything.

He recalled the man he had seen outside the door. He couldn't help but wonder if the man really had been allowed inside the house. But if that was true, where was he now?

When the dark suspicions crept into his thoughts, he thrust them away and concentrated on the idea of playing his dad's guitar. He remembered everything he'd been taught, and now he went through it all in his mind. When he played the guitar, the music was in his head and in his heart. When Casey listened to his own music, he felt incredibly happy, happier than at any other time. It was magic, feeling the smooth wood, warm and alive, against him. When he moved his fingers along the strings and the guitar began to sing, it was so hauntingly beautiful, it made him want to cry.

He had told his dad how he felt, and his dad explained, 'That's because the guitar is speaking to you, bringing your senses alive. Music is an age-old language. It speaks to everyone, young and old. It lifts the spirit and touches the heart, and when it stops it lives on inside you, making you richer in mind and spirit.'

Casey understood. Daddy made it all so easy to understand. He adored his dad, but sometimes he didn't like his mam. She shouted a lot, and she told lies. Just now, she said he could play the guitar, but only because she wanted him to go away. But why did she want him to go away? Why couldn't she just come down and give him the fish-and-chip money?

At the back of his mind, he knew why, but it was such an awful thing, he didn't even want to think about it.

Instead he made himself think of playing the guitar, and he was filled with such excitement, he could hardly breathe.

He now ran into the front parlour and closed the door behind him. He was happy in here, especially when he was allowed to play the guitar. Mam could shout and scream all she liked, but he wouldn't listen.

~

'We're rid of him at last.' Lying across Len's nakedness, Ruth tantalised him, licking his mouth with the tip of her tongue. 'We'd best be quick, Len!' With the minutes swiftly passing, she was growing nervous.

'Stop panicking. There's time enough.' He was enjoying the foreplay.

'There isn't time,' she whispered. 'We can't have Tom finding us naked in his bedroom. Can you imagine the ructions if he found his wife and best mate wrestling about in his bed?'

Hearing a noise outside the bedroom, she sat back on her haunches. 'Ssh! What was that?' She glanced nervously towards the door. 'If we're not careful, he'll be bursting in here, any minute.'

She had no real affection for Tom. He was not an exciting man, while she was a woman who positively thrived on excitement. She liked the thrill of the chase, and she enjoyed the attention of other men, even though she knew they were only after one thing – which they got in abundance, and paid for in ready cash. Steady, affable Tom hardly ever made demands on her, but that was his loss, not hers.

The thing was, she liked her men feisty, willing to take risks and grab life by the horns. Tom was not like that. He was, however, a good provider, and an excellent father to Casey, while she had no time for the brat. If it hadn't been for Tom looking after his wellbeing, Casey would be left to his own devices.

Thankfully, Tom was always there for Casey, and the boy idolised him. They each had the same interests, in music and football, and in creative things. They had made a den in the cellar, every wall painted a different colour and every square inch of the ceiling carefully pinned with cut-out pictures of aeroplanes all heading the same way, as though in a mass exodus.

They spent precious time together down there, talking music, playing the guitar, making the cellar into a wonderland.

Whenever they tried to include her, she didn't want to know. The one time Tom and Casey managed to persuade her down to the cellar, she ridiculed their efforts and couldn't get out quick enough.

Ruth realised her jealousy of the happy childhood Tom was trying to provide for Casey was because of her own impoverished childhood.

Still, Tom was a good father to Casey, and when some

years ago she had been in a desperate situation, Tom had unwittingly proved to be a godsend.

Thinking of Tom now, she smiled to herself. If only he knew what she was doing right now. And who with. Oh, but it would give her so much pleasure to shock him with the truth. But what if the truth damaged her more than it damaged him? Still, the thought of Tom walking in on her and Len gave her a shiver of wicked delight.

'What are you smiling about?' Reaching up, Len grabbed her by the buttocks and roughly drew her closer to him. Unlike Len, Tom had never been, nor ever would be, man enough for her.

'I'm smiling at you . . .' She answered, 'at the pair of us being together like this.'

'Hmm . . .' Also aware that Tom could burst in at any minute, Len concentrated on the matter in hand, while Ruth's devious mind inevitably strayed back to Tom.

In all the years she'd known him, Tom had never done her wrong, and she believed he never would. But if it was not for her shady sideline she felt her life would be unbearable. Even so, she was happy in the knowledge that when she grew unattractive, and the men who excited her were gone, Tom would still be there to provide for her.

Right now, though, she gave herself freely to the men who used her yet had no real feelings for her. Len in particular could take her to dizzy heights, the like of which she had never experienced with her undemanding husband.

'Ssh! Did you hear that? It sounds like there's somebody out there.'

'There's nobody out there. It's the birds on the roof, or summat. Or it's the kid playing games to wind yer up. Yeah, that'll be it. If yer ask me, that lad o' yours wants keeping in check! If 'e were mine I'd give 'im a right slap. Irritating little bastard.'

'Hey!' she giggled. 'If you're itching to slap somebody, why don't you slap me?' Grabbing his hand from her breast, she clamped it over her buttocks.

He liked that. 'Yer a wicked bitch, Ruth Denton, a woman who'd sell herself for a shilling.' He sniggered. 'If Tom ever upped and left, I wouldn't be surprised if you flogged the kid to the highest bidder.'

She chuckled. 'It wouldn't bother me to be rid of the brat,' she confessed. 'Come to think of it, old Foggarty might pay me more for him than he'd pay for that damned guitar!' She gave a low, throaty cackle. 'I'm sure the old devil would find a good use for the boy . . . one way or another.' Sometimes the nastiness in her took even her by surprise.

Rolling her over, Len climbed on top, biting and caressing her neck and giving of himself in such a way that the passion became too strong for him to hold back.

Afterwards, when he rolled away from her, he told her, 'Yer a bad example to women, you are. In times past, you'd 'ave been tarred and feathered. To tell the truth, I don't know how poor Tom puts up with yer.'

He meant it too. Having worked alongside Tom for a good many years, he knew what a decent sort he was. He even felt a pang of guilt.

Ruth gave him a playful slap. 'Hey! What's all this about "poor Tom"? Forget him! All I need to know is . . . did you get yer money's worth?'

His answer was to grab her about the waist and roughly draw her to him. 'You certainly know how to please a man,' he admitted. 'Matter o' fact, I might even go for another helping. What d'yer say, eh?'

'It'll cost yer.' She giggled, snaking her arms round his neck.

~

Headed home, Tom was deep in thought, his face dampened by the drizzle and his mind alive with thoughts of what he'd decided.

It was a moment before he realised that he'd actually walked right past the bus stop. Turning to go back, he was dismayed to see the bus had already set off. 'Dammit!' That would put another half-hour onto the journey home.

No matter. At least he now had more time to think, and to plan. There must be no regrets, and he must make sure that the boy was safe. That, above all else, was the important thing.

When the slight rainfall became a real downpour, he quickened his steps through the town to King Street, where he saw the queue in the fish-and-chip shop. When the aroma drifted towards him, his stomach began rumbling.

I wonder if Ruth's cooked us a meal, he thought, quickening his pace towards the lights of the chip shop. I bet she hasn't. I bet our Casey's not been fed . . . again.

Countless times he'd got home to find that Ruth was out and Casey was searching the cupboard for food. Keeping house and seeing to the boy's welfare were never his wife's priorities.

He ducked into the fish-and-chip shop. When his turn came, he ordered, 'Fish and chips three times, please.'

'Got caught out in the rain, did yer?' The woman had a round, rosy face and a kindly voice, much like his own mother, who had died shortly before he'd married Ruth. Suddenly, Tom wondered if his mother, looking down, would be ashamed at his plans. He truly hoped not.

He forced a smile. 'The rain's coming down hard,' he remarked. 'I reckon it'll settle in for the night now.' He found it amazing how he could converse so casually about something and nothing, when he was intent on a deed so dark and drastic that lives would be changed for ever.

The woman dished the food into the paper bags. 'D'yer want salt and vinegar, young man?'

'Yeah . . . go on then, but not too much, eh?'

'Have yer far to go wi' these?'

'Only to Henry Street.'

'Hmm! That's still a good long stride an' no mistake.' She regarded him with interest. Seeing how wet he was, and how sad he seemed, she suggested, 'You go and sit yersel' in that chair over by the window. I'll put these on the fryer to keep warm, then I'll mek yer a pot o' tea . . . no charge, mind. It's on the house.'

'I need to get back,' Tom explained graciously. 'I missed my bus so I've had to walk, but I'm almost home now. Fifteen minutes and I'll be in the warm. Thank you all the same.'

She was genuinely disappointed. 'Aye, well, I expect you're eager to get home to yer good woman, eh?'

Tom gave a wry little smile. 'Something like that, yes.' He wished Ruth could realise how she had damaged his love by her rejection of Casey, together with her infidelity to himself.

Often it felt to Tom that there were only two people in the whole world that mattered to him now. They were his father, Bob, and his son, Casey; and may God forgive him, for he was about to hurt them badly.

'There you are, son.' The kindly woman tapped him on the shoulder.

'Oh!' Tom apologised, 'Sorry, I was miles away.'

'Are you all right?' She'd seen the faraway look in his eyes and, being a mother herself, she suspected he was unhappy. 'A trouble shared is a trouble halved,' she said quietly. 'I've a son about your age, and I know how some things can get you down.' She smiled. 'Money worries, is it?'

'No, we manage well enough, I reckon,' Tom assured her.

'Oh, well then, it'll be woman trouble,' she tutted. 'It's allus woman trouble . . . at least with my son it is. She's already left him twice and come back with her tail between her legs. I tell him straight, you'd be better off without her, but he never listens—'

She would have ranted on, but Tom interrupted, 'No, it's not woman trouble, but thanks for your interest.' She meant well, he thought, but from what she was saying, it sounded as though she might have troubles of her own.

'Right then!' She handed him the bag of food. 'I've double-wrapped them in newspaper so they should still be nice and hot by the time yer get home.'

Wishing her well, Tom opened his wage packet, settled the bill, and left.

He knew Ruth would not be too pleased about him dipping into the wage packet. No doubt she would launch into one of her tantrums.

Besides, he had no intention of being drawn into an argument, especially not tonight of all nights, when he had other pressing matters on his mind.

With the three meals bagged up and tucked under his coat to keep warm, he quickened his pace towards home. The sooner it's done, the better, he told himself. There's no turning back. Not now. Not ever.

It wasn't long before he was approaching Henry Street.

As he crossed the little Blakewater bridge, he paused, holding the meals safe with one hand, while with the other, he frantically searched his coat pockets for the front door key.

Still digging about in his pockets, determined to find the key, he set off again. By this time, he was only minutes away from his front door.

The closer he got to the house, the more he despaired at the thought of what he must do, and how it would devastate those he loved.

Oh, Tom, have you really thought it through? Not for the first time he questioned himself. You must know what it will do to that lad o' yours?

Momentarily distraught, he leaned against the wall, his eyes closed and his heart heavy. It's a terrible thing you're planning, Tom, he admitted . . . a terrible, sinful thing.

Raising his gaze to the skies, he asked softly, 'Please, Lord, don't punish the boy for my bad actions. Look after him, Lord. Don't let him come to any harm.' When the tears threatened, he took a deep breath and continued on; his pace now slow and laboured. But his determination remained unswerving.

Nothing, not his crippling sense of guilt nor the deep concern he felt for his father, nor even his complete devotion to the boy, could change his mind. Not when the alternative could prove to be even more painful. Not when he knew that whichever road he took, all would be lost anyway.

~

Upstairs, Tom's wife and the trusted workmate were parting company.

'Ssh!'

While the man frantically dressed, Ruth ran onto the landing and listened. Nervous, she fled back into the bedroom. 'There's somebody outside the front door. You'd best be quick!'

She grabbed the money he was offering, then took him by the arm and led him quickly and silently onto the landing, where she peered down.

'It's all clear . . . hurry!' She ran him down the stairs. 'Go out the back way.' Keeping one wary eye on the front door, she hissed, 'Through the scullery and out, along the ginnel. Be quick, dammit!' She shoved Len towards the back rooms.

Relieved to hear that Tom was chatting with someone outside the front door, she fled swiftly back up the stairs and into the bedroom where, breathless and excited, she hid her shameful earnings in a purpose-made slit in the hem of the curtain linings.

She then went to the mirror, where she wiped away the heavy make-up and tidied her hair.

On checking herself in the mirror, she wagged a finger at the reflected image. 'One o' these days, my girl, if yer not careful, you'll be caught out, sure as eggs are eggs!' The thought of her conquest fleeing through the alley-ways with his underpants on back to front and his trouser-belt dangling, had her stifling a giggle.

Outside, Tom bade the neighbour good night. 'Mind how you go, Mick, lad.' The amiable old man was away to get his regular pint of ale at the local. He was often too early, but the landlord always let him in, and no one ever complained. Even the local bobby looked the other way.

Impatient, Tom struggled with the fish and chips, finally found his key, and slid the key in the lock. Just then, out the corner of his eye, he thought he saw someone running out of the ginnel some way down the street. For a split second he thought he recognised the figure. But it was dark, the man was quickly gone from sight, and now he was not altogether certain.

Tom shook his head, No . . . it couldn't be Len, he thought. What in God's name would he be doing running out of a ginnel, and here of all places? Besides, as I recall, he sent word to the foreman, to say he was having some teeth taken out.

Looking again at the shadowy place where the figure had disappeared, a niggling thought crossed his mind.

Then he glanced up at the front bedroom, where the light was on. 'No . . .' He dared not allow himself to believe what was running through his mind: the shocking idea of his wife and Len . . . up there in his own bed. All the same, he knew from experience that it was not an impossibility. Don't be so bloody stupid! Len's a good mate! he angrily dispatched the wicked idea from his mind.

But the seed was sown. Maybe it really was Len running out of the ginnel. 'You're wrong.' he muttered angrily. 'Take a grip of yourself, man!'

Opening the door, he entered the house, and called out his son's name. 'Casey! Casey, where are you?'

When there was no answer he closed the door, went down the passage and called up the stairs, 'Ruth, I'm home.'

Ruth came rushing from the parlour, where she'd been congratulating herself on her conquest of Len, and her quick wit in covering her tracks. But then she'd had enough practice over the years.

Tom was surprised to see her coming from the direction of the back room. 'I thought you were upstairs.'

'Really? Well, now you can see I'm not.'

'Did you know the lights are on up there?'

She feigned surprise. 'Oh, are they? Well, yes, I was up there changing the beds, but I came rushing down when I heard you at the door.'

Cursing herself for leaving the lights on, she wisely changed the subject. 'Anyway, you're late! Where've you been?' Keeping a distance, she groaned, 'The tea isn't ready yet, but I've been up to my neck in ironing, and I've been catching up on a multitude of things.'

Tom was not surprised. 'So there's no tea ready, then?'

'Like I said, I've been that busy I haven't even had time to go to the butcher's and get the sausages I planned for your meal.'

Eager to vindicate herself she began to whine, 'You've no idea of the time it takes to run a house.' She held out her hand. 'Oh, and I'll need some money if I'm going to buy some food from the corner shop. You go and talk to Casey.' She stretched out her hand, 'come on then!' waiting.

'Where's Casey?' Normally, the boy would be at the door, looking for his dad.

'He's in the front parlour. He said something about cleaning your guitar.'

At that moment, soft musical tones emanated from the front parlour.

'Well! The little sod!' Ruth said angrily. 'I warned him not to play the guitar, but you know what he's like . . . doesn't listen to a damned word I say.'

Oblivious to the fact that Tom was standing in wet clothes, she screeched at him, 'Did you not hear what I said? If I'm going to the corner shop, I'll need money.'

'For pity's sake, woman, let me catch my breath, will you!' Not once had she asked how his day had been, or noticed that he was wet to the marrow. 'I need to dry myself off . . .'

'Oh, yes . . . you're soaked, aren't you!' Stepping back a pace, she feigned concern. 'You'd best dry yourself on the towel in the kitchen, while I go to the shop.' She thrust her open palm beneath his face. 'I'm waiting! The quicker you give me some money, the quicker I'll be back.'

When she leaned forward to collect the little brown packet containing his wages, Tom could smell the other man on her; the thick tobacco odour that clung to her skin and lingered in her hair. Ruth smoked Woodbines, while it seemed this man rolled a stronger brand of tobacco.

The image of the man running from the ginnel raised a suspicion in his mind. He knew Len smoked roll-ups.

Was it possible that he and Ruth had . . . No! It was too loathsome to imagine. Besides, any number of men smoked roll-ups.

He knew his wife had been with a man, though. The telltale tobacco odour had a woody smell, while her Woodbines were much sweeter. Over the years, Tom had learned to tell the difference.

With her wanton ways and devious nature, she had caused him a deal of misery, but now it no longer mattered. Now he had a plan. Whatever happened, Ruth was a survivor and would come through. It was young Casey he worried about, and to that end he had made contingencies.

Reaching into his coat, he took out the bag of fish and chips and handed it to her.

'What's this?' She sniffed. 'Fish and chips!' Her face fell. 'Don't tell me you've spent good money on fish and bloody chips? Especially when I'd already planned sausage and mash. But, oh no! You had to take matters into your own hands, didn't you, eh?'

Tom ignored her goading. 'You just said yourself, you haven't got the meal ready, so now you don't have to bother, do you?' Giving her a way out for not cooking a meal was becoming a regular occurrence.

He handed her the open wage packet. 'There you are. Count it, if you like, while I go and put these out on plates before they get too cold to eat.'

'Hey!' She caught him by the arm. 'You seem to forget, there are bills to be paid and I need to get your trousers out of Foggarty's pawn shop. What you've given me is not enough. Oh, and while we're at it, your son needs new shoes. How he wears 'em out so quick, I never will know!'

But with his troubling thoughts elsewhere, Tom was not listening.

'Hey! I'm talking to you. What's wrong with yer?' Tom

seemed too calm to her, too quick to back away from her attempt at an argument.

He looked up. 'There's nothing wrong with me except I'm starving. And, no doubt, so is Casey. And, as I recall, it wouldn't be for the first time.'

'Don't you dare have a go at me!' Ruth snapped. 'I've already told you . . . I had a pile of ironing and other stuff to see to. Then some man came to the door, looking to sell me some rubbish. I got rid of him, though. Ask Casey, I'm sure he'll tell you.' She knew he would, and her idea was to get in first. '. . . And another thing, I'm really surprised at you opening your wage packet. You never do that as a rule.'

Tom looked her in the eye for what seemed an age. He wanted to tell her so many things. He needed to share his troubling thoughts, but she was not a woman to care one way or the other, so instead he answered in a quiet voice, 'You're right. I don't open my wages as a rule, but sometimes, we need to break the rules, don't we?'

Her face reddened with guilt. 'That's a strange thing for you to say.' There was something really different about him tonight, she thought . . . something worrying. 'Are you sure you're all right?'

She couldn't help but wonder if he'd found out that she was having a fling with Len. She nervously toyed with the idea that he might be saving the confrontation for later; possibly after Casey had gone to bed.

'Course I'm all right.'

Tom threw off his coat, hung it on the back of the chair, and went into the scullery. He was surprised to see the back door wide open, and the rain coming in.

'What's going on, Ruth?' There it was again, that niggling suspicion.

Panicked, she stuffed the wage packet into her pocket. 'What d'you mean? There's nothing "going on".'

'It's raining, and the back door's wide open.'

'Oh, I see.' Greatly relieved, she gave the first answer that came to mind. 'I forgot to shut it after I came up from the yard . . .'

'I thought you said you'd been changing the beds?' Now he was in no doubt she was up to her old tricks again. She had been entertaining a man and, by the looks of it, he must have left in a hurry. Tom recalled the figure he'd seen running from the ginnel. He hoped the man was not Len, because that would be humiliation twice over.

Smiling sweetly, Ruth explained, 'I changed the beds earlier, and then I remembered I'd left the back gate open. I was running in from the rain, and didn't remember to shut the door behind me. Besides, Casey was yelling for me.'

Closing the door, she made a show of sympathy. 'Aw, Tom! Just look at the state of you. Come 'ere . . . I'd best tend to you before I go.' She lifted the towel from the rail and tenderly ran it through his wet hair, then over his hands and face. 'That's better. Now then, husband, you'd better fetch Casey while I put the fish and chips out. There's nothing so urgent from the corner shop that it won't wait till tomorrow.'

In truth, she felt too exhausted to go traipsing all the way down the street. That Len was too energetic and demanding for his own good, she mused with a sly little smile.

When Tom took the towel from her, she felt pleased with herself at having duped him yet again. 'I'm sorry about not having the meal ready.' Leaning forward, she brushed his face with a fleeting kiss.

Tom could not forget the figure running from the ginnel, and even now the thick aroma of rolled tobacco lingered on her.

When she pecked him on the cheek he simply nodded and moved away. Just now, the touch of her hands was repugnant to him. Making his way out of the scullery, he slung the wet towel into the laundry bin as he went.

As Tom headed for the front parlour, he could hear Ruth loudly complained, 'I already had sausage and mash planned and now, what with you spending money on fish and chips, I've no idea how I'll stretch it for the bills and everything.'

He called back, 'You forget, I did that overtime. So you'll manage. There's more than enough money to pay the bills and get Casey's new shoes. As for my trousers, you needn't bother.'

He was convinced that she and Len had lain together, but he thrust the ugly suspicion aside andwith a quieter heart he quickened his steps.

Life could be very cruel, as he had recently learned only too well, and there was much to be afraid of. But this evening he could spend precious time with his son, and that was all he cared about.

For now.

CHAPTER TWO

OUTSIDE THE FRONT-ROOM Tom paused to listen. Casey had the heart and fingers of a true musician. His technique was not yet perfect, but his artistry was enchanting.

Leaning on the door jamb, his face suffused with pride, Tom murmured as though to the boy, 'You do your daddy proud, my son. You're not quite there with the chords, but it's only a matter of time. More importantly, you've got a magic that can never be taught. And that's what really counts.'

His eyes filled with tears. He despised what he must do. Time and again, he had tried desperately to think of an alternative, but there was none. So now he was resigned; impatient, even, to do the awful deed.

When the music stopped, Tom took a deep breath and gently pushed open the parlour door. 'That was wonderful,' he told the boy. 'I've no doubt that one day you'll make a fine musician.'

Happy to see his father, Casey put aside the guitar and ran to meet him, laughing out loud when Tom swung him in the air before hugging him close.

In that precious moment, with his son close to him,

Tom almost lost sight of the path he had chosen. But nothing he could do or say would change what was already set in motion.

'Was I really good?' Casey asked when Tom set him down. 'I asked Mam if I could play the guitar and she said yes. You're not cross with me, are you?'

Faking a frown, Tom spoke sternly. 'I should think so! Coming in here, playing my guitar without so much as a by-your-leave! Yes, of course, you're in trouble. After we've eaten, you're to wash all the dishes, and when that's done, you'll set about scrubbing the floor till I can see my face in it. After that, the back yard needs sweeping . . .'

Casey broke into a grin, and then both he and Tom were laughing out loud. 'I knew you didn't mean it,' Casey giggled. 'I knew you were only playing. Was I good, though, Daddy?' he persisted. 'Did I really play well?'

'You did, yes. You've still a lot to learn, but you're getting there, and I'm proud of you. Matter o' fact, you've taken to the guitar like you were born to it.' He ruffled the boy's thick, brown hair. 'Y'know what, son?'

'What?' As always, Casey hung on his every word.

'Well, for what it's worth, I reckon . . .' Tom paused, wondering how to put it, '. . . yeah, I reckon the angels must have smiled on you.'

'Really?' Casey wasn't sure what to make of his daddy's comment, but he thought it might be a good thing.

'Yes, really.' Tom looked him in the eye, his voice low and meaningful. 'I'll tell you something . . .' Then he thought of what he was about to do, and how it would affect this darling boy, and he was racked with pain.

Impatient, Casey caught his attention. 'Go on then . . . what were you going to tell me?'

'Listen to me, son. You must never forget what I'm about to say. I need you to think about it, and believe it. And when you think about it, I want you to keep it in your heart. Can you do that for me, Casey?'

Intrigued and excited, Casey promised. So Tom told him. 'First of all, I'm very proud of you, Casey. You're a wonderful son, and I love you so very much.'

'I love you too, Daddy.'

Tom smiled. 'Would you like to know something else?'

'Yes, please.'

'Well, then. From the first day you came struggling into the world, I always believed that the angels had smiled on you. Y'see, when the angels smile on someone who they think is extra special, they also sprinkle a little bit of magic.'

The boy was mesmerised. 'Do they? Do they really?'

'Oh, yes. But they don't always smile on everyone.'

'Well, I don't think they smiled on my teacher, because he shouts and he never laughs, and when the bell goes for playtime, he throws us out in a heap.'

Tom chuckled. 'I expect that's because the poor man's had enough of you by playtime, eh?'

'Did the angels smile on you, Daddy?'

Tom thought about that. 'I reckon they did,' he answered solemnly. 'Not because they thought I was anything special, but because they gave me an important assignment. Y'see, they wanted me to take care of you. And I'm very happy with that.'

'So, how did the angels smile on *me*, Daddy?'

'Oh, that's easy.' Tom felt a mingling of joy and great sadness. 'When you pick up that guitar and make music, it's a beautiful thing to hear. You're one of the few people who can touch the heart and lift the soul.'

He cast his mind back to his own childhood. 'When I was your age, my daddy – your granddad Bob – taught me to play the guitar. I learned quickly and, just like you, I really loved it. But I could never make the guitar sing quite like you do. I could make people listen and I enjoyed it, but you, Casey, you *live* it. You're part of the guitar and together you create a magic all of your own. Believe it or not, there are very few people who can do that. You see, Casey,' he tapped his chest, 'when you play, the music comes from deep down inside of you. Something amazing happens, because you have a way of reaching people . . . of touching them with your music. You make them happy and sad, and uplifted all at the same time. Tell me, son, is that how *you* feel when you play?'

'Yes.'

'So, you understand what I'm saying then?'

'I think so, Daddy.' Up to now, he had never told anyone how he felt when he played the guitar. 'When Granddad Bob plays, it makes me sad, and I want to cry. Then I feel happy and I want to laugh out loud. I want him to play for ever, because it's . . .' Lost for words, he fell quiet for a moment, '. . . Granddad must have the magic, eh?'

Tom smiled. 'Yes, son. And after the angels had sprinkled the magic on Granddad, they saved some of it for you. The thing is, Casey, you've been blessed with a gift that can never be taught.'

'Does Granddad Bob think the same?'

'I don't know; he's never said, but though you've each been given a gift and you play with the same passion, there is a difference between you and Granddad. You see, Granddad Bob never had ambitions to play big halls or travel the world. I would have liked to, but it didn't work out. But you will. One day, when you're ready, you'll take your music to the people, and however long you play for them, they will always want more.'

'What? Y'mean like when they asked me to play for the Scouts' party, and they wanted me to play again?'

Tom chuckled. 'Well, yes . . . sort of. Only, I'm talking huge halls, like the size of the Ritz picture house, with hundreds of people listening to you play, and afterwards they'll clap so loud the rafters will shake.'

'Oh!' In his mind, the boy conjured up a frightening image. 'That's too scary!'

'All right then, maybe the rafters won't shake,' Tom reassured him, 'but when the people stand up, clapping and shouting, everyone will hear, and then your name will be known across the world. "Casey Denton," they'll say, "oh, but he's got the magic."'

Afraid and excited and all at once lost for words, the boy didn't know what to say. What his daddy told him just now, was overwhelming. He could not begin to take it in.

Bringing the exchange to a close, Tom remembered Casey would be hungry. 'Come on, son. It's time to put the guitar away.'

A few minutes later, after the guitar was safely replaced in its cubbyhole, Tom took his son by the hand. 'Now that we've set the world to rights, I reckon it's time we got summat to eat, don't you?'

He could see how Casey had been astonished by his vision of the future, while he himself had never been in any doubt as to his son's musical talents. From Casey's first attempt at playing the guitar, Tom had been convinced that one day his boy would make his mark in the music world.

Casey had been mulling his daddy's words over in his mind. 'If they ask me to visit different places away from here, you will come with me, won't you?'

'If it's possible, I'll be with you always. Everywhere you go,' Tom answered cagily. He gave Casey a gentle warning. 'I'm not saying success will be handed to you on a plate. Oh, no! In this world, if you give nothing out, you get nothing back. That's the way it is, but if you work hard and stick at it, I can honestly promise that, in time, you'll play the guitar better than I ever did; and, dare I say it, better, even, than your granddad Bob.'

The boy caught his breath. 'I'll never be as good as you and Granddad. Never!'

Pausing outside the parlour door, Tom stooped down and, gently wrapping his work-worn hands about the boy's face, he gave a quiet, knowing smile. 'We'll just have to wait and see, won't we, son?'

'You'll help me, though, won't you, Daddy?'

'Haven't I already helped you?' He hoped so. Oh, he did hope so. Brightening his smile, he announced jovially, 'My stomach's playing a tune of its own, so now can we kindly go in search o' them fish and chips?'

Ruth was just putting out a pot of tea and various condiments.

'It'll be your own fault if the food's gone cold!' she snapped. 'What the devil 'ave you been up to?'

'Daddy's been listening to me play the guitar,' Casey announced proudly. 'When we've finished our tea, will you come and listen, please, Mam?'

'I haven't got time!' Taking a piece of bread and butter, she took a huge bite and, still chewing, she told him angrily, 'I've told you before, I've got more to do than listen to you making a row on that damned guitar!'

She felt peeved. The brat had spoiled her fun with Len, and then Tom had taken it on himself to open his wage packet. It was clear that the pair of them were getting above themselves, and she was determined to nip that in the bud.

'Please, Mam?' Casey reminded her. 'You *never* listen to me play.'

'That's because I've got better things to do.' Angrily slicing a fleshy chunk from the fish-belly, she stabbed it with her fork and rammed it into her mouth. 'You're getting above yourself, my boy!' A flake of fish escaped down her chin and she angrily wiped it away. 'What right had you to play that guitar? Especially after I warned you not to?' She was determined to stir up trouble between father and son. They were always cosying up together over the wretched guitar.

40

Shocked at her blatant lie, Casey again reminded her, 'You said I could play it.' He turned to his father. 'Honestly, Daddy, I would never play your guitar without asking. Mam said it would be all right.' Close to tears, he appealed to his mother. 'Tell him, Mam . . . please?'

'You're a wicked little liar!' Leaning towards him, she raised her hand, but when Tom fastened her with a hardened look, she dropped it and began viciously hacking at the fish. 'I might have known you'd believe him against me,' she ranted. 'I'm telling you, I never said he could play it. I told him he could clean it, and that was all!'

Fixing Casey in a direct glare, she warned, 'Don't you dare make me out to be the bad one! You'd best own up and shame the devil. Go on, own up to what you did!' She envied their close relationship, and it gave her a sense of achievement when she was able to come between them.

'It doesn't really matter,' Tom intervened. 'Stop bullying the boy, Ruth!' He knew she was the one who was lying; he could see it in her face.

'So, I'm "bullying" him, am I?' Slamming down her knife and fork, she glared at Tom. 'He's calling me a liar, and you're doing sod-all about it! That boy is turning out to be a bad 'un, but you just can't see it, can you?'

'Honestly, Daddy, I'm telling you the truth,' Casey sobbed. 'I would never play your guitar without asking. I went to the bedroom and asked if I could clean the guitar. But Mam got angry, and told me to go away.' Something else came into his mind. 'She didn't want me outside her bedroom door. She said I could sell your guitar to old Foggarty . . .' He paused, remembering. 'She told me to go away . . . that she was busy . . .' He began to falter. 'I heard something else, I mean . . . I think I heard.'

A hostile glance from Ruth was enough to put him on his guard, but then fear became anger. 'It's Mam who's telling lies. Not me!'

Believing enough had been said, Tom soothed the boy. 'That's enough, Casey. Eat your tea now. It doesn't matter if you did play the guitar without asking, because I would have said yes anyway. But, if you like, we can talk about this later, eh?' He gave a little smile. 'All right, son?'

The boy gave a nod. His mam did things that worried him. There had been other times when he'd thought she had someone in her bedroom. He wondered if he should tell the whole truth: how this very afternoon, he thought he'd heard her talking to someone there. And what about the man she said she'd sent away?

Casey suspected she had not sent the man away at all, yet he fretted about telling, because he didn't want to cause another argument. His troubled young heart urged him to confide in his daddy about men sneaking in and out of the house, and voices whispering in her bedroom. One time there was money lying on her bed after she'd had a visitor. That made him curious. It puzzled him, but he never said anything about it.

Casey knew his mother was doing bad things, and his every instinct told him to speak out. But common sense and a deep-down dread warned him not to reveal what he had seen and heard.

Across the table, Tom wondered how much Casey really did know. It was painfully obvious that Ruth intended to cover her own guilt by throwing the blame onto her son. It was a shocking, shameful thing for any mother to do.

With a heavy heart, Tom found it all too easy to fit the pieces together in his mind. He had suspected for some time that Ruth was cheating on him, but like a fool he had let it drift; choosing instead to put it down to his imagination. Now, though, on this night of all nights, he had no choice but to face the truth: that his wife was not only cheating on him, but she was a barefaced liar and a bully into the bargain.

Tom realised, though, that he had to be careful not to make a wrong move. These past few days he had been forced to think things through. For reasons of her own, Ruth was a hard-hearted, vengeful woman, who would make the boy's life a misery if it suited her purpose. Above all else, Tom was determined his son's future safety must be ensured.

Again, he wondered about the man he saw fleeing from the ginnel. Now he had little doubt but that the man was Len Baker, his long-time workmate. Angry and disgusted, he imagined Len and Ruth together, and his stomach churned.

He felt ashamed, and dirty. He wanted to shake her, to make her tell him the truth, but with Casey already distressed he kept his silence. Later, though, he meant to root out the truth, and deal with the consequences.

Having decided on the road he must take, he felt stronger and calmer.

The meal continued in an uncomfortable atmosphere.

Having wolfed down her food, Ruth angrily pushed her chair back. 'Look at the wasted food!' she raged at the boy for his meagre appetite. 'All that money down the drain! You're a useless brat . . . causing rows and making up stories. You need a bloody good hiding, that's what you need!' She caught him by the hair.

'Leave him!' Tom's sharp warning sent her muttering and swearing into the scullery with her crockery.

Casey remained silent. He had seen his mother in a bad temper before, but this time she was like a mad thing.

'You've eaten next to nothing,' Tom told his son. He gestured to the food on Casey's plate. 'Try to eat a bit more, if you can, son. And don't worry, whatever's going on here, your mam and I will deal with it.' Standing up, he too pushed his chair back.

'Where are you going, Daddy?' Casey was anxious.

'I'll only be a minute. When I get back, I want to see less on your plate than there is now. OK?'

'You're not going away, are you? You won't leave me, will you?' Casey glanced nervously towards the scullery. What if Mam came back to beat him, and Daddy wasn't there to stop her?

Tom tried to reassure the boy. 'Do as I ask, will you, son? Try and eat up your food, and I'll be back soon enough.'

He turned away to leave the room, and went slowly upstairs.

Pushing open the bedroom door, he stood for a moment, his gaze falling on the bed. The eiderdown was ruffled and untidy, as though the bed had been made in a hurry.

When he drew the eiderdown back, Tom was not surprised to see the undersheet was heavily crumpled, with both pillows in complete disarray.

The unmade bed was all the more suspicious because, while Ruth was not a good housewife, she was very particular about keeping a neat, attractive bed.

Then Tom noticed a small object peeping out from beneath the edge of the eiderdown. Curious, he stooped down and, taking hold of a small, black leather strap, he withdrew a set of keys: one a brass door key; the other, smaller and silver.

Turning the keys over in the palm of his hand, he realised he'd seen them before. It took him a moment or two to remember. Yes, of course! It had been just a few days ago.

Tom thought back. He and his fellow workers were on their tea break, and he had seen these very keys lying on top of a packing case. He had actually moved the keys aside so he could sit down.

He recalled then how Len had come back looking for

them. There was no mistaking them: these were definitely Len's keys. It was him all right . . . it was Len! In his mind's eye Tom could see Len running from the ginnel, and his heart sank.

So! Ruth had been cheating on him yet again, this time in their own home. In their own bed.

Even worse, their son had been right there, outside the bedroom door, while she and her fancy-man were . . . Sickened, he shut out the images. He daren't even bring himself to think that Casey could have found them lying together.

Just as he was thinking of Casey, he heard his son cry out, 'Please, Mam, don't! You're hurting me . . .'

'Casey!' With the keys in his hand, Tom ran down the stairs and along the passageway to the back parlour.

Casey was cowering at the table, while, standing over him, Ruth was battering him with such force it seemed she meant to kill him.

With both arms across his head in an effort to protect himself, Casey was sobbing, 'I weren't gonna tell . . . I weren't!'

'LIAR!' She bent to look him in the face, lowering her voice to a harsh whisper. 'The minute my back was turned you would 'ave told all right. Admit it, damn you!' Her hands round Casey's neck, she began to squeeze. 'Yer a troublemaker! Yer should never 'ave been born!'

'For God's sake, are you mad!' Surging forward, Tom grabbed the boy and swung him out of her reach. 'What the hell d'you think you're doing?'

'He needs teaching a lesson!' Ruth made to grab the boy, but Tom was quicker as he lowered Casey behind him, out of her reach. 'Leave him be!' He held out a hand to ward her off.

Like a crazy thing, she went for him, her sharp talons drawing blood as she scraped them down his face. 'Why d'you always believe him over me?' she screeched. 'What's he been saying? What lies has 'e told, that's what I want to know!'

Shocked by her vicious attack, Tom grabbed her by the arms and held her still. 'Listen to me. It doesn't matter any more!' Forcing her down into a chair, his voice and manner became suddenly calm. 'Whatever Casey has to tell me, or however many men you choose over me, none of it matters any more.' Leaning down, he put his face close to hers and, speaking in a soft, almost kindly voice, he told her, 'It's over, Ruth. You and me . . . it's over and done with. For good.'

His sudden change of mood had her worried and she pulled away from him. 'What d'yer mean, "none of it matters any more"? What's your game, eh?' In the depth of her crazed mind, she could see him throwing her out, turning her onto the streets without money, or a roof over her head. 'You'd better not be threatening me,' she whined. 'I've done nothing wrong!'

Ignoring her, Tom turned to Casey. 'Are you all right, son?'

His face streaked with tears, Casey nodded. 'I'm all right, Daddy.'

'Good. Then I'd like you to go in the scullery and wash your hands and face. Comb your hair and make yourself look respectable. And don't open the door until I call. Me and your mother need to talk. Can you do that for me?'

Casey gave a nervous little nod. 'Yes.' Trembling, he never once looked at his mother, but as he closed the scullery door, he heard her screeching and ranting and, incredibly, she was now pleading.

'Don't go all cold on me, Tom,' she was saying. 'It's all summat and nowt. I don't want it coming between the two of us, and if you try and throw me out on the streets, I'll make you rue the day, you see if I don't!'

'Oh, I see. You think I might throw you out and leave you destitute, is that it? Well! You could not be more wrong, but that's not to say I shouldn't throw you out. No, it's me and Casey who are leaving. We can't go on like this. After what just happened, I've got to mek sure the lad is safe.'

'You're not thinking straight, Tom. I'm the boy's mother, and he belongs here, with me. The truth is, you couldn't give a bugger what he wants, or you wouldn't be so intent on splitting the family up.'

'Don't make the mistake of painting me with your own brush, Ruth,' he told her. 'All I want is for our son to grow up, safe and secure. He can't do that here, not with you. In my father's house he'll have love and security. He'll be allowed to choose what he wants in life, and he'll be helped to achieve it, without threat or anger.'

Ruth was as determined to keep the boy with her, as Tom was to take him away. She had never wanted the child, but she couldn't bear the thought of Tom and Casey sharing a life from which she was excluded. Well, she'd make damned sure Tom didn't have it all his own way. 'To hell with what you want! He's staying here, and that's an end to it!' She ranted.

Fearing that his mother would escalate the row, Casey remained locked in the scullery, running the tap and splashing water over his face in an effort to drown out the sound of his parents' angry voices.

He was afraid. He sensed something awful was about to happen, and he blamed himself. He must have done something wrong, something so terrible that he had set his parents at each other's throats.

Outside, Ruth would not let up. 'You're up to some trick or other, I know you are. So, what is it? What spiteful thing are you planning?' Made increasingly uneasy by Tom's quiet mood, Ruth suspected he was not telling her the entire truth. But that was not the total sum of her fears. It dawned on her that if he left her and she was forced to make her own way, how would she manage? She had no work-skills. Through all the years they'd been wed, Tom had always provided for her, so she had never once needed to work. And she had no desire to start now. The idea of not having Tom there to bring in the money was a frightening prospect.

Oh, yes, she could always sell herself; she had done so often enough. But that was simply a sideline; a rewarding pleasure she was free to indulge in whenever the mood took her.

And anyway, what would she do when her figure went to seed, and the wrinkles ravaged her face? No man would look at her twice then, let alone lie with her. However old and unattractive she got, Tom was a man who would always do his duty and bring in a regular wage.

'Please, Tom, don't leave me,' she played on his softer side. 'I'll change my ways, I really will.'

In all her married life she had never once belittled herself to plead with him, but the prospect of losing that wage packet on a Friday was too daunting.

'Sit down, Ruth.' Tom's voice was surprisingly gentle.

Gesturing to the chair, he waited, but she made no move.

'Please, Ruth. Sit down. There is something I need to tell you.' Though after everything that had happened here, he was beginning to think it might be unwise to share his own troubles with her.

Increasingly unnerved by Tom's manner, she did as he asked. 'The boy is a liar,' she stoutly insisted. 'The little bastard wanted to make you think I had a man in the bedroom, didn't he, eh? Well, don't listen to a word he says. Let me talk to him, and I'll make him tell you the truth.'

Realising yet again that the time was not right to reveal his troubles, Tom decided to keep his own counsel.

'Listen to me, Ruth,' he said firmly instead. 'I really

don't care whether you had a man in the bedroom or not.' Reaching into his trouser-pocket, he took out the two keys and threw them onto the table, gratified when she shrank back in shock.

'Whose keys are they? Where did you get them from?' she asked, trying to regain her composure.

'From the look on your face, you already know whose keys they are,' Tom retaliated. 'They belong to your new man friend, and I'm sure I don't need to tell you where I found them.' He smiled knowingly. 'I reckon you'd best get these back to him at the first opportunity . . . before his missus realises they've gone missing.' He spoke in a disarmingly casual manner.

'I'm truly sorry, Tom.' Ruth feigned a tear. 'All right! You caught me out, but it's the first time Len's been here, and I swear it will never happen again. You have my word on it.'

'I really don't care what you do any more,' Tom reminded her. 'The truth is, he can have you, because once me and Casey have gone from here, we won't be coming back . . . ever.'

Tom was all too aware that in the greater scheme of things, there were other urgent issues they should be discussing. But even now he felt it wasn't the moment to tell her.

Today, as always, she had managed to create a situation that prevented him from confiding in her. Instead, he had no option but to make other, drastic plans, with regard to their son.

He believed that, in view of what had taken place here tonight, he quietly smiled to himself. If he confessed the truth to her, he realised that Ruth would no doubt welcome his news.

All day, he had been in emotional and physical torment; aching to come home and share his news with her. Instead, he had finally discovered that there was no doubt she felt no love or feeling towards him at all.

That was a hard and painful thing for him to learn.

'I know I've done wrong,' Ruth persisted lamely, her voice trembling. 'But you have my word, it won't happen again. It were Len's fault. He kept bothering me . . . coming to the door when he knew you wouldn't be in. But nothing happened. I would never cheat on you with another man.' Lies came so easily to her.

'Enough, Ruth, I don't want to hear any more.' When she fell silent, Tom went on, his voice cold and unforgiving, 'I've already said, you're free to go with whichever man takes your fancy, and God only knows there have been enough of them over the years. Fool that I am, I've put up with your infidelities for too long, but no more. But all that aside, I won't stand by while you take your spite out on the boy. That's all over now. And so is our sham of a marriage.'

'Please, Tom! You can't mean that. We need each other. You love me, I know you do.'

'Well, you've tested my love to the very limit. In the back of my mind, I think I knew what you were up to, but I hoped I was wrong. I didn't want to risk losing you. But now Casey and I are going. I don't care any longer what you do.'

He gave a small, whimsical smile. 'I do care about our son, though, and having witnessed how you enjoy hurting him, I'm determined to get him away from here. He'll be safe enough with his granddad Bob. Oh, and if you so much as show your face there, I'll inform the authorities how you mercilessly beat the boy for nothing more than telling the truth.'

'I won't let you take him! You can bugger off if you want to, but you're not taking the boy. He's staying here with me. He's nearly nine years old; before you can turn round he'll be fourteen and off to work. That's when he'll be old enough to make up his own mind about where he wants to go, and who with. Till then, I'll decide what's best for him. He's staying here, with me, where he belongs!'

'Oh, I can see it all now. The truth is, you can hardly wait till he's off to work and bringing home a wage packet. Of course, that's why you're so desperate to keep him. You see him as taking my place and earning the money to keep you in fags and idleness. You intend him to support you in the manner you're used to, while turning a blind eye to the men friends you entertain under this roof.'

'You're wrong! I want him to stay here with me, because I'm his mother, and this is where he should be.'

'Like hell, he should! You don't give a damn for the boy. You never have. Five years from now, you'll be too far gone to attract the men, and Casey will take over from me as breadwinner. Well, you can forget it. I've no intention of leaving my son here so's you can ruin his life like you've ruined mine.'

Leaving her to reflect on his words, he crossed to the scullery and opened the door. 'Are you ready, Casey?'

Casey switched off the taps. 'Yes, Daddy.'

'Right, then go upstairs and get what you need. You're coming with me to stay with Granddad Bob.'

Keeping his gaze to the floor, Casey hurried across the parlour and up the stairs, where he began collecting a few belongings. He wasn't sorry to be going, as long as he was with his daddy.

Downstairs, Ruth ranted on. 'I'll have him back before you know it,' she warned. 'I'm not done with you yet.'

'Is that so?' Tom was also determined. 'Well then, I'll make you a promise, shall I? If you try any of your tricks or if you go anywhere near him, I'll make sure the authorities know what kind of a useless mother you are. They'll know about the men you entertain, here in our home, with your own son able to hear what's going on. And I'll make sure they're aware of what happened here today. You've never had any real love for that boy, and if I was to leave him here with you, I dread to think what might happen.'

Having filled a canvas bag with his few belongings, Casey emerged from the bedroom. He sat down on the stairs, listening, waiting for the angry voices to subside.

It seemed like an age before he dared venture to the parlour door, but when he felt his mother's eyes on him he kept his gaze averted.

'Are you ready, son?' Tom placed an encouraging hand on the boy's shoulder.

Casey looked into his father's kindly face. 'Are we taking the guitar?'

Tom smiled down on him. 'Yes, so you go and fetch it, while I have a quiet word with your mother. Then we'll be away from here.'

Relieved and happy that they were going to stay with Granddad Bob for a while, Casey made his way to the front parlour.

Turning to Ruth, who appeared to be in a quieter mood, Tom told her, 'Oddly enough, I still have feelings for you, but I could never again want you as my wife . . . not in that way. Not after you've shared yourself with other men time and again.'

Ruth made no answer. Instead, while seeming to listen, she slyly glanced to the door, where Casey was now waiting, the guitar safe in its soft cover, and clutched tightly in his arms.

'Ruth, d'you hear what I'm saying?' Tom was slightly unnerved by her suddenly calm manner.

'I'm listening.' Her smile crept over him.

'Once I leave here, I'll be out of your life for good. I will never again set foot in this house, but it goes without saying I can't speak for our son. Whatever he decides in the future is up to him, but he will always have a place in my father's house.'

He desperately needed to share his close secret with someone; a secret that was playing heavily on his mind, especially now. He felt angry, and guilty and so alone. Sadly Ruth had never been the kind of woman a person might confide in.

Sensing a weakness about him, Ruth turned on the tears. 'Please, Tom, don't leave me destitute. I can't afford to rent this house on my own. I love you both. I couldn't bear it if you left.'

'Sorry but the decision is made. Whatever the cost to me, I intend doing what's right for Casey.' Aware that Casey might hear, Tom lowered his voice. 'The way you went for the boy was shocking. It showed real hatred. I must have been blind or stupid not to have seen it before.'

Realising he'd seen right through her, she boldly admitted, 'You're absolutely right, I do have a powerful hatred for the boy, so much so that I shrink inside whenever he comes near me. What's more, I feel the same way about you . . . always have done.'

When he looked away she sidled up to him, her voice taunting. 'So y'see? I don't give a bugger whether you stay or go, but if you think I'll hand you a divorce so you can opt out of supporting me financially, you've another thought coming.'

Tom instinctively drew back. 'You don't have a cat in hell's chance of keeping him.' Taking her by the arms, he held her tightly. 'When did you ever show him any tenderness or guidance? Whenever he brought friends home, you couldn't wait to get rid of them on some pretext or other. You made them feel uncomfortable, making nasty comments and belittling Casey in front of them, and now he has no friends at all. So, what does that say about you, eh?'

'You're twisting things! I was right to get rid of them! Besides, they weren't real friends! They were cunning little buggers, and they were not welcome in my house.'

'*Your* house, is it?'

'Yes! *My* house, *my* son, and *my* decision. Besides, it's a mother's place to vet her son's friends. What I did was for his own good.'

'So, tell me, Ruth, if he's your son, and you know what's best for him, why did you never cuddle him or sit down and talk with him about school or the music he loves? Why do you never ask how he's doing at his lessons, or praise him when he achieves something he's proud of . . . like the time he played the guitar in assembly. Do you remember, how he came running home all excited, and you just brushed it aside, like it was nothing?'

'All right! I'll tell you why I didn't want to make a fuss. It's because, unlike you, I don't want him turning into some kind of softie. Besides, any fool can tap their fingers against a piece o' wood and make some kind o' noise. It doesn't mean they're summat special.'

'How would you know? That day, in front of all those parents, teachers and even classmates, our son poured his emotions into the music and the music touched a cord in everyone. He made me proud, but then I expect that's something you could never understand.'

His words sent her mind reeling back to when she was younger. He was wrong to tell her she could never understand Casey's talent, because she did understand. She had always understood and hated him all the more for it. In spite of her searching for the bad in him, she found only good. He was a normal boy, back-chatting at times and grating on her nerves when he stood up to her. Occasionally, he had proven to be as disobedient and aggravating as any other boy, but for all that, she recognised something special in him. Something intangible, which awakened the best in everyone, except her. In truth, she envied him.

Casey was everything she was not. He was kind while she was cruel. He needed her but she had never needed him. Unlike her, he had the capability to love, fiercely and with great pride, as in the way he loved Tom and Granddad Bob; while she was incapable of loving anyone. Over the years, she had watched the boy grow into a fine young person under Tom's guidance, and every day she was punished because of it. Yet, she had never told, and never would.

Even as a baby, when Casey held up his chubby arms for a cuddle, she would turn away – much as she had turned away from her family, where she had looked in vain for love, and even from Tom, a man of principle. A hard-working man, who had always provided for her, and who had, from an early age, loved her without question.

Tom and the boy were not of her world. They were too safe, too predictable. Since childhood she had never wanted a safe world.

And for that, she had neither regrets, nor peace. She had hardened her heart, vowing never to let others hurt her, but they had hurt her, and the pain was like a living thing inside her. It had taught her that love could only ever bring pain.

'RUTH!'

'What now?' Startled out of her reverie, she raged at him, 'I won't change my mind. I mean to keep the boy, and there is nothing you or your father can do about it. When the time comes, I'll make sure he knuckles down, and learns a useful trade. *You* might be running away, but I won't allow him to go. It won't be long before he'll need to take up his responsibilities. There'll be no more time wasted on music and such, I'll make sure of it.'

'Not if I can help it, you won't! His granddad thinks as I do.'

'For pity's sake, what's wrong with you? He's a boy, he

should be outside playing football or fighting in the playground, or being trained for summat that might earn him a living, like building or plumbing. Instead he's wasting his time holding a piece o' wood and making noises that no one cares about. He's useless, and the sooner he gets out of school and into a proper job, the happier I'll be, and that's the truth.'

Casey had retreated into the passage to lean forlornly against the far wall. 'Look at him!' Ruth screeched. 'Hugging that damned guitar like it were summat precious. It's nothing but a piece o' wood, that's all. Useless . . . like him!'

Deeply hurt, Casey stepped forward. 'You don't understand. When I played in assembly, everybody stood up and clapped. Miss Hardwick said it was beautiful, but you never heard me because you weren't even there. You don't care about anything I do.' When the tears began to flow, he wiped his eyes and brought his sorry gaze to the floor.

Unmoved, Ruth rounded on Tom. 'Now, see what you've done. You've got him thinking he's summat special. He thinks that piece o' wood is his future, but it's not and never will be. It won't earn him a wage, and it won't make him a man. It's nothing! D'you hear me?'

Suddenly she rushed across the room and grabbed the guitar out of Casey's arms. Fighting Tom off as he tried to stop her, she smashed the instrument against the wall where the cover split open, shooting out splinters of wood and tangled strings.

'That's what I think of yer precious guitar.'

When she tried to raise the guitar again, Tom wrestled her onto a chair, his voice trembling with anger. 'You know how much that guitar meant to Casey. Why would you do such a wicked thing?'

'Huh! I don't know why I didn't smash that thing long ago,' Ruth sneered.

Tom wrapped an arm about Casey's shoulders. 'It'll be all right, son,' he assured him. Carefully placing the broken instrument into its cover, he handed it to him, saying. 'Take it with you, and wait for me at the end of the street.'

'Yeah, go on!' As the boy made his way along the passage, his mother's vicious rantings followed him. 'Get off to yer granddad Bob. Tell him not to mek you too comfortable, 'cause I'll be along soon enough to fetch yer back!'

With Casey out of earshot, Tom turned on her. 'What kind of creature are you?' He remained outwardly calm, though he would gladly have throttled her there and then. 'If I had any doubts about taking Casey away from here, you've just proved that I've made the right decision.'

Without another word, he walked out of the room and along the passage.

Ruth ran after him. 'Think you're the man, don't yer, eh? If you try and take my son, I'll 'ave the police on yer! You've no rights, d'you hear me? You've no rights!'

'I've every right! Casey is my son, and I'm responsible for his safety. If you interfere, I warn you, Ruth, you'll be starting something you might regret.'

'Really? Well, I think you should know, if you try and fight me, you'll be sorry. You can be sure o' that.'

Tom was not impressed. 'I know what you're up to, but it's not on.'

'Huh!' Her manner changed suddenly. With a sly, triumphant smile on her face, she spoke slowly, so the words would cut deep, 'Casey . . . is not . . . your son.'

For what seemed an age, Tom gave no reply. He felt shocked and numbed, unable to comprehend what she had said.

Turning the knife, Ruth elaborated in a harsh and cruel voice. 'Truth is, you raised another man's bastard. After he was born, I used to watch you doting on him, hugging him like he was something precious. You never knew how much I longed to tell you the truth . . . to take the smile off yer face, but I never did. I'm telling you now, though. He was never yours, and he never will be.'

'You're a damned liar!' Tom was shocked, then enraged. 'You've stooped to many a dodgy thing in your time, but this is really evil. You'd better take back what you said. Take it back . . . now!'

'I'm not lying, Tom. Not this time.' Delighting in his distress, she pressed home her own version of the truth. 'I've no idea who his father is, but I do know it's not you, because it happened a short time before you and I lay down together. I tricked you, and like the gullible fool that you are, you never suspected; not even when I lied about him being born early. He's an unwanted little bastard . . . made down a dark alley with some stranger who had more money than he knew what to do with.'

Stricken to the heart, Tom took her by the shoulders. 'You're a wicked, destructive woman, and your lies won't get Casey back.' He gripped her so tight she winced with pain. 'He's my son. Mine! D'you hear what I'm telling you? Casey is mine and he always will be. Nothing you say or do will ever change that.'

'Oh, but you're wrong. You're not listening, Tom! It isn't your blood that runs through the boy. It's the blood of a stranger who never knew what he'd made, and probably couldn't care less anyway. When the pleasure was over, he went his way and I went mine.'

Her words were like a knife through Tom's heart. In his mind he went back to the day she told him she was pregnant. Had he really been so gullible?

Now the truth was out after all these years, it was as if a dam had broken in Ruth and the words poured out. 'Do you remember all that time you were after me, and

I turned you away; but then you finally came in useful . . . if you see what I mean?' She gave a sly little grin. 'When I found I were up the duff, I moved Heaven and Earth to be rid of it, but for some reason it wouldn't be budged, more's the pity. But there you were, all doe-eyed and in love. I never had any real feelings for you in that way. You were simply a way out of my dilemma. When I told you we were having a baby, oh, you were over the moon. So excited, planning this and that . . .' she laughed out loud, '. . . and you never knew that your joy had been another man's pleasure before we were ever married.'

While Tom took all this in, she watched his agony and felt nothing. 'The thing is, I've done you a favour. You won't want to be saddled with him now, will yer, eh? Not now you know the truth. He's not so special after all. Think about it, Tom. For all we know, his real father might have been a dodgy sort with a badness that could rise in the boy at any time. Then there's the matter of my own blood running through his veins . . . the blood of a woman you believe to be wicked. Maybe the boy's a chip off the old block. What if his real father turns out to be some sort of villain, a wanted killer, even?' The thought amused her. 'What about that, eh?'

'Never!' Though reeling from what she'd told him, Tom ferociously defended the child's good nature. 'Casey is nothing like you! He's good and fine. I've raised him to know the right way to live. I'm proud of his every achievement, and I've always encouraged him into doing what he loves and what he's good at. That's what a father does, and that's what I am: Casey's father. I held him when he was born and I've nurtured him ever since. I love him and he loves me, and there's a powerful father-and-son bond between us. No man alive could be prouder of his son than I am of Casey . . . my son.'

The more distressed he became, the more Ruth revelled

in it. 'Tell him!' she urged. 'Go out there and tell him he's not your son. Then we'll see who he'll want to stay with. Tell him he can be with you – someone who had no part in creating him – or he can stay here where he belongs, with his blood mother, the woman who carried him inside her for nine months; the woman who gave birth to him, and raised him, and made sure he had a roof over his head. Tell him how I was made to use my wiles and make sacrifices, to be with a man I didn't love, so he would always be provided for.'

When he made no move, she rounded on him. 'Go on! Tell him the truth! Because if you don't, I will!' She would much rather Tom told the boy, because then Tom would be outcast instead of her.

But Tom was determined. 'Casey is my son and I'm his father, and if you tell him anything other, I swear I'll kill you!'

Seeing him like this, so cold and unforgiving, she took an involuntary step back. 'Big words for such a little man.'

Tom wisely ignored her remark. 'I mean it. That boy has gone through enough already, without you telling him he was spawned in some dark alley by his tart of a mother and some stranger who's long gone.'

'Sorry, Tom, but the boy has a right to know. So, like I say, if you don't tell him, I surely will.'

In that moment Tom actually entertained the idea of putting his two hands round her neck and strangling the life out of her. By God, he was sorely tempted.

'Alongside my own father, Casey is the only good thing in my life,' he told her. 'I need to know he's safe and secure.'

Thrusting her aside, he started down the passage, Ruth right behind him, ranting and raving, telling him how he could not stop her from getting to the boy.

'If not today, then tomorrow. Either way, you've lost

him, Tom. But then, he was never yours anyway.'

When Tom tried to get out of the door, she leaped forward to catch him unawares. Grabbing his hair, she caught him off balance and fought him down. But Tom was the stronger. Having swiftly wrestled her to the carpet, he made a dash for the door.

When she clambered up, intent on forcing him back, he instinctively hit out and sent her sprawling. Before she could get up, he was away down the street, the only thought in his mind to find Casey.

Spread-eagled on the floor, Ruth made no effort to get up. 'You won't have him for long!' she shouted after him. 'When I tell your dad the truth, he won't even want the little bastard in his house!'

Tom ran down the street, leaving her yelling obscenities. 'You've not heard the last o' me! I'll get him back, even if I have to fight you in court.'

Deliberately closing his ears to her screeching, he grew increasingly anxious that Casey might have overheard what she'd said earlier, and her vile threats played on his mind. She's lying! he tried to convince himself. Casey is *my* son. She would say anything to suit her own ends; even labelling her own child a bastard. But she won't get her claws into him, not if I have anything to do with it.

But he knew that keeping her at bay would not be easy and because of his own unfortunate predicament, might even be beyond his control.

'Dear Lord, what am I to do?' Slowing his steps, Tom glanced up at the shifting skies and, for the strangest moment, he felt a great sense of peace. The kind of peace that warmed and reassured; easing the restless soul.

But then he thought of the jeopardy Casey was in, and his peace was short-lived.

~

As he went down the street, calling out for Casey, the next-door neighbours were at the front door looking out. Sylvia Marshall and her husband, William, had lived next to the Denton family these past nine years. Having soon learned that she was trouble, they had given Ruth a wide berth, but they always had a smile for Tom and his son, Casey.

'I'm worried.' William was anxious. 'Something went a hell of a bang. I'm wondering if somebody might be hurt.'

'Well, thank goodness it's not Tom or the boy, because we've just seen them go off down the street . . . poor little devil, having to put up with a mother like that! And if Tom's given that wife of his a good slapping, then it's no more than she deserves.' Having overheard a snippet of the argument that had raged on, she could only guess at the rest.

'I ought to go and see if everything's all right.'

'You keep your nose out of it and don't interfere. They've rowed before, and no doubt they'll row again. She thrives on trouble, you should know that by now.'

Sylvia, however, found herself talking to thin air as her husband followed the shouts and abuse that came from the Denton house. 'Oh, my!' At the door, he saw Ruth lying there, still loudly complaining. She appeared half dazed and there was a trickle of blood running down her face. When she madly struggled to get up off the floor, the ornaments fell off the side table one after the other.

'Whatever's happened? Here . . . let me help you . . .'

As William began to make his way into the house, Ruth gave him a barrage of abuse. 'Bugger off out of it!' Snatching a small ornament, she sent it flying through the air, to land at his feet. 'You'd best clear off before I get up . . . or you'll rue the day!'

When he came running back indoors, his wife was in fits of laughter. 'You silly old fool! I told you not to go, but you never listen, do you?'

'Hmm!' Without another word, he skulked into the parlour, lit up his pipe, and sat there, contemplating life and thanking his lucky stars he had married a sensible, understanding wife.

~

Away from Henry Street, Tom was growing frantic. Casey was nowhere to be seen. He was not in the street, nor was he at the bus stop, and each time he called out, Tom was greeted with silence.

After widening his search beyond Penny Street, he wended his way back to Henry Street. At the back of his mind Tom worried that the boy might have overheard the row. If so, it would have been a devastating shock, flooding Casey's young mind with all manner of imaginings. Tom hoped with all his heart that the one thing Casey had not heard was his mother's shocking confession.

Suddenly Tom recalled the place where Casey would go whenever he wanted to be alone or quiet; mostly after school and before his daddy was home. That was the time when Ruth might send him out – so she could entertain her men friends, Tom now knew.

He remembered how much Casey loved the peace and quiet of the Blakewater, a long, winding brook that ran behind Henry Street and on through the lowlands of Blackburn. He quickened his steps towards the place.

Once there, he paused to look over the little stone bridge, and was greatly relieved to see Casey below. A small bundle of humanity scrunched in a heap on the wet cobbles, he was sobbing bitterly, his arms wrapped round the guitar and his head bent low.

Saddened at the sight of that small, innocent child hunched up in the cold and so deeply distressed, Tom thought of where the blame lay. He suspected the worst:

that Casey must have heard his mother's damning confession; that the man he had always known and loved as his father was not his father at all.

Tom felt helpless. While he himself was trying to come to terms with her wicked claim, he could not even imagine the trauma Casey was going through. His heart went out to him.

'Casey!' Tom called out.

When there was no answer, he took off at a run, over the bridge and down the slope, where he slithered and slipped on the shifting cobbles. 'Casey. You had me worried, son. I've been searching everywhere for you!'

Casey appeared not to have heard or, as Tom suspected, he chose not to respond.

A few minutes later, Tom was seated cross-legged alongside the child.

'I'm sorry about earlier, about the shouting and the things that were said, but none of it was your fault, son. Don't ever think that.' Deciding it might be wiser not to elevate the situation, Tom slid a comforting arm about Casey's shoulders. 'I'm just glad you're safe. When I couldn't find you, I got really concerned.'

Tom waited for him to speak. The boy, though, remained silent, afraid to open a conversation that might prove his fears were all too real.

Tom understood. In some inexplicable way he, too, felt immensely safe in those familiar surroundings, and, again like Casey, he was momentarily lost in the peace of that place.

This dark, dank area beneath the Blakewater bridge could never be described as beautiful. Beneath life's traffic, and surrounded by brick buildings and stone walls, a visitor might be forgiven for thinking he was deep in the bowels of the earth. The air was thick with a pervading stench of rotting food and other perishables routinely thrown into the water from the bridge, yet, for all that, there was something magical about this place. Here an unquiet soul felt safe and uniquely comforted. Unlike people, this ancient bridge would not desert or hurt you.

Now quieter of heart, Tom glanced about him at the tall, ancient walls that had stood for an age, thick and solid, and strong enough to support the houses that had rested on those reliable stone shoulders for many an age.

At certain times, after heavy rains, the shifting stream of Blakewater would rise to cover the walls and flood the passageways into the back yards. Carried by the high water, rats would swim through into the house cellars. Many scampering rodents lost their lives when the frightened residents beat them with spades and threw their corpses back into the swirling, stinking waters.

When the water receded, the rats were carried off, and the walls were left covered in a coat of dark slime, which dripped relentlessly until a brighter day arrived to dry it off.

Now, softly breaking the silence, the delicate splashes of water trickled over the cobbles to create a unique melody. Above them, with the evening closing in fast, the streetlamp cast a flickering, eerie shadow over the fading day.

'You love it here, don't you?' Tom said softly. 'I can understand why.' He chided himself for not searching here earlier for the boy.

'Yes, it's my favourite place.' Casey did not look up.

Tom smiled. 'Mine too.'

Surprised by Tom's admission, the boy peeped at him out the corner of his eye. 'When you were little, did you ever run along the bridge wall?'

'I did, yes.'

'Were you frightened?'

Tom laughed out loud. 'I were terrified!'

'So, why did you do it then?'

'Because . . .'

'Because what?' Casey kept his gaze averted, his arms wrapped round his knees and his head bent as before, but now his face was turned sideways as he gazed up. He felt a deeper sense of security now that Tom was there.

'Well . . . because . . .' Momentarily lost for words, Tom cast his mind back over the years. 'Because I think I must have taken leave of my senses.'

When Casey laughed at that, Tom laughed with him, and the sound rippled softly through the air, causing some frightened creature to scurry away under the bridge.

There followed another small silence, before Casey confided his secret. 'They wanted me to do it, but I never did.'

'Well, thank God for that!' Tom shivered inwardly at the way these children regularly risked life and limb, running along a six-inch-wide wall some twenty feet above the water. 'So, who was it that wanted you to do it?'

'School pals.'

'Who were they?'

'There were two Brindle brothers, and another boy who lives on King Street.'

'Oh, the Brindles . . . big family. Yes, I know them.'

'Well, the Brindle brothers had a race in bare feet. One of them ran on the far wall, and the other ran along the opposite wall. I had to count from one to ten, and see who got to the other side first.'

'So, who won?'

'Nobody. They got to the other side at the same time. On a count of eight.'

'A draw, eh? Well, I think that was OK, don't you? At least it stopped them from arguing.'

'No, because they still argued. They said I must have counted wrong, but they were so fast, it was frightening. They ran like the wind . . . slipping and sliding all over the place, they were. I thought they might fall into the water, but it didn't even bother 'em! They kept their balance, and made it to the other side.' When he looked up at Tom, the light from the lamp caught the excitement in his eyes. 'You should have seen them go, Dad!'

'I can imagine.' The Brindle family was boisterous, with the boys, in particular, always up to something.

'They made it look so exciting, I really wanted to try.'

'You never did, though, did you?'

Casey gave a huge sigh. 'No, but sometimes I wish I had.'

'So, what stopped you?'

'I tried once, but my foot slipped and I could hardly keep my balance, so I chickened out.'

'That was very brave.'

The boy gasped. 'How could it be brave, when I chickened out?'

'Because sometimes it's better to admit that it's too dangerous and stop, instead of going on when your instincts warn you not to.'

'Honestly?'

'Yes, really. It takes a wise man to admit when he's made a wrong decision.'

When Casey suddenly leaned his head on his father's broad shoulder, it was a tender, deeply bonding moment in which each relived the awful situation that had brought him here.

Eventually the child asked hesitantly, 'She hates me, doesn't she?'

'Are we talking about your mam?'

'Yes.'

'I see.' Tom carefully considered his next words, because whatever he said, he could not deny that Ruth had caused a great deal of pain and confusion especially with her cruel revelation to himself.

Casey's next words only proved the damage Ruth had done. 'I don't want to stay with her. I want to be with you and Granddad.'

'That's fine, then, because that's where we're going.'

Another awkward moment of silence before Casey needed to know, 'Are you my daddy? Are you *really* my daddy?'

Choking back the rush of emotion, Tom turned the boy round to face him. 'I want you to listen to me, son. I want you to hear my every word and never forget it. Can you do that for me?'

When Casey nodded, Tom held him tight before telling him softly, 'In every way that matters, I truly am your daddy. Your name is Casey Denton, and you are the son of Thomas Denton . . . that's me. I was there when you were born, and I was the first one to hold you, after the nurse. Then I placed you tenderly into your mammy's arms, and the two of us loved you so much, we never wanted to let you go. So, you see, it's always been the three of us.'

'So, when I was born she held me. That means she must love me, eh?'

Tom assured him that it was so.

Casey was unsettled, however, his mind questioning everything that Tom said. 'But if she loved me when I was born, why doesn't she love me now?'

It was a difficult question for Tom. On the day when Casey was born, Ruth had held him for less than a minute, her manner cold and hard as she returned the baby to him. 'I don't want it! Take it back.' The vehemence in her voice had shaken him to the core.

Unconcerned, the nurse had taken the baby from him and placed him tenderly into the prepared cot.

Afterwards, when he was leaving, the nurse had urged Tom not to be upset by his wife's words. 'I promise you, your wife is not the first to reject her newborn. She's had a very long, painful labour and an extremely difficult birth. Rejecting the baby in the first flush is not an unusual reaction. She'll come round. They always do.'

After a while, Ruth appeared to have accepted the boy, and no more was said.

Through Casey's formative years, however, there were occasions when Ruth had shown hostility towards her son. Tom had chosen to dismiss it, but tonight, when she claimed to hate the boy, the awful truth was driven home to him. Ruth really did harbour a sense of hatred towards her son.

'I don't think she loves me at all.' Casey's voice startled Tom out of his thoughts. 'Why doesn't she love me?'

Taking that small face between the palms of his hands, Tom gently wiped away the tears. 'In all honesty, I don't know what to tell you, Casey, except that I'm sure she does have feelings for you. The thing is, do any of us know what love really means? Y'see, son, it can mean different things to different people.' He felt totally out of his depth; wanting to comfort the boy, yet not wanting to lie to him. 'As for myself, I believe that when you love someone, you have a deep urge to protect them. You want them always to be happy, and never to get hurt, and you'll do anything to make them safe. That's what I personally believe love means.'

He paused to gather his thoughts, before going on. 'But y'see, Casey, not everyone thinks of it in the same way. Someone else might think that love means moulding a person so that he or she can learn to protect themselves and be safe from harm. They want their loved ones to be strong enough to reach their potential in life. They believe that being hard and demanding to their loved ones is the right way to be, even though it could make them appear cruel.'

'But she *is* cruel. She never cuddles me. She likes to hurt me, and make me cry.'

Tom was deeply saddened by the child's words. 'The thing is, Casey, people like your mother don't know any other way. They think that cuddling and being soft is wrong, and that their way is best.'

For what seemed an age, Casey remained silent. Then, looking Tom in the eye, he told him in a clear voice, 'I don't like her, and I don't like that kind of love, and I don't want her to be my mam any more.'

'That's your choice, son, and I respect that. You have every right to speak your mind. But you must never hate, because hatred is a terrible, destructive thing. It's like I was saying, we're all different, and we all deal differently with particular situations. I agree . . . some people's kind of love is complicated. It isn't for you and it isn't for me either, but people can't help the way they are, and though we might not care for their kind of love, we have to accept it. That's just the way it is.'

'So . . .' in his young mind, Casey tried to make sense of it all, '. . . you're telling me that my mam really *does* love me, only in a different way?'

'Well, yes. That's exactly what I'm saying.'

'So, why did you take me away from her? Why did you say you never want me to live with her again?'

Realising that Casey had heard more than he'd first thought, Tom gave him a simple explanation that he hoped would finish the conversation right there. 'Well, the way I see it is this. You said yourself that you didn't like her kind of love.'

'I don't!'

'OK. So, if you stayed with her, you would be unhappy, is that right?'

'Yes!'

'And you might refuse to accept her kind of love and

even fight against it, because you think she's cruel and unkind. So, there might be arguments and fights and she would get angry and hit out. And the whole situation would escalate into a war between you. Am I right?'

'Yes. I don't want to live with her, because she's too cruel. She tells lies, and she hit me with her fists, and she smashed up the guitar.' Scrambling to his feet, he began to cry. 'I don't want her to love me any more. I'm glad you took me away because I don't want her. I only want you and Granddad Bob.'

'And that's your final decision, is it?' Tom was satisfied that his attempted interpretation of Ruth's 'love' for Casey had somehow helped; making him realise that, his mother had proved herself to be more than capable of making his life a misery, and that it was all right for him to leave.

It was a huge source of comfort to Tom that his boy would be out of harm's reach, and safely settled with his granddad.

'Come on then, son.' Securing the guitar over Casey's shoulder, he swung him into his arms. 'We'd best go and tell Granddad Bob.'

'Will you tell him how Mam smashed up your guitar?'

'Oh, I'm sure he'll see that for himself.'

'He won't be pleased.'

'You're right. He won't.'

'What else will you tell him?' Casey remembered the man who he heard in his mother's bedroom, and the others who had been there before him.

Suspecting the reasoning behind this question, Tom feigned a chuckle. 'I'll tell him he's got two smelly lodgers from the Blakewater, and that we both need a hot bath.'

'And that we're cold and hungry, eh?' Casey was excited.

'OK, that too.'

'Yeah!' Casey was famished. 'If Granddad's made a meat and potato pie, there might be some left over.'

With that in mind, they headed for the nearest bus stop, where they sat on the wooden bench to wait.

When, some ten minutes later, the bus arrived, the two of them climbed aboard and seated themselves on the seat furthest from the doors. 'We'll be far enough away from the draught here,' Tom decided.

Tom bought two single tickets to Preston New Road. From there, they would walk down to Addison Street, where he was born and grew up.

Realising how much was at stake following his decision, he was deeply apprehensive. So many things to think about. So much responsibility. Of late, he had been called upon to take the most important decisions of his life. Heart-breaking decisions that would affect those he loved. He had never wished to be in this situation, but now that he was, he had to face it with hard determination, or be lost.

There was too much to think about, too much that he did not understand. He was forced to act, and he did so after long deliberation, and with a sad heart. There was much regret and, more importantly, too much left unsaid.

'Daddy!'

Casey's raised voice startled him. 'Ssh! Don't be so loud, Casey. There are other people on this bus.'

'I'm sorry, Dad, but I need to ask something.'

'All right, I'm listening. What is it you want to say?'

'I just wanted to know . . . if you were sad?' The memory of that awful row between his parents had really unsettled him.

Smiling assuredly, Tom answered, 'Well, I might have been just a little bit sad, but I'm happy enough now. What about you?'

'I'm really happy now, 'cause I'll be with you and Granddad.' Easier of heart, the boy resumed looking through the window; and while he counted the streetlamps as they flashed by, Tom turned his mind to other, burning issues.

His thoughts were torn between his own dear father, and this darling boy whom he loved with a passion. They were his responsibility, and he could not help but be afraid for them.

Ruth was a born survivor. With tooth and nail, she would always find a way. Surprisingly, even though she had caused him anguish over the years, Tom was still able to think of her in a kindly way.

A long time ago he had stopped trying to fathom her sudden bouts of wicked temper and the spiteful manner in which she flew at the boy for any reason. Yet though her behaviour maddened him at times, he could find no lasting hatred in his heart towards her.

Through the years, his love for her had been tested many times, but he could not deny the affection he felt towards her. Yes, she was a cheat, and yes, she could be cruel and violent at times. But even though the boy might have come from another man's seed – though Tom hoped that was not the case – Ruth had still given him the best gift any woman could give her man. She had offered him a son to love and raise, and he had come to love the boy, heart and soul.

Soon, though, young Casey would be sorely tested, and right now Tom prayed he had provided him with the right tools to deal with life. Because all too soon, it would be time for him to leave.

When Tom looked up, Casey smiled at him, a trusting, innocent smile.

Tom returned the smile, but behind it lay a great reservoir of loneliness, and a forlorn hope that he might be forgiven for what he soon must do.

CHAPTER THREE

FOR A MAN in his mid-sixties, Bob Denton was both strong and able, though, as was to be expected, he suffered the aches and pains of increasing age.

A contented man, he considered himself to be fortunate in having married the girl he loved and fathered a wonderful son. He would have liked more children, but Tom was destined to be the only one. The joy he brought was immeasurable and he had been a huge comfort to his father when, some nine years ago, Tom's mother had died of TB.

That had been a desperately trying time for both Tom and his father, and, sharing the grief as best they could, they drew strength from each other.

Tom had married Ruth about that time, and his marriage and the birth of his son had given him a degree of consolation. Bob, meanwhile, feverishly immersed himself in his work at the quarries, and when young Casey was born, the old man's heart was happier than it had been for months. Seemingly gifted with a deep love and a joyful ability for music, the boy had given him another reason to keep going. Bob still missed his lovely woman – that would never change – but he tried to move on in life as best he could.

The previous year, Bob had retired from work, so now all he had was his son and his grandson, two people he loved more than life itself. As for Ruth, he had tried many times to befriend her, but she was not an easy woman to get close to. In the end, he had no choice but to give up trying, yet it was a situation he still fretted over.

Like it or not, Ruth carried the name of Denton. She was his daughter-in-law, the wife of his only son, and the mother of his only grandchild, but because she had little time for him, he hardly knew her.

He had always considered that to be a great pity.

Having eaten his dinner and washed the dishes, Bob was now putting them away in the cupboard. Got to keep the place tidy, he thought. As my lovely woman used to say, 'You never know when you might get visitors.'

Like the rest of this lived-in kind of house, the kitchen was a homely place, not 'posh', and certainly not pristine. A well-worn, crinkled mat was at the door, and a row of pretty floral teacups decorated the shelves of the kitchen cabinet. More often than not, there was a used cup on the draining board, next to the tea caddy, and beside that was a barrel of biscuits.

Many things were naturally reused. Every morning Bob would scrunch up yesterday's newspaper and spread it beneath the wood and coal in the fire grate. Later, when he slumped in his favourite armchair to smoke his pipe and read his paper, he would light the fire, and enjoy the evening warming his toes, and eating his hot stew. If there was any stew left over, he'd always take it down to the butcher, who would be very grateful. 'I'll give it to the pigs,' he would say. 'Mek the meat taste that much richer, eh?' Bob told him he didn't want that information, thank you. It was enough to know that the leftovers were of a use to him.

This little house was Bob's castle. It had known much

love and laughter – a house adorned with mementoes of good times – and when you went inside it was like a pair of strong arms wrapping themselves about you, covering you with warmth and love, which over the years had steeped into the walls for all time.

Arranged on the sitting-room walls were many beautiful sketches of local landscapes, each and every one lovingly created by Bob's talented wife, Anne.

With much love and a true painter's eye, she had sketched the green, meandering fields around Pleasington: the town hall on a sunny day; the canal with its colourful barges; even a painting of Addison Street, with its loaf-shaped cobbles and tall iron streetlamps, which lit the way home at night, and provided the supports for children's swings during the day.

It was said that once you'd enjoyed the unique experience of Addison Street, you would never forget it. If you approached the street from the bottom, you had to lean your body forward at a sharp angle, in order to climb to the top.

But if you approached Addison Street from Preston New Road at the top, you would need to be feet first and leaning backwards, in the opposite direction.

Negotiating the street from top to bottom was either foolhardy, or an act of sheer bravery, the locals claimed. It was so impossibly steep that you could never adopt a leisurely pace, though with legs slightly bent and your whole body leaning backwards for balance, you might start off with that intention. The first few steps might give you the confidence to accelerate slightly, but unless you had a desire to be catapulted into Never Never Land, you would be well advised to take it slowly; though that might be harder than you envisaged.

Inevitably you would find yourself increasing pace, going faster and faster, until you started running; by that point, in an uncontrollable and terrifying manner. With your best hat flown away, and hair standing on end, your last resort would be to pray you might get to the bottom without injury.

Once there, with shattered nerves and a fast-beating heart, you'd be anxious to resume your journey on level ground, promising yourself that never again would you be so careless of life and limb.

Some wary adults learned to negotiate the street by walking sideways with their backs to the wall as they edged along; others were known to hang onto the door handles as they inched their way down. And a few staunch heroes might brave the ordeal with a forced smile on their faces.

Most adults dreaded the ordeal of negotiating Addison Street, but chidren would happily throw caution to the winds as they ran from top to bottom, whooping and hollering. When it seemed they might take off and launch themselves into the wild blue yonder, they would catch hold of a passing lamppost and swing round and round until they fell in a dizzy heap on the pavement.

Some said it was better than a free funfair, while Granddad Bob claimed it was his beloved Addison Street that kept him 'fit for owt'.

~

Having just tidied the kitchen, Bob planned to amble his way to the back parlour, where he would settle down with pipe and paper, and choose a likely winning horse from the racing page.

As he went into the passageway, he was surprised and slightly irritated by a determined knock on the door.

He opened the front door, delighted to see Tom and Casey.

'Well, I never!' Opening his arms, he took the boy into

his embrace before inviting him to, 'Get yer coat off an' help yourself to a ginger biscuit from the barrel in the kitchen cabinet. Oh, and by the way, your comics are still in the drawer, if you're wondering.'

Curious, he glanced at the mantelpiece clock. It was almost 8 p.m. At this time of evening, the boy should be at home, getting ready for his bed. And when Tom hung his coat up, the old fella noticed that he was still in his working clothes. That was odd, he thought worriedly. 'Come through, lad. Looks to me like we need to talk, eh?'

Leaving the boy to his biscuits and comic, Bob led his son to the back parlour, where Tom stood with his back to the fireplace, while his father sat himself in the big old armchair.

'What's wrong, lad?' Though a working man, married with a child, Tom was always referred to by his father as 'lad'. In an odd way, it gave him a sense of comfort, but not tonight, because tonight, there was nothing on earth that might comfort him.

'I've left her.' Tom spoke softly so the boy might not hear. He was not proud of his decison, however justified it might be. Nor was he proud of the awful burden he was about to heap on this dear man. 'We're not going back, Dad. Not ever!'

When his father made no response, Tom saw the worry in his face. 'I'm sorry, Dad. I know it was a drastic step to take, but this time, she's gone too far.' In his mind's eye he could see Ruth wildly attacking Casey, and the boy flinching from her, his arms held high in a feeble effort to protect himself.

'I see.' Bob gave a small, understanding smile. 'You had another bad set-to with Ruth, am I right?'

'Yes.' He had no intentions of revealing the shocking thing Ruth had confessed to him about the stranger in the alley being Casey's true father.

'Hmm. Well now, with you and Ruth at loggerheads, and all things taken into account, I can mebbe understand *you* not wanting to go back, but have you considered what Casey wants? Oh, I know he's not yet of an age when he can reason for himself, but he has a quick mind and a voice with which to express his own views. I trust you've taken his feelings into account when you say you're "never" going back? And besides, who's to say this upset with Ruth won't blow over, like they've done many times before?'

'Not this time, Dad.'

'So, why not this time? What's gone on between the two of you that's so unforgivable it can't be put right?'

Tom felt the anger rise in him. 'It can't ever be put right, Dad, because, like I say, this time she's gone too far altogether!'

'But in what way?'

'It doesn't matter. All you need to know is, she's shown her true colours. Take my word, Dad, me and Casey are well out of it. I want nothing more to do with her. It was Casey himself who asked me to bring him here, so he could live here with you. He told me he never wants to go back there.'

For a long, tense moment, the air was thick with Tom's outburst. Then, almost in a whisper, Bob revealed what was on his mind. 'This upset between you and Ruth . . . a man, was it?'

For some time now, he had overheard snippets of worrying gossip. He kept them to himself, because like many a parent, he believed any problems should be taken care of inside the relationship, though it seemed in this particular case that might be too much to ask. 'That's it, isn't it, lad? That wandering wife o' yourn has been cheating on you again.'

Tom was shocked. 'What makes you ask that?' He had

no idea that his father was aware of Ruth's seedy other life.

'Oh, lad! I might be long in the tooth, but I'm not a fool.' When under pressure, Bob had a habit of biting his bottom lip, which he did now. 'The thing is, I've heard mutterings now and then. I had hoped it was just idle gossip amongst folks who'd got nothing better to do. I'm sorry, Tom. I should have known there's no smoke without fire. So, is it true then . . . what they say?'

Tom merely nodded, his sense of shame increasing tenfold.

Getting out of his chair, Bob went to the door and softly closed it. Then he laid his broad, comforting hand on Tom's shoulder. 'You and the boy can stay 'ere as long as you need to. I'll not ask any questions, and I'll not intrude in your marriage . . . unless o' course you need me to. Whichever way you want to handle it, lad, I'm here for you.'

'Thanks, Dad.' Tom was deeply moved by his father's support. 'I promise you, Dad, I haven't taken this step lightly. For a long time now, I've tried to keep the marriage together, mainly for Casey's sake – you've no idea how I've tried – but she doesn't love us . . . not me, and certainly not the boy.'

In that moment, he believed he was the one who had failed, and that things could only get worse. It broke his heart to realise that, out of all this chaos, the person who would be hurt most was young Casey.

As Tom hung his head and choked back the tears, his father held him close. 'It'll be all right, son,' he said. 'Whatever it is, we'll face it together, me and you . . . and our precious boy.'

Tom gave no answer. Instead he kept his head buried in his father's shoulders until his sobs began to subside.

The old man also had tears in his eyes. 'Hey, come on

now, lad. Don't let the boy see you like this. Best get to your bed, eh? Right now, your mind is all over the place. In the morning, we'll all be thinking clearly, then we'll talk it through, and deal with it.'

Holding Tom at arm's length, he was relieved when Tom smiled back at him. 'That's better, son. So, is my plan a good 'un, d'you think?'

'Yeah, Dad. As good as any I've heard.'

When his father seemed relieved, Tom regretted not being able to tell him about the other matter that haunted him. For some time now, Tom had been on the brink of confiding in that dear man, but he could not bring himself to burden him with such crippling news, even though he knew his father would move Heaven and Earth to bring him a measure of peace.

So now, as he thanked his father for accommodating him and Casey, Tom managed a smile; though it was a shallow effort.

Tom was well versed in putting on a brave face, so the old man had no idea that his son was carrying a much heavier burden than he was yet ready to reveal.

Sometimes in life, bad things happened and there was no real explanation as to why. All Tom knew was that these past weeks had been almost unbearable. There was no way for him to ease his mind, and no way he could share the load. So, he carried the burden alone; praying that somehow, his instincts might lead him to do the right thing, for everyone; especially his son.

Somewhere deep inside himself, Tom wanted to believe that Ruth did love the boy, and yet her every word, look and action showed only hatred. Casey felt her rejection of him, and in turn he began to lose both respect and love for his mother. It was a difficult situation, which over the years, had widened the rift between Tom and his wife, and made him love his son even more.

His thoughts now turned to his father. The truth was that however the darling old man might want to 'work out' his son's problems, there was no way that could ever happen. What was done was already done, and there could be no turning back.

In her seemingly cruel way, Fate had intervened.

The dice were thrown and there were no winners.

'I reckon you'd best get the boy to bed, afore he falls asleep on the kitchen floor.' Tom was jolted out of his thoughts by his father's timely reminder.

'I'll do that right now,' Tom answered. 'Mind you, I don't suppose he'd care much if we left him there till morning.'

'Well, we're not having that. So, go on, you put your son to bed, and meantime I'll get us a drop o' summat good to warm the cockles.' Reaching out, he patted Tom on the arm. 'How does that sound, eh?'

'Sounds good to me.' Tom looked into those kindly blue eyes and for one precious moment he felt incredibly safe; even strong enough to take on the world all by himself. 'I can never thank you enough, Dad, for taking us in like this.'

'Oh, give over. You and me, we look after each other. Always have, always will.' He gave Tom a friendly push. 'Now then, be off and get the lad to his bed.'

As Tom hurried towards the kitchen, Bob called after him, 'You needn't worry if you didn't have time to pack a bag for the lad. Casey allus keeps a spare pair o' jamas here. And I've enough shirts upstairs to open a shop. Find one that doesn't altogether drown him, and he'll come to no harm. Now then! Don't forget to fetch him in 'ere, so's he can say good night to his old granddad.'

Tom found Casey on the kitchen floor, with the comic spread out in front of him, but he wasn't reading it. Instead, he was lying flat, with his arms stretched out, and his head resting on his arms. 'It's time for bed, son.' Tom stooped down beside him. 'Granddad Bob needs you to say good night.'

Big, soulful eyes looked up at Tom. 'Did Granddad Bob say we can stay here then?' His voice was suspiciously shaky, and from the smudges round his eyes, Tom suspected he'd been crying.

'We can stay here as long as we want, that's what he said.'

'Can't I stay up a bit longer?'

'No, son. You've had a rough time of it. You need to get your sleep. You look shattered, and besides, me and Granddad Bob need to talk . . . grown-up stuff, if you know what I mean?'

'About that man?'

'About all sorts of things.' Tom wisely skirted the reference to 'that man'.

'Dad?'

'Yes.' Taking the boy by his arms, Tom drew him up. 'What is it, son?'

'I don't think I can go to sleep.'

'Oh, and why's that?' Tom needed to satisfy himself that, tonight of all nights, his son should sleep well and be safe from harm.

One thing was certain: there would be no sleep for Tom himself. Not with his mind in such turmoil. He needed space and quiet in order to think things through. He had to be sure he was doing the right thing for everyone, and not just for himself. Caught between the devil and the deep blue sea, he had made an agonising decision, which was bound to cause further pain and regrets for those he loved.

To his surprise, he found himself counting Ruth in that group. He knew she could be unbelievably cruel, and he deeply regretted the shame she had brought to their marriage. Moreover, he had seen at first hand her uncontrollable dislike for the boy. And yet, for some reason, Tom was surprised to find that he still had feelings for her.

Angry and confused, he thrust away his thoughts and concentrated on Casey. 'Right then, son, let's have you. First, you can say good night to your granddad, then it's off up them stairs.'

'OK.' Without further ado, the boy replaced the biscuit barrel to the shelf, then he folded his comic and tucked it under his arm, before giving a long, lazy yawn. 'Did Granddad really say we can stay here?'

'If we want to, yes.'

'Well, I want to, 'cause I never want to go back home.'

'All right, son, but for now, I need you to put it all out of your mind and get some sleep. Tomorrow is another day, isn't that so?' He thought it surprising that, even after all the turmoil and troubles, the boy still referred to that unhappy dwelling on Henry Street as 'home'.

Granddad Bob held Casey a moment longer than he might normally have done. 'You've had a bit of a rough time,' he said, 'but it's all behind you now, so put it out of your mind, lad. And while you're here, you and your dad must treat this place as your own home. D'you understand?'

'Thank you.' The boy hugged him. 'I love you, Granddad Bob.'

'Mek sure you do, or you'll get no more ginger biscuits.' He gave a little wink. 'Right?'

'Right!'

Giggling, Casey ran across to his father. 'Granddad Bob is really funny.'

Tom laughed. 'Until you leave the bathroom in a mess, then you'll find out differently.'

'I don't leave the bathroom in a mess.'

'Ah, well, that's a good job then, isn't it?'

As the two of them went up the stairs, chatting and laughing, the old man remained deep in thought.

The boy's overheard remark about 'that man' had only confirmed his suspicions about Ruth's continuing affairs.

Yet Bob wondered whether that was just one reason for Tom's distress. He couldn't help but feel that Tom was keeping something back. Something he was not yet ready to share. What else besides his marriage had gone wrong?

The idea of Tom carrying some deep problem he felt unable to share was deeply worrying to the old man; so much so that he began pacing back and forth across the parlour.

Upstairs, Tom lingered by the bathroom door while young Casey squirted a measure of toothpaste onto his finger before rubbing it into his teeth. 'If we're staying here now, I'll need a new toothbrush. I don't want to go back and get my old one. Is that all right, Dad?'

'Fine by me, so long as you stop talking and get on with the business of cleaning your teeth.'

A few minutes later, Casey was done. He then wiped the basin over with a flannel. 'That's all clean now, eh, Dad?' Combing his tousled hair, he smiled at Tom.

'Why yes! I don't think I've ever seen such a clean basin. I reckon Granddad Bob will be very pleased with that. You know how fussy he is about his bathroom.'

As they made their way to the small bedroom, Casey wanted to know, 'Why is Granddad Bob so fussy about his bathroom?'

Tom gave it some thought. 'I reckon it's because, for a long time, we never had a proper bathroom. My mother – the grandma you never knew – well, she always dreamed of having a proper bathroom, instead of bringing in the tin bath that hung on the wall outside. So anyway, when they finally got the boxroom turned into a bathroom, Mam was so happy that she was very particular about having it left clean and tidy.'

'Why was she so puticlar?'

'I think you mean "particular".'

'Hmm! Well, why was she so . . . you know . . . *that*?'

'I'll answer your question when you say the word properly.' Tom sounded it out: 'Par-tic-u-lar.'

'All right then. So, why was she so par-tic-u-lar?'

Laughing, Tom clapped his hands. 'Well done! Mum was so proud of the bathroom that she wanted visitors to see it in all its shining glory, polished up and clean as a whistle. Your granddad remembers that, and it's why he, too, wants the bathroom always to be left clean, just the way Grandma would have liked it.'

'Oh, I see.' Casey was happy with the explanation.

Tom turned back the bedclothes and Casey climbed in.

'Dad?'

'Yes, son?'

'I love it here, with Granddad Bob.'

'Good.'

'Can we stay for ever?'

'Maybe.'

'Would you like to stay here for ever, Dad?'

'I think so.' If things were different, he wondered if his answer might have been more definite.

'And d'you think Granddad Bob would be willing to put up with us, if we stayed for ever, I mean?'

'Yes, 'cause we'd be sure and look after him, wouldn't we?'

'That's right! You could take him to the pub sometimes, and in the summer we could go on picnics; he'd like that. And I could run errands and fetch in the coal. We could go to Blackpool on Sundays and ride on the hobby-horses and after that, we could make sandcastles on the beach. Oh, and then—'

'Whoa!' Tom laughed out loud. 'That all sounds too exhausting and wonderful, and I'm sure Granddad Bob would love it, but I don't think it's a good idea to get all wound up just now, when I need you to go to sleep.' He added cautiously, 'No doubt there'll be time for all that later on.'

The memories of his own wonderful childhood flooded Tom's mind and lifted his heart. Lately, though, he had discovered that sometimes life was really cruel.

When the boy yawned again, Tom tucked the bedclothes over him. 'I'm so proud of you, son.' He sat on the edge of the bed, his fingers twining through the boy's thick hair. 'No man ever had a more wonderful son.'

'Dad?'

'Go to sleep, Casey.'

'But I want to ask you a question.'

'Aw, go on then. But that's the last one.'

'Are you proud of me when I play the guitar and sing?'

'Of course. How could I not be proud of you, eh? You have a gift, and you must always use it. But I'm not only proud of you for that. I'm proud of you because you're a good boy. It makes me feel special to have a son as fine as you.'

For a moment he paused, looking Casey in the eye. 'I want you to tell me the truth, Casey. Are you sorry we left home . . . and your mam?'

'No, Dad, I'm not sorry. I can't be happy at home, because Mam won't let me be. She gets angry and she makes me cry, even when I haven't done anything wrong.'

Tom received the boy's answer with mixed feelings. 'Do you think you might be able to forgive her . . . some day in the future?'

Lowering his gaze, Casey considered Tom's question

before answering quietly, 'I don't know. Sometimes, I don't like Mam very much, and sometimes . . . well, I think I might love her. Only she doesn't want me to love her, and she won't love me back.'

'I understand what you're saying,' Tom reassured him. In his heart he was content to think that Ruth might never again get her claws into this boy. Then again, Casey was her son, and he needed a mother. And yet, if Ruth really had no warm feelings for him, he might be better off without her altogether.

'It's difficult to love someone, isn't it?' Tom said now. 'Like you, I'm not really sure if she wants us or not. But there's always the chance that she'll change her mind. And if that happens, it would of course be for you to decide whether or not you want to forgive her.'

'I'll never forgive her!' Casey had not forgotten. 'She called me a liar, and I know what I heard. Anyway, she doesn't want me. She said so.'

Before Tom could reply, the boy asked quietly, 'She meant it, didn't she, Dad?'

Tom shrugged. 'Yes, I think she did . . . at the time, but when we're angry, we all say all kinds of things we don't mean.'

'Well, if she doesn't want me, then I don't want her. I've made up my mind, and I won't go back.'

'All right, son. That's enough now. We're here at Grand-dad's, and he said you can stay as long as you want. So, let's leave it at that, shall we?'

'All right.'

'I love you, Casey, and all I want is for you to be happy.'

'But I can't be happy just now, 'cause I'm a little bit sad that I can't play the guitar any more.'

'Then we'll just have to get it mended, won't we?'

'How can we do that?' He looked up at Tom with wide eyes, the tearful words tumbling one over the other. 'It's all busted, and the strings have jumped out, and . . . it's no good any more.'

Tom gathered him into his arms. 'Trust me, son,' he murmured, 'it can be mended.'

'But, it's all in bits.' Casey's tears spilled over. 'It can't ever be mended. Never, never!'

'Hey!' Tom wagged a finger. 'Have I ever promised to do something that can't be done?'

The child shook his head. 'No.'

'Right! So trust me now. Tears and tantrums won't mend anything. But there must be a man out there who can mend whatever needs mending; even a guitar with "jumped-out" strings, and bits of wood missing.'

'Where is he, then?'

'Well, I can't be really sure, not yet, but there must be someone out there. I mean, there are clockmakers to mend clocks; tailors to repair clothes, and mechanics to mend broken engines. So I reckon that means there must be someone who mends guitars. Isn't that so?'

Tom was rewarded with a bright, happy smile. 'Yeah! And we'll find him, won't we, Dad?'

Relieved that the boy's spirits were up again, Tom gave an encouraging nod. 'Now close your eyes and go to sleep.'

'Dad?'

'What now?'

'Will you tell me that story, about when you were a little boy, and Granddad used to take you to Mill Hill bridge, where you watched the trains running underneath, and all the steam blew up into your faces?' He grinned at the thought. 'You said you felt invisible.'

'That's right, son. Oh, but they were wonderful times. I was a very lucky boy to have those adventures.' Just now, when Casey mentioned the railway bridge at Mill Hill, Tom's heart had almost stopped, because that particular place from his childhood had played heavily on his mind lately.

Now, though, because of the boy's curiosity, he was made to revisit Mill Hill bridge in his mind once more. The thought of his father and himself walking under that picturesque viaduct and onwards, up the bank and along the curve of the bridge itself, was one of Tom's most precious memories.

When other, darker thoughts clouded his troubled mind, he smiled at the irony. 'Are you sure you want that particular story, son?'

'Yes, please.'

With mixed emotions, Tom told the story about the days when he and Granddad Bob had regularly stood on the bridge for hours, watching the trains as they made their noisy way beneath, sending clouds of steam upwards and outwards. There was always much laughter when the steam enveloped the two of them, before quickly evaporating in the air.

While Casey laughed aloud, Tom blinked away stinging tears. 'Soon the next train would come along,' he went on, 'and sometimes we'd lean over the bridge wall, with your granddad Bob hanging onto my pants to stop me from falling headfirst onto the railway lines below. The steam was everywhere. When we finally came away, my hair would feel really damp to the touch. Then Granddad Bob would always threaten to turn me upside down when we got home.'

'Why would he turn you upside down?'

'So's he could wash the kitchen floor with my damp hair . . . or at least that's what he said.'

Casey laughed out loud. 'He wouldn't really do that, would he?'

'No, it was just his idea of a joke.'

Having been persuaded to tell the tale for the umpteenth time, Tom's heart was heavy.

Nevertheless, he told it as promised, right to the end; by which time Casey was fast asleep.

Tom stayed with him for a while. He held his hand, and watched him sleeping. His tearful eyes roved over that small, familiar face, and for a precious time he lay beside him, oddly content just to watch him sleep.

In those precious moments of quiet, he could almost hear the boy's heartbeat, as regular as a clock counting away the minutes.

Tom closed his eyes and whispered a prayer. 'Dear Lord above, please help me to be strong, and forgive me if you can. And it would give me some peace if you could find your way to making Casey's wishes come true. Could you show him the way to become a fine musician? It isn't much to ask, is it, not when he's already losing so much in his turbulent young life?' He felt guilty and so very sad.

When, a few moments later, Tom found himself falling asleep, he clambered off the bed and, after making sure Casey was resting easy, made his way downstairs.

His father was sitting in the armchair beside a warm, crackling fire.

'Oh, 'ere you are, Tom. I were beginning to think you'd gone to bed, an' all,' he remarked cheerily. 'Mind you, I nearly nodded off meself a minute or two back. I'll not be long afore I make my own way up them stairs, I can tell you.'

'It was a while before Casey closed his eyes,' Tom explained. 'He had so many questions. His main worry was how to get the guitar mended, after Ruth smashed it to pieces.'

The old man tutted angrily. 'Smashed it to pieces, eh? Shame on the woman! That was a terrible, wicked thing to do, even for her!'

Tom, too, had been astonished at the violent way in

which she'd smashed the guitar into the wall; almost as though she was taking her rage out on a living thing . . . a person, maybe.

Bob went on thoughtfully, 'Don't say anything to the lad just yet in case it comes to nothing, but I recall somebody talking in the pub last week. They're thinking of having a piano player of a Sat'day night, and it seems there's a fella round these parts who knows a great deal about musical instruments and such. Mebbe he can rebuild that guitar?'

The idea gave Tom a deal of contentment before the feeling of sadness took hold again. He closed his eyes and thought of Ruth, and he regretted with all his heart the pain she had caused that young boy.

His own pain was of no importance compared to other issues, but he felt really hurt for Casey, who had his whole life ahead of him, with all its unexpected twists and turns.

The old man had seen the change in his son's manner. 'You look like somebody lost,' he said. 'Sit yersel' down, lad. I've poured you a drop o' gin. It'll help wash your troubles away.' He gestured to the tumbler on the small table. 'Get it down you, lad. It'll do you a world o' good.'

Making a smile, Tom took the glass and settled in the opposite armchair beside the fire. Being closer now, he observed the rosy glow in his dad's weathered old face, but it was the twinkle in his eye that gave him away. 'Looks to me like you've started without me,' Tom laughed. 'Not that I blame you, because we both need a tipple after what's happened.'

The old man nodded. 'There's nowt wrong wi' a drop o' the good stuff now and then, so long as you don't let it become a habit. Everything in moderation – isn't that what they say? A little drop occasionally, that's the trick. Enough for you to celebrate when you're on the up, and lift your spirits when you're down.'

Tom agreed. 'So, where are we now, up or down?'

'Well, with you having to leave your wife, I'd say we were down a while ago, but now that you and my grandson are 'ere with me, safe and well, I reckon we must be on the up. So, to my mind, that calls for another little tipple.' He held out his empty glass. 'Not too much, mind. We've things to talk through, and I need a clear 'ead on me shoulders.'

So, they had a second little tipple, and talked into the late hours. Tom explained how Ruth had been sleeping with one of his workmates, and that she'd entertained him in their own house, in their own bed, and worse, 'Young Casey was right there, outside the bedroom. He actually heard the man's voice from inside, and when he felt the need to tell me, she started on him. Like a wild thing she was.'

The old man was shocked. 'Aye, well, there's no accounting for some folks, and if you ask me, you did right in leaving. I'm glad you brought the boy 'ere. I'd have done exactly the same!'

A moment later, having knocked back his tipple, he got out of his chair and gave a long stretch. 'I'm off to me bed, son, afore I drop off in the chair. See you in the morning, eh?'

Tom gave a little nod. 'Good night, Dad.' He watched his father amble across the room. 'Sleep well, and thanks again. If it hadn't been for you taking us in, I don't know what might have happened.'

The old man turned round. 'It's what any man would do for them as he loves.'

His kind words struck a deep chord with Tom. On a sudden impulse he went across the room and, taking his father into a deep hug, he told him, 'All my life you've been an example to me. I hope I've done the same for my boy.'

Surprised by Tom's fierce display of affection, the old

man held him at arm's length. 'I know you're upset about everything, but you're not to worry, son. As for being a good father to your own son, nobody could have done better. I promise we'll be fine, all three of us. One way or another, we'll sort it out and, like you, I'm determined young Casey will get his chance.' He smiled sincerely. 'Even if it means me trying to mend that guitar meself. Trust me, son, that little lad will have his time.'

Patting Tom on the back, he confided, 'It's you I'm worried about. You look like you've been through the wringer. I noticed straight off, from seeing you last week, you've lost weight. Oh, I can understand how this business with Ruth would bring you down . . . bring any man down, I'm sure!'

He lowered his voice. 'The thing is, I can't help but feel you're not telling me everything.'

Resting his hands on Tom's shoulders, he asked him outright, 'Be honest with me, son. Is there summat you're not saying? Summat else that's caused you to turn your back on house and home? Though God knows, what with yer wife carrying on like that, and then upsetting that little lad, that's more than enough to send a man off the rails. All the same, I need you to be honest with me. So, is there summat?' He looked Tom in the eye. 'You can trust me, son. Whatever it is, you know I'm here to help.'

Sidestepping his father's direct question, Tom shook his head. 'You already know the problem, and now here you are, right in the middle of it, when I should be dealing with it myself. I'm sorry, Dad. I truly never meant for that to happen.' Casting his gaze to the floor, he finished lamely, 'Truth is, things have got on top of me, and I can't help but wonder . . . how will it all end.'

'Tom, now you listen to me!' Struck by Tom's heartfelt words, Bob told him firmly, 'I'm all right with being caught up in your troubles. When a family's in need, we all pull together, isn't that the way it's allus been? If I needed a home, I know you would never turn me away. We're family, and families look after each other. God willing, I'll be here for you for as long as the Good Lord sees fit to let me live. D'you understand me, son? If you're in trouble, it's my trouble as well, and so long as I've got a roof over my head, so have you and the boy . . . even Ruth, if she ever saw fit to mend her ways. So, we'll 'ave no more o' this thanking me, and worrying yerself stupid.'

He paused, before speaking firmly: 'I've asked you once, and now I'll ask again. Is there summat you're not telling me?'

'What d'you mean?'

'What I mean is, while I understand about Ruth and her bad ways, I can't help but feel, in here,' he thumped his chest, 'that you're deliberately holding summat back. Are yer?'

Again, Tom skirted the question as honestly as he could. 'Dad! I've told you what happened,' he said.

'And that's everything, is it?'

Tom forced a cynical little laugh. 'Isn't that enough?'

'Mmm.' The old man was still not altogether satisfied, but as he was dog-tired, anything else could wait until morning. 'All right, son.' He patted Tom on the shoulder. 'I'm off to my bed now, and from the look of you I reckon you need to do the same.' He was concerned at Tom's appearance: the dark, hollow patches under his eyes, and that forsaken look that took away his smile. 'We'll talk tomorrow. Good night, son. Don't stay up too late, and remember, you and the boy are all right here with me. I'm well suited wi' that.'

'Good night then, Dad. Thanks.'

Still troubled, Bob went carefully up the narrow, winding staircase. At the top, he turned towards the bedroom where Casey was sleeping soundly.

For a while, he stood by the bed, looking tenderly down on that strong little face. Well, lad, it sounds like you and yer father have had a real bad time of it, he thought. 'But thank God, you're safe now, and while I'm 'ere to watch over yer, you'll come to no harm. I don't know what he's hiding, but I'm not such an old fool I don't know when my own son is troubled.'

Looking on the boy again, Bob's face wreathed in a smile.

Mind you, I'm old and addled, and I could be imagining things. I mean, I've been wrong afore, an' who's to say I'm not wrong now? Not to worry, eh, lad? The truth is, we all need a good night's sleep. Things will likely look a whole lot better in the morning.

Leaning down, he gently kissed the boy's forehead. 'You've no need to fret about the guitar, lad,' he whispered, 'because your old gramp will get it fixed. You'll see, one way or another, you'll be playing like a good 'un in no time at all.'

He gazed fondly on the boy a moment longer, then he went softly to the door, where he gave a last look back before ambling on to his own bedroom.

Walking carefully to avoid the creaking boards on the landing, he heard the clock strike the eleventh hour, and the downstairs radio playing soft music.

'Go to bed, son,' he muttered under his breath. 'Today was a bad 'un, but tomorrow is a new day altogether.'

With that thought in mind he went to his bed hoping that, when tomorrow came, his son might be more able to confide in his old dad.

~

Downstairs in the back parlour, Tom sat at the small table. With his eyes closed and the palms of his hands covering his head, he made no attempt to wipe away the tears that ran freely down his face.

Instead, he searched his mind for a way out; a way that would cause the least distress; a way that might allow them to forgive him.

But there *was* no way out, and he was mortified at the thought of what he was about to do.

In the comfortable familiarity of that small room, alone and deeply troubled, he remained still, his mind going over the remnants of his life, while the only sound breaking the silence was the insistent ticking of the clock on the mantelpiece.

Allowing the rhythmic sound to ripple through his body, he thought it reminiscent of the constancy of Casey's beating heart.

'Casey . . .' He softly murmured his name. 'I hope you'll forgive me, in time.'

Raising his head, he glanced about the room, his gaze lingering on the armchair where his father often sat and did his football pools, or picked his horses for the Saturday races.

Decorating the sideboard were his mother's much-loved ornaments. There was a brown and white pot dog, and beside that a large, framed photograph of his parents and himself as a boy. The picture was a happy one, taken by a beach photographer on a day out to Cleveleys. In pride of place was the big, painted vase that Tom had bought his mother, along with a bunch of flowers to put in it. He remembered, sadly, that birthday had been her last.

Each and every item in this cosy room held a memory. Normally, he found great comfort in that. But not tonight.

Sadness overwhelmed him, but then he looked again at the photograph, and he remembered those happy times. Over the years, this little house had always been a haven to him. Here with his parents and his friends, he had experienced laughter and joy. He had learned from his parents both practical matters and the freedom to dream.

Above all else, he had grown through childhood to manhood, being blessed with a great sense of belonging. Treasures such as that were priceless.

He remembered his fortunate boyhood, and his heart broke for Casey.

Getting up from the table, he absent-mindedly wiped the drying tears from his face. He then went to the sideboard where he lifted the photo frame. Taking a moment to gaze down on those three happy faces, he gave a whimsical smile. With the tip of his finger he traced the younger faces of his beloved parents, and he remembered that wonderful day out like it was only yesterday.

Replacing the photograph, he then opened the tiny drawer in which his father kept his notepaper and envelopes. They were hardly ever used these days, as he had little reason to write letters. But every now and then an article would appear in the newspaper that would stir up the fight in him, and he would pen a long and carefully crafted letter, spelling out his agreement or disagreement.

Taking the writing paper, together with three envelopes, a pot of ink and a fountain pen, Tom returned to the table.

For what seemed an age, he sat at the table with the articles before him. He had known for some time that he must write these letters, but now that the occasion was actually here, he found it difficult to think straight. His mind was too scrambled. All he could hear was the grandmother clock in the hall, striking the half-hour.

He arranged the notepaper; unscrewed the lid of the ink bottle, and took the top from the fountain pen. What to say? He stared at the paper for a while, searching for the right words. Then he began.

'My dearest Son,'

When Ruth's cruel words came into his mind, he viciously scrunched up the paper.

Distressed, he put the pen down and sat for a while going over her claim in his mind: 'Casey is not your son . . . I've no idea who the father is, but I do know it's not you . . . a dark alley . . . some stranger . . .' Her voice echoed in his brain. 'Casey is not your son . . .'

Picking up the pen, he started the letter once more.

My dearest Casey,

I have things to tell you, some of which no man should ever have to say to his beloved son.

Since the moment you were born, you have brought me such pride and joy, and I have loved and protected you, with every breath in my body.

Throughout your life, and even when you are very old – God willing – please remember these words, for they're spoken from the heart.

I have to tell you something now, that will make you sad, and that is the last thing I would ever want to do.

By the time you get this letter, your granddad Bob will have spoken with you and explained the reasons why I did the awful thing I'm about to do. When you know the truth, I hope you will understand, and find it in your heart to forgive me.

My love will always be with you, son, and if it's possible, I will be ever by your side, watching and guiding you. When you're worried and sad of heart, you might hear

the softest rush of sound about you. It
will be me, come to encourage and help
you.
Be brave, my son. Follow your heart,
and know always that I love you.
Dad XX

After a while, Tom got up from the chair and paced the floor; his painful thoughts on the boy, whom he feared might never understand. What if he thinks me a coward? What if he turns against my memory, he wondered.

He was certain of one thing: if he changed his mind now, his loved ones would suffer the most.

So many times he had agonised over his decision. If he went one way, he would be creating a physical and emotional burden, with no closure in sight.

If he kept to his original plan, there would still be the emotional burden, but he hoped that would ease with time. But there would also be closure, which would be quick, decisive, and of his own choosing.

Returning to the table, he picked up the pen and set out a new sheet of notepaper. This time there were no tears. He felt only a peculiar sense of isolation, almost as though it was someone else sitting there, and not him.

His father loomed large in his mind. He had always seen Bob Denton as a man of stature and consequence – everything he now believed himself not to be.

Casting all doubt aside, he remained true to his plan. There was no going back now.

Dear Dad,
Your instincts were right when you asked
if I was hiding something from you.
The truth is, some time ago, after a
short bout of illness which you may

remember, I was obliged to go for a check-up, and they discovered a disease of the bones, which though it might be treated, can never be cured.

Lately, the condition has got much worse, and I fear that very soon I will be unable to work, and eventually unable to walk without assistance. Consequently, I'll need the use of a wheelchair.

My future is bleak. It means that my life as an able man who provides for his family will not only come to an end, but the disability will also render me entirely dependent on my loved ones. And though I know you would accept the responsibility gracefully, I can't let that happen.

You can be sure, Dad, that I have spent many hours thinking of a way to deal with this cruel situation.

I don't want to suffer the ordeal of just biding my time before the inevitable happens. More often of late, I've felt the disease creeping up on me, and it haunts my every waking thought. Not just because my own life will be changed for ever, but because it will affect the lives of those who love me.

I can't accept the idea of the pain it will cause you and Casey to watch me deteriorate.

Constantly thinking about it proves how much it's already beginning to shape my life. Sometimes at work, I'm so troubled that my thoughts begin to drift away, and I'm not aware of what's going on around

me. Things will never be the same again.
I'm frightened, Dad.

You are a proud and strong man, and
you have always been a great inspiration to
me. Sadly this time, there's nothing you can
do to help except to take care of my boy,
as I know you will. And if you can find it
in your heart to keep an eye on Ruth,
even if only from a distance, I would rest
easy.

Ruth is a troubled woman, Dad. She's
impulsive, driven by anger and hatred, but
I would not want her to come to a bad
end. She is after all, Casey's mother.

Please forgive me, Dad. Teach my son,
the way you taught me, and tell him I'm
so sorry. And that I love you both, always
and for ever.

Your grateful and loving son,
Tom XX

There was a third, and final letter.

This was for his wife, Ruth. It was a letter of reconciliation.

In many ways, this was the most difficult one to write, because she had hurt him in the cruellest way possible by claiming he was not the father of this wonderful boy he had raised.

Even now, he found it hard to forgive her. He desperately wanted to write the letter, and yet at the same time, it was the last thing he wanted to do.

He was still angry, and also concerned that, whatever he might say, it would be of no consequence to her. She was his wife, and he still felt a stirring of love for her. Yet for some time now she had been almost a stranger to him.

He pined for that long ago love, and for what might have been.

After a moment's thought, he decided he must try to make the letter brief and to the point. That was his intention, but emotions were a powerful force.

Dear Ruth,

Please, don't disregard this letter. These words will be the last I ever say to you, and I have many things to tell you. First, how much I regret not being the husband you wanted. I regret many things: working too long and hard, and not keeping time aside for the two of us. I'm sorry for not being the man you could confide in.

I have been lacking in trust, because I have never told you the truth. I have long been aware of your many affairs, but each time I tried to talk with you, the anger and distrust got in the way. I should have fought harder for your love, instead of giving up on you.

None of that matters now, because our life together is over.

There are important things I need to ask of you, Ruth, for all our sakes.

By the time you get this letter, you will know the circumstances. I am truly sorry it had to come to this, because even after all that's happened between us, I want you to know how I truly feel about you, Ruth. How I have always felt about you.

The plain and simple truth is, I still love you. And though he'll be feeling bruised and frightened at the moment, Casey also loves you.

Because of my actions, he'll need you more than ever. You and his granddad are now the only people he has in the whole wide world.

I've convinced myself that the awful thing you said about a 'stranger in the alley' was just a wicked way of hurting me. Casey has always been my son, and always will be. And because of that, I ask – no, I'm begging you, Ruth – please don't ever give the boy a reason to doubt who he is. When it all comes down to it, you need him, far more than you yet realise. Like you, he has a strong and determined mind. I believe he's destined for wonderful things; if not through music, then something else. He has a passion for life. He's far-sighted, and caring. And he's your flesh and blood. Please, Ruth, look out for each other.

Show him that you really do love him, because I know you do. How can you not love him? He's your son, after all.

I wish with all my heart that I could be there to make amends, and bring the family back together. But Fate has decreed that I should choose between the devil and the deep blue sea.

In the end I am following my instincts and choosing the only way that I believe and hope will lessen the pain for my loved ones.

In spite of all the rage inside you, Ruth,

I know there is also goodness, if only you will stop fighting it.

I always wanted to see you content, and sadly all I saw was torment. Make peace with yourself, Ruth. For your own sake, and for Casey's sake too. Help each other, because even if you don't realise it, you need him, and he needs you. More now than ever. God bless, and please, my darling, think about what I'm asking of you. I want this for you and Casey. I hope and pray that you will do the right thing.

And, Ruth, if only we had trusted each other, it could have been so very different. But it isn't too late for you and Casey.

Remember the good times, and remember I loved you,

Tom XX

Tom carefully folded each letter and placed it in an envelope. He then wrote each recipient's name, together with the same instruction, 'This letter to be opened only by the person named below.'

Agitated, he paced the floor, wondering where to put them. He had to place them so Casey would not find them, but where they could be easily found by his father. It was Tom's intention that his son would be told the awful truth by his beloved grandfather, after he himself had learned of it. With that in mind, he realised there was only one place he could safely leave the letters.

Just now, though, for some inexplicable reason, he had a sudden urge to sit in his father's armchair. Nervously, he went across the room, and for a long moment he stood looking down on that much-loved and well-worn chair.

Now, as he sank into its cavernous depth, it was almost as though the chair wrapped itself around him and held him there. With a sense of joy, he closed his eyes and allowed himself to be one with it. This old chair. His father's chair. Something that was always there, like the walls of the house or the ground beneath his feet, calm and welcoming, even while chaos reigned all about.

A great sadness came over him, and then he was overwhelmed with all manner of emotions: joy and reassurance, because he felt closer to that wonderful man; pride, because that man was his own father, and grandfather to Casey.

There was a sense of grief too because of the awful thing he was about to do, and the pain he would surely leave in his wake.

Sitting there in that big, squashy chair, he was aware of the normal, familiar sounds in this homely little house: the insistent ticking of the clock; the soft rush of air forced through a gap between the top of the door and the framework – a fault his father had long meant to put right, but never did.

When Tom offered to do it, Bob would have none of it. 'That's my job, lad!' That was his pride talking. So Tom never offered again, and the draught got worse. But in the end, in the greater scheme of things, what did it matter?

Just now, his father's snoring gentled into his thoughts. Outside, the night air was disturbed by many high-pitched whines as the neighbourhood cats hunted for mates. Comforting, familiar sounds that he would never hear again.

In this house where he grew up, everything was exactly the same. Now, though, for him, everything was changed. Changed for ever more.

Taking the three letters, he went up the narrow staircase.

On the landing he trod carefully, so as to avoid the creaking floorboards. Going first to his son, he entered the room silently.

Kneeling down beside the sleeping child, he tenderly kissed the boy's forehead. 'I could tell you a million times that I love you. And still, you would never know how much.'

He made his way along the landing to his father's room, where he silently inched open the door. He could see his father's bulky figure, lying flat on his back, mouth wide open, sending out a series of tuneful snores. It made Tom smile.

Going quietly to the bedside, Tom watched his father for a while, then, with his father's letter uppermost, he put all three letters down on the bedside cabinet. He made sure they were well positioned, so that on waking his father would see his own letter first.

Tom's whispered goodbye was tearful. 'Look after our boy, will you, Dad?' he murmured. 'And please forgive me, if you can.'

He then made his way downstairs, and along the passage to the front door, where he collected his coat from the peg.

Shrugging it on, he took a moment to fasten the buttons, then gave one last, lingering glance up to where his loved ones were sleeping. *'Take care of them, Lord'*. When the tears threatened, he choked them back.

Taking a deep, sobering breath, he went softly from the house, making sure the door was secured behind him.

Shivering in the night air, Tom drew the lapels of his coat together and hurried down Addison Street. His mind was alive with all manner of memories from his childhood: of the way he used to laugh and shout as he raced with friends down this steep path; of the visiting funfair at Easter, with all the noise and merriment.

And how could he not remember the Blackpool trips with his parents, eating ice cream on the beach, and the first donkey ride he ever had? Once, when the donkey ran off with him, his dad caught up and saved him from a fall.

He recalled his and Ruth's wedding day, when his father wore a proper shirt and tie for the first and last time ever. He recalled the wonder they had all felt when Casey was born, and the proud moments when each of them first held little Casey in their arms.

Like moving pictures, all these precious, priceless moments rippled through his heart and filled his mind, making him all the more determined to save his loved ones from what he believed would be an agony worse than even he could imagine.

Striding away from Addison Street, he cut through the cobbled backstreets, making for Whalley Banks and King Street. Determined, yet somewhat nervous, he never once looked back.

He didn't need to look on what he had once had, because he was taking it all with him in his mind.

In no time at all, he was leaving all the familiar haunts behind: Leyland Street, where the boys played footie on the cobbles; the Ragged School, for ragged children; Craig Street, where he and friends became miniature cowboys and villains. The little bike shop, where you could pay a few coins to hire a rusty old bicycle for the weekend. And of course, the cinema, where all the naughty kids, including Tom, would sneak in for a free show.

Going swiftly on, he passed the familiar run of shops, including Mrs Martin's flower and bric-a-brac shop, then across the cobbled ginnel and the old tripe shop, and on towards Mill Hill.

He dared not let himself think about what had gone before. Nor did he fret about things that might have been in the future. Instead, he cleared his mind of everything that might deter him from his intention.

With every strong, purposeful stride, he drew nearer to his destination.

Soon, he was passing the Mill Hill pub and Bower Street. Only a few more steps, and he was on the railway bridge.

~

Dolly Pritchard lived in the corner house on Parkinson Street, a long, busy street of terraced houses situated alongside the railway lines.

Having married at the age of twenty, Dolly and her new husband moved into the terraced house and lived there together for thirty-five years. Having lost her husband five years ago, to a swift and unforgiving illness, she remained in the house. It was her home, and having now turned sixty, with greying hair and a few extra pounds round the middle, she thought herself past the upheaval of setting up somewhere else.

Instead she got herself a loyal little dog from the dog pound, on the very day he was due to be put down as an unwanted stray. Dolly loved Bartie at first sight. He was a hairy, misshapen little creature, with an insatiable thirst for adventure.

Most nights she had to cajole him back inside with a juicy titbit. Only this time, he refused to come in, and when next door's cat popped its head round the corner, the dog took after it, and the pair of them were soon scampering out of sight.

Dolly called Bartie several times, and promised him the world, but that wily little dog was not about to come home; at least not until he'd taught that cat a lesson it would never forget.

'You little minx!' Dolly was well known for her sergeant-major voice. 'You come back here this minute, or I'll give you what for, and no mistake!'

The dog, however, was long gone.

Muttering angrily, Dolly put on her hat and coat, and collected the dog lead from the drawer in the sideboard. Ready for war, she made her way down the passage, and out onto the step, key in hand. She turned to look up and down the street in case the dog had started his way home.

It was then that she noticed the figure on the railway bridge.

In the hazy light from the streetlamp she recognised it to be a young man. What was he doing, hanging about there at that time of night?

Curious, she remained in the doorway, watching, one eye directed up the street for her dog, and the other on the young man. She could see how his head was bent, as though he was looking down at the railway lines below. 'What can he see down there, I wonder?'

A horrible thought crossed her mind: Oh, my God! That little scamp has got on the lines!

Dropping the door key into her pocket, she ran to where Tom was standing.

'Is there a little dog down there?' she asked breathlessly. 'Can you see him? The little devil ran off to chase a cat, and I can't find him. Is he down there?' She edged her way forward. 'Bartie, come on, boy!'

Tom was startled by the sudden appearance of this kindly looking lady. He shook his head. 'I haven't seen any dog,' he told her quietly. 'I was just looking . . . well . . . for nothing in particular, I suppose. I didn't see any dog, though. I should think he got tired of chasing the cat and went home. He's probably waiting for you at the door.' Regrettably, this woman had managed to disturb his mood.

Dolly's curiosity was heightened. 'So, if you didn't see a dog down there, what exactly were you looking at?'

Tom gave a little shrug.

Dolly was persistent. 'Have you got someone to meet at the station?' she asked casually, 'because if you have, you'd best get along there now. If I remember right, the last train is due in about five minutes or so.'

'I'm all right for a while yet,' Tom replied. 'Don't worry about me, just go and find your little dog.'

Ignoring his suggestion, Dolly took a closer look at this young man. She noticed how jittery he seemed, and the intent way he kept glancing down towards the rail tracks. Also, the way his hands were wrapped tight over the wall, almost as though he was bracing himself for something. Something she dared not even think about. What was he doing there, at that time of night? And why was he staring down at the rails, seemingly oblivious of her presence?'

'Are you all right, son?' she asked him.

Hearing her use of the word 'son', Tom was deeply shaken. 'I really think you should go and find your dog, before it gets itself in trouble,' he told her.

'But are you sure you're all right?'

Tom nodded, and so she bade him good night. 'You've only got a few minutes to get to the station and meet your friend,' she warned on parting. 'You don't want to keep them waiting.'

Tom was not listening. He had heard the train whistle from far off, and he knew what he must do.

Tom was touched by the way the lady had addressed him in that same easy, familiar way his own father did.

Tom recalled the day he and his father came right here to this very bridge, to spot the trains.

He'd been so excited, he'd leaned far over the wall in order to see the trains better, until his father had swiftly hoisted him back with a gentle reprimand. 'Don't you ever do that again, son. Them trains don't stop for nothing, least of all for a scrap of a boy like you.' He'd led Tom away. 'I'm sorry, son, but you gave me a real fright, leaning over like that.' He'd marched Tom to King Street and into old John's toffee shop, where he treated him to a glass of sarsaparilla.

Just then, in his tortured mind, Tom could clearly see himself and his father on this very spot where he stood now. For a moment, the image hurt so much he could hardly breathe. But the moment passed, and his intention remained strong.

This was the place where he had known such joy and laughter. He belonged here, together with all the wonderful memories.

He heard the woman bid him good night. He watched her walk away, calling out as she went, 'Mind how you go, young man!'

The train whistle sounded nearer. Feeling strangely calm, Tom sat on the wall, his legs dangling over; his gaze following the rising steam as it approached.

Just a short distance away, Dolly was greatly relieved to find her little dog. 'You naughty scamp!'

Threading the lead through his collar, she turned to make her way back, when she heard the scream of the train whistle. It was very close. Some deep inner instinct urged her to quicken her steps. On nearing the bridge, she tried to make out the young man, but the steam rose and hid him from sight.

As the train sped towards him, Tom waited for the right moment. When it came, he hesitated for just a split second, then with a forgiving heart, he leaned forward, loosened his hold and slid softly away.

His last thoughts before the train hit him full on were for Casey and his father.

His last *words*, however, were for the woman who had caused her son and himself such torment. 'I love you, Ruth. I always have.'

Dolly was just a short distance away, when she saw him let go of the wall. And then, in the blink of an eye, he was gone.

'Oh God, NO . . . NO!' Shocked and tearful, she ran forward, but it was too late. Realising what his intentions had been all along, she now understood his anxiety to send her away.

How she wished with all her heart that she had stayed, and talked a while longer. If only she'd persuaded him to confide in her, she might have prevented him from doing such a shocking thing.

Shaken to her very bones, she remained momentarily transfixed to the spot. She wanted to peer over the wall, but was terrified of what she might see. Through the turmoil in her mind she knew it was too late. Mere flesh and blood could never have survived such an impact.

With the initial trauma beginning to ebb away, she began violently shaking. Then she was sobbing uncontrollably. 'I should have stayed with him. I should have stopped him.' She blamed herself.

Screaming out to raise the alarm, she crossed the street at a run. 'Help! Please . . . somebody.' Reaching her next-door neighbour's house, she banged her fists on the door and yelled at the top of her voice, 'Billy! Open the door.' She stole a nervous, fleeting glimpse at the bridge where the young man had been, 'BILLY! For God's sake open this door!'

When the door was opened by a sleepy, middle-aged man in his pyjamas, she rushed past him, the words tumbling out in a rush as she told him what she had seen. Then she was sobbing helplessly, holding onto him, telling him about 'that sad young man' and how she had an idea

113

of what he meant to do. 'I should've stayed with him. I should have stopped him . . .'

When she grew hysterical, Billy firmly urged her to stay calm and speak clearly.

When he understood the details he asked quietly, 'Are you sure he meant to jump? Could he not have accidentally slipped from the wall?'

Dolly shook her head. 'No . . . no!' Thinking back, she could see the incident so clearly in her mind it was too shocking to comprehend. 'He just . . . let go of the wall and slid over the edge. He . . .' she took a deep breath, '. . . he told me he was going to meet a friend at the station, but I know now that was a lie. There was no friend. He waited for the train to come . . .' her voice quivered, '. . . he was waiting for the train to get close enough to the bridge, and then he just . . .'

Momentarily silent, she knew she would never forgive herself for not staying there to keep him company, to talk with him. 'I blame myself,' she murmured. 'I should have realised . . .'

'Hey, it's not your fault,' Billy calmed her. 'If that young man truly meant to jump from the bridge, there's nothing whatsoever you could have done to stop him. If you'd stayed, he might have moved away, but probably only until you were out of sight. From what you tell me, I reckon he was determined.'

Dolly was past listening. Instead, she was rocking back and forth in the chair, quietly sobbing and chunnering to herself.

After gently quietening her, Billy firmly advised, 'We'd best call the police. When they get here, you must tell them exactly what you just told me.'

114

CHAPTER FOUR

Casey was out of bed and eager to see his father, when he heard a car door slam shut in the street below.

Having already pulled one sock up to his ankle, he now hopped awkwardly to the window, while continuing to pull it up to his knee.

For a fleeting moment he thought about his mother, and the awful row that had brought him and his dad here. He had stayed over with his granddad Bob many times before, but never with his dad in the next room. Now, though, he needed to talk to him about his mam and everything . . .

Throwing open the curtains, he closed his mind to the bad things his mam had said. Instead, he chose to concentrate only on what his dad had told him afterwards: that he was his son, and always would be.

Curious now, Casey pressed his nose to the windowpane. Looking down, he noticed one police officer standing by a black car, and another policeman climbing out of the other side and making his way round to the pavement. He saw the severe expressions on their faces, and when the two officers went to the front door of Granddad Bob's house, a sense of dread came over Casey.

Why were they here? What did the police want with Granddad Bob? Was he in trouble? Then Casey thought of the row between his parents. *'It's Mam! She's called the police to come and take me away.'* Or had she sent them for his dad? Had she lied and claimed that he'd hit her? Casey knew she'd lied before. But how could the police take his dad away when he had done nothing wrong?

He had to go down and tell the police . . . his dad had done nothing wrong. It was his mam's fault. Look how she'd punched him with her fists, and when Dad tried to stop her she went mad and broke Granddad Bob's guitar. It was all her fault.

Quickly, he grabbed his other grey sock and, sitting on the edge of the bed, he struggled to put it on.

Rushing to the other bedroom, Casey was surprised to see that the bed was made and his father was nowhere in sight. Assuming he must be downstairs with Granddad Bob, he ran towards the stairs.

He could hear Granddad Bob at the door. He was talking to the officers, and then they were inside, going down the passage. Peeping over the banister, Casey could see them: Granddad Bob had his head bent, and was going ever so slowly towards the back parlour, with the two police officers following behind. It seemed to Casey that they were moving too slowly, too quietly, and the silence was almost deafening.

The feeling of dread that Casey had experienced earlier was much stronger now; like a hard, choking lump in his throat.

Softly, nervously, he crept down the stairs and sat on the last but one step. From here, he could listen without being seen. He was angry. *She* had done this. She wanted his dad to be put away, but Casey was adamant he wouldn't let them do that. When he told them the truth, they would understand. His mam was a liar and a bully.

In the back parlour, Tom's father fell heavily into his old armchair, his ashen face stained with tears and his heart heavier than any man could bear.

For what seemed an age, he did not utter one word, nor did he look at the two men. Instead, keeping his face down, he reached out and taking Tom's open letter from the side table, he held it up to them.

The senior officer took the letter and read it, then handed it to his colleague. 'I'm sorry, Mr Denton.' Sympathy was all he could offer. 'I'm very sorry.'

The officer went on, 'From the papers your son had in his pocket, we discovered his home address. We went round there first, but there was no one in. The neighbour said there'd been a row of sorts, and soon after your son left, his wife took off and hasn't been seen since.'

Straining to listen, but unable to hear clearly what was being said, Casey shifted down to the next step. Peering carefully round the corner, he saw Granddad Bob in the chair, looking older and sadder than he had ever seen him before. The two stern-faced officers were standing over him.

Casey wanted to go to find out why Granddad Bob was crying, but he was too afraid. Something was very wrong. If his mam really had sent them to take his dad away, they would be asking where he was, and Granddad would show them the door. But it wasn't like that, and Casey's fear was heightened.

What did they want? Why were they here?

Casey quickly pulled back when the officer addressed the old man.

'When did you know about this letter?'

'I found it this morning, when I woke up.' There was a muffled sob while Granddad Bob discreetly wiped his eyes. 'It was propped up on my bedside cabinet.'

'And before you found this letter, did you have any idea of what he meant to do?'

The old man shook his head.

'And you had no idea of what he's explained in the letter . . . the obvious cause of his distress?'

He was greeted with silence.

'I'm sorry, Mr Denton, but I have to ask these questions. I know this is painful for you, but even though we now have the letter, I am obliged to verify the reason for us being here and, like I say, I know how difficult this must be for you.' His voice was warm, his manner caring. 'You did understand what I was saying to you at the door?'

The old man looked up, his voice breaking as he said softly, 'I know what you told me, and I have the letter. But . . . I can't seem to get it into my head.' His face was haggard. 'I can't make myself believe . . . ?' Racked with grief, he lowered his head and sobbed; unable to discuss it any more.

Leaning forward on the step, Casey was aching to go to his granddad, but when he saw the younger officer glance his way, he dodged back, his instinct to remain hidden.

Deeply moved by the old man's distress, the officer stooped to his level. 'It's all right, old fella.' He laid his hand over Bob's trembling fist. 'I'm sorry . . . I truly am, but you do need to hear what I'm telling you, because sadly, I'm afraid it is true, although as I'm sure you understand, there are other steps to be taken before we know for certain.' He was careful not to go into detail of how they had discovered the pitiful remains of a young man, together with proof of his identity.

He explained in reverent tone, 'Mrs Dolly Pritchard gave us enough of a description to tie it all together as best we could under the circumstances.' He went quickly on, 'Also, we recovered the remains of two documents, which we've already shown you, and which you've identified as belonging to your son.'

Leaving Casey's granddad to reflect on that, the officer lifted his gaze to the photograph on the sideboard. It tied in with the smaller, damaged photo they'd discovered on the tracks earlier that morning.

'That's your son, isn't it, Mr Denton?'

The old man looked up, his eyes raw from the crying, 'Yes, that's Tom,' he confirmed. 'And there's his own darling son alongside.' He pointed a shaking finger at the figure of Casey.

His thoughts were now for the little boy. Dear God above, how would he tell him that his father had thrown himself under a train and was killed instantly?

How would the child cope when, even to his own weathered old mind, it beggared belief that Tom would do such a wicked thing? But then, who was he to know how a man's mind might work, when faced with the agonising decision that had haunted Tom?

Still reluctant to believe it, he asked the officer for the second time, 'Tell me again . . . what happened?'

'Like I explained, we investigated a call some hours ago. A woman living nearby was out looking for her little dog, and she stopped to talk with the young man, who we now believe to be your son. As she walked away, some instinct made her turn back, and she actually saw him slide from the bridge wall. She then ran to a neighbour's house, and he raised the alarm. We responded swiftly, but it was already too late. There was absolutely nothing anyone could do. I'm so sorry.'

Crouched down out of sight on the step, Casey was confused. Sometimes when the officer spoke quietly he could hardly hear what was being said, but he could hear his granddad's quiet sobbing, and it tore through him like a rush of cold wind.

'This woman . . .' His granddad's trembling voice was so low, Casey dared to lean forward in order to hear him,

'. . . who is this woman? What exactly did she tell you?'

Now the younger officer stepped forward, while the first one was grateful for the chance to take a deep breath and compose himself, for although they were used to such visits, this particular duty was especially harrowing. 'As my colleague said, her name is Dolly Pritchard. She's a widow, and she lives opposite the railway bridge at Mill Hill . . .'

While he explained the event in a sensitive, careful manner, Casey sat bolt upright on the stairs, his heart racing as he tried to make sense of it all.

His mind was flooded with all manner of questions. That officer said some woman called Dolly had stopped to ask his dad about a dog, and now the police were here, and Granddad Bob was crying. What was all this about? When did it happen, and why was his dad on the railway bridge at Mill Hill? And, where was his dad now?

'Where did you say he was when she stopped to ask him about the dog?' The old man was trying hard to piece it all together, but it was difficult. His reasoning was all over the place and it was all too much. Way too much! He didn't want to listen, but he knew he had to. 'My son . . . where was he when he spoke to the woman? Where was he . . . exactly?'

'Like I said before,' the officer was more than willing to explain again in view of the old man's distress and confusion, 'the young man we believe to be your son was standing on the railway bridge at Mill Hill.'

For a minute, Bob remained silent, appearing not to have heard, and then, as the information settled in his mind, the fragments came together and formed a heartbreaking picture. 'The railway bridge at Mill Hill you say? Oh, dear God, no!'

In his mind, the old man drifted back to the days when he would take Tom to watch the trains going under Mill Hill bridge. Anne would pack them a bag of sandwiches and a flask, and they would camp out on the bridge, waiting for each train as it came flying in. They would laugh when the steam rose and momentarily shrouded them, and later they would take the long walk home to Addison Street, talking through their happy time when trainspotting.

Bob smiled through his tears. 'Mill Hill were allus a special place to me and my boy.'

Suddenly it was like he could not hold in the pain any longer, and his cries were heart-rending. 'All them years I took him to that bridge. It were ours . . . our own special place, and now I don't know what to think.' His voice was hoarse with emotion. 'Why in God's name would he do such a terrible thing?' He began to rock back and forth.

Moved by the old man's pain, the older officer leaned close and in a gentle voice he told him, 'Maybe it was the only place he could go, because in his mind he imagined he would be with you. Maybe that bridge and the train were the last things he needed to see, because that was where he spent some of the happiest times of his life.'

Leaning into the chair Bob gave a whimsical little smile.'Aye . . . mebbe.' He hoped that was what Tom had thought: that he would leave this world with a picture of himself and his father in that very spot. They were good memories, and maybe that truly was the reason why Tom had chosen that place. The thought offered him small comfort, though at the same time, he felt angry and sad. And, oh, so very lonely. And yet, he had young Casey, Tom's son, his own dear grandson.

'This woman, Mrs Pritchard, what exactly did she see?'

The officer answered in a quiet voice, 'Only that he was leaning on the wall, and when she turned round, he appeared to have climbed up onto the wall, and then he just . . . well, she wasn't sure whether it was done on purpose, or whether he fell accidentally.' He pointed to the letter. 'As to that, I believe your son's letter appears to answer that question.'

Listening on the stairs, Casey understood his dad had been sitting on the wall on the railway bridge at Mill Hill, and that something might, or might not have happened.

But what was that to do with his dad, and what was the letter they kept talking about? Granddad was crying, but why? And where was his dad?

Suddenly he could bear it no longer. Bursting into the room, he demanded to know, 'Where's my dad? What's happened to him? I WANT MY DAD!' When the tears flooded his eyes, Granddad was on his feet, holding out his arms to take him.

'Oh, lad! Were you listening? Tell me what you heard.'

But Casey was adamant. 'Where's my dad? I want my dad!'

The old man moved towards him, his arms open wide and his voice trembling. 'Oh, lad let me take you back upstairs. Then we'll talk, you and me.'

Backing away, Casey would not be quietened. 'I want my dad!' He confronted the police officers. 'What 'ave you done with my dad? Where is he? What's happened to him?'

When the younger officer made towards him, Casey ran along the passage and out the door, yelling as he went, 'Leave me alone! I'm going to find my dad, and you can't stop me!'

Bob was frantic. 'He heard us talking. I tell you, he knows! Find him.' Impatient, he began yelling, 'GO ON, GET AFTER HIM. HE'LL BE HEADED FOR MILL HILL!'

The officers hurried out to the car, the old man following. Glancing down the street he saw Casey, running as if the devil were on his heels. 'Casey, come back, lad!' Bob called, but Casey had to find his dad, and he was in no mood for listening. A few more steps and he was away round the corner, headed for the backstreets, and Mill Hill beyond.

'I'm coming with you.' Following the officers, Bob was determined. 'The boy's distraught. Who knows what he overheard?'

'No!' The officer was adamant. 'Leave it to us. You need to stay here in case he comes back.'

'If I stay here, do you promise you'll find him, and fetch him back to me?' Already emotionally and physically exhausted, and now desperately afraid for his grandson, he knew the officer was right. What if Casey came back and there was no one here? Seeing the state he was in, that would be unforgivable.

'All right, I'll stay and wait to see if he comes back. But you get off to Mill Hill as quick as you can. Search him out. Look everywhere. The thing is, I don't know how much he heard.' He waved them away. 'Don't come back without him!'

His shoulders hunched with the weight of sorrow, Bob shuffled inside the house. Tom loomed large in his mind. How he wished to God his son had confided in him. Even then, he could not have changed the harsh fact that Tom had a sorry future ahead of him.

Deliberately leaving the front door slightly ajar, Bob returned to the parlour, where he fell into his chair and picked up the letter. He read it for the umpteenth time, a few words leaping out of the page at him: '. . . My future is bleak . . . The disability is bound to render me entirely dependent on loved ones . . .'

'Aw, lad!' Shaking his head in despair, he laid the letter down. Leaning back into the chair he reflected on the morning's shocking events. Yesterday he was thrilled to have his son and grandson here with him, and now his whole world had fallen apart.

He looked towards the mantelpiece at the snapshot of his wife in her younger days: a handsome, dark-haired woman with sparkling eyes and winning smile. 'God help us, Anne, lass,' he whispered. 'Look what's happened to us now.' He rubbed his head with the palms of his hands, while still confiding in his beloved late wife. 'Did he think we wouldn't take care of him, eh? Does he not know that I would've given my own life to save his?'

He tried so hard to put himself in Tom's shoes, and in a strange way, he understood. Just enough, maybe, to forgive.

Overwhelmed and feeling helpless, he sat there, quiet and reflective. Inevitably the tears came again, and this time they would not stop. 'Look after our boy, Lord, wherever he is,' he prayed. 'And please, bring that little lad home, safe and well. Me and Casey need each other now. More than ever.'

For a long time he remained in the chair, trying to come to terms with the news that Tom had most probably taken his own life.

Aw, lad, why did you suffer it all on yer own? he thought. Why couldn't you share yer troubles with yer old father, eh? Surely to God, between the two of us, we might 'a' found some other way.

Over and over, he ran the officers' words through his mind. It was so very hard to take in the stark truth.

~

Outside, while the police car took the main route to Mill Hill, Casey made for the backstreets. Unknowingly following the same route his father had taken before him, he ran fast and furious, winding through the cobbled ginnels and onto King Street, then through the alleyways and ginnels, towards the railway bridge.

After passing the pub, he wended his way through the shortcut he and his father took when they came here with Granddad.

Every few minutes he looked about, keeping a wary eye open for any police car. In his young mind, going to the railway bridge was the only way to find out what had happened.

Even then, he was afraid to know, yet more afraid not to.

As though for his very life he ran on, his chest hurting with every breath he took and his heart fit to burst. His legs ached, the sweat ran down his face and his shirt stuck to his back.

In Mary-Anne Street, he was forced to pause and catch his breath, but he daren't stop for more than a minute in case the police caught up with him.

'Are you all right, son?' a man walking by asked with concern.

'Yes . . . thank you.'

Casey ran on with determination, his feet hardly touching the ground. Being sure to keep well away from the main thoroughfares, he dodged under hedges and leaped over walls. They said his dad was on the bridge. What was he doing on the bridge, and why had he gone there alone? He must be in trouble, he thought! His dad would explain, but first, he must find him.

That bright, burning thought drove him on.

When he swung past the familiar row of trees, he knew he was not far from the railway bridge. But what if Dad wasn't there? And still he wondered, what had happened at the bridge, because it seemed to him that something had happened. Something frightening.

His young mind was constantly troubled with questions. Why was the bed neatly made up this morning, as though no one had slept in it? Had his dad simply left it tidy when he woke up? Or had he not slept in it at all, and if that was the case, why not?

Maybe Dad had stayed downstairs with Granddad Bob last night. Maybe they were talking and planning, about what to do now Mam and Dad had parted company. Maybe Dad might have changed his mind about living with Granddad for ever.

Now, the doubts began to set in, until Casey wasn't sure what he expected to find at the bridge. He reminded himself of what he had overheard when the policemen were talking to his granddad. They mentioned his dad and the bridge, and Granddad was shocked and upset. And there was a woman . . . a widow by the name of Dolly something.

With every step his fears were heightened.

All he could think of was finding his dad. Then everything would be all right, because it always was.

Soon he was running up the street to the bridge; then he was at the foot of the bridge. He paused, making sure the police were not already there, waiting to pounce on him.

Going cautiously forward, he was curious to see a straggled line of people leaning over the wall; they appeared to be interested in what was going on below. Now Casey saw that nearby was a police car, and a long, thick rope cordoning off the area. Two helmeted police officers patrolled the scene.

Casey approached a man in the crowd. 'What's going on, mister?'

'You don't want to know, lad.' Having children of his own, the man was concerned by Casey's appearance. His face was red and stained with sweat, and his breath was laboured, as though he'd been running hard. 'You'd best clear off away from 'ere!'

'Leave him alone, Dave!' His wife stooped to speak with

Casey. 'He's right, though. Does your mother know where you are? Don't you know something bad happened here? They're saying a man went off the bridge last night . . . that he was killed by a train . . . It doesn't bear thinking about. So you'd best get off, lad. Get off home, where you belong . . .'

Just then a police car came screeching to a halt at the kerbside, and a young officer came running towards them.

'Stay there, son!' Making a beeline for the boy, the officer called out, 'We're not here to hurt you. Your granddad wants you home, that's all.'

Cautiously narrowing the distance between himself and the boy, he pleaded, 'I'm sorry, son, but we need to get you back home, where you belong. Come on now . . . your granddad needs you.'

'No!' Casey backed away. 'I'm not going home till I find my dad!' What the woman had just told him was burning in his mind. 'Tell me what happened to my dad.' Growing hysterical, he demanded. 'Was it him who got killed by a train? Was it? TELL ME THE TRUTH!'

On seeing the looks exchanged between the two officers, he suspected the truth, and it was more than he could deal with. Backing off, he began sobbing, 'No, it's not true! It wasn't my dad. It couldn't have been. Do you hear me . . . it wasn't him!' Distraught, he edged away. 'You're lying . . . all of you . . . LIARS!'

When the young officer came forward to calm him, Casey took to his heels and fled. Deep down, he knew his father was gone, yet he could not let himself believe it.

Instead, he clung to the fantasy that they'd made a mistake, that his father was somewhere else, safe and well. Yes, that was it! His dad was not the man killed by that train. He couldn't be.

Some small instinct in the back of his mind forced him to accept the possibility that maybe, just maybe, his dad really was the man that had . . . that was . . . ? Angry with himself for even entertaining the idea, he pushed it away.

He had to run, yet he didn't want to leave, because this was the place they'd told Granddad about. He didn't know how, but somehow, he would find his dad, and everything would be all right. Just now, he couldn't think straight.

'Come on, lad,' the older officer addressed him softly, 'you need to go home now. You need to be with your granddad . . .'

When the officer was almost close enough to touch him, Casey took off again. 'Leave me alone!' he shouted as he ran. 'I'm not going back till I find my dad!' He was concerned about his granddad, though. He had seen him sobbing, but while his granddad played on his mind, his dad was paramount in his thoughts. He could not let himself believe the worst. He would find his dad, he *would*. His mind was in chaos.

Casey was soon out of sight of the policemen.

'The little sod!' Scrambling into the car, the two officers were concerned for the lad. 'I expect he'll make his way back to his granddad,' the older police officer was convinced, 'but we need to be sure he gets there safely.' Starting the engine, he slammed the car into gear and surged forward. 'We can't have the kid running loose all over the place.'

'Do you really think he heard . . . back at the house?' The young officer was worried. 'It would be a shocking thing if he overheard us saying how his father appeared to have taken his own life.'

'It would, yes.' Taking the bend at speed, the older man shook his head. 'Look! I don't know what the boy heard. Maybe he really did overhear something, and it got him guessing. And just now, there was a woman talking to him. When all's said and done, happen the boy knows enough to put two and two together.' The older policeman felt bad about the boy. 'I reckon he'll be on his way back to his granddad. When we get to the house, we should ask the old fella to tell him. It's better for the lad to know the truth.'

~

Keeping a safe distance from the tracks, and greatly relieved that no one could see him, Casey remained very still.

From his hiding place in a crevice beneath the bridge, he could see the big police vans arrive, and soon after that the people retreated.

The officers kept them moving, and once the onlookers had gone, the cordons were taken down and packed into the waiting vans. Eventually the vans were gone; then the police cars and the body of officers followed, while two of them stayed behind to check round and be sure that everything was as it should be. Soon, they too were leaving, and the bridge was emptied. After the noise and bustle, it now seemed eerily silent.

Carefully climbing up to the bridge, Casey felt as though he was the only person in the whole wide world. Because of the barriers, the traffic had been diverted earlier, and as yet had not found its way back along this route. There was not a train or a person in sight, while down the street, a solitary dog relieved itself against a lamppost.

Spreading his two arms over the bridge wall, Casey looked to the rails below. He recalled the many wonderful times he and his dad, along with his granddad, had leaned over in this very spot to watch the trains go by.

Somewhere in the darkness of his mind, he couldn't help but wonder if they would ever again do that, all three of them together. But he knew the truth, and a great, overwhelming sadness took hold of him.

He felt the cold stone under his fingertips, and he imagined his father being where he was right now, arms stretched and his fingertips holding onto the rim of the wall, so that he could pull himself upwards.

Since hearing the police officers talking with his granddad, and seeing that dear old man distraught, Casey had drawn an invisible shield over his mind in a desperate bid to keep out the terrifying truth.

Now, though, as he lay across the wall, his head hanging over the track and his mind flooded with thoughts of his beloved father, it was as though the shield had slid away, and he could see the truth laid bare, terrifying and shocking. It emblazoned itself on his heart and mind, and tore him apart. His dad was never coming back. Not ever. In the whole of his life he would never see his dad again.

With his heart breaking, he slid to the ground, the sound of his sobbing echoed in the cool, quiet air. All he could think about was his father, and the idea of him going over the bridge wall. Distraught, he sat cross-legged on the cold ground, rocking back and forth, his heart like a lead weight inside his chest.

Suddenly, when a tabby cat was beside him gently rubbing its head against the boy's face, it gave him a sense of comfort.

Raising his head, he looked straight into the cat's dark eyes and then he slid his arm round the cat, and the cat snuggled up to him as though sensing his grief.

Then, as stealthily as he'd arrived, the cat was gone, and the boy was alone again.

Casey watched the cat stroll away, and when it was eventually out of sight, the sense of loneliness and desolation was unbearable here on this familiar bridge, with all its fond memories; here in this lonely place, without the people he loved.

In that dark moment he thought of his mother, and he hated her. Yet at the same time he loved and needed her. Then he despised himself for even thinking that she might care.

But he called for her all the same. 'Mam!' The tears fell fast. 'Oh, Mam . . .' Once again he dropped his head to his knees and wrapped his arms about his legs. He wasn't really sure where his dad was, but just then, he so much wanted to be with him.

~

Across the street, Dolly was just waking.

She had mostly lain awake through the dark hours, snatching a wink or two here and a half-hour there. Twice she had gone down to the kitchen to make a cup of tea. The night had been long and painful, and guilt plagued her mind. Eventually she fell into a troubled sleep, and now, waking with a start, she was horrified to hear the grandmother clock strike four times.

Half an hour later, having washed and dressed, she entered the kitchen to make herself a pot of tea. When the tea was brewed and her cup filled, she wrapped her two hands around it and carried it to the window, where she looked out.

Something on the bridge quickly caught her attention. Collecting her spectacles from the sideboard, she put them on and squinted towards the bridge once more, at what she imagined was a bundle of rags on the ground.

She leaned forward to get a better look. It was a child . . . a small child. Laying down her spectacles, she ran to the front passageway and collected her coat. Outside, she looked up and down the street, but could not see anyone who might belong to the child.

The memories of what had happened to that young man had badly shaken her. And now there was a child sitting on the cold ground beneath that very same spot where the young man had slid to his death.

She chattered to herself as she went out of the front door and across the street. She knew she would never forget what she had seen. 'Why didn't I realise what he meant to do?' she tormented herself. Even now, she could see Tom's quiet smile in her mind. She could hear his reassuring voice, yet still she blamed herself for not realising his intention. And what about his family? The thought of their sorrow made her feel all the more guilty.

Now, she was hurrying across the street, noticing how the bridge was already cordoned off. 'Soon they'll be out here in their droves, I dare say.'

Dolly realised that was inevitable, given the circumstances. Drawing closer to the bridge, she could see the child crouched down against the bridge wall. Close enough now, she realised the child was a boy, probably no older than seven or eight years of age. She looked about, wondering if the parents might be close, but there was no one else in sight.

She advanced quietly and carefully, afraid that when he saw her approaching, he might suddenly run away.

Casey was so lost in thoughts of his dad, he had not seen Dolly coming, but when he heard her call out to him, he was on his feet in an instant. Ready to run, he stood with his back to the wall.

'Please, lady, I'm not doing anything wrong. Leave me alone.' As Dolly drew nearer, he took stock of her, relieved to find that she was just an old woman.

'I know you're not doing anything wrong.'

Dolly stood still on the pavement, afraid he would take off if she took one more step. 'It's just that I heard you crying, and I noticed there was no one with you. I'm sorry, child, but I was worried. I only want to help you.'

She could see he was agitated, ready to flee at any moment. She needed to calm him. 'It's just that . . . well, it's so cold out here, I thought you might like to come inside my house and warm yourself. I can make you a nice cup of hot cocoa, if you like? You needn't worry, there's no one else in the house . . . only me.' Her smile was warm. 'I promise, I truly don't mean to harm you.'

To her bitter disappointment, she had never been blessed with children of her own, though over the years she had been an adopted auntie to the neighbours' children. 'Just so's you know, my name is Dolly. What's yours?'

Her name jogged Casey's memory. 'Dolly? Is that really your name . . . Dolly?' He tried to remember what the policeman had said, and he uttered the first thing that came to mind: 'Did you find my dad?'

Dolly was completely taken aback. Tearfully she came forward. 'Oh, dearie me, you're looking for your father, aren't you? That's why you're here, isn't it? Oh, child, what are we to do, eh?'

Raising the cuff of her sleeve she wiped away her tears. 'Come with me, eh? Trust me. You can ask me anything you like . . .' she opened her arms to him, '. . . please, child. Come home with me now, eh? I don't mean you any harm. I only want to help you.'

Suddenly the boy was in her arms, sobbing, clinging to her, as all the pent-up emotions poured out, 'Where is he . . . where's my dad?' He looked up at her, his eyes big and sad. 'They won't tell me what's happened, and I can't find him.'

Fighting back her own tears, Dolly held him tight. 'First things first, m'darling,' she coaxed. 'Come on now. Let's get you inside, in the warm. Then we'll decide what to do . . . the two of us.'

Together they walked across the street, and into that cosy little home. Closing the door behind them, Dolly held his hand as they went down the passage and into the back parlour. 'Here we are, bonny lad!' She looked into that sorrowful little face and her old heart ached for what he must be going through.

Casey remained anxious. 'Where's my dad? I want my dad.' Even while he asked the questions, he already knew. 'Is it true what they said? Did my dad fall . . . ?' He choked on the words, not wanting to know the truth, yet desperate to be told.

Dolly's heart went out to him. She didn't really know how to tell him the truth, or even whether she should. To her mind, it was the responsibility of a close relative to break the awful news. So she answered his question with another instead. 'What's your name, child?'

'Casey.'

'Well, now, that's a fine name, an' no mistake.' She kept her hold on him, loose yet definite, in case he decided to run. 'D'you know what I think, Casey?'

Casey shook his head. 'No.'

'Well, first of all, I think I should make us both a cup o' cocoa. Then we'll sit down together, and you can ask me any questions you like. I don't promise to know all the answers, but I'll do my best. So, what d'you say to that?'

Needing to trust her, Casey gave a small, if reluctant nod.

'Right then.' Dolly was grateful. 'That's good. You sit in the chair by the fireside, and I'll set about making us that cocoa.'

She watched him go over to the fireplace, where he hoisted himself into the big old armchair. Feeling easier now that she'd managed to persuade him this far, Dolly went into the scullery and put the kettle on.

'Are you hungry?' she called out to him. 'I've got short-cake biscuits, or apple pie . . . all home-made.' Still nervous that he might decide to make a dash for it, she kept a wary eye on him through the adjoining door.

Casey, though, was willing and even thankful to sit there for a while. He was cold, and hungry, and he needed to think. And anyway, she'd promised that he could ask her questions about his dad, and that she would do her best to answer them. He was starting to think that this kind lady would reassure him, and that the police had got it all wrong.

A few moments later, Dolly came through to the back parlour. 'Here we are, Casey. I've brought both biscuits and a slice of my apple pie as well. It won't matter if you leave it, because I'm sure it won't go to waste. Billy next door is very partial to my home-made apple pie.' She wagged a finger at him. 'Mind you, I'd much rather you had it, because that Billy's put on too much weight of late. I keep telling him it's bad for his heart. But will he listen?'

When she set the tray on the table, Casey saw the food and his stomach began quietly growling. The biscuits were thick and crumbly, and the apple pie was plump and dripping with juice. He couldn't remember his mother ever baking anything like that.

Not for the first time, he thought of his mother. Then he recalled the frightful scene back at the house, and he shut her from his mind. All the same, he was sorry about what happened. In truth, he blamed himself.

'Come and sit at the table, child.' Dolly set him a place. 'There you are.' She watched as he climbed onto the chair. 'You just help yourself, while I pop to the front room for a minute.'

'You're not going outside, are you?' Nervous that she might not come back, Casey began to panic.

'Oh, now don't you worry, child. I've just remembered I forgot to open the curtains in the front room.' She gave a nervous little chuckle. 'Folks'll begin to think I'm still abed, an' we can't have that, can we, eh?'

Still a little anxious, Casey shook his head.

Dolly breathed a sigh of relief. 'You help yourself to the cakes and biscuits, and I'll be back before you know it.'

When he now reached out for a biscuit, she sneaked quietly away. Once inside the front room, she softly closed the door, then quickly went to the sideboard where the big black telephone stood. It was Billy, her next-door neighbour, who had suggested that she get a telephone, 'So you can call out if ever you need to,' he told her.

She now picked up the big heavy receiver and placed the earpiece to her ear. With the tip of her finger, she began dialling the police number. She still hadn't got used to using the telephone, and was somewhat nervous.

It rang for a moment before a very officious woman answered at the other end. 'Blackburn Police Station. Can I help you?'

Holding the telephone slightly away from her face, Dolly told her, 'This is Dolly Pritchard speaking. I live in Mill Hill, and I was the woman who saw that young man fall from Mill-Hill bridge. I have his son here. He's run away, d'you see. The poor lad is looking for his father. I, er . . . I mean, I don't like to tell him what's happened, d'you see?' she began to stutter.

'Mrs Pritchard, you say you were the one who reported the man falling from the bridge at Mill Hill? . . . Thank you, I have your name. Please could you tell me your full address . . . ?'

Ashamed and guilty for having called the police, Dolly

slammed the receiver down. This was not the right way to help the boy.

When she returned to the back parlour, Casey was seated in the big old armchair, staring into the fire grate, but seeming not to be looking at anything in particular.

Dolly glanced at the table, where sadly not a thing had been touched; not even the cocoa she'd made to warm him up.

With an aching heart, she went to him and, placing her chubby hands about his face, she caused him to look up at her. 'What are we going to do with you, eh, child?' He looked so small and lost.

'Please . . . will you tell me where my dad is?'

'I don't know where he is,' she answered softly.

'You saw him, though, didn't you?' When she gave no answer, he scrambled away from her, his voice loud and angry. 'YOU'RE JUST LIKE THE OTHERS . . . YOU'RE LYING! I HEARD WHAT THE POLICEMAN TOLD MY GRANDDAD.'

'What did you hear?'

'You saw him, didn't you?'

'I saw a young man, yes that's true. But I don't know if he was your father. I don't know what your father looked like. The young man on the bridge seemed very troubled. We spoke, and he urged me to go and look for my little dog. He'd run away, you see, and I needed to find him before he got lost. He does that sometimes, and he doesn't like a lot of noise and fuss. Which is why Billy's keeping him next door just now.' Slightly panicking, she took a deep breath, 'Your father worried me,' she admitted.

'Did my dad fall?' Calmer now, Casey was desperate to know. 'Did he get killed by the train?'

'Like I said, I don't even know if it was your dad at the time.'

With heavy heart, Dolly decided she had to get the boy

back to his family. 'Let me take you home, child. Your mother will be so worried.'

'I haven't got a mother!' The words that came out of his mouth shocked him. He did have a mother, but if she didn't want him, then he didn't want her.

'I'm sorry to hear that.' Dolly suspected he might be lying, but that was not her business. 'But a while ago you said that you wanted your granddad.'

'I do.' Casey was still concerned about his granddad Bob.

'Of course you do, and he's bound to worry because he doesn't know what's happened to you, does he?'

'No.'

'Well, there you are then. Your granddad will be waiting for you, looking out the window and getting himself into a state. And besides, I'm sure he'll be able to answer all your questions, because if the police have been to see him like you said, he'll probably know a great deal more about what happened to your daddy, than I do. Please, Casey, let me take you to him.'

'Tell me, *was* it my dad who got killed?'

'I truly don't know,' Dolly answered. 'All I know is there was a young man on the bridge. He told me he was waiting for a friend and that he would be going to the station to meet him. The next thing I know, I was chastising my little dog, then I heard the train. I turned round and I saw . . .' when the image rose in her mind, she took a deep, calming breath, '. . . I saw the young man fall. I did not know he was your father, and that's the God's honest truth.'

Casey knew, though. He knew it in his heart and soul that his dad had been killed by that train. And now something was happening to him. He felt different from before. He wanted to cry but he found he couldn't. He wasn't even able to think any more. He felt confused and frightened.

When, unexpectedly, Dolly took him gently into her

chubby arms, he held onto her. He felt safe somehow, although in that moment, nothing seemed to matter any more.

Inside him, there was a strange, sweeping coldness; as though he, too, had died.

When she felt him trembling, Dolly held him close for a while, softly talking to him, reassuring him.

Then he was looking at her, pleading, 'Please! I want my granddad . . . I want him now, please.'

His childish plea pierced her old heart and, as she turned away, the tears threatened. But she would not let herself cry in front of the boy. Not when he was already being so very brave.

'All right, child. We'll get you home now, shall we?'

A short time later, they were ready to leave. 'So, what's your granddad's name?' Dolly had kept on talking, though the boy had lapsed into a deep silence.

Casey gave no answer. Instead, he waited patiently while she locked the front door. He wanted his dad. He needed to see him, and talk with him, and play the guitar. But his mother had broken the guitar, and his dad was gone. Why did he go? Why did he leave me?

So many questions, and no answers.

The police car was just pulling up outside, after a message had come through from the station.

When Dolly and Casey turned from the front door, they saw the police approaching.

'Don't worry, child,' she said, holding onto Casey. 'They're here to help, that's all. I expect your granddad sent them to find you.'

Casey was through running, and when the older officer stooped to talk with him, he offered no resistance.

'It's all right, lad, we've come to take you home. Your granddad's waiting for you. He's been worried.'

When the officer led him to the car, Casey glanced back at Dolly, looking forlorn in her hat and coat, and the key still poised in her hand. There were tears in her eyes.

'I'm not going without Dolly!' In the short time he'd spent with her, Casey had come to trust and love her.

'Mrs Pritchard, do you want to come with us?' The officers could see how these two had formed a bond of friendship.

Greatly relieved, Dolly returned his smile and nodded; then she looked at the boy's childish face and smiled encouragement to him as she walked to the car, where the officer carefully helped her inside.

To the boy the older officer said, 'You've a lot to thank this lady for, my lad. We were just about to send out the search team for you.'

He saw how the boy held out a hand to make sure Dolly was safely inside. He saw how the woman wrapped an arm about him the minute she was seated, and he was gratified to see how the boy leaned against her. And knowing what trauma the child must have suffered alone out there on the streets, the friendship between these two brought a swell of emotion to his throat.

PART TWO

~

Loving Arms

CHAPTER FIVE

GRANDDAD BOB WAS waiting at the window. These past hours, he had thought long and hard about what Tom had done. Slowly, he had come to see how tormented his son must have been, when learning the devastating news of his illness. He was deeply saddened, but he was also very angry.

'Oh, Tom, lad . . . why couldn't you have confided in your old father?' Time and again he uttered those words. Time and again he tried to persuade himself that Tom had taken what he believed to be the best and only option. But it was bad, and so wrong, and it would take his father some long time to forgive him. But forgive him he would. When you love someone with all your heart, that precious love will endure through thick and thin, good times and bad. To the end of time, and maybe even beyond.

Several times he'd gone to the front door and looked out, hoping to see his grandson coming down the street, and each time he'd closed the door with a heavy heart.

In between, he'd paced up and down close to the window, and every other minute stopping to look out. But there was no sign of Casey. 'Where are you, lad? Come 'ome to yer old granddad, eh?' He had a yearning to wrap his arms about that little bundle of humanity. He needed to keep him safe, and talk with him about what his father had done, and why.

He cast a sorry gaze at the other two letters lying face up on the sideboard. He wondered about the letter addressed to Ruth, and he hoped that in the harsh words that must be said, there might be a small gesture of forgiveness for the part she had played in hurting the ones who loved her.

As for Casey, he knew every word in that letter would be like a knife to his heart; as his own letter had been to himself.

The pain of losing a son, and in such a way, was the most unbearable thing.

After what seemed endless pacing up and down, he saw the police car draw up at the house, and he rushed to the front door as fast as his old legs would carry him.

When Casey climbed out of the car and ran to him, the old man clasped him so tight to his chest, the boy could hardly breathe. 'Oh, lad! I've been that worried. I didn't know where you were, or whether you'd come back to me. Oh dear God, I'm so thankful you're home.' The tears he'd been holding back ran freely down his face. 'Come inside, lad; come inside with yer old granddad, eh?'

Then the old man saw the police officer helping Dolly out of the car. 'Who's this, then?' He was pleasantly surprised to see this woman, with her warm, reassuring smile and kindly manner.

'She's my friend.' Breaking loose, Casey ran to Dolly and, taking her by the hand, he told his granddad, 'She took care of me. Her name's Dolly. I know the police told you . . . how she saw . . .' he trailed off, unable to actually say it.

Nervously, Dolly stepped forward. 'I found Casey on the bridge,' she explained. 'I took him home, and we talked a lot. Then he wanted you, his granddad Bob.' She smiled. 'I know he'll be safe now, and I can rest easy.'

Behind her, the police officer stood by the open car door, waiting to take her home again. 'Oh, no, thank you all the same,' said Dolly, turning to him. 'I've taken up enough of your time. You go about your business. I'll go back on the bus.'

'Are you sure? It's no trouble for us to run you back.'

'Yes, of course. To tell you the truth, I don't feel comfortable riding in a police car.' She smiled again. 'You never know what the neighbours might think.'

Bob thought he had never seen such a lovely smile; it lit her pretty blue eyes and warmed his heart. 'I wouldn't even hear of you going back without a cup o' tea and a kindly word. I'm grateful to you for looking out for my grandson.' He gently ushered her along. 'Come inside, won't you?'

When Dolly hesitated, Casey took a firm hold of her hand. 'I want you to come in,' he told her. 'I don't want you to go yet. Please, Dolly?'

Secretly delighted, though feeling just a little jaded after everything that had happened, Dolly gave in to his request. 'All right then, child. Being as you've asked, and your granddad's offered, I'll stay awhile longer, only if it's all right with your granddad. I'm not one to make a nuisance of meself.'

She thought the boy's granddad to be a pleasant and caring soul, although the depth of sorrow etched in his face was a pitiful thing to see. Maybe her staying on for a while might be a blessed thing for the old man. While he might not be able to open his mind to the boy, he'd perhaps feel easier talking to her.

Unwilling to let her go, Casey led Dolly through the door, and they both followed Granddad Bob along the passageway and into the back parlour.

The police officers drove away, their work done for now.

Inside the house, the three were at ease in each other's company, although recent events were not yet mentioned. But there would be time enough to talk about that.

Before Casey could see the three letters, the old man covered them with his newspaper. 'Right! I'll mek us a drink and yer can talk me through everything.' He was eager to know exactly what Dolly had seen on that bridge.

And afterwards, he thought, it would be only right to give the boy the letter his father had left for him.

A short time later, after Casey had finished off his glass of sarsaparilla, and his elders had drained their teacups, Dolly informed them of her fateful meeting with Tom on the bridge. She confessed how she felt guilty about not having suspected there was something wrong.

'He smiled, but there was a kind of sadness in his face. It was as though, even when he spoke to me, his mind seemed far away . . . like he had something more important to think about.'

Not wishing to add to their grief, she kept the detail to a minimum.

'I blame myself,' she confessed. 'He told me he was waiting for a friend to arrive on the train, but deep down I don't think I believed him. I should have talked with him a while longer. I should have asked if he was all right, but I just accepted what he told me. Oh dearie me, what an old fool I am . . .' Taking a folded handkerchief from her pocket, she dabbed at her tears. 'I'll never forgive myself for not staying with him.'

'Don't cry, Dolly.' Running to sit on her knee, Casey squashed up against her, his small body trembling as he took hold of her hand and held it tight. 'It's not your fault.' When his voice caught in a sob, he tried so hard to be brave, but he could not stop his sorrow from spilling over.

Dolly held him close, rocking back and forth with him,

while the old man looked on, his face smudged and raw with the tears he too had shed since hearing the news. He glanced across to the side table where the letters lay under the newspaper, and shook his head forlornly. Like Dolly, he wondered what he could have done to prevent Tom from taking his own life.

Try as he might, he could not draw his attention away from the table. In his mind's eye, he could see the three letters that lay hidden; one opened and the others waiting to be delivered.

He knew every heartbreaking word in the letter addressed to himself, and his fear grew at how that young lad might receive such a letter.

When his thoughts turned to Ruth, he felt a rush of hatred for the part she had played in Tom's distress. He recalled how Tom had asked him not to turn against Ruth, but though he wanted to forgive her, he was not certain he ever could.

He shifted his gaze to Dolly and Casey. In a slow, rhythmic manner, she rocked back and forth, softly singing, eyes closed and her arms tight about the child. Comforted, the boy hid his face in her shoulder and quietly sobbed. It was a beautiful yet harrowing scene, one that the old man thought would stay in his heart and mind for ever.

He desperately needed to ease the boy's pain, but then he reminded himself of the one thing he must do before the healing might begin.

'Casey?' In a gentle, broken voice, he called the boy's attention. 'Come 'ere to yer granddad, there's a good lad.' He wanted to collect the boy in his embrace, but when he tried to raise his arms, it was as though all the strength had gone from them.

Dolly released the boy, and watched him go to his granddad, her heart aching for them both.

When the boy came to him, the old man held him by the hands. 'Listen to me, young Casey. There's summat I need to tell yer,' he informed him softly. 'Summat that might hurt you all over again, but it's important. D'yer hear what I'm saying?'

Casey nodded. 'Yes, Granddad. What is it you need to tell me?'

'Well . . . it's summat yer dad wanted you and me to know, only he never did tell us. So far as I'm aware, he never told anyone, but now I know, and he wanted me to mek sure that you know as well.'

Taking a deep breath, he explained to the boy how his daddy was very ill, and that the illness would have got much worse because there was little the doctors could do.

'. . . So y'see, lad, your daddy knew he might end up being unable to care for himself. He would not be able to work any more, or pay his way, and it would only have been a matter of time afore he ended up in a wheelchair.'

As his cutting words unfolded, he saw the light go from the boy's eyes. He saw him physically cringe, and then the tears rose, to spill over.

Bob spoke softly, 'Aw, lad, it grieves me to have to tell you these things, but I can't imagine what terrible thoughts must have been going through your daddy's head . . . knowing all that, and making the decision to take his own life. He didn't want to live the rest of his life helpless. Nor did he want us to see him struck down like that. Not able to stride down the street, or pick you up and swing you round, or play football with you. And mebbe not even have the strength in his fingers to play his beloved guitar.'

He went on, 'Yes, it's true your daddy did a terrible thing, but it was his decision and however hard it might be, we have to do our best to respect that. And d'you know what, lad, I've asked myself how I might have dealt with such a terrible illness, and I can't honestly say what I would have done in the circumstances.'

Drawing the boy closer, he explained. 'I didn't know about your daddy's illness until this very morning. Y'see, when I woke up and your dad were gone, I found summat on the bedside cabinet. Summat very special. Summat yer dad left for us.'

Still reeling from what he'd been told, Casey remained silent.

'Hey!' The old man placed his fingers under the boy's chin and lifted his face in such a way that he could not avoid looking up at him. 'D'yer want to see what yer daddy left for you?'

'No!'

'Why's that then? Is it 'cause yer angry? Is that it?'

'I would have looked after him, I would. I really would!'

'I know you would, and yer daddy knew full well that you would want to look after him – he knew we both would – and that's the very reason why he did what he did. He had his pride and he did not want to become reliant on anyone to feed and clothe him, take him to the bathroom or clean his teeth. Oh, lad, try an' understand if yer can. Because y'see, however hard it might be, we have to forgive what he did, because we love him.'

'I . . . won't ever forgive . . . him, *I won't*!' With his heart breaking, Casey clung to his granddad while, nearby, Dolly felt for these two darling people, but was powerless to ease their pain.

After a while, Casey asked tentatively, 'What did my dad want me to have?'

The old man was greatly relieved. 'He left you a letter. In fact, there were three letters in all. There was one for me, and there was one for you . . . and . . .' He decided to leave the boy's mother out of it for now.

'What did the letters say?'

'Well, o' course it weren't for me to open anyone's letter but my own. In it, he told me about his illness, and how it were creeping up on him. He asked me to tell you before you read your letter, so it wouldn't come as such a shock.'

'Where is it then, Granddad? Where's my letter? I want to read it, please, Granddad.'

The old man had dreaded this moment.

Dolly was desperately sad, 'Might it be best if I leave now?' she whispered.

His answer was a vigorous shake of the head, which told her exactly what she wanted to hear: that she was needed; that they had accepted her.

Having collected the letters from the side table, he then went to sit on the sofa. Patting the area beside him, he told Casey, 'You can sit 'atween me an' Dolly while yer read the letter.' He beckoned Dolly to the sofa, and she was more than willing to do as he asked.

On catching sight of Ruth's letter, Casey asked angrily, 'Why is there a letter for *her*?' Grabbing it from the old man's fingers, he threw it across the sofa.

'That's not for us to question, is it, lad?'

From what Tom had written in his father's letter, he obviously favoured a reconciliation between Ruth and Casey but, to the old fella's way of thinking, it was not a good idea. Recovering Ruth's letter, he laid it on the side table. 'It's best if you don't concern yourself as to why your dad left your mam a letter. I'm sure he had his own good reasons.'

Taking hold of the boy under the armpits, the old man hoisted him onto the sofa, where Casey busily opened the envelope.

'What does it say, Granddad?'

'All kinda things. But look, lad, why don't yer let me or Dolly read it out loud for yer?'

Clutching his letter tight, Casey shook his head. 'No. I want to read it myself. I can. I'm good at reading.'

'I already know that. So go on then! Get on with it.' He laid a cautionary hand on the boy's arm. 'It's a hard letter for a boy to read, mind. Are you sure you wouldn't rather I read it quietly to yer?'

The boy was adamant. 'No, Granddad! It's my letter, and I want to read it by myself.'

And so, he did; silently and with his expression slowly changing as he read through the painful words at the end:

> My love will always be with you, son, and if it's possible, I will be ever by your side, watching and guiding you. When you're worried and sad of heart, you might hear the softest rush of sound about you. It will be me, come to encourage and help you.
>
> Be brave, my son. Follow your heart, and know always that I love you.
> Dad XX

Suddenly, Casey was up on his feet. Throwing the letter across the sofa, he ran out of the room, through the scullery and down the outer steps to the cellar.

A few minutes later, that was where Granddad Bob found him, hunched in a dark corner, sobbing his heart out.

'Hey, lad . . . Oh, come on now.' With great difficulty, he slid down beside Casey. He did not put his arm about him, nor did he say anything more. Instead, he sat there with the boy, the two of them close together, side by side, while Casey sobbed as though his heart would break.

'I've got summat for you, lad.' Bob opened his hand

to reveal a photograph. 'It's a picture of you with yer mam and dad. It were your first birthday, and I took this picture with my old Brownie camera. Keep it in your pocket, lad. Whenever you feel sad, look at it and remember the good times. It's not a brilliant photo, but it's the only photo we have of you with yer mam and daddy.' Tenderly, he closed the photo into the boy's hand.

Upstairs, Dolly had gone into the scullery and, after realising that the two of them were in the cellar, she took it on herself to fill the kettle from the cold water tap and pop it onto the hob. Locating a small box of matches on the shelf above, she struck one alight and set it to the gas ring. Next, she set about preparing teapot and cups, and afterwards searched the cupboard to find suitable ingredients to make some cheese sandwiches. She knew it could be hard to deal with things on an empty stomach.

A short time later, with the kettle merrily boiling, and the sandwiches set out on the plate, she turned down the gas, cleared up the mess she'd made, and patiently waited.

Minutes passed, then it was a quarter of an hour. Then it was half an hour, and still there was no sign of them. I expect they're talking things through, she thought. I'll not go down – it's not my place to do that – but I'll be here when they come up, an' no mistake. Her mind was made up: she was going nowhere until she knew they were safe and well. So she waited. First she paced the scullery, then she paced the parlour, and now she was halfway down the steps, then she was back up in the scullery again.

Dolly, however, was wrong in her assumption that the old man and the boy were 'talking things through', because three-quarters of an hour after Bob had given him the photo, not another word had been spoken in the cellar. Instead, Casey sobbed until he could sob no more, and the old man remained beside him, silently keeping him warm.

After what seemed an age, Casey snuggled closer still to the old man. 'I don't hate my dad.'

'I know you don't, lad.'

'Where is he now, Granddad? Is he in Heaven?'

'I'm not really sure, but I should think he's safe enough, wherever he might be now. I don't believe he'll come to any harm. Your daddy is a good man, d'yer see? And they do say that, while we can't see them, they can still see us.'

'Oh!' Casey's eyes grew bigger. 'D'you think Dad's here, in the cellar, with us?'

'He might be. Who knows?' The old man gave a dry little chuckle. 'Mind you, if he is down 'ere with us, I hope he's not sitting on this damp floor, 'cause I can feel the cold right through me trousers.' He gave a groan, 'D'yer know what, lad?'

'What, Granddad?'

'I reckon if I sit 'ere much longer, I'll never be able to get up, ever again!'

'Why not?'

'Well, 'cause me ol' bones will 'ave set so 'ard, they'll be stiff as chair legs, that's why.'

'Do they hurt, Granddad?'

'Not yet, but I'm sure they will, soonever I try an' move.'

'D'you want me to help you up?'

'Aye, go on then.' The old man held out his hand. 'One big tug should do it.'

There followed a deal of grunting and groaning, and quiet cursing too, but after a bit of a struggle, the old man was on his feet and carefully limbering up, ready for the long journey up the steps and into the scullery.

First, though, he drew the boy to the small basement window, where he examined the scars of grief streaked across his pale little face. 'I'm so sorry, lad.' His old heart was deeply pained. 'I'd 'ave given anything for your dad not to have left us like that.'

The boy looked up at the lovable, weathered old face, and those blue eyes that usually twinkled and smiled, and which were now so quiet and sad. 'Me too, Granddad.' He didn't know what else to say.

'Come on then, m'boy.' The old man forced a smile. 'Your friend Dolly will think we've deserted her.'

'She's your friend too, Granddad . . . isn't she?'

The old man smiled properly then. 'Aye, I reckon she is, an' all.'

Dolly was greatly relieved to see the two of them coming steadily up the steps. 'I thought you'd set up home down there,' she chided light-heartedly. 'Look at the pair of you. Good Lord! You must be frozen to the bone.'

Hobbling into the scullery, the old man was cheered by the kettle boiling on the hob, and, there on the kitchenette, a plate of sandwiches. 'By! That looks grand!' He spread his hands out to the flickering light beneath the kettle. 'Come 'ere, lad, warm yersel' afore we sit down again.'

When Casey went to him, Bob gathered his small hands into his, rubbing them to pass on the warmth he'd gathered from the stove. 'There! That's better, isn't it, eh?'

Casey looked up at his granddad's smiling face and, for the first time since losing his dad, he felt safe, with this darling old man and also with Dolly, who had already shown herself to be a true friend. 'I love you, Granddad.' He turned to smile at Dolly. 'I love you too.'

'And I love you back.' Dolly felt the tears prick her eyes.

'And, do you love Granddad Bob?'

Surprised by his innocent question, Dolly felt embarrassed. She looked at the old man, at the bright, sincere eyes and that way he had of smiling right into your heart, and she gave her answer.

'How could I love you, and not love your granddad

Bob?' It was said light-heartedly, but she meant it, because something had happened to her here in this homely little place, with these two very special people. Something she did not yet understand. Something surprising, that brought a spring to her step and a warm blush to her heart. And that had not happened to her in a very long time.

On arriving here, she had wanted to be quickly gone, yet now, the thought of leaving these two and going back to her lonely little house was a prospect she did not care to think about. But go she must, and soon.

~

The policeman was thorough as he questioned the neighbour in Henry Street. 'And you say you heard rows and arguments, is that so, Mrs Kettle?'

'Yes. It was shocking. Look, I've already told you people how Mr Denton went after the boy, leaving Mrs Denton on the floor, yelling and screaming. Oh, and the language was awful!'

'And you say she went out later on?'

'She did, yes. Left the door wide open, she did, with nobody there to look after the house. When she'd gone, my husband went along and pulled the door to. Oh, and she looked a right sorry mess as she flounced away down the street. No coat, and her hair uncombed. If you ask me, she wants locking away. The way she treats that boy, it's a disgrace!'

'What are you saying – that she beats him? Abuses him?'

'I'm saying she screams at him. Oh, and she has men back to the house. We've seen them sneaking out the back door. Shameful, that's what it is . . . shameful!'

'So, when she left, she didn't by any chance say where she was going, did she?'

'Not to us, no. Well, she wouldn't, would she? I mean, we try not to have anything to do with her. Mind you, young Mr Denton is a different sort altogether. Nice man. Hard-working, and a positive angel to put up with her goings-on. My husband asked her if she was all right, but she just swore at him. I told him not to speak to her. We all know what she's like. Gives the street a bad name, she does.'

'I see. And is there another neighbour who might know where she's gone?'

She shook her head. 'No. As far as I know, they don't have any truck with her, and who can blame them?'

Before he satisfied himself that the Dentons' house was secure, the officer reminded her, 'If she returns, would you please ask Mrs Denton to contact the police station? It's very important.'

'I see.' Curiosity got the better of Sylvia. 'Is it to do with her husband? Because he hasn't come back, and nor has the boy. I expect they might be at Tom's father's house. The two of them often go round to see the old man. Happen she's gone there to follow up on the row and cause even more aggravation. She's never satisfied, that's her trouble.'

'Mrs Denton is not at her father-in-law's house. We've been there. We've spoken to the boy, and also to Mr Denton senior. They haven't seen or heard from her.'

'So, what's going on? Why are you searching for her? Huh! Don't tell me she's got herself into even more hot water?'

Avoiding her question, the officer tipped his hat. 'Thanks for your help, and as I say, if she does turn up, do please ask her to get in touch with the police station.' With that he promptly left.

In no time at all, Mrs Kettle was inside, informing her husband of what had been said.

'There's summat strange going on,' she told William.

'They're still looking for her. They've even been round to old Mr Denton's, and from what I can make out, the boy is there with him, but there was no mention of either Tom or Ruth. Strange, don't you think?'

Her husband shook his head. 'It's nowt to do with us.'

He had his own suspicions about young Tom Denton's whereabouts.

Earlier today, when he went to the pub for a pint, there was talk of a suicide last night on Mill Hill bridge. And though William hoped he was wrong, he still couldn't help but wonder, especially as Tom Denton had not been seen since. And now the police were desperate to get hold of his wife, who was probably in some stranger's arms in a seedy little room at the back of some pub or other.

He felt a deal of sympathy for Tom Denton, because while he appeared to be unaware of his wife's carrying-on, everyone else knew of her tainted reputation.

~

At that very moment, Ruth was at the other end of town, curled up in an alleyway on a back doorstep.

Dazed, dishevelled, and unaware of her surroundings, she tried to gather her thoughts. Where had she spent the night, and who with? And where was she now?

She gave a shiver as the cold bit through her flimsy clothes. *He's left me . . . him and the kid!* It was all coming back now. *They've buggered off and left me!* She didn't know what to do, or where to go. The idea of going home to that empty house was more than she could bear. I'll find Tom. I'll tell him I'm sorry and then he'll come home, she decided. The old man can keep the brat, though.

Just then the door was flung open. 'What the devil . . . ?' The man was surprised to see what had looked like a sack of rags on his doorstep.

Startled, Ruth scrambled up and accidentally tripped forward, hitting her head on the wall as she fell.

Shocked at her dishevelled appearance, the man helped her up. When she struggled, he held her tight. 'Hey! There's no need to be frightened o' me. But what in God's name are you doing out here? It's a bitter cold morning, and you haven't even got a coat to your back.' He was alarmed at the trickle of blood running down her forehead. 'You'd best come inside and clean up. I'm sure the missus can find an old coat to keep you warm. Where d'you live? Once we've got you warm and seen to that cut on your forehead, I'd best run you home . . . if that's what you want?'

Disorientated and angry, Ruth stared at him. It was all coming back to her now. She remembered being in some backstreet pub, making merry, when a good-looking fella paid attention to her. She was flattered when he began flirting with her; then he bought her a few drinks over the bar, and the more she drank, the merrier she got. After a while, he offered to take her home, and she was more than willing to go with him.

When they got to his place, she was surprised to see what a filthy tip it was, yet even then she was so angry at Tom leaving her, and so full of booze, that she brushed aside all the warning signals.

The man turned out to be a monster, who viciously took what he wanted and smacked her about before throwing her out on the streets.

She felt oddly humiliated because that had never happened before. It had always been a matter of enjoying herself with the men she took up with until now.

This time, though, dazed and hurt, she wandered about, walking the streets until, too weary to walk further, she fell asleep in this doorway.

Now, allowing herself to be led inside by this man who

appeared to be kind and considerate, she asked him grog-gily, 'Where am I? What street is this?'

'You're on Preston New Road, and you appeared to have fallen asleep on my doorstep.' His smile was genu-inely friendly. 'I'm Jim Ellis.' A retired pub owner, he was a small man in his late sixties, with balding head and pert manner. 'I'm afraid you've had a fall and cut your head. My missus will take a look at the cut . . . if that's all right with you?'

He could smell the streets on her clothes, and it was not pleasant. Also, he suspected from the look of her that she'd been knocked about quite a bit. Certainly the fall outside could not be blamed for the bruises on her neck and arms.

They entered a room off the hallway. Well furnished, with deep armchairs and a sofa of wide proportions, it contained a handsome old display cabinet, crammed full of all manner of pretty china artefacts.

Covering most of the far wall was a beautiful fireplace with high mantelpiece, and red velvet-fringed runner stretching from one end to the other. Standing centre of the mantelpiece was a clock of immense proportions, with two moulded figurines flanking either side of the face.

Ruth imagined this place to be the home of people who, though maybe not wealthy, had no financial worries.

Just as he'd promised, the man's wife treated the cut on Ruth's forehead. Then she was given tea and cakes, and an old coat to fend off the cold, though, unlike her husband, the wife was not kindly of manner.

'What were you doing, sleeping on our doorstep? Have you no home to go to?'

'I got lost, that's all.'

'Drunk, were you?' The smell of booze lingered in the air.

'Maybe, maybe not.' Irritated by the woman's questions, Ruth lashed out. 'So, what if I *were* drunk? What's it got to do with you?'

Sensing trouble, the woman's husband warned her, 'Leave it, Judith. I'm sure when our visitor is fed and feeling warm again, she'll be in a hurry to get home.'

Having recovered somewhat from her earlier ordeal, Ruth changed her tone. 'I'm not in a hurry. What have I got to go home for? My husband's cleared off and left me. Mind you, he took the little bastard with him, so good shuts to the pair of 'em, that's what I say!'

'I'm sorry for your troubles,' Judith Ellis said, refusing to be drawn further into this woman's confidence. 'If you're feeling better now, you might want to go into the bathroom and clean up. Afterwards, I think it best if you make your way home.'

'Hmm!' Swigging the dregs of her tea, Ruth replaced the teacup into the saucer. 'Where's the bathroom then?'

Jim stood up. 'I'll show you.'

She followed him down the passageway and when she went into the bathroom, her benefactor returned to his wife, who was already regretting their charity.

'I wish you hadn't brought her into our home,' she said, flustered. 'There's something about her . . . I've seen her before somewhere, but for the life of me, I can't think where.'

'Don't worry, dear. At least we've done our duty and helped a poor soul in need. Soon, she'll be away from here, and you'll never see her again.'

'I hope not!' Sometimes, her husband was too kind and far too trusting, and it was a real source of worry to her.

A few moments later, Ruth appeared, looking and feeling more like her old self. 'I could really get used to this place.'

The man quietly took stock of Ruth. With the grime of the streets now stripped away, and having raked a comb through her hair, the woman looked almost human; handsome, even, Jim thought. But there was something else . . . The more he looked at her, the more familiar she looked.

'I know you!' he exclaimed. 'You're Ruth Denton. You used to visit our establishment, the Rose and Crown, on King Street.'

Ruth laughed out loud. 'Well, bugger me! I didn't recognise you. By, you've not aged well, either of you. The Rose and Crown, eh? Good grief! That seems a lifetime ago.'

'Ruth Denton, of course!' The woman was shocked. 'What's happened to you? How in God's name could you bring yourself to go out drinking, wandering the streets and sleeping in doorways? Have you lost all sense of decency? You should be at home, looking after your child. It's shameful, especially at a time like this.' She gave a loud tut. 'Does your poor husband's memory mean nothing to you?'

'What the hell are you going on about?' Ruth stared at her, angry and confused. 'My "poor husband's memory" – what kinda talk is that? Just 'cause I told you he'd buggered off and left me, doesn't give you the right to say a thing like that!'

Shocked, the woman looked to her husband, who stepped forward. 'I'm sure nobody meant to be disrespectful, least of all us. Only—'

'Only . . . what?' Panic rose up in Ruth. 'What's going on 'ere? What the devil's she talking about, my "poor husband's memory"? ANSWER ME, DAMMIT! WHAT DOES SHE MEAN BY THAT?'

'All right, calm yourself.' Taking her by the shoulders, Jim adopted a sympathetic voice. 'I imagine from your reaction that you haven't been home for some time. But . . . have you heard what's being said? Have you had a chance to look at the papers?'

Ruth began to imagine all manner of things. 'What are you trying to say? Tell me. Has something happened that I should know about?'

'Just a minute, please.' Jim went to the sideboard and took out the late edition of the day's newspaper, which he placed on the table for her to see. 'I think you should prepare yourself, my dear. They're not altogether sure of the facts yet . . . but there's a lot of speculation regarding your husband, Tom Denton. I'm sorry.'

Ruth quickly read the article about the young man who had committed suicide. The name Thomas Denton was mentioned more than once.

'No . . . no, it can't be Tom.' The blood drained from her face. 'It can't be . . .'

When the man stepped forward to comfort her, she pushed him away. 'Leave me alone! It's not him. I know it's not him . . . it can't be!' Then she was running; down the passageway and out of the front door.

When she was clear of the house, she fell against the wall and sobbed bitterly. 'It can't be Tom . . . he would never do a thing like that.' But then she remembered that shocking row, and the hateful things that were done, and she was disgusted, with herself, but mostly with him.

'Tom Denton, you cowardly bastard!' She thumped the wall with her bare fists. 'How could you do that to me? How will I manage now, eh? How am I supposed to keep a roof over my head?'

After a while, when the shock had run its course, she walked down the street, cursing and blaming him, and wondering what would happen to her now. *You can't have loved me. If you did, you would never have abandoned me . . . and in such a way. What made you do it, Tom? What possessed you?*

An overwhelming sense of pain rose above her anger. She blamed herself, and regretted she had not done right by him. Right from the start, she had pretended to love him; pretended to cherish their every moment together, when all the while she felt nothing for him. Instead she had leaned on him, and when it suited her she had given herself to other men. Hard and selfish, she had leaned on Tom like no woman should ever lean on her man, and when she lay with strangers, she never gave her long-suffering husband a moment's thought.

From the day he put a ring on her finger and even before then, she had no love in her heart for him. And in all the difficult years that followed, there had never been any love for him.

Time and again over the years, she had heaped humiliation on that good man. She had taken his hard-earned money; she had given thanks because he had raised the brat in the belief that he was the father. And she had gladly taken his money, and when that was spent, she had taken other men – even his friends – into her bed.

Standing there all alone in that empty street, she saw herself as she really was. And when the weight of her treachery threatened to overwhelm her, she reluctantly headed for Henry Street.

As she hurried there, dark rage rippled through her. She blamed Tom for not being man enough to see what she was like. She blamed him for putting up with her all these years. She blamed him for not realising that the brat was not his, but came from the loins of another man; a man he never knew and never would. A man she had never forgotten. A man who had taken her love and betrayed her, in the same callous way she had betrayed Tom.

Thinking about it all now, she was filled with hatred. The world was an ugly place and she did not fit in any more. Penniless and alone, she now had some very hard decisions to make.

One thing was certain: the brat needn't think he could rely on her. If she hadn't wanted him when Tom was here, why would she want him now? In fact, he was the one to blame, because he was at the root of all the heartache. That was why, if she never again clapped eyes on him, it would not bother her.

It seemed an age before she arrived at her front door. For a long, reflective moment, she stood on the pavement, her eyes sweeping the house, as she recalled memories of the years she had spent behind that closed door. Like a film, the scenes rolled through her tortured mind.

In her mind's eye she saw the time when, as his bride, Tom carried her over the threshold. He was so happy then; loving her like any man loved his new wife. He was proud to have his arms around her; proud when she told him she was carrying his child. And even then, he never knew how much she wished she was not there; weighed down with a shiny new wedding ring on her finger, and the strong arms about her body were like a chain choking the life from her.

Tom's arms were not the arms she needed about her.

From that first night as man and wife, and through all the hard years afterwards, her heart and soul slowly began to die, until after a while she felt nothing for Tom, and gave nothing to him. And she knew that for the rest of her life she would always feel like that.

On that first day as her husband, and on the days and weeks following, Tom never knew how much she resented him. She had never loved him; though at first she did try, but there was no love in her heart; not for Tom, and not for the life form she carried inside her. In those first few, unbearable months, all her efforts to be rid of the unborn came to nothing.

It was as though she were being punished, and even before the child was born she felt no motherly love for it. When she first looked down on the child's face, she was shocked. He had a look of his father. He was a constant reminder of how that man had deceived and abandoned her; just like Tom had abandoned her now.

'Mrs Denton, are you all right?' Mrs Kettle had seen Ruth arrive and was puzzled by the way she just stood there, staring at the door. But then, after the awful business of her husband's suicide, who could blame her for acting strangely?

'We're so sorry to hear about your husband . . . I mean . . . oh, but what a shocking thing. Is there anything we can do? Would you like to come inside . . .? I've got the teapot freshly warmed . . .'

With her memories shattered, Ruth shook her head. 'No . . . thank you all the same.' That woman was the last person she would ever sit down with.

Quickly climbing the steps she went inside the house. She didn't even notice that the front door was unlocked.

Closing the door behind her, she stood still for a moment, her back to the door and her eyes scouring the way before her. She looked along that seemingly endless passageway, then her gaze travelled up the stairs, and now she was climbing the stairs until she was at the top, looking down, unaware that the tears were rolling down her face.

In her confused and twisted mind, she imagined Tom standing on the Mill Hill bridge. She imagined him waiting for the train and then leaping to his death.

Wasn't that what it said in the paper? How he had seemingly jumped from the bridge into the path of a train. They could not be sure at this stage, but because of an eye-witness account, they were currently treating it as a suicide.

She knew the truth, though. She knew in her heart

and soul that Tom had ended his life because, at long last, he had given up on her.

Slowly, but with purpose, she went into the bedroom. Her gaze fell on the bed and she realised with shame the bad things she had done there; with Tom's workmates, and even with strangers that she'd found in the pubs and dives.

She had done all that, and even now, she needed to blame Tom. 'It was all your fault, Tom. You should never have loved me. I didn't want you to love me,' she murmured brokenly. 'You should have left me long ago. You should have taken the boy and gone away from me. Maybe then we might all have had a chance at happiness.'

She knelt down at the side of the bed, where she lifted the hem of the eiderdown and threw it up over the bed. She then reached under and drew out a small, plain brown package tied with string. There was nothing to indicate what it was, but it was a precious thing all the same; far more precious than Tom, or the boy, or even herself.

With the package in her hands, she sat on the bed and gazed at the package, then she turned it over. After a while she held it against her face in a loving manner. Rocking back and forth, eyes closed, she softly murmured to herself, 'See what's happened to me? See what you've done?'

Eventually she laid the package on the bed, took hold of the ends of the string and, very gingerly, opened up the package.

Taking out the items one by one, she laid them out on the bed. There was a dried rosebud, picked one summer evening and given to her, she thought, with love. There was a pretty floral handkerchief still in its box; a memento from a wonderful day in Blackpool, in the height of summer, many years ago.

When the tears started again, she rammed the items

back into the package; all but one: a black-and-white photograph of herself and a man, holding hands. Smiling and content, they were seated on a bench in the park.

There was no denying that he was the boy's father because it was clear to see; in their strong, handsome features; the same thick, wild mop of hair, and that same beautiful, heart-breaking smile.

Over the years, whenever the boy smiled, it cut Ruth's heart to shreds. She had learned to ease the pain by closing her heart to him.

Over these past few years, she had quickly come to realise that the boy's love of music came from his true father. He was part of a band playing at the Palais that fateful night, when she'd gone there with a friend.

She brought her gaze once more to the photograph in her hand. She recalled the very day – indeed, the very moment – of this photograph. They had paused to sit on the bench and had asked a passer-by to take the picture.

On that day, their love shone out for all to see, and Ruth thought her world could not be more perfect.

They arranged to meet that same night, to make plans for the future.

The next morning he was gone, and she never heard from him again. She tried every which way to find him, but then she learned that the band had left town and she didn't know where they'd gone.

Saddened, she now kissed her fingertips, and placed the kiss on the man's mouth. 'I loved you then, and even though you deserted me, I still love you . . . fool that I am!' Her heart was his and always would be, that was why she could never love Tom.

The whisper of a smile crossed her features. There was no feeling of hatred. No more regrets. It was as though she had been burned out from the inside, and now she was empty. Only anger and a sense of self-destruction remained. The same self-destruction that had crippled her all these years. The same self-destruction that stopped her from loving, and took away her joy.

Tearful now, she snatched up the photograph and tore it into the tiniest particles, until soon it was just a heap of rubbish on the bed.

Collecting the shredded pile, along with the package and its contents, she carried them to the fireplace, where she placed them very carefully into the grate.

Reaching for the box of matches on the mantelpiece, she then set fire to the items.

Seated cross-legged on the rug, she watched the flames flicker and dance, and when the papers were reduced to ashes, she buried her head in her hands, and sobbed as though her heart would break.

After a while, she clambered up and calmly made the bed and tidied round. That done, she went downstairs and satisfied herself that the house was presentable. Taking a notepad and pencil from the dresser, she wrote a letter for the next-door neighbour, asking that she might, please, 'return these house keys to the landlord'.

She then addressed an envelope to her neighbour Mrs Kettle, she then placed the note and keys inside, and sealed it.

Another moment of quiet contemplation, then she went to stand at the door. Looking down that familiar street, she felt a pang of loneliness at leaving this place that had been her home for so long; but then some driving instinct urged her to leave quickly. She'd be lonelier still if she stayed.

Momentarily closing her eyes, she gave a deep replenishing sigh. A few moments later, after dropping the envelope through her neighbour's letter box, she took a moment to think about the enormity of what she was doing.

With head held high, she then hurried away, leaving Henry Street behind for ever.

She took no luggage, no mementoes, and not a single item of clothing or belongings. She left just as she had arrived some years ago: with empty pockets and an empty heart. The day of her wedding to Tom had been the start of what felt like a lifetime of punishment.

Willingly, deliberately, she had committed one wicked act after another. First, she had employed every effort to end the pregnancy; then, when that was unsuccessful, she had trapped her man and foisted the unborn child onto him. From then on, her whole life was a lie, and through it all, she felt no love for the boy or for her husband, nor did she feel any sense of guilt or regret. Instead, she felt used and lonely, and enraged with the circumstances that had brought her to this lonely moment in time.

These past eight years or so had been unbearable.

Every day she was made to look at the boy and realise what she had lost. And every night she was made to lie in the arms of a man she did not love.

Her life had been intolerable, but now, with Tom having taken his own life, she was free at last.

As for the boy, she could only assume that he was with Tom's father.

Right now, she had no idea where she was headed. All she knew was that her life here was done. She must get far away from these parts. Away from the bad memories. Away from where it all went wrong, for her, and for Tom, and in many ways, for the boy.

Next door, Mrs Kettle looked out of the window, the open letter clutched in her hand. Seeing Ruth linger a moment before heading off, she was sorely tempted to run out and ask where she was going, and had she heard anything more about her poor husband's death.

But she thought twice and decided it was not worth the aggravation she would get in return. Even at the best of times, she had thought Ruth Denton to be mentally unhinged.

When for the briefest moment Ruth turned to look at her, she swiftly dodged back behind the curtain.

Yes, of course she would give the landord the keys, as requested in the note. And she hoped that was the last she might see of Ruth Denton, although there would be less to complain about with her gone.

All the same, she wouldn't want Ruth Denton to discover she'd been spreading gossip about her, though she felt cheated that Ruth Denton had not found the common decency to confide in her about why she was handing in the keys, and where she was headed. And wasn't it peculiar that she had neither bag nor portmanteau with her?

Moreover, what about the furniture, which Tom Denton had worked hard to provide? And where was the boy?

What had she done with the boy, who was never seen to enjoy a kiss or a cuddle, or even a kind word, from his mother? He was certainly not with her just now.

If he wasn't with her – and he was certainly not with his father – then he must be with his granddad Bob.

Growing irritated, she went off to get herself a cup of tea. If young Casey really were with his granddad Bob, then she'd be thankful for that much at least. Especially when, apart from his daddy, that darling old man was probably the only person who had ever really loved him.

CHAPTER SIX

'WHERE IS SHE then?' Casey blamed himself. 'Has she run away? Was it my fault?'

'No, lad. If she has run away – and we don't know that for sure – then it wouldn't be your fault, or anyone else's. Yer mam has a mind of 'er own, we all know that.'

'But when we went round to give her Daddy's letter, Mrs Kettle said that Mam gave her the keys, and asked her to give them to the landlord. That means she's not coming back.' The tears welled up in Casey's eyes. 'It's all my fault. I made her mad, and then Daddy got angry, and now she's run away, and Daddy's . . . Daddy's . . .' Choked with emotion, he threw his arms around Bob's neck. 'It is my fault! It is!'

'No, lad, it isn't.' Holding the boy for a moment, he then eased him away to look him in the eye. 'You believe your old granddad, don't yer?'

Casey nodded, his face lined with grief.

'So, if I tell you that it isn't your fault – that it's nobody's fault – then you really should believe me . . . isn't that right?'

Again, the boy nodded, his voice trembling as he asked, 'Why's she gone away then?' He recalled his father's letter, and how he had asked him to 'forgive'. But he didn't know how to. All he knew was that both his parents had gone away, leaving him and Granddad all alone.

The old man was saddened by the boy's suffering. 'Look! I'll be honest with you, lad. I truly don't know why your mam's gone away, and I certainly don't know why she's handed in her house keys. Mebbe she just needs to get away and think about things.'

The old man had been haunted by the very same questions, and now his voice was almost inaudible, almost as though he was speaking to himself. 'Mebbe she can't handle what's happened. Who can get inside anybody else's head and know what they're thinking, eh?'

It was painfully obvious to him that Ruth Denton had no intention of returning to the house on Henry Street.

He turned the boy to face him again. 'Casey?'

'Yes, Granddad?'

'I want you to promise me that you'll stop thinking any of this is your fault, because it really isn't.'

When the child gave no answer, he gave him a gentle shake. 'Casey! Do yer understand what I'm saying?'

The boy nodded.

'It's not your fault, and it isn't anybody else's fault either. Whether we like it or not, folks will do what they mean to do, and nobody ever knows the real truth of it. D'yer see what I'm telling yer, lad?'

'Yes, Granddad.'

For a moment or so, the old man held his grandson close. 'It's just me an' you now, lad. So we need to look after each other, don't we, eh? We need to help each other through these next few days especially, 'cause it's gonna be real hard to go to that church and say goodbye to yer daddy. I reckon it'll be one of the hardest things we've ever had to do.'

When he felt the tears rising, he decided it was time

to change the subject and try something new. 'Hey, d'yer know what I reckon, lad?'

'What, Granddad?' Casey could sense a new determination about the old man, and it was comforting.

'Well, I've been thinking we should tek a look at that guitar, see if it's repairable. What d'yer say?'

'Oh, yes, please, Granddad!' The boy's eyes it up. 'Daddy would like that. He was really sad when Mam broke it . . .'

'Aye, well. Let's not think too much about the bad things. Let's just think right now about what yer dad would want us to do.' He gave a wag of his finger. 'Mind you, if you do happen to think about the bad things, I don't want you to think about 'em on yer own. You an' me can talk, and sometimes when yer talk, it does help, doesn't it?'

'Yes, Granddad. Thank you.' Casey thought his granddad was very special. Whenever he was around, it felt safe, as though nobody in the whole wide world could ever hurt them again.

'Aw, lad . . .' The child's open gratitude caught the old man in the heart. 'There's no need to thank me. I only want to help . . . like you want to help me when I'm sad. 'Cause when all's said an' done, you really are all I've got left now.'

'I know, Granddad, and you're all I've got left, and I love you lots.' He smiled eagerly. 'Please, Granddad . . . can I fetch the guitar now?'

'Aye, but there's summat else we need to get clear first. Then we'll set about that guitar.'

The boy listened while the old man tried to prepare him for the ordeal in the next couple of days.

'When we go into that church, we'll be together, you and me. There'll no doubt be some of yer dad's work-mates and a smattering of good neighbours, an' happen yer mam might even turn up. If she does, we'll be kind to 'er, won't we?' He recalled what Tom had said in his letter, and it had touched a chord with him.

When the boy gave no answer he went on, 'If she does turn up, we'll ask what her plans are, and whether you and me have any place in them. And we'll do what yer daddy asked, and try to forget about all the rows and the cruel words spoken in the heat of the moment . . . Casey, lad?'

When the boy still remained silent, Bob persisted, 'I know it will be hard, lad. But if yer mam turns up, we should try and be kind to her like yer daddy would want. Oh, I know she can be a bad 'un, and I know she lashes out for no reason, and whatever punishment she might get, it would serve her right. But we mustn't forget she's your mammy after all, and she's been hurt as well. She's lost her husband, just like you've lost your daddy, and while you've got me, she has to start her life all over again, on her own. Oh, I know that's mebbe what she wants, but we really should try and be a bit easy on her . . . if we can.'

He asked gently, for he knew it was awfully hard for Casey to forgive her. 'Will you try at least not to be cruel to her, like she's been cruel to you? Yer know what they say: two wrongs don't mek a right.'

Not altogether sure what was expected of him – Casey thought he might find it too hard to be kind to his mam, even if he wanted, but he gave a curt little nod all the same.

'Aw, that's champion, lad. Y'know, I reckon, when it comes right down to it, we're all of us different. Mebbe we should try and allow for that, eh?' Yet even he found it hard to forgive Ruth's behaviour.

Casey felt angry. He didn't even want to see his mam any more, and he hoped with all his heart that she would not turn up at the church.

'Casey?' The old man could see the boy clenching and

unclenching his knuckles. 'Answer me, lad. If yer mammy turns up at the church, you won't let her see how angry you are . . . will yer?'

Casey took a moment to think. 'All right, Granddad. If she's friendly to me, I'll try and be friendly back. But only because you and Daddy want me to.' He was hopelessly mixed up inside. In his head he could still hear her calling him 'liar' and 'little bastard', yelling at his dad like a crazy thing. And whatever Granddad Bob said now, he still believed that he must be partly to blame for everything that had happened.

The old man gave a rueful smile at the boy's honest answer. 'All right then, lad. So if she's friendly, you'll return the compliment. That'll do me. At least for now.'

'Now can I get the guitar?'

'In a minute. There's one other thing we need to talk about, an' it's to do with you in particular. After we've . . . what I mean is . . .' It was so hard to say. 'After the church . . . we've got to start thinking about getting you back to school.'

'I don't like school. I don't ever want to go back there!' These past few days, Casey had been content to stay at home with his granddad. 'I don't want to leave you. I hate school!'

'No, you mustn't say that, lad. School is where you learn things. It's where you get the chance to prepare for what you want to do, once you're out there in the big wide world. Besides, I'm sure it won't be long afore the authorities need to speak with the two of us . . . about you staying with me, and meking sure you go to school. Meantime, we'll keep you off school for a few days after . . . well, until things 'ave settled a bit. Then I want to get back to as normal as possible, and that includes you going to school.' He added, 'An' who knows, yer might even get music lessons at school.'

'They don't do music lessons.'

'Mebbe not, but they let you play your guitar in assembly so that's a start. They might be thinking about proper music lessons. Just ask your teacher. Then we'll see what happens, eh?'

'I don't want to go to school. I don't like to leave you.'

'Ah, well now, if you're worried about me being on my own, don't give it a second thought.'

'Why not?'

The old man gave a cheeky grin. ''Cause I'll not be on my own. Y'see . . . your friend Dolly said she'll come round regular an' keep an eye on us.' He winked naughtily. 'To tell yer the truth, I reckon she fancies me.'

'What?' Casey gave an embarrassed little laugh. 'No she doesn't!'

'Well, I reckon she does!'

'Doesn't!'

'Does!'

Soon they were both laughing out loud, until inevitably the sombre mood of the day brought them down.

'Well, then!' Bob wisely changed the subject. 'Yer asked if yer could fetch the guitar. So go on then, off yer go.'

As the boy ran to collect the broken guitar, the old man heaved a great sigh, Look after us, Lord, he prayed, 'cause me an' the boy are a bit lost at the minute.

~

It was ten days since Tom was lost to them.

Having been quickly established that Tom Denton had taken his own life 'while the balance of his mind was disturbed', the coroner had given leave for the service to take place, and now everything was ready.

Unable to sleep, Bob had been up and down the stairs half the night; one minute seated in the scullery, thinking about things, and the next minute looking in on the boy. Then he was tiptoeing away, unaware that Casey was every bit as wide awake as he was himself.

At eight thirty, after eventually snatching a few hours' sleep, the two of them were seated at the small table in the back parlour, where Casey was toying with his boiled egg and toast.

'Try and eat summat, lad,' Bob urged. 'There's not much of you already, and if you don't eat you'll end up skin and bone.'

'I'm not hungry, Granddad.'

'No, and neither am I, but if we don't get summat down us, we might faint in the church, an' we wouldn't want that, would we, eh?'

'I won't "faint".'

'Yer might . . . if yer don't eat some o' that egg yer fiddling with.'

To set an example, he dug his spoon into the top of his boiled egg and, drawing out a sizeable bite of yolk, he pushed it into his mouth. 'See that! Now, it's your turn.'

So, just to please his granddad Bob, the boy did the same; although it took a huge effort for him to actually swallow the food.

An hour later, the table had been cleared, and the two of them set about getting ready. The old man put on his one and only suit, a grey tweed effort, which had hung in the wardrobe since his dear wife had been laid to her rest.

'Does it look all right, lad?' Going into the boy's room, he stood by the door. 'Do I look decent enough?'

The boy could not recall ever seeing his granddad Bob looking so formal, and so different that he could hardly recognise him.

No longer was he an old man with untidy grey whiskers,

and a wild sprouting of hair. Instead, his whiskers were smartly trimmed, and his hair was combed through, and his usual baggy brown trousers were replaced with a suit that fitted him, and even made his round tummy seem smaller.

Casey could not take his eyes off him. 'You look . . .' he couldn't find a fitting word, '. . . you look . . . lovely, Granddad.'

The old man chuckled. 'No, lad. That won't do! What I need is to look smart. Do I look smart, that's what I want to know?' He drew in his tummy, tightened his belt, straightened his tie and stood to attention. 'Well?'

'Yes, you look really . . . smart.' Suddenly, Casey saw the telltale signs on the old man's face. 'Granddad?'

'Yes, lad?'

'Have you been crying again?' He would never admit that he, too, had spent most of the night in tears, his head buried in the pillow.

'What? No, o' course I haven't been crying.'

In truth, he had hardly stopped crying this past week or so. If it hadn't been for the boy, and the lovely Dolly popping round at times, he might have followed his son in the self-same way, God forgive him for the thought.

'Do I look smart as well, Granddad?' Casey had on a tidy little jacket with three brass buttons up the front, and for the very first time in his young life he was wearing long trousers. Bought from the second-hand shop on Montague Street, the trousers and jacket were dark blue, and fitted him perfectly.

'Aw, lad, yer look grand. In them trousers you look more like a little man than an eight-year-old. By, yer daddy would be that proud of yer.'

At his granddad's encouraging words, Casey's chest felt like it had grown another inch, he was that chuffed.

A short time later, the hearse arrived to lead them to

the church. Patrick Riley, a long-time friend of Bob's, had offered to take him and his grandson to the church. So now, as the two climbed into Patrick's old wagon, Patrick doffed his flat cap and gave his condolences.

'All right, are yer, Bob?'

'I'm fine, Patrick, thanks. Me an' the boy are as fine as can be expected, under the circumstances.' A moment later they were driving behind the hearse and headed for the church.

With an ache in his heart and a strong arm about Casey, Bob thought it was a nightmare of a journey, especially for this wonderful boy, who was like a shivering little wreck beside him.

In his silent prayers, the old man vowed then and there that he would use the years he had left to guide and nurture his grandson, and bring out the God-given talent he had been blessed with.

'I'm frightened, Granddad.' The boy's voice trembled. 'I don't know what to do.'

'Yer don't need to do anything, lad, except just hold onto me,' Bob's voice broke, '. . . and mebbe say a little prayer that your daddy is on his way to Heaven, and that when he gets there, he'll be watching over us, just like he promised.'

His kindly words appeared to settle the child. When they arrived, the priest was there to welcome them, and to offer his sincere condolence, as he had done on the two occasions when he had visited Bob's house.

The church was full to bursting. As a kindly act of respect, many of Tom's closer workmates had been given a brief respite from work, in order to witness his being laid to rest.

The old man was pleased to see a respectable number of neighbours there, too. Many of them were just curious, though others did really care. All had been shocked at the terrible way in which old Bob had lost his only son and the boy, just eight years old, had lost his beloved daddy.

When everyone was seated, the priest began the service, although the old man and the boy hardly heard a word he was saying because their eyes were glued to the wooden box that held their beloved son and father. Above that, the magnificent crucifix, with open arms and golden heart, appeared to be reaching down, embracing Tom, and then the boy alongside his granddad.

The kindly voice of the priest resonated to the high ceilings, touching the hearts of the mourners, and offering faith and love and trust in the ever after.

For one brief moment while they stood to sing, heads bowed and thoughts heavy, the congregation remained silent. Then the organ struck up 'All things bright and beautiful', and the voices rang out.

It was a bitter-sweet beginning.

~

Outside, Ruth Denton made a solitary figure.

Without coat or hat, and wearing the same clothes as when she left Henry Street for the last time, she looked haggard and forlorn. Her once-shining and well-groomed hair was piled up in a kind of bird's nest, uncombed and unwashed.

Her handsome face, usually pampered, bore the marks of turmoil and sleepless nights spent in dark, damp alley-ways. All the fight had gone from her.

Now, as the music and voices rang out, she nervously made her way to the partially open church door. She inched forward to peep through. Surprised to see so many people there, she stood on tiptoe, searching for two figures in particular.

After a moment, her curious gaze alighted first on

Tom's father, who, though of an age when he was beginning to bend slightly at the spine, was still a man of some
energy and stature.

Just then the old man turned his head. When he seemed
to look towards the door, Ruth quickly dodged away.

After a while, when the music stopped and the priest
addressed the gathering, she dared to step forward and
take another peep inside.

Like everyone else, she listened to the priest talking
about Tom Denton, the family man; how he was known
to be a hard-working and good man, who was loved and
respected by those who knew him.

Moved by the words, Ruth listened, and when the priest
was done and the people stood up to sing again, she
inched forward until, unnoticed and nervous, she tiptoed
into the back of the church, being sure to stay in the
shadows, while all her attention was fixed on the place
where her husband lay.

She recalled the last time she and Tom had exchanged
words, and the spiteful things she had said; especially
when, in the heat of the moment, she had confessed that
the boy was not his son. Now, she prayed for his forgiveness in silence. Though it was true, she should never have
taunted him with it.

She had seen the devastated look on Tom's face, especially when she had lied and said Casey was the son of a
stranger she had coupled with in a dark alley. She had
felt his pain, and even then she could not find it in her
to offer him a single crumb of comfort. From the moment
the words had tumbled from her mouth, she had wished
she could have taken them back. But she couldn't, and
the guilt had crept up on her, until now she could hardly
bear it.

For all that, she still carried a deep and crippling bitterness inside her. After all these years, the need to hit out

and harm others seemed stronger than ever. Yet the only people that she could punish were the two who truly loved her.

Now, after all her ambitions for the future, and because of hopes and dreams long gone, she was left with nothing. No family. No home. No self-respect. Yet though she missed the security of being taken care of, she knew it was right to leave. She had punished Tom and the boy too much, and now she was paying the price.

Steve Bates had done that to her; the man she had trusted and loved with every fibre of her being. But he was gone for ever, and she was left with a burden that at times drove her to the point of madness.

Her curious gaze wandered back to her son.

Whenever she looked at him, like now, she did not see Casey, the innocent boy. Instead, she saw his true father: the same strong features; the same deepest brown eyes.

She had loved that man so very much. She had given her heart and soul to him, and he had destroyed her without a shred of conscience. Then he went away and she never saw him again.

She had tried so hard to forget him, but each time she looked at the boy, the father was there, taunting her, making her remember. When his name came into her mind now, she tried to push it away, but like the memories, it clung to her. 'Steve . . .' she murmured his name. For one fleeting moment she felt a need to search him out, but where would she even begin to look? And if she found him, what then?

Suddenly, for the first time, she felt a kinship with Tom and Casey. Now, as she looked on that small, frightened face, she had an overriding urge to go to him, to assure him that everything would be all right; that she and his granddad would look after him . . . that she would even try her very best to love him.

But with that thought, her heart grew cold again. No, she could never love him. It would be a lie, and there had been enough lies already. Lies about loving, and keeping, and caring for the one you believed would be there for ever. So many cruel lies. So much pain. And a callous betrayal that she would never forgive.

Just a short distance away from his mother, Casey could not rest. With everyone listening to the priest closing the service, he felt someone watching him. He wondered, just for a moment, whether it might be his daddy. Like his letter said, 'When you're worried . . . the softest rush of sound . . . will be me . . . to encourage and help you.' The words were emblazoned on his heart.

Instinctively, he turned, and she was there looking straight at him. At first, he hardly recognised her because of her wild hair and unkempt appearance.

When she realised he'd seen her, she dodged back outside, and disappeared from sight.

Casey was about to tell his granddad that his mam was here, but the moment was lost when suddenly everyone stood up to walk slowly down the aisle and on towards the door. When his granddad took hold of his hand, he went with him, his eyes peeled to catch sight of his mother. But she was already gone.

Outside, they followed the procession across the path and onto the grass, and when Granddad looked down to him, Casey told him excitedly, 'She was here. Mam was here!'

The old man glanced about, trying to catch sight of Ruth. He looked down the path to the gate, then across to the church porch, but there was no sign of her and, head bowed, he concentrated on the priest's closing prayer.

A few moments later, it was all over. The mourners lined up to shake the old man by the hand. 'You've still got a part of your son in that little lad,' they assured him, and Bob knew he was lucky in that respect.

They smiled on the boy, and promised, 'Your granddad will take good care of you.' Knowing it was true, Casey was content enough, though he sorely missed his daddy. Far too much for anyone to understand except maybe Granddad Bob.

When everyone else was gone, the old man and the boy remained, a sorry pair, deeply unhappy and wishing this day had never been. Still holding hands, they turned away from the grave, and the bond between them grew even stronger.

As they walked down the flagged path and on towards Patrick Riley's wagon, Bob asked, 'Was she really here, lad? Yer mam . . . did you honestly see 'er?' He had hoped she might be there, but if she really had come to see her husband laid to rest, why had she not willingly shown herself to him and the boy?

Yet again he glanced about, but he could see no sign of her, or even anyone closely resembling her. In the end, he was made to wonder if the boy might have imagined her.

From behind some beech trees, Ruth watched them make their way down to the wagon. In all her life, she had never felt so alone; except maybe once, but that was a long time ago, and not even worth remembering.

Going to stay with Tom's father had crossed her mind, but had been swiftly dismissed. It was not the answer, and anyway, she felt no kinship or affection of any kind for him. She had to survive and come to terms with the trauma of being left on her own. Yet again. Just like the other time, only that was worse, because then it was just her. There was no husband, no father-in-law, and at that time she had not yet learned that she was already with child.

And now, here she was again, made to start over, and no idea which way to go. She knew the old man would not turn her away. She only had to ask and he would give her a place in his home. But she did not want that.

There was too much water under the bridge; too many bad memories to resolve. It would take a long time, maybe for ever, before she could ever become part of a loving family.

She shivered at the idea that one day she might be expected to take responsibility for her son. She did not want the boy. She would *never* want him.

At the van, Casey turned and saw her watching them. 'She's there, Granddad. Look!'

But by the time the old man looked up, she was gone.

'She was there, Granddad!' The child was adamant. 'She really was!'

Bob believed him. 'Here, lad!' Taking Tom's letter addressed to Ruth from his jacket pocket, he handed it to the boy. 'This path down to the gate is the only way out, so she can't be too far away. Go after her; give her this. Tell her, it's for her, and it's a letter from your daddy. Hurry, lad. HURRY!'

The boy ran as fast as his legs could take him, up the path and through the shrubbery, but there was no sign of his mother. He looked back at his granddad, and slowly shook his head.

When the old man gestured towards the church, Casey understood and ran to the church door. He was about to go inside, when his attention was drawn to the place where his daddy was laid. At first, all he could see were the two men already shifting the earth and replacing the many flowers.

And then he saw his mother, standing a little way off, looking tearful and sad as she watched the men go about their work.

For a moment, Casey was upset by what the workmen were doing. He wanted to go to them and tell them to stop. It wasn't right. They should not be moving things about and trampling over his daddy's place. It was not right! He needed someone to hold him and, almost without realising it, he ran to his mammy, startling her as he threw his arms round her middle. He held on, his tears covered by the folds of her dress.

She did not push him away. Instead, for that one, precious moment, she held on to him. Soon, though, she eased him away, telling him coldly, 'Go back to your granddad.'

Casey shook his head. 'Please, Mam, I'm sorry if I upset you before. Please . . . come back with me and Granddad Bob?'

Affected by his tear-stained face, she began to retreat. 'I'm not coming back, Casey. I am *never* coming back!'

As she prepared to brush past him, the boy handed her the letter. 'Granddad said I have to give you this. It's from . . . it's—'

She glanced at the handwriting, and she did not need telling. 'I can see who it's from, and I don't want it. Take it back to your granddad. Tell him, I want nothing from any of you!'

Her harsh words cut through the boy's hopes, making him angry. 'You have to have it! It's for you . . . from Daddy. YOU'RE WICKED . . . AND I HATE YOU!' Sobbing, he turned away; then he was fighting and struggling as she took hold of his shoulder, relenting.

'All right, give me the letter. I'll read it, I promise.'

Subdued by her promise, Casey handed her the letter. 'Please, Mam, please, come back with me and Granddad,' he asked again. 'He wants you to, I know he does.'

Having already said more than she was comfortable with, Ruth shook her head. 'I can't. I've got things to do, so leave me the letter and go back to your granddad. Go on! Don't keep him waiting.'

'Can I fetch Granddad here? He wants to talk to you. He won't be angry, he really won't. So, can I fetch him?'

Against her instincts, she found herself caught in an emotional trap. 'All right then, just for a minute, but I mean it: I'm not coming back with you. As long as you both understand that, then, yes, fetch him.'

Jubilant, the boy ran to get his granddad. 'She says she wants to see you,' he yelled as he ran down the path. 'Quick, Granddad! Mam says you can come and talk to her.'

The old man hoped this might be the start of a reunion between Ruth and her son. It's what Tom would have wanted. 'I'll just be a minute,' he told Patrick Riley. 'Can you hang on for us?'

'Course I can. Tek as long as yer like, mate.' Patrick drew his newspaper from between the seats. 'Meantime, it'll give me a chance to choose the winner in the two-thirty.'

The old man and the boy hurried up the path, each excited, and hoping the badness was at an end. But when they got to the place where she'd been, there was no sight of Ruth. 'She's gone!' Tugging at the old man's hand, Casey yelled for his mammy. 'COME BACK . . . YOU PROMISED!' He was frantic. 'She's left us, Granddad. She's gone!'

Bob shook his head in disgust. 'Let her go, lad. She's not worth yer tears.'

His heart breaking, Casey walked away with his granddad. Twice he glanced back to see what the men were doing. He so wanted everything to be as it was; even the rows, and his mammy yelling all the time. At least he was not alone then. But now, even with his darling granddad holding his hand, he felt so alone, and it was frightening.

In that moment, because she had not wanted his daddy's letter, and because she didn't want him either, the boy made himself believe that he never wanted to see his mam again; not for as long as he lived.

As they climbed into the wagon and sat, silent and upset throughout the journey, Patrick Riley was also upset.

He had witnessed the entire episode and, as a father himself, he could not believe the extent of that woman's wickedness.

~

Ruth remained out of sight until the van was gone. She then came out of her hiding place and made her way back to the churchyard.

For a long time, she stood at the foot of Tom's grave, her eyes glued on the wooden identity cross placed there by the workmen; until a permanent structure could be laid.

The inscription told Tom's name and the length of his life; which was pitifully short.

For a while, she stood there, looking down, trying to imagine what he must have thought of her at the end.

'I never thought you would do such a terrible thing,' she chided angrily. 'You took the coward's way out. You left me and then you couldn't face the shame.'

She held out the letter. 'I don't have to read this because I can imagine what you've said – that I'm a trollop, and you'd be right. That I'm a no-good mother, and you'd be right again. You've probably slated me for making you believe that you had a son, when all the time he belonged to another man. You have every right to slate me. But I was desperate, and I know you had long fancied me. I had no money, and no one to help me, so I grabbed the opportunity. You were so crazy about me, you never even questioned when I told you the baby was born early.'

She laughed out loud. 'You were so besotted, you would have believed anything I told you . . . anything! You were a fool, Tom Denton, and I used you. But you never once found me out. You were too stupid, so blind you couldn't even see what was right in front of you.'

Having held her emotions back since leaving Henry Street, Ruth now sobbed bitterly, quietly at first, then as though her heart would break. She told him tenderly, 'You were a good man all the same, Tom Denton. You did not deserve me, but I'm what you got, and I could have searched the world over and not found a man who loved me as much as you did. I tried to love you back, I really did, but I couldn't. I'm sorry. I'm sorry, too, about the boy, because he reminded me of something that I needed to forget. Like it or not, I was forced to see him, every day and night for all those years. And because I couldn't bring myself to love him, I made myself hate him.'

Stepping back, she wiped her eyes with her sleeve. 'Sleep well, Tom Denton. Try not to hate me too much, eh?'

As she turned to walk away, the breeze heightened and caught the letter from her grasp. She watched as it was carried through the air, spinning and dancing, into the small, wooded area.

Curious, she watched it go out of sight. Then she smiled down on Tom. 'So, you took it back, did you? Well, that's OK. I didn't need to read it anyway.'

Somehow, it felt right, that the letter should be free.

Unlike her, because as far as she could tell right now, she would never be free.

But what did it matter? The fires of Hell could be no worse than the Hell she was living here on earth.

PART THREE

~

A Hard Road

CHAPTER SEVEN

'But I need to come with you, Granddad. I won't be any trouble.'

'I don't reckon it would be a good idea,' Bob told Casey. 'It'll be painful enough for me, let alone for a young lad like you. After all that's happened, it's best you stay away from there.'

'But I have to get my comics and stuff.'

'I'll get them for yer. And don't worry, I'll be careful. Anyway, I've already asked Dolly if she'll be kind enough to stay here with you while I go and sort out the other house.'

Four weeks tomorrow! thought Bob in disgust. That's all it's been and already the landlord's on me back! He wants the house emptied today, or he'll charge another month's rent, cheeky bugger! It seems he can't pack another family in fast enough!

Putting on his spectacles, he checked the list, which had been delivered by the landlord. 'Look at that! He reckons he owns the double bed, and both armchairs in the sitting room. That's the first I've heard o' that!'

'Me too,' Casey declared stoutly.

'Well, I never!' Though the situation was disappointing,

Granddad Bob was secretly amused by the boy's quick remark. 'Yer mean to tell me, yer mam and dad never thought to inform yer as to whether or not they owned all the furniture?' He gave an aside wink at Dolly, who was also amused by the boy's contribution.

'Bless his little heart.' She smiled at Casey. 'You're only trying to help, isn't that right, sweetheart?'

'Yes, Granddad!' In his own little way, the boy chided, 'You shouldn't ask me, 'cause I were never told anything like that.'

In truth, he was surprised as anyone to learn that the landlord owned his mam and dad's bed, and two chairs.

'Yer absolutely right, lad, I should not have asked you, and I'm very sorry, I must say. As it happens, though, we're both of us in the dark, 'cause nobody told me neither.'

He gave a convincing scowl. 'So it looks like between the two of us, we've no idea what furniture the landlord owns, or doesn't own.' He looked across at Dolly. 'We've only got his word for it. Moreover, to my recollection, some landlords have been known to claim things that weren't even theirs in the first place!'

Dolly was always a practical soul. 'Well, Bob, if you don't mind me saying, it seems to me that if no one knows, and as your daughter-in-law can't be found, you've little choice but to accept the landlord's claim. Then later on, if you find out he's lied, you can have him, good and proper!'

The old man laughed out loud. 'What with you and the boy, I reckon I'm caught between the devil and the deep blue sea. But yer right, lass. There's nowt I can do for now, except tek his word for it.'

'That's what I think an' all!' Casey liked to be involved in serious conversations, even though sometimes he was out of his depth. 'Maybe Daddy wrote it all down in his papers and stuff.'

The old man was intrigued. 'What "papers and stuff" would that be then?'

'The rent book, I think, and papers . . .' he gave a shrug '. . . just papers. And sometimes, when Daddy was writing things down and I was waiting to play the guitar, he would put the papers into a big envelope and ask me to put it in his special place, while he got the guitar tuned and everything.'

'I see.' The old man lapsed into deep thought. He couldn't help but wonder what kind of 'writing things down' his son might do; especially when his income was modest and he owned next to nothing.

'I know where it's all kept,' Casey persisted, 'so you do need me to help, and Dolly can come too. She can help pack stuff into the boxes, and I know what stuff was ours. I can write on the boxes, so everybody knows what's inside.'

'Oh, I see.' Bob gave a contrived little groan. 'Looks like I'm being nagged from all sides. All right then, we'll all go. All three of us. Satisfied, are yer?'

'Well, I think that's a very good idea,' Dolly said. 'Thank you, Casey.' She told the boy. 'For a minute there, I thought I'd never be asked.' Picking up the teapot, she poured another cup of tea for Bob. 'Me and the lad knew all along that you'd get it right, though, didn't we, Casey?' When she gave the boy a crafty wink, he understood and grinned back at her.

He liked Dolly. It was good to have her here.

'Right, lad,' said Bob, 'you go and get yourself ready. And don't forget to comb your hair properly and make yourself look decent, in case them nosy neighbours are watching.'

'What about the guitar, Granddad?'

'What about it?'

'When are we taking it for the man to mend?'

'When we get back. But listen, lad, don't get yer hopes up, in case it's too far gone.'

'But you said the man was really good at mending things.'

'I know that, son, and he is, but he's not a genius, and if a thing is past mending, he'll say so.'

'But he won't say the guitar is "past mending", will he, Granddad?'

'I honestly don't know, lad. Don't forget that guitar took quite a battering.'

Bob had never given his grandson false hope, and he wasn't about to give it now. 'A guitar, like any musical instrument, is a delicate thing. Even if it got put back together, there's no guarantee it would ever sound the same.'

'But we have to try, Granddad. We have to!'

'I agree. We'll do all we can, lad. I made you a promise on that.'

Reassured, the boy went up to get himself ready.

Once inside the bedroom, he sat before the mirror, suddenly low in spirit as he thought of what they were about to do.

'I don't want the landlord to take back the house, but I don't ever want to live there again,' Casey spoke. 'But what if Mam wants to stay there? How can she do that, without any money for the rent? Granddad says she's made her choice, and that he's sure if she needs us she'll be in touch, but she won't need us and she won't ever get in touch, and I don't know if I even want her to.'

His mind and heart were heavy with all manner of guilt and blame, and when he thought of his daddy's loving letter, he wondered how he was able to forgive her when he was finding it so hard to do.

'I don't want to go back to Henry Street, and then I do, and then I don't,' he muttered. He closed his eyes, remembering the last time he was in that house. In his mind's eye he could hear Mam shouting at Daddy. Telling her bad things. He could remember her grabbing hold of him when Daddy was out of the room, and how very much she had wanted to hurt him.

Disturbed by the images in his mind, he opened his eyes and stared at himself in the mirror. Suddenly, he imagined it was not himself looking back from the mirror, but his daddy, smiling at him, willing him to be brave. 'I don't know how I'll feel when I go inside the house. I'm frightened, Daddy. I'm worried I might run away, and upset Granddad . . .'

For one precious, fleeting moment, Casey felt as though his daddy was right there, in the room with him, and his presence gave him such great strength of heart that suddenly his fear was gone, and then his daddy was gone.

He tried hard to stop the tears from falling, but he could not. This time, though, unlike before, they were not sad, because he was not sad.

Eventually, he brushed the tears impatiently away. 'I love you, Daddy.' His fingers traced the spot where he thought he had seen his daddy's face, and his heart was calm again.

He would try hard to be brave, because his daddy would be there just as he had promised in the letter. He would be there to help him.

Downstairs, Bob and Dolly were talking. 'I'm still not sure I'm doing the right thing, lass . . . tekking the boy back there.'

Like Bob, Dolly kept her voice low. 'You do right to take him, Bob. From what you told me, Henry Street is the only home he's ever known, and to my mind, it's best he's allowed to say goodbye, once and for all. Y'see, Bob . . . in doing that, he won't be forever hankering after what once was, or what might have been, because now, with his daddy gone – God rest his soul,' she made the sign of the cross on herself – 'and with his mammy gone off who knows where, Casey has no choice but to start again. But he'll have you, thank goodness, and I'll be there whenever either of you need me.'

'Oh, I see!' Bob had come to value Dolly like he never thought he would value another woman since his dear wife was gone. He was happy in Dolly's company, and he looked forward to having her here. And now the two of them were so familiar with each other, she felt she had the right to speak her mind, which she did whenever she thought it necessary. 'So, now I'm being got at from all sides, am I?'

She answered tenderly, 'I'm not getting at you, Bob. All I'm saying is, young Casey is a sensible lad. If he feels able to deal with seeing his old house again, then why not let him? I'll be there as well. You know I'm more than willing to lend a hand. And you know that if the lad is upset at being back there in that house, I'll take him out of it, while you carry on and do the necessary work.'

The old man was deeply uncomfortable about the plan. 'I don't know, Dolly. I'm not altogether sure it's right for the lad to be there.' He lowered his voice to a whisper. 'Bad memories and all that.'

'Well, of course it's entirely up to you, and I really shouldn't interfere. But have you thought that, in order to get past the "bad memories and all that", the lad might really need to go back and say goodbye for that one last time? It won't be easy for you either, Bob, but between the two of you, I know you'll get through this.' Having witnessed first-hand the close bond between the old man and the boy, she was filled with warmth and admiration.

Bob looked up at her, and what he saw was the kindliest, prettiest face smiling down on him; and he felt like the luckiest man on earth to have found her, especially at this time in his life. 'Yer right, lass. The boy has a mind of his own, and if he's sure it won't test him too much, then we'll tek him back, like he asked. Besides, it'll save me a job, 'cause then he can sort out his own comics, eh?'

And so it was decided. All three of them would go.

~

Some half-hour later, like three souls on a mission, they went off down the street, the boy going in front, and the two old folk coming up behind, chatting about things in general, and privately thinking about each other and the future.

The boy, however, was strongest on their minds. They knew it would be an ordeal for him to go into the house on Henry Street.

The very same thought was running through Casey's young mind. It was strange to think that when they left Henry Street, it would be for the last time. That little terraced house where he was brought up was very special to him, the only home he had known until a month ago.

It was only now that he came to realise the many boyish adventures he'd enjoyed in Henry Street. He'd learned to play football on the cobbles; race a playmate from the top of the street to the bottom, and to swing round the lampposts with a makeshift wooden seat fastened to a rope, the rope carefully looped over the arm of the lamp.

It was where he first learned to ride his bicycle, with his daddy running close behind, ready to catch him if he should fall.

As he ran in front of Dolly and Granddad Bob, he recalled many good happenings inside their house, things that made him laugh out loud. Like the time he and his daddy had been working down in the coal cellar.

The idea was to clean a small area, then they would paint the walls and partition it all off, so they could play the guitar and make music down there without bothering anyone with the noise. It would be their very own little hideaway.

First, they needed to clear away the thick layers of soot, which over the years had stuck to the damp walls like a second skin.

After a couple of hours' scraping and shovelling, they had almost cleared one wall when a solid blanket of soot slid off the upper area and covered them from head to foot.

Panicking, they fled up the back stairs to the house, but when Ruth saw them through the window, she ran out, screaming and yelling and waving the house brush at them. 'You're not fetching that muck in 'ere!' she yelled angrily.

Casey remembered his daddy's face was coal black, with two white rings round his eyes where he'd rubbed away the soot. 'You look like a panda!' the boy laughed, and then his dad threw a fistful of soot at him, and he threw a fistful right back, until Mam shouted from the back door, 'You can stay out there all night, for all I care. I mean it! If you're not soon cleaned up, I'll lock this door, and leave you out there to freeze!'

So, not wanting to stay out there all night in the cold, the two of them stripped off and washed under the yard tap, splashing soot and water at each other, and laughing till their sides ached.

'Casey!' Granddad Bob's voice startled him.

'What's wrong, Granddad?'

'Look! There's the bus. Quick, lad, don't let him go off without us.'

'I won't!'

Casey ran on and asked the conductor to wait. 'All

right, but only for a minute or two. I can't afford to be late.'

Puffing and panting, the old man arrived to thank him, then he helped Dolly and the boy onto the platform, and led them to the long seating at the sides. After settling Dolly, he sat the boy between them. 'All right, are yer, lad?'

'Yes, Granddad, and what about you?'

'I'm all right.' He turned to Dolly. 'All right, are yer, lass?'

'Right as rain, thank you, Bob.'

'Good.' Though he loathed the circumstances that had brought her to his home, he felt a degree of contentment. With himself and Dolly and the boy all together, it felt like he had been given back a little family.

He firmly believed it was true what they said: the Good Lord takes with one hand and gives with the other.

Collecting the fares, the conductor addressed the boy. 'On a trip with the grandparents, is it?'

The boy smiled at that. He looked at Granddad Bob, with Dolly beside him, and his emotions were a mingling of sadness and pride. 'We're going to Henry Street.'

'Henry Street, eh? This bus doesn't go all the way. You'll need to walk from Penny Street.'

Granddad Bob held out the loose change. 'That's all right,' he acknowledged. 'Penny Street will do. Besides, it's nobbut a spit and a jump from Henry Street.' He watched the conductor roll off the tickets from the machine round his neck. 'Happen the short walk will do us old 'uns a world o' good,' he said.

As they travelled to Penny Street, all three became thoughtful, with Casey growing ever more nervous.

Bob was also troubled. Try as he might, he could not rid himself of the idea that Ruth might have actually gone back there. But then he couldn't see how or why she would, especially as she'd handed in the keys and the house was about to be emptied of its contents.

He'd noticed how the boy was increasingly agitated, shifting about between himself and Dolly, and constantly fidgeting. He was beginning to regret having brought the child with them.

'Worried are you, lad?'

'I'm not worried, Granddad.' Casey's voice dropped to a whisper. 'I'm just a bit sorry, that's all.'

'Aw, lad, that's understandable. We're all a bit sorry. But we need to be strong as well, don't we?'

'Mmm.' Casey gave a little nod, and turned to gaze out the window.

It felt so very strange, coming back here. He wished his daddy was waiting for them at the house. He needed him.

Sensing his anguish, the old man was deeply sorry he could not change things for this hurt little lad. He realised how difficult this journey must be for his grandson, having lost both his parents in different ways. Soon, the only home he had ever known would be gone for ever.

'Hey!' He took hold of the boy's hand. 'It'll work out all right, I promise you. Trust yer old granddad, eh?' His face crumpled in a smile. 'Well, are yer coming in or not?'

'Yes, Granddad. Anyway, I want to get my comics and I need to make sure the landlord doesn't take things that don't belong to him.' He had not forgotten about the chairs and the bed. Also, there were personal things belonging to his daddy.

The old man understood. 'All right then, yer must come inside, but I'll tek care of yer daddy's personal things,' he promised. 'You just root 'em out for me, an' then they'll be for me to worry about. You have my word, the landlord won't get his hands on anything that's not his to take.'

'I'll get the papers for you, Granddad. I know where they are.'

'Good lad!' He gave the boy's hand a friendly little squeeze. 'Between the two of us, we'll have this business sorted in no time at all.'

When, at that moment, Casey glanced up, he was greatly embarrassed to see a pretty schoolgirl, with long plaits and a smiley face, looking right at him. Blushing bright pink, he quickly slid his hand away from his granddad. He didn't need his hand held; he was not a baby! And he didn't want to look like a big sissy in front of that girl.

Bob and Dolly saw Casey's embarrassment and exchanged knowing little smiles.

Soon, much to the boy's relief, the bus shuddered to a halt, and it was time to get off.

Granddad went first, then Dolly, and then Casey. But as he left, the girl watched him go, and when he turned round, she unnerved him with her cheeky little smile. Rushing forward to get out that much quicker, he lost his footing and tripped headlong into the conductor.

'Whoa! Steady there, lad.'

Hoisting him up by the arms, the conductor set Casey upright, but when Granddad went to help him down onto the pavement, Casey was having none of it. 'I can get down myself, Granddad. I'm all right!'

Feeling foolish, he couldn't get away from there quick enough, especially when the girl passed them by and turned to smile right at him.

All the way to Henry Street, he remained silent, his head hung down, and his eyes crinkled in a little grin. He thought the girl was very pretty, and he wondered what her name was.

~

'You're a wicked little girl, Susie.' Having seen the chaos his niece had caused with her lovely smile, the man teased her, 'You're too free and easy with that smile of yours.'

'I don't know what you mean.' She had seen the boy trip and she was really sorry. 'It wasn't me who made him fall down the step.'

'Really? Well, it certainly wasn't me.' Tall, with kindly features, thick brown hair and dark eyes, Steve Bates was a fine-looking man. Mischievously teasing the girl now, his smile was every bit as captivating as the one his niece had showered on Casey.

'Poor little devil. I'm not surprised he fell down the step.'

The girl deliberately ignored him.

'Susie?'

'I'm not listening!'

'All right. Please yourself.' He knew how to deal with this little bundle of mischief. Ignore her, and she would soon come back at you.

He turned his mind to the new enterprise and his blood raced with excitement. He had done well in the music business. Having worked his way up the ranks as a professional guitarist and folk singer, he had the ambition and now the money in place to create a recording studio of such magnificence that it would be renowned throughout the music and entertainment worlds.

He knew the pitfalls, but he also knew that this was what the music industry needed, especially now, with new groups and solo artists bursting onto the scene. A new age was emerging; a different style. And he was determined to be a part of it.

He planned to have the best-equipped, purpose-built recording studios in the land, and his instinct and experience told him that players, composers and management from every part of the music industry would travel miles to use them.

Getting the project off the ground would be a huge financial drain on his resources, which was why he had chosen to look north, where land and manpower were relatively attainable, while land in the south was far more expensive, making it impossible to find a suitable site without his taking on potentially crippling loans.

He was not too proud to take advice from performers themselves. After all, they would be the ones using the facilities, and he knew from his own experience that current studios left a lot to be desired. Moreover, the better ones were nearly always booked up months in advance.

Also, he knew this area. He felt confident here, having spent some time in this part of the country many years ago, when he was a struggling musician. Growing melancholy, his thoughts wandered back to a particular time some nine years ago, and the girl he deserted.

After all this time, he suspected that, like himself, she would be long married and, unlike himself, she probably had children.

He gave a wry little smile. He recalled her to be a hot-blooded girl, whom he had not found it easy to leave behind. In fact, he would not be surprised to find she had a whole little army of children in her trail.

A wave of sadness rippled through him, as he recalled a recent conversation he and his wife had shared; during which she had made her thoughts very clear. 'I told you from the start I didn't want children, and I still don't!'

From day one she had told him that, but he'd married her because he thought he loved her, and because he hoped one day she might love him enough to change her mind. But she never did, and unfortunately for him, he never would.

Little by little, moment by moment, they had grown apart.

～

He had never forgotten the girl he'd left behind here, in the north. He had secretly kept a photograph of her hidden away in the back of his wallet. In his mind's eye, he could see it now. They had spent the day together, and he had never been happier, not before or since.

But life and his musical ambitions got in the way. When, unexpectedly, a once-in-a-lifetime opportunity came along, he deserted her. He was not proud of that.

Her name was never far from his thoughts. He often wondered what might have happened if things had been different, if he'd been a little more mature, or if he had not chosen his budding career over her.

As it turned out, he'd been right to take that first unexpected and exciting opportunity when it came up. But in putting his career before her, he now believed that he had lost something very precious; something he could never get back.

Even now, after all this time, and because the memories were still raw, he had been reluctant to return to this particular area. But he was first and foremost a musician and a businessman, and to that end, as always, he would put his career and music before anything else.

If truth be told, he still had regrets over the sudden and cruel way he had left her. But life marched on relentlessly; that was the way of things. Or so he told himself. Business-wise, he had achieved what he used to think was unattainable; in his private life, however, in all honesty, he was not a contented man.

'All right then, what were you going to say?' The girl jolted his thoughts.

'When?'

'Just now, you were going to say something to me.'

'Oh, yes, that's right. And you said you were not listening.'

'I'm listening now.'

'And I'm supposed to remember what I was about to say, is that it?'

'Yes! So, tell me.'

He knew well enough what he was about to say, but for her impudence he decided she should be made to wait. 'Mmm . . . let me see, what was it?'

'Stop it, Uncle Steve, you know very well.'

'Oh, do I? Well then, if I remember rightly, we were talking about the boy. I asked why you didn't say hello. I mean, he seemed friendly enough.'

'I didn't say hello 'cause I didn't want to,' she fibbed. 'Anyway, Mummy said I should never talk to strangers.'

'Quite right too! And the boy might have wanted to be friends, and then, just as you begin to make friends, he would have gone off with the old fella. Then, before you know it, you'll be gone back to London with your mother . . . after the two of you have emptied all the shops in Lancashire! And all that time you spent getting to know the boy would be wasted.'

'Why are you angry?'

'I'm not angry.'

'You sound angry.'

'Well, I promise, I'm not.' For a moment there, he had been thinking of himself and the sweetheart he'd left behind. 'I tell you what, Susie. When we get off this bus, the first thng we'll do is go and get an ice cream. What d'you say?'

'Ooh, yes! I'd like a cornet, please.'

'OK, we'll each have a cornet.'

Steve grew melancholy. The girl was right: he had been angry. Angry that he gave his wife everything, while she gave him nothing. Angry that some nine years ago he had walked out on an innocent young woman who cared deeply for him.

But that was in the past, and he put the past behind him

in the belief that the young woman he'd left behind was probably happily married and had forgotten all about him.

'Uncle Steve, I don't want to go back home. I want to stay here with you. I want to see where you're building your music studios.'

'No, Susie, I told you before we came here, I could be up north for some weeks. It may well take that long to locate the site I need; assuming I do find one. If I can't find a suitable site here in the north, I'll have to look elsewhere.'

'Uncle Steve?'

'Yes?'

'Mummy wanted Auntie Connie to come with us. Why did she not come? She should have, because they're sisters, and it's good for sisters to spend time together.'

'They're not sisters, sweetheart. They're sisters-in-law, because your daddy is my brother . . . It's complicated.'

'Well anyway, Mummy asked her and she said no, and I think that was mean, even if she is your wife. Besides, I don't suppose Auntie Connie was doing anything else, so she could have come with us.'

'And Mummy was disappointed, was she?'

'She said she wasn't, but she was really.'

'Well, I'm sorry about that, but I think your Auntie Connie didn't come with us because she really was too busy to come.' His mood darkened. 'I'm sure she would have come otherwise.'

'Mummy told Daddy that Auntie Connie should be with you on this trip because it's really important to you. She said you might as well not be married, because Auntie Connie acts like she . . .' screwing up her face, she tried to remember the exact words, '. . . er . . . like she's footers and fancy three.'

Steve laughed out loud. 'I think you mean footloose and fancy-free.'

'Well, anyway, that's what Mummy said. She was angry.

She said Auntie Connie always likes to go her own way, and she doesn't care about your music.'

Steve was not best pleased to hear that, although he knew it was true enough. 'Your mummy really thinks that, does she?'

'Yes, and I think so too.'

'I see.'

This delightful little girl was the apple of his eye, a breath of fresh air, and everything she relayed to him was not new. He was only too aware of his wife's faults, and even his own, where this failing marriage was concerned. How could he not, after years of being married to a woman who had little concern for others and could not see past his wallet?

'Well then, my little know-all, if you think it must be true, who am I to argue? So, now that you've put the world to rights, will you kindly give it a rest and stop nagging me?' Turning his head away he couldn't help but give a little chuckle at the wisdom of a seven-year-old.

When, curious, the girl looked up, he made out he was having a coughing fit.

'Mummy says you don't take care of yourself . . . always flying about and running off and playing your music.'

'Hmm! Your mummy certainly has a lot to say, don't you think?'

'Yes, and I think you should listen to her because she knows best.'

Chuckling again, he gave a little shake of his head. 'What am I gonna do with you, eh?'

'I don't know.'

'Well, what with your mother wanting to buy out all the women's shops in Blackburn, and you wanting me to take you everywhere I go, I wish I'd left the pair of you at home.'

'Uncle Steve?'

'What?'

209

'You shouldn't say that.'

'Shouldn't say what?'

'You shouldn't grumble about Mummy. And Mummy shouldn't grumble about Auntie Connie, although Auntie Connie's not as nice as Mummy, because sometimes she makes people fed up with her.'

'Oh! And don't I know it! It was your Auntie Connie who talked me into bringing the pair of you up here with me. I must be the only man who would bring along his sister-in-law, and a little chatterbox who can't stop talking, even when I'm supposed to have my mind on business. I'm supposed to be getting the lie of the land from this bus trip, not arguing with you.'

'It's not kind to say that. And anyway, you're my uncle, and uncles should be kind to their nieces.'

'Oh, is that so? Well, how about nieces being kind to their uncles? You haven't once smiled at me, in the way you smiled at that boy,' he teased. 'You gave him the most beautiful smile I've ever seen you give anyone.'

'I never!'

'Yes, you did.'

'Hmm!' She was done arguing.

But she thought about the boy and how sad he looked, and she really wished she had spoken to him.

But it was too late now, because the boy had gone off with his granddad, and most likely she would never see him again.

Somehow, the thought of never seeing him again made her feel really sad, too.

~

As he neared Henry Street, Casey thought of his dad and the reason they were here, and he secretly felt sick with nerves.

When they arrived at the house, Dolly noticed Casey's reluctance to go up the two steps to the front door.

She had a suggestion. 'Casey? What if your granddad goes in first, and you show me the place down by the water, where Granddad said you used to play . . . what was it called now?' She feigned a memory loss. 'I can't remember the name of it . . .'

'Blakewater.'

'Oh, yes, that's it, Blakewater. So, do you want to show me, and maybe Granddad could make a start on listing things in the house? What d'you say?'

Casey welcomed her suggestion. 'All right . . . if Granddad doesn't mind?'

'I don't mind one bit.' The old man was thankful for Dolly's suggestion. 'You two get along, and I'll mek a start on sorting things out here.'

Dipping into his jacket pocket, he took out the envelope that he'd received from the landlord, took out the house key, turned it in the lock and threw open the door.

'We'll not be long,' Dolly assured him.

Casey was concerned. 'I don't like leaving you on your own, Granddad.'

'Aw, don't you worry about that, lad, 'cause I'll not be on my own for long. Patrick Riley will be turning up in his old wagon any minute now and, knowing him, he'll have enough gossip to keep me busy for at least half an hour. So, if you two want to make your way back after that, it'll work out right.'

By the time he turned away, Dolly and Casey were already making their way over the little bridge, and on, towards the narrow path that led down to the Blakewater.

Dolly was anxious that she had done the right thing in bringing him here. According to what the boy had told her, he and his daddy had spent many a pleasant hour in this place so this was bound to be difficult for him, yet she

211

thought he might be glad of reliving his memories. That way, in the future, whenever he felt sad or lonely, those wonderful memories would comfort and gladden him.

As they came onto the lower ground, the boy's mind and heart were flooded with those precious memories.

He recalled how, in the summertime, he and his daddy would sometimes wade barefoot in the water, squealing and holding hands when the pebbles hurt their feet. Other times they would just sit and quietly talk, watching the water flow and dip as it went on its busy way. That was the time Casey liked best. They talked about fishing and football, and how he was doing at school – small, seemingly unimportant things – but to the boy, they were even more precious now, because those lovely times down here with his daddy would never happen again.

For the next half-hour, Casey and Dolly sat beside the water. For a time they remained silent. Dolly was saddened by the turn of events that had brought them here. And Casey was moved by a mingling of sorrow and love; but along with these emotions, he was filled with a deep sense of joy at reliving the Blakewater memories, when he and his daddy had learned to know each other, man and boy; father and son.

And now, he would always have that, locked in his heart for ever.

'I'm glad you brought me here, Dolly.' He daren't look up in case she saw his tears.

Dolly, however, heard the tears in his voice. Without a word, she slid her arm round his shoulders, and when he leaned into her and sobbed as though his heart would break, she held him close until the emotions died down, and he was able to smile and eventually to confide in her.

'In his letter my dad promised that he would be with me when I'm worried or sad. Is it true, Dolly? Can he do that?'

Dolly was honest in her reply. 'I don't know, Casey. None of us knows what we're able to do once we're gone from this life. But tell me something, did your father ever lie to you?'

The boy shook his head. 'No, I'm sure he never did.'

'So you always trusted in him, is that right?'

'Yes.'

'So, trust him now, Casey. Believe what he told you – that he will always be near. If it is truly possible to be with you in spirit, your daddy will find a way.'

Shyly, Casey kissed her on the cheek. 'I'm so happy that you and Granddad are friends.'

Dolly smiled warmly, 'What if Granddad and I were to became more than friends – would that bother you?'

'What, d'you mean . . . get married?' He was not altogether surprised.

'Well, what if it happened some day, would you mind?'

'No, because Granddad really likes you. He said you were . . .' he carefully recalled the very words, '. . . "the best thing to come into my life since Grandma".'

Dolly blushed a deep shade of red. 'Did he really say that?'

'He did, yes.' Embarrassed, Casey turned his attention to the flow of water over the pebbles; it made a weird sort of rippling pattern in the water, much like the pattern on the backs of seashells.

Seemingly content, the two of them sat quietly for a while.

Dolly was still thinking about what Casey had told her. She was so thrilled that Granddad Bob had confided to his grandson that he liked her, because she liked him as well. She too had been lonely since losing her own loved one, but lately she was happier than she'd been for a very long time.

~

Back at the house, Bob was still looking out for his old friend. I bet he's gone the wrong way, or the engine's packed up, and he's stuck in some godforsaken ginnel, he thought. Useless, that's what he is. Useless an' unreliable!

At that moment he heard the wagon coughing and spluttering as it bumped over the cobbles.

'You wouldn't believe what's happened to me!' With clutches of wild red hair jutting out from beneath a flat cap, and his head stuck out the window, the little Irishman brought the wagon to a juddering halt. 'You silly old divil, Bob. You led me on a wild-goose chase, so ye did!'

'What are you talking about? I gave you the address and you've got here, haven't you – late as usual?'

'Don't you blame me, Bob Denton! Sure, it's a wonder I'm here at all. I've been up hill and down dale looking for you. Why didn't you tell me it was Henry Street I wanted?'

Clambering out of the wagon, he stood, hands on hips, his flat cap askew, and a grimace on his face that was more comical than threatening. 'I had to ask all over the place before I got it right, so I did.'

'Patrick, yer a damned idiot.' Standing toe to toe with his mate, the old man wagged a finger at him. 'I said to come to Henry Street, so how did you go wrong?'

'It were you that got it wrong. You told me to go to Emily Street. You said nothing at all about Henry Street.' Taking out a grubby hanky from his pocket, the little man blew his nose. 'I went up an' down and all around, and couldn't find Emily Street nowhere. I must 'a asked a hundred people – "Do you know where Emily Street is?" I said. And they told me they had no idea. Then somebody said there was a Henry Street, and here I am. So y'see, I'm not as daft as you make me out.'

'All I can say is, you must be deaf as well as daft. Anyway, I thought you knew where my son lived?'

'Don't gimme that!' With the back of his hand Patrick wiped a trickle of sweat from his forehead. 'How the divil am I supposed to remember where your son lives? I don't even know where my own son lives. Since the idle bugger moved out, I've seen neither hide nor hair of him.'

'Forget all that, Patrick. We'd best get started, or the landlord will be here for his pickings.'

Bob ushered him inside. 'I hope you've cleared all that rubbish outta yer wagon, 'cause there'll be quite a big load to tek down the second-hand shop.'

'A big load, y'say?' The little man was nervous. 'So, how much stuff will there be, d'you reckon?'

The anxious manner in which Patrick asked the question made the old man curious. 'You sound worried. Why's that, I wonder. Oh, Patrick! Don't tell me you've not cleared out the back of yer wagon, like I asked?'

'No! Well . . . I didn't take it all out. Sure I've a few things to take to the second-hand shop meself. I thought it were a good opportunity, what with you already going there, an' all.'

'I knew it! I should have realised it could never run smoothly . . . not where Patrick Riley's involved.'

'Hey, you two! What's all the noise? You woke my 'usband, with yer goings-on!' The neighbour was up in arms.

Patrick shouted back, 'It's all right, missus . . . you go back inside. Tell your old fella he's no need to worry, 'cause me an' this fine gent are dealing with it!'

With an angry toss of her head, she told him in no uncertain terms, 'He will not be pleased, I'll have you know . . . he's not been well these past few days.'

'Ah, well then! You'll need to drag the poor ol' thing back into bed, so ye will! Get into your prettiest nightie an' put a smile on his face, why don't you?' Smiling broadly, Patrick gave a naughty wink, which left her in no doubt as to what he meant.

'Oh! You filthy beast!' With a toss of her hairnet and a wicked gleam in her eye, Mrs Kettle slammed shut the door and went at a run down the passageway, trying to remember where she last put away her 'prettiest nightie'.

The two men were still arguing when Dolly and Casey arrived.

'Hey!' Dolly quickened her steps to the back parlour. 'Instead of arguing and shouting at each other, why don't you both go and see how much room there is in the back of the wagon, and while you're there, give it a tidy-up?' Having taken a peek inside the wagon, she realised they would have to be inventive in order to fit in the stuff from the house. 'You'll be surprised at how much room you might create when you put your back to it. Oh, and if you want another two pairs of hands, me and Casey can help . . .'

'No!' Bob put a stop to that straight off. 'Whatever needs tekking out to the wagon, me and Patrick will see to that. As for you and Casey, well, there's more than enough for the two of you to be getting on with.'

'Such as?' Dolly liked things to be clear. That way she could not be blamed if it went wrong.

'Well, let's see. For starters, all the cupboards an' wardrobes need emptying, so's we can see what we're dealing with. Then there's the carpets to be rolled up; curtains to come down and be folded. Anything hanging on the walls needs tekking down, and any food in the scullery that's not gone off we'll tek back with us. Oh, and—'

'Stop!' Dolly was out of breath just listening. 'That'll do to be getting on with. You and Patrick can get on with your work, while me and Casey get on with ours. Right?'

Stopped in his tracks, the old man was filled with

admiration. 'Sounds to me like yer more than capable, so I'll leave you to it.' He glanced at Casey. 'See if yer can find them papers and such, lad, while me an' Patrick check the back of his wagon. Mind you, it wouldn't surprise me if it weren't still packed floor to ceiling with his old rubbish . . .'

'Hey, you ol' divil! Stop showing me up in front o' the lovely lady, or I might tell her a tale or two about yourself!' Suffering a headache got from a night on the town, and now with a bad start to the day, Patrick was feeling a bit precious. 'D'you want my help, or don't you?'

'Well, o' course, or I would never have asked you, would I?'

'Right then, so let's get on with it!'

'That's fine by me, my old friend. I've been too long on tenterhooks waiting here for you. And now that you've managed to find me, it seems all yer after is to start an argument.'

'Start an argument? Don't talk outta your hat, Bob Denton. If I wanted an argument, sure I wouldn't be pussy-footing about, I can tell ye that much. So, what is it to be then? Are we working, or arguing?' Puffing out his chest, he visibly bristled.

Sensing Patrick's mood, Bob backed off. He'd seen the little Irishman start an argument on less than the exchange of words the two of them had so far enjoyed. 'That's enough of the fighting talk, Patrick. Especially when we should be working.'

'Get a move on then, matey. It's time we climbed into the back o' the wagon so's ye can see if there's anything lurking there that shouldn't be.'

As it happened, there were several big cardboard boxes in the back of the wagon. A few were bulky and a few were empty, and others were strewn about with their contents trailing out.

'We can fill the empty ones with curtains and smaller stuff.' The old man was feeling more optimistic. 'Then we need to sort the others out.'

He was not best pleased to find that two of the boxes were so heavy it took a lot of pushing and shoving to get them into the corner.

'What 'ave yer got in them boxes, Patrick, the crown jewels?'

Tapping the side of his nose, Patrick gave a cheeky wink. 'That's for me to know and you to find out.'

'Why is everything thrown about?' Bob asked. 'Why haven't you kept it all in one place?'

'Ah, well now, that's your fault, so it is! It were you that told me to go to Emily Street, when all the time I should 'a been going to Henry Street. It's thanks to you that I got stuck down a ginnel. I had to bump along in reverse for half a mile, so I did. Me mirror got broken on the wall, then I took a wrong turn, ended up on a demolition site, and it were a nightmare; crashing over brickbats and piles o' rubble. Then the boxes fell over, and some of the contents rolled out.' He gave an almighty sigh. 'Jeez! It's a wonder I got away wit me life, so it is!'

'Don't be so dramatic.' Bob tried not to chuckle, but he couldn't help himself. He roared with laughter, as did Patrick.

'Did you send me to Emily Street on purpose, you old sod?'

'I never sent you to Emily Street in the first place.'

'Well, then, it must 'a been my mistake. But it's got me so I don't know where I am. What is this place? Where are we now?' He glared about with a gormless expresssion.

'Don't act daft. We haven't got time to play games.' The old man was used to Patrick's warped sense of humour, especially after a late night out with his drinking pals. 'We need to get the stuff tidied, then fetch the other stuff outta the house and into the wagon. When it's all out, we'll get it back to Addison Street. It'll not be as big a load as I feared, 'cause the landlord took a claim on the double bed and two armchairs.'

Emotions set in and his voice fell to a whisper. 'Our Tom worked hard for what he put into this house, and now he's gone to his maker, and his wife's took herself off. Gone to Hell, I shouldn't wonder.'

'What's that y'say? Speak up, man.' Patrick hated it when folks grumbled under their breath. 'Me hearing isn't what it used to be.'

The old man smiled. 'Ah, well, there yer go then. That's the reason you went to Emily Street instead o' Henry Street.'

'Don't try wriggling out of what you did.' The little Irishman stuck to his story. ''Twas you that sent me to Emily Street, and that's God's truth, so it is.'

'If you say so, but I know different.' Weighed down by other worries, the old fella scratched the back of his neck. 'To tell you the truth, Patrick, I'm not right sure what to do with all this stuff. Even with the landlord claiming a few items o' furniture, that still leaves a sizeable load to go somewhere. It'll be hard to fit it all into my little house. As it is, we haven't got room to swing a cat. To tell you the truth, Patrick, I'm not really sure what I should do with it all.'

'Sell it!' Patrick advised him. 'That's the best way, if ye ask me. Instead o' storing the stuff, why don't you just sell everything, and put the money aside for when Ruth comes back?'

'That's a bad idea. How can I sell stuff that isn't mine? That's tantamount to stealing, and what would Ruth say if she came back to find everything gone?'

'Ah, sure, she might never come back at all, have you thought of that? And besides, if she does come back, I'm sure she'd prefer to have the money and buy new stuff,

219

rather than be presented with dust-ridden furniture that might not be worth tuppence. Whereas, if you sold it now, and put the money into the bank, that money could well grow into a little pot worth having.' Patrick felt very proud of himself. 'See, there! I'm not so daft as ye tink I am.'

'I'm not doing it, Patrick. I wouldn't be able to sleep at night.'

'Hmm! Well, if it were me, I'd sleep better than I would if my house was chock-a-block with a lot of old stuff that didn't belong to me. Especially if nobody came to claim it, and so it's left there for ever.'

'Look, Patrick, I'm not altogether dismissing your idea. It's just, well, I wouldn't feel comfortable selling off what belongs to my son's wife; however unreliable and ungrateful she might be.' Though in truth Bob was tempted to do what his old friend suggested. It made a lot of sense.

Patrick wanted to get the job done and be off home. 'We'll sort the stuff and cart it off. As to where we're carting it, I'll leave that to you, my old friend.'

'You're right, Patrick. We should just get it on the cart and then decide what to do, though right now we'd best head for Addiston Street.'

He was still thinking of what Patrick had suggested. Maybe selling the stuff and keeping the money safe was the best idea after all.

Either way, he had a few hours to think about it.

While the two men packed the boxes at one end of the wagon, Dolly and Casey made a start on the upstairs. They emptied all the cupboards and wardrobes in all three bedrooms, and filled some of the bags and boxes that Granddad Bob and Patrick brought up.

After a couple of hours' working, all four of them were ready for a break. 'Luckily, they haven't yet switched off the electric, so if you'll kindly do the honours, Dolly, we might all enjoy a nice cup of tea together?' Bob suggested.

Dolly soon had the tea made, and, seated at the table, Bob had a quick perusal of the paperwork Casey had found.

'It's clear enough,' he reported as they sipped at their tea. 'From what's written here, the landlord has every right to claim the double bed and two armchairs, seeing as they were already in the house when Tom and Ruth moved in.' He pointed to an entry made in Tom's own hand. 'Our Tom's got it all written down here, God rest his soul.' And the two men made the sign of the cross on themselves, while Dolly and the boy momentarily hung their heads.

After pausing a moment to compose himself, the old fella went on, 'As far as I can tell, everything apart from what the landlord claims, belonged to Tom and Ruth.'

'But they're not here, are they?' Patrick was taking it all in as best he could.

'That's very true, me old friend, so as yer can understand, it's giving me a real headache, trying to work out what's best to do.'

'Well, I've given ye my opinion, so I have,' Patrick reminded him. 'Sometimes in situations like this, others can see what's right and what's wrong, where your emotions might get in the way of doing the right thing.'

The old man nodded. 'That might be true, Patrick, my old friend. Ralph, the pub landlord, said more or less the same thing. He came to deliver his condolences over our Tom and, what with him being a successful businessman, I asked his advice. He said much the same as Patrick: that I should sell everything and put the money away safely for the day when Ruth and Casey might need it.' He went on in serious tone, 'He reminded me not to do anything in a hurry, though. He pointed out that with family belongings, and especially with the situation I find myself in, I might need to see a solicitor.'

'Well, maybe he was right, Bob.' Dolly had been of the same mind, but chose not to say anything, considering she had not known Bob long enough to give advice.

'Mebbe, but solicitors cost a fortune, and I don't have a fortune. Like I told Ralph, as Tom's father, I think I'd know more about what our Tom would have wanted than any stranger would, solicitor or not. I believe I'm the only one who can decide what's right, for the boy and his mam.'

Dolly was spurred into speaking her mind. 'You're right. I felt the very same after I lost my husband. I did what I knew he would want me to do. I sold what I didn't need and got myself a few pounds in the bank for a rainy day. If you go to a solicitor, they only look out for themselves. They don't know us, and they don't know what's best for the family. They just look at the cold, hard facts and charge you the earth for telling you what you already know. I think you should do what you think best for your son's wife, and your grandson.'

Bob fell silent for a while. When he spoke again, it was to inform the gathering: 'As it happens, my own first thoughts were to sell everything off and divide it up in the only fair way I know how. In fact I even wrote it down.'

He took the list from his pocket and read it out. 'First, all of Tom's personal stuff should be put aside and kept safe for Casey when he gets older; or for Ruth if she ever comes back. Secondly – unless, of course, Casey had any objections – I would sell everything else for the best price possible. Then, with the money I got, I thought I should do three things. Our Tom had no insurance of any kind, 'cause he couldn't afford it. Therefore, we would need to use some of the money for a memorial stone, to be placed over his resting place. It won't be expensive, just simple and proud.'

With heavy heart, he continued, 'Tom's wife must have her half of the money put safely away to hand to her the minute she might return. If she hasn't returned by the time our Casey is eighteen, it will naturally go to him. That's my thinking anyway. Then I thought – after our Tom's memorial stone was got, and Ruth's share of money is put away – we pay to get our Tom's guitar mended. That would then go to Casey, as I'm sure our Tom would have wanted.'

Feeling emotionally exhausted, Bob finished, 'As for what's left, I intend putting that aside for Casey, for when he's older. So, altogether, Ruth would get her half, then, apart from the memorial stone and paying for the guitar repair, our Tom's half would be safely put away for his son. I hope you think I've done the right thing by everyone.' He looked from one to the other. 'So, what's yer opinion? Is that a good plan or not?'

To his great relief, they each supported his plan.

'It's a really good plan, Granddad,' said Casey. 'Only I don't want anything. I want you to have it. I'll just be happy to have Daddy's guitar fixed.'

The old man was insistent. 'I'm doing what yer dad would have wanted, and that's to mek sure you've got summat in the bank for a rainy day.'

Dolly was close to tears as she gave her opinion. 'I think you've done right by everyone. It's well thought out and fair, especially to your daughter-in-law, what with her having left you and her son behind.'

'So, d'yer think our Tom would have approved?'

'I'm sure he would. And I'm sure no one could have done any better.'

'I never knew you had such a clever head on them shoulders,' Patrick said. 'As for me, I will never have that problem. That's because I haven't a penny to spare, nor a pair o' Sunday shoes to leave behind when I'm gone. I pay the rent, and I live from day to day, earning a bob or two where and when I can. Sure, the only thing I own is meself.'

Puffing out his chest, he told them, 'What ye see is what ye get. Patrick Riley's the name, an' he's a poor man without roots, so he is! He works with a clapped-out wagon, and he struggles through from day to day. He answers to nobody, and he's got no time for fools. Moreover, he doesn't give a tinker's cuss who knows it!'

'Well, thank you for that, Patrick,' the old man chuckled. 'And thank you all for your support.'

Bob was greatly relieved that at least this part of the proceedings was sorted.

He would not delude himself, though, because things were bound to get harder. Anxious, he glanced up at the boy. For young Casey's sake, he prayed that once they had got through the immediate painful business, life might be a little kinder to them.

CHAPTER EIGHT

PATRICK WAS IMPATIENT to get started. 'Right then, me lovelies! We've settled one important dilemma, so what say we get on with shifting furniture and stuff, before the day's gone altogether?'

Bob was relieved to have got the thumbs up on his little plan. 'I'm satisfied I'll be doing the right thing by our Tom and Casey . . . and, of course, Tom's wife, Ruth.'

'We don't even know where Mam's gone,' Casey commented. 'She might never come back.'

'Hey, now!' Clambering out of his chair, Granddad Bob went over to him. 'Yer want 'er to come back, don't yer, lad?'

'I don't care, and anyway, she won't come back, even if I want her to.' He had not forgotten how she turned him away at the churchyard.

'Well, I think you do care, the same as I do. Oh, I know she can be a tyrant at times, and it's bad that she's gone off, like she doesn't care about us any more. There's no denying you've plenty to be upset about, lad, and to tell yer the truth, I'm the very same. I'm sad, and I'm angry, and I've no idea how this will all turn out. But we have to carry on the best we can, and see what happens. We

225

have to be brave and strong, you and me, because we both know your daddy would want that.'

He felt he had a duty to spell it out to the boy. 'As far as yer mam's concerned, I've no idea what's on 'er mind, nor why she's deserted everything and everybody. There might well come a day when she just turns up, unexpected like. How d'yer think you'd feel if she did? Would yer ask her to stay, or would yer want her to go?'

The boy took a while to reflect on this. In his mind he could see his mam's face, all angry and shouting. He knew she wanted to hurt him; she always wanted to hurt him, and he wasn't sure why. And what about the last time? That was the worst ever. In his mind he could see his daddy dragging her off him, and he couldn't help but wonder why his mam hated him so much; because she did, otherwise she would never look at him like that, as though she wanted him dead.

Sometimes, he didn't like her at all, and sometimes he loved her, because she was his mam.

Just now, though, he didn't want to think about her. All he wanted was his daddy back. But his daddy was not coming back. That made him hurt so much, he could hardly breathe. Deep down inside, where no one else could see, it was like a door had closed for ever.

When the tears rose in the boy's eyes, Granddad Bob wrapped a strong arm round his small shoulders. 'I want yer to know that you can talk to me any time, about anything. And remember, you've allus got me, and Dolly, and you're very much loved. You do know that, don't yer, lad?'

'Yes, Granddad.'

'Good! And for what it's worth, I reckon we should all try hard not to give up on yer mam. I've a strong feeling that one o' these fine days, she might just turn up on the doorstep. Oh, I know well enough what she's like, and I know she might want to take what's hers and go away again, and that'd be her choice. Or, she might want to make a fresh start, and that'd be her choice, too. But whatever she decides, we can deal with it if and when the time comes. Until then, it's you and me, lad.'

He smiled at those two wonderful people who had watched the display of emotion and trust between him and the boy. 'And aren't we lucky to have our very good friends Dolly and Patrick?' These two had consoled him through his own grief, just like he had tried to console his grandson.

But now, there was something else he had to tell the boy. Something that, in the light of recent events, he was aching to clear from his mind.

'Casey, lad?'

'What, Granddad?'

'Being as we're already talking about things that are not very pleasant, I think we should get it all over and done with in one foul swoop. Y'see, there's summat I need to explain to yer, and I reckon now is as good a time as any. After I've told yer, we can then put it all behind us and get on with our lives. The thing is, over the years me and your grandma got together a nice lot of knick-knacks. Things like furniture and ornaments, and suchlike. What I'm trying to say is, well, I've written things down in a letter . . . just so there'll be no misunderstanding, and I need to tell yer now.'

Taking a deep breath he got out what he had to say as quickly and as plainly as he could. 'The letter is in an envelope tucked underneath my bed. It's signed and everything. What it says is that when the Good Lord decides to tek me, everything will be yours, to do with as yer like.' He smiled at the boy. 'There! It's done, and now we need never mention it again, because I intend to live 'til I'm a hundred!'

Casey was horrified. 'I don't want anything, Granddad! I only want you. I don't want "the Good Lord" to take you away from me.'

When the boy began to panic, Granddad Bob took him by the shoulders. 'Now, you listen to me, young Casey.' He spoke firmly, but kindly. 'For starters, like I said, it's important for you to know these things. And don't you worry about me going to the Good Lord just yet, 'cause like I said, I intend being about for some long time. And besides, I've got you to look after, and you've got me to look after, an' all . . .'

Hoping to ease the tension, he gave a raucous laugh. 'I'm warning yer now, lad, I want at least a dozen great-grandchildren off yer!'

Everyone in the room laughed at that. 'Twelve childer? Jeez!' Patrick went white at the thought. 'Sure, you'll have the lad collapsing at the very idea, so ye will.'

Happier now, Casey hugged his granddad. 'I love you, Granddad.'

'I love you too, lad. Allus 'ave, allus will.'

'Honest, Granddad . . . you're not leaving me, are you?'

'Not on your life! Oh, and while we're getting things straight, I might as well tell yer summat else. It's a little secret I were saving for another day. Only I reckon yer should know right now. Especially as our friend Patrick is 'ere to share in it. And because it will show how long I mean to be here, to look after yer and keep an eye on what yer up to.'

'What secret, Granddad?' The boy's eyes lit up. 'Tell me.'

'All right then, I will!' He gave a happy little whoop. 'The thing is, I'm hoping that in the not too distant future, me and Dolly might mek a life together. I've asked her, but like any woman, she's playing hard to get.'

He turned to look at Dolly, who was blushing like a

young girl. She had not expected him to blurt it out, especially as they'd only talked about it last night.

'Well, lass, what d'yer say? D'yer want us or not? Are yer willing to tek on a grumpy old bugger, and a bright young lad, both of who love yer? It's no good being coy, 'cause now's the time to speak out. So, is it a yes, or a no?'

Thrilled and delighted, Dolly gave her answer. 'It's a yes, but only if Casey is ready to accept me as his new grandma?' She was only too aware that he had lost both his mam and his dad, and right now, his emotions must be raw. She remembered what he'd said at the stream, and her heart was full.

'I knew it!' Casey ran to her and, flinging his arms round her neck, he snuggled up to her. 'Oh, Dolly, I'll be so glad for you and Granddad to be together, 'cause I love you both . . . so much.' Already she felt like a grandma to him, and it seemed natural that she and Granddad Bob would be together.

Granddad Bob's smile lit up the room. 'Right then. Looks like we've wedding plans to mek, lad. But not just yet, 'cause we've still got a thousand things to do.'

His eyes were suspiciously moist as he winked at Dolly, who gave him a reassuring smile.

'Best move yerself then, Bob Denton,' she chided. 'We can't be romancing when there's work to be done.'

～

Within two hours, everything was packed into the wagon and safely secured. The house was cleaned and swept out, and when he turned the key in the door for the last time, Granddad Bob told the boy, 'Don't think of this as the end, lad. Think of it like a new beginning, eh?'

Casey gave no answer, because if he spoke now, he was

sure to cry. So he just nodded. And Granddad Bob smiled, and it was all right again.

After they had delivered the key to the neighbour, Granddad Bob helped Dolly up into the cab of the wagon, then Casey, and finally climbed in himself.

'We're packed in here like a can o' sardines, so we are!' Patrick never liked his space to be invaded. 'Are youse lot gonna be all right?'

'Right as rain.' Granddad Bob had Casey on his lap, and Dolly beside him. He considered himself to be somewhat fortunate that, after losing one family, he had all but gained another. He hoped with all his heart Casey might also find a degree of contentment.

'All right, are yer, lad?'

'Yes, Granddad.'

'That'll do me then.' The smile he gave Dolly was warm and wonderful. 'You all right there, are yer, Dolly?'

'I'm fine.' Reaching out, she reassured him with a gentle touch on the back of his hand. 'You all right, are you?'

'Aye, lass. We've a long way to go yet, but we'll get there . . . all three of us.'

'Don't ye mean four?' Patrick was having trouble keeping the wagon steady.

'Four?' Granddad Bob was confused.

'Just now, ye said you'd get there . . . all three of youse. So, am I not part of this family? Am I only good for shifting and carrying, and then to be chucked out on me ear?' When he turned to give his old friend a disapproving scowl, the wagon ran up the kerb. 'Jesus, Mary and Joseph, will ye look at that. You very nearly caused an accident, so ye did!'

'For pity's sake, Patrick, keep your eyes on the road. All right then, all four of us will get through it together . . . if that's what you're upset about. So, will yer please now get us all safely to our destination, because if we all get mangled, it won't matter if we're three or four, or an army on the march!'

Patrick was satisfied. 'All I can say is, I'm proud to be a part o' this family; thank you.'

He then concentrated on the road and the traffic, until he began to worry again. 'Where did ye say we were going?'

'Patrick, will you stop that! I've already told you: we're going to my house on Addison Street. What's wrong with yer? Were yer boozing heavy last night, or is there summat wrong with your hearing?'

'There's nothing at all wrong wit' my hearing, and if I choose to have a pint or two wit me good friends, who's to say I shouldn't? Jeez! I never know where I am with you. So, just to be on the safe side, let me get this straight. We've just brought the stuff from Henry Street, and now, we're taking it to your house on Addison Street. Am I right?'

'Well, there you go. You knew all along.'

'Look here, Bob, me old friend, what with one thing and another, I've had enough trouble today. The last thing I need is for you to be changing your mind all the time.' He had not forgotten that awful business down Emily Street. 'I don't ever want to get stuck in some narrow ginnel again. That's all I'm saying.'

'You won't get stuck in a ginnel on my account. Just keep driving, and don't go too fast or you'll topple the boxes, and don't go too slow or we'll never get there. Oh, and—'

'That's enough o' the dos and don't's! I do not appreciate your advice on how to drive my wagon, thank you. And since you were good enough to explain, just to be on the safe side, I'd best go over it again. We've come from Henry Street, right?'

'Right.'

'And now we're on our way to Addison Street?'

'That's right.'

Patrick repeated to himself, 'We've been to . . . Henry Street, and now . . . we're going to . . . Addison Street.'

Bob gave a sigh of relief. 'Just be sure not to take any wrong turns.'

When, a short time later, Patrick turned the wagon into Addison Street, Bob was able to relax. 'Yer did well, Patrick.' But his relief turned to frustration as the engine began spitting and groaning. When the wagon came to a full stop in the middle of the street, Patrick informed them, 'You'll need to get out and push, so ye will.'

Seeing how they were stranded at one end of the street and his house was at the other, Bob knew they had little choice. He was not best pleased, but he was sensible enough to know that the engine packing up could not altogether be Patrick's fault; that is, until Patrick grumbled, 'I thought I'd put enough petrol in the tank to get us all the way back, so I did . . .'

One look at his old friend's disbelieving expression, and Patrick wisely turned away. 'Casey, lad. D'ye think you could steer the wagon, while I get behind and help the others push it along to the house?'

'Yes, Patrick, I can do that, if you show me how.'

So, after Patrick showed him how to steer, Casey was confident enough, though he was so low down, he could hardly see above the steering wheel.

'Sit still a minute. I'll soon 'ave ye comfortable, so I will.'

Patrick climbed into the back of the wagon and began throwing things about.

'What the devil are you doing in there?' Bob was horrified to see all his carefully packed boxes being ravaged one by one.

A few minutes later Patrick emerged, triumphantly

brandishing a pillow. 'This'll do the trick!' he told them. He folded the pillow, placed it on the driving seat, and Casey sat atop it. 'Now then, are ye able to see above the steering wheel?'

When Casey sat up straight, his view of the road ahead was perfect. 'Yes, I can see right down to our granddad's house.'

Patrick was proud of himself. 'All it takes is a bit o' common sense and a clear head, an' a man can solve all the problems in the world, so he can!'

He went on to give Casey a quick résumé of the next steps. 'Now then, young 'un, all ye need to do is steer the wagon to the house. Ye must keep as near the kerb as possible, but make sure ye don't run over it. D'ye understand?'

'Yes, Patrick, I understand.' He repeated the instructions to Patrick's satisfaction.

'Good! Now then, I'm going back to help push the wagon. We're all relying on you to do a proper job, so we are. Oh, and don't forget what I told ye. When we're getting closer to the house, me or your granddad will shout for you to stamp your foot hard on the brake.' He pointed. 'That's the one, right there. And don't you worry, 'cause we'll give ye plenty o' warning.'

'I can't do it, Patrick.'

'What d'ye mean, ye can't do it? Course ye can!'

'Patrick Riley, yer dafter than I thought.' Bob's voice rang out from behind. 'Look at where the boy is! How the devil can he be expected to slam his foot on the brakes from where he is?'

Patrick followed his old friend's gaze. When he saw the boy's little legs dangling in mid-air, he was shocked. 'Jesus, Mary and Joseph! What's happened to his legs?'

Bob burst out laughing, '*You've* happened, that's what! You've hoisted him up with the pillow. Now he can see above the steering wheel all right, only his legs are hanging in mid-air. In order to slam his foot on the brake, he'll need to climb down, but if he climbs down, he won't be able to see where he's going.'

Patrick was taking it all in. 'Well, I never!'

Hearing the fracas, Dolly came to see, and she tried hard not to laugh. 'Trust a man to get it wrong,' she murmured.

Embarrassed, Patrick reviewed the situation. When he took note of how Casey was sitting atop the doubled pillow, with his legs swinging back and forth, he started to titter, then he was chuckling, and now the three of them were roaring with laughter.

The raucous laughter echoed down the street, and in a matter of minutes, the windows and doors were being thrown open for neighbours to see what was going on.

'Want a hand, do you?' That was Mr Barnes from number fourteen. 'Looks like you've got trouble.'

Having watched their progress from the window, he couldn't imagine why they were laughing. Now though, having got the gist of it, he was impatient to get down to the pub that night and relay the comical tale to his mates. He had never met Patrick before, but he instantly warmed to him.

'I can help to push the wagon forward, or we can get the boy down, and I'll steer the wagon. Just tell me where to go. Like I say, I'll do whatever helps most.'

'Ah, now, wouldn't that be grand. Thank you kindly.' Patrick promptly recruited him to help push the wagon from behind. Patrick then helped Casey down and climbed into the cab, while Casey was assigned the job of walking along the pavement and keeping an eye on progress.

Unaware that he was just being kept safe, he felt really proud to be helping.

Mr Barnes and Bob positioned themselves at the rear of the wagon, taking the weight at the corners, while Dolly was in the middle, helping as best she could, without unduly straining herself.

It was a good plan in the circumstances and though they were going downhill, the wagon and its heavy load made the short journey somewhat painful.

'I've a petrol can in the back.' Patrick was thinking ahead, 'Youse can make a start if ye like, while I make my way to the garage.'

'No need for that.' Mr Barnes was puffing and blowing as he bent his back to the wagon. 'It's a long walk to the nearest garage. When you're ready I'll run you down to King Street garage.'

'You'd best ask my mate Bob. He's the boss – on this occasion, anyway.'

Bob was grateful for Mr Barnes' further offer of help. 'That would be much appreciated. Also, we've a pile o' furniture and a load of heavy boxes to carry into the house. Another pair o' helping hands would get the job done in a quicker time, if you're sure yer don't mind?' He was conscious of how everyone in this street knew what had happened to his son, and that each and every one of them had been genuine in their sympathy.

When they drew up at the house Patrick flung open the wagon doors. 'Right then, mateys, let's get started.'

No sooner were the doors opened and the first items of furniture brought to the lip of the wagon, than seemingly out of nowhere, people appeared to offer help in their droves.

'All right, are you, Bob?'

'We'll give you a hand, Bob.'

Soon, there were more curious people than was comfortable, everyone barging one into the other.

'What 'ave you got in there . . . enough bricks and

concrete to build a couple of houses I shouldn't wonder?' That was Frances Armitage, a sour-faced but big-hearted woman who was never happy unless grumbling.

Bob explained how he'd had to empty Tom's place, and that he'd brought all the furniture and stuff from inside.

'It's got to be sold,' he said. 'I haven't got room to keep it all in my house for too long.'

Mr Barnes asked if he had a double bed to sell.

'Sorry.' Bob apologised. 'The landlord took it back, but there's a single bed, and a wardrobe from the boy's bedroom. Casey won't need it at mine, 'cause his room's already fitted out.'

'How much are you asking for the two?'

'I haven't really thought about it yet.' Bob put his thinking cap on. 'Well, they're in good condition. I can't afford to let them go for . . . what . . .' he was careful not to let his excitement show, 'say, er, fifteen quid the pair, and that's a bargain . . .'

'Done!' Mr Barnes was delighted. They shook hands on it, the furniture was removed from the wagon, and promptly delivered to Mr Barnes' spare bedroom.

The crowd of neighbours were curious as to what other bargains might be tucked inside that old wagon, and they were prepared to part with a shilling or two.

Patrick helped out and got so excited that he sold all his own stuff at the same time. Within the hour, the wagon was empty.

'Well, now, wasn't that a turn-up for the book, eh?' Patrick counted his own earnings, while his old friend counted the rest.

'Well, I never!' Bob was delighted. 'I thought I might be lucky to get half that amount, and I expected it might tek a month or so, afore it were all gone.'

He gave Casey and Dolly a cuddle. 'Half the battle is won.'

He was pleased at the transaction, but then immediately swamped by a rush of sadness at the reason for the selling.

Casey, too, was very quiet. 'Well, lad,' Granddad Bob slid an arm round the boy's neck, 'I don't know about you, but I'm glad that's over and done with.'

'Me too, Granddad.' Even so, he could not imagine never seeing Henry Street again.

And Henry Street and the Blakewater would always be there.

'Granddad?'

'Yes, lad?'

'Do you think we could go back sometime, Granddad?'

Suppressing emotion at the boy's question, the old man answered softly, 'Whenever you're ready to go back there, just tell me, lad, and we'll be off like a shot.' When Casey's eyes lit up, the old man reached down to ruffle his mop of hair. 'Can I ask yer summat, lad? And if yer not happy about it, then we'll just forget I ever said it.'

'What is it?' Casey could see how uncomfortable his granddad was. 'Go on, Granddad, ask me.'

'Well, I were just . . . I mean,' quickly glancing about, he lowered his voice, 'I were wondering if yer might want to bring Dolly along as well. I know she'd like that.'

Casey did not hesitate, 'Course we can, Granddad. I'd like it too.'

'Oh, that's grand! I'm right pleased. And now that's been settled, I reckon we'd best get on.'

As he went away, the old man wiped his eyes with the cuff of his shirt.

That brief exchange with his grandson had touched him deeply, and he suddenly felt incredibly lonely. He had lost his son, Tom, and as for Ruth, he didn't even know where she was, or if she would ever again show her face round these parts. If that turned out to be the case, then the lad had no parents at all, and that was the saddest thing.

Just then, seeing Dolly and Patrick arguing about something and nothing, he was made to smile. Then, the two of them were laughing, and a moment later Dolly made her way to where young Casey was examining an item he'd picked up from the ground.

Casey handed it to Dolly and she turned it over in her hands. Then she brushed it clean with the hem of her dress, and the two of them chatted about it, as they made their way to the house, Dolly with her hand on the boy's shoulders, and the boy looking up at her, seemingly happy.

Engrossed in each other, they did not realise that Granddad Bob was watching them. With a full heart and a smile on his face, he turned away. 'Yer get days when it never stops raining, and your heart weighs heavy,' he murmured. 'Then yer get days when the skies are clear and yer can't help but smile.'

Pausing on the doorstep, he stole another glance at the two of them approaching. 'Yesterday it were raining, Lord, and today we've got sunshine. 'Cause we've got each other – me and the boy – an' now we've got this lovely lady who's come into our lives, just when we need her the most.' He chuckled aloud. 'The Three Musketeers. That's what we are.'

~

Later that evening, while Dolly was happily getting their tea, Granddad Bob made Casey a promise.

'Tomorrow morning, you and me – and Dolly, too, if she's a mind – we'll make our way into Blackburn town.'

'Are we going shopping, Granddad?'

'In a way, yes. We're going to see Frank, the pawnshop man. I've heard that he knows a thing or two about guitars. So, we'll show him what needs doing, and if he can't do it, we'll find somebody who can. Does that idea please you, lad?'

From the excitement in Casey's face and the way he threw his arms round his granddad's leathery old neck, he was delighted with the news.

'I can't wait to play Daddy's guitar again,' he said. 'I think it will make him really happy.'

'Aye, lad. So do I.'

That night, as he lay in bed with the broken guitar beside him, Casey could hardly believe it. 'Did you hear where we're going in the morning, Daddy?' His gaze was drawn to the window. 'Granddad's getting the guitar fixed, and I'll be able to play again.'

He was so excited, he could hardly wait for morning. When he thought of the guitar being mended, his heart beat faster, and several times he got out of bed and looked out of the window at the darkening skies.

'I love you so much, Daddy. I miss you.'

Somewhere deep inside he loved his mammy too. But he didn't know her like he knew his daddy, and she didn't love him like his daddy loved him.

And, try as he might, he could not think of what he had done that was so very bad that she didn't want him.

Some time later, when he was sleeping, his granddad and Dolly looked in on him on the way to the bedrooms. After a long day, Dolly was staying over.

The old fella was saddened to notice the stain of tears down Casey's face. 'He's been through so much,' he whispered to Dolly as they left the small bedroom. 'Getting that guitar mended will be the turning point for him, I know it!'

'And will it be the turning point for you as well?' Dolly had seen how strong Bob had been for the boy. 'I've caught you crying when you think no one's looking. I know how brave and generous you've been with Casey

. . . always there for him, always ready to hold and advise him. But what about you, my dear? Who have *you* been able to turn to?'

Having no real answer, he hunched his shoulders. 'A man just has to deal with things.' She would never know how hard it had been, he thought sadly; but then it could not have been easy for her, when she lost her husband.

Dolly brought him to a halt. 'Listen to me, Bob, please. I know the boy lost his daddy, but you lost a son. You've had to carry the pain alone. I understand, I really do. But you're not alone now, Bob Denton, because I'm here, and now you've asked me, I intend to stay.'

Taking hold of her hand, he squeezed it tight. 'You don't know how glad I am about that,' he admitted.

'So, I'll take care of you. I'll share your pain and take some of the weight off your shoulders.'

Her kind words brought tears to the old man's eyes. 'You're right, lass. This shocking business has rocked me to the heart,' he confessed. 'I've lost my only child, and my daughter-in-law's tekken off to God knows where, and back there is a broken little soul, who desperately needs us both. I've lost an awful lot, Dolly . . . me and the boy both.'

'I know that, and there's the very reason why I want to take care of you . . . and the boy.'

'I'll tell ye what, Dolly, lass.'

'Go on then.'

'How about me and the boy . . . taking care of you and each other? So, d'you reckon that's a good plan?'

Smiling softly, she acknowledged his 'plan' with a tip of the head. 'I've never known a man make so many plans,' she admitted, 'but I'll tell you what, Bob Denton. I reckon that must be one of your very best.'

'Well, thank you.' He believed there was a 'plan' for every eventuality, and right now, he dared to seal this particular plan with a little peck on Dolly's rosy cheek. 'It goes to show, doesn't it, Dolly?'

'What's that, then?'

'Well, how Fate can tek with one hand, then give back with the other. Y'see, you lost your husband, and now me and the boy have lost something precious as well, but because o' that, you found the boy, and now the three of us have been brought together. So now, I've got you in my life, and young Casey's got a new and wonderful friend. D'yer see what I mean? We've all been hurt, and now we're looking after each other.'

'I know, and it's wonderful, don't you think?'

'Aye, lass, it's more than wonderful. And we do love you, me and the boy.' He smiled coyly. 'I don't think you realise how much I love you . . . in another way, o' course.' He blushed.

'I love you too,' she confessed shyly.

Wondering if he might take that as an invitation to walk her to his bedroom, she wagged a finger. 'Oi! If you think that means I'm about to let you take adavantage of me, you'd best think again.'

The old man chuckled. 'It never even crossed me mind. In fact, after all this time, I doubt if I'm even capable o' tekking advantage. All I meant was, I love you as a man might love his wife. I didn't mean I was about to ravish you.'

The idea of him physically carrying her to his bedroom made him laugh out loud. 'Chance'd be a fine thing!'

'Aye, well. You'll get no "chance" from me, at least not until we're man and wife, and happen not even then.'

Wrapping her two hands about his face, she said softly, 'Mind you, if needs be, I'd settle for a little cuddle now and then. So, seeing as you're fond of "plans", what d'you think to that little plan, eh?'

He loved her all the more. 'That's a fine little plan,'

he said. 'D'you know what, Dolly? Yer a woman after me own heart.'

He watched her go into her bedroom. 'Good night, Bob.'

'Good night, Dolly.'

As he made his way down to the far bedroom, he smiled to himself. 'She's a good 'un,' he muttered under his breath. 'Once we wed though, who's to say it will all go as planned? As a matter o' fact, I might have completely forgotten what I'm supposed to do. An' even if I haven't forgotten, me poor old parts might 'a given up anyway.' He chuckled.

Truth was, having been without a woman these many years, the last thing he needed was to make a fool of himself.

In bed, he lay awake for a while, thinking about Dolly, and how it would all turn out. The idea of him having a real, warm woman in his bed after all this time was really nerve-racking. Even more, the idea of his being a masterful lover struck him as hilarious.

His thoughts turned to the morrow and to Casey. He was determined that, whatever it took or however much it cost, he would keep his promise and get the guitar mended.

'The boy needs to be playing again,' he reminded himself, 'and the sooner, the better.'

That was the right and proper thing to do because, Bob knew for certain, it was what Tom would have wanted.

In his mind's eye he pictured the boy playing the guitar, and singing to the music. When he had that guitar, and he began to sing, it was like he drifted into a world of his own. There was something magic about him, and when he held the guitar, it was almost like a part of him. His fingers caressed the strings and the strings were made to shiver with emotion, the essence of which could silence a room full of people.

And when he sang – whether it be soul, country or slow ballad – it was almost as though he was unaware of everyone and everything else around him. And those who heard him felt the magic, and were swept along with the mood of it.

Bob had seen the boy's talent nurtured and blossom, and even Tom had spoken of his amazement at the way in which Casey had taken to the music.

'He's far more talented than I could ever be,' Tom had once confided in his father. 'I teach him a chord or two, and he's away as if he's been playing it for ever.'

Lying in bed, in the silence of evening, Bob remembered his son's words. And they made him wonder, not for the first time, about how young Casey had acquired such a powerful instinct for the music.

He himself loved to play, though he had not played for some time. Tom also, had shown early promise, but neither of them had ever played with the heart and soul that Casey did. With Casey, it was in the blood. It was like a hunger or a thirst that could never be quenched.

Thinking about it now, he softly voiced his thoughts. 'Where did yer get such musical ability, lad? Where did it come from? Lord only knows, because there's never been anyone in the family possessed of such an instinct for the music.'

Over the years he had often wondered about that.

Tonight, inevitably, Ruth came into his mind. Yes, he'd heard the rumours, and yes, at times he'd been suspicious, but he had mostly been angered by the gossip; preferring to see the rumours as just spiteful whisperings, spread by bitchy women with loose tongues. Now, though, having recently learned a truth or two about Tom's wife, he was made to consider the possibilities.

After a while, a more disturbing suspicion crept into his thoughts. All these years, whenever he'd looked at young Casey, he'd seen his own son, Tom: that same sense of fun; the same wonderful smile. He'd seen the same sincerity in his own son and in his grandson, and each of them shared the same sense of decency and goodness.

'Yer a silly old fool, Bob Denton!' he chided himself. 'You need to remember, you bred a fine son in Tom, and Tom bred a fine son in Casey. There's nowt in this world as can change that . . . ever.'

With that thought warming his heart, he closed his eyes and drifted off to sleep; but it was not a peaceful sleep.

PART FOUR

~

Chance Encounter

CHAPTER NINE

THE MEETING WAS held in the dining room of a smart hotel in one of the quieter areas of Blackpool. It was progressing well, and as the conversation deepened, Steve was convinced that he'd made a good choice in appointing this particular land agent to oversee the purchase of a suitable site for his recording studio.

The agent outlined his plans. 'Following your brief, I have located three prime sites. I believe any one of them could be suited to your purpose.'

A middle-aged man of medium build and homely face, Edward Mull was an established land agent, well known and respected in the area.

'All we need now is to sort out a time when you're able to take a look at them.'

Steve was delighted, though he was careful not to show too much enthusiasm in case the agent thought to increase his commission. Although, according to the contact who had introduced him to Edward Mull, the man could be trusted.

'I was due to receive plan sets this morning, only there was a delay at the other end of the chain – a simple dispatch hiccup, nothing for you to be concerned about.

I will have the plans by tomorrow morning, even if I have to collect them myself. I've asked for current council notes on change of use and other details: reference planning and small restrictions regarding use of premises.' He was quick to assure his client, 'I've already had a sight of the original documents and, as far as I can tell, there should be no legal reason why you can't choose whichever site would suit your purpose.'

Though slightly irritated by the plans not being available, Steve appreciated how these things could often get caught up in red tape.

So, how far apart are the sites exactly?' Time was important to him. 'If possible, I'd like to see them all in one day. That way, if they're not right we can keep on looking. Or if I find one of them is just what I'm searching for, I can get it all tied up quickly.'

The other man drew a small map from his jacket pocket. 'Let me show you where we are in relation to the three sites.' Pushing aside the used crockery, he spread the map across the table. 'Providing we can make an early start, it should be easy enough to see all three in one day.'

Tracing with a finger from their present position, he said, 'D'you see how they form a triangle? The first port of call will be this one.' He pointed to a site a few miles from the centre of Blackpool.

'I spent some time up here in Blackpool when I was younger,' Steve told him. 'Me and a couple of mates did a few short tours, singing and playing music hereabouts. I remember we sometimes invited girls back to our hotel overnight.' He smiled. 'It was memorable, to say the least.'

'Girls, eh? Aren't you the lucky one – free with the girls and touring with your group into the bargain? My father was far too strict to allow me such pleasures.'

Edward gave a weary kind of smile. 'I was born and bred in a quiet little hamlet some way from here. My father was a vicar and my mother a school teacher. Going to Blackpool was not their idea of a day out. Oh, no! Their day out was a long train ride and four hours touring museums and walking round historic houses. Oh, I'm not saying there's anything wrong with that, because I learned a great deal that I wouldn't otherwise have done. The trouble was, although it was their idea of heaven, I was never given the choice.'

'Well, there you go then.' Steve sensed his regret, 'as for me the one and only time I went to a museum, I did enjoy it, though I would much rather have been playing my guitar, alongside my dad with his flute. We always made good music together, even back then.'

A wave of nostalgia engulfed Steve. 'He's been gone for years, but I still have his flute. And I have the passion for music that he bred in me and nurtured. I'm immensely grateful for that. If it hadn't been for him, I wouldn't be here talking to you now.'

'It seems to me, Steve, that your father not only encouraged your natural musical talent, but he left you a wonderful legacy,' Edward said.

Steve had to smile at that. 'The *only* legacy though! Sadly he was never good with money. He was in and out of work, and how my mother coped, I will never know. But anyway, we managed, and of course my brother and I got jobs as soon as we could, and somehow we bumbled through.'

When the memories grew painful, he took a moment to reflect. After my father died, Mother changed. She missed my dad so very much; as I did, although I tried hard never to cry in front of her. But then, three years later, she followed him, and I was out on the streets making my own way. My brother is older and was already running his own business by then.'

'Oh, that must have been so hard. How old were you?'

'Too young to be fending for myself, but I soon learned how to take care of number one.'

'Toughened up, did you?'

'You could say that, yes. I survived; more than that, I enjoyed the challenge.'

Edward was impressed. 'You've obviously had a hard time of it, but you appear to have come through it well. You might not believe it, but in a way I envy you. You had the freedom to make your own way in life, whereas my own early years were mapped out from the start, whether I liked it or not. Even after my parents were gone, they still controlled me.'

'How do you mean?'

'Both my parents were dead by the time I turned twenty-five. I was left a deal of money, but I was not allowed immediate access to it. The solicitor kept it in trust and oversaw any purchases I made. I was ordered not to "fritter away" the legacy, but to use it to "improve" myself, in readiness for a suitable career.'

'And how were you supposed to know what that might be?'

Edward gave a shrug. 'The answer is, I didn't. Anyway, at that time I was working for a reputable old firm of land agents. When the owner decided to sell up, I bought the business with my father's money, and I've never looked back. In the end, it all worked out handsomely.'

Steve did not envy him. 'It seems to me that we're both content with our lot. My future was never mapped out. Instead, I was forced to make my own way the best I could. I was left nothing but my father's flute, and the guitar he bought me.'

'What were your parents like?'

Steve smiled. 'Volatile. Forever rowing. Couldn't live together; couldn't live apart. They were quick-tempered and passionate. Oh, they loved each other, and neither of them ever looked at anyone else, but they had different views on everything, and one wrong word was enough to fire up an argument. But there was also laughter and fun, and music. Always the music. Most weekends me, my dad and my brother would go fishing and walking, and sometimes Mother would come with us and we'd take a tent and live like nomads.'

'It sounds wonderful!'

'Oh, it was. So many adventures; so many memories to cherish. Whenever we went camping, Dad would always take his flute. I took the guitar, and together we would play music while Mother cooked sausages on an open fire that my brother made. He was not at all musical.'

'Did your father ever play professionally . . . like you, I mean? Did he ever tour in a group in his younger days?'

'Not that he ever said. He was a grafter, though. His first duty was to work hard and provide for his family. But ever since I can remember, he had the music in him. In the pubs they'd call for him to entertain them. He would sing at the drop of a hat, and played the flute like you would not believe. Oh yes, my dad certainly had the magic.'

'He sounds like a contented, happy sort of chap.'

'Yes, he was, and he gave me an appetite for the music. It was in my soul then, and it still is. I took every opportunity to learn the guitar, and once I'd mastered that, I moved on to other instruments.' He gave a knowing smile. 'I could never master the flute, though. I could never make it sing the way he did.'

His gaze wandered to the map, and suddenly his thoughts were sharper. 'Blackpool, eh? Me and the boys played here several times and were a great success. I remember a certain girl; dark-eyed she was, with masses of wild hair and a smile to knock you backwards. She was here on holiday, and we kinda clicked . . .' he gave a cheeky wink, '. . . if you know what I mean?'

'I think I do, yes.' That was one thing Edward missed in his lonely life: an understanding and loving woman.

'Her name was Ruth. Lovely name, lovely girl . . .' He could see her now in his mind's eye.

Unsettled by his thoughts, Steve quickly turned his mind to business. 'Right! So, you think we'll be able to cover all the sites in one day?'

'Er, well . . . yes, I should think so.' Temporarily caught off guard by the abruptness of his client's manner, the little man swiftly adapted his mood to suit. 'My intention was to start with the nearest one, and work our way round.'

'So tell me again, what's the history of these sites?' He had not forgotten, but he was keen to put from his mind thoughts of Ruth, the girl he had loved and left all those years back. He had wanted to stay with her, but at that particular time in his life, his music and his career were paramount.

When their manager rang to say he'd secured the band a slot in a London club, there was no time to say goodbye. For a time he regretted that. But then he met his future wife and it was all too late.

Having scrutinised his notes, the agent informed him, 'As for the sites, the two larger ones are ex-industrial. The smaller of the three was a holiday camp, closed down some three years back.'

'And the locations . . . if I remember rightly, you mentioned how any one of them would suit my purpose?' Steve desperately wanted to rid his mind of the girl who had haunted his thoughts. He must now concentrate on the matter in hand. If he was to make a success of this project, the past had to be left where it was, and besides, he was a married man. There was no room in his life for regrets.

Edward reminded him, 'As I said when we spoke on

the telephone, the first two are sites of approximately four acres. They are well-positioned, just outside town, with excellent communication and transport.'

'And the other?'

'That one lies about three miles from the centre of Blackpool. It is equally well served, but has only half the land.'

'OK. And you say the asking prices are all negotiable, is that right?'

'Yes, but things can change from day to day in this game. As I'm sure you understand, good sites like these are hard to come by, and much sought after.'

'Understood. And are all three sites clear?'

'Absolutely! There is nothing to demolish, no unsafe or derelict buildings, and no piles of rubble to shift.'

Steve was impressed. 'Sounds like you've done your homework.'

'Of course. That's what I get paid for.' Putting away the map and paperwork, Edward finished, 'So now, unless you have more questions, I need you to tell me when you'd like to view them and I'll clear my diary to suit.'

'Tomorrow.' Steve was champing at the bit. 'From what you just said, we'd best not hang about.'

'Quite! And yes, tomorrow is absolutely fine by me. I can arrange that. We'll need to make an early start, so as to be sure and cover all eventualities.'

'Such as what?'

'Trust me, it's a distinct possibility that there could be other viewers there. On big, commercial sites like these, the owners often instruct the selling agents to arrange multiple viewings. It's a clever way of boosting the competition. It can often undermine your offer, or even trigger a bidding war right there on site. Also, it has been known for the owner to be hovering about somewhere incognito, trying all manner of tricks to push up the price.'

Steve was shocked. 'It sounds like a real dirty business to me.'

'I'm not saying these things happen all the time, but yes, it can be a bit dirty.'

'Well, all I can say is, I'm glad I'm in the music business.'

'So, an early start is OK with you then?'

'Absolutely. The sooner I get the site secured, the better. What time were you thinking?'

'Eight o'clock OK with you? I'll pick you up from your hotel.'

'Fine. I'll be ready and waiting at the main doors.'

After Steve insisted on paying the bill, the two of them walked to the front door where the agent had a taxi waiting. 'Hopefully by this time tomorrow, you'll be set up with a suitable site for your studios.'

'We'll see.' Over the years, Steve had learned never to count his chickens.

The two men shook hands and the agent climbed into the taxi. 'Good night then. I'll see you tomorrow at the King's, eight a.m.'

Steve nodded. 'See you then. Good night, and thanks.'

Turning up the collar of his overcoat, he watched the taxi drive off. A few moments later it was out of sight altogether.

For what seemed an age, Steve stood there, his mind filled with thoughts of long ago, and a girl named Ruth. He could see her so very clearly; the smile that lit up her face. The laughter that made everyone smile, and those amazing, brooding eyes.

He remembered her as being very special. Unlike the woman who later became his wife, she had loved him with a passion. On that all too short and wonderful day and night, she had shown him what true love meant.

He now felt ashamed that even though he had loved

her with the same passion, he had turned his back on her; choosing his career instead.

Sadly, while his music had flourished, he had never found the same excitement and passion with any other woman as he had with Ruth.

'I'm sorry for deserting you,' he whispered. 'You might not believe it, but I did love you, Ruth. We might even have made a life together, but things got in the way. Music was my future, and I had to put it first. I was free of responsibility, and far too selfish to tie myself down.'

Sighing inwardly, he thought of the woman he finally took as his wife. It had been the biggest mistake of his life.

Growing angry with himself, he did not feel much like going back to his hotel.

He felt ashamed, and guilty. And now he was so cold he began shivering. How long had he been standing there, reliving the past? Why was it haunting him so?

He looked about. The night had grown dark and chilly, and the streets were eerily quiet.

Considering the wrong choices he'd made and the chances he'd missed, his heart grew heavy. No doubt she was also committed to someone now.

Plunging his two hands into the pockets of his coat, he began walking.

Strolling along aimlessly, he chided himself: you have to leave the past behind, and concentrate on the future. You're here to find a way of creating the best recording studio this side of London. Back then, you might well have thrown away a good thing. Now, make sure you don't throw away another.

Deep in thought, Steve had no idea where he was headed. All he knew was that he needed to walk, to feel the cool night air on his face, while he tried to clear his mind.

He followed the main street to the end, then, lured by

haunting music, he turned into a side street. The light emanating from a pub window lit his way, and the music caught at his heartstrings. With his spirits uplifted, he stood outside the pub enjoying the music, and his foot merrily tapping against the pavement.

'Hey! Are you staying outside, or are you going in? Because if you're going in, you need to move yourself. And if you're staying out, then step aside and let them in as wants to go in.'

From his strong accent, the man was obviously of Scottish origin; in his senior years, and of short, lean build. Two thick, grey tufts of hair protruded from either side of his head, and haphazardly perched on top was a checked flat cap, the brim drawn low above his strong, dark eyes.

He was also possessed of a deep, chesty cough, which almost shook him off his feet as Steve allowed him to go inside before him.

A few minutes later, as he hung his overcoat on the door peg, Steve saw him approach the bar still coughing badly.

Steve also made his way to the bar. 'A pint, please, bartender.'

Beside him, the man in the checked cap was frantically digging into his pockets, obviously searching for money, and obviously not finding any. Steve discreetly addressed the bartender. 'Oh, and whatever our good friend here is drinking.' Steve smiled at the little fella. 'That's if my offer doesn't offend?' he asked cautiously.

'Not at all.' He nodded at Steve. 'Mine's a whisky,' he told the bartender, 'and, seeing as the laddie's paying, you can make that a double.'

Grinning cheekily, he displayed a set of smoke-stained and gappy teeth. 'I can't remember the last time anyone bought me a drink,' he told Steve. 'Thank you kindly!'

'You're very welcome.'

In truth, Steve had taken a liking to the old Scotsman, and when he saw him lighting a cigarette, he added cautiously, 'If I were you, I'd be thinking of packing the cigarettes in. Especially with the cough you've got there.'

'Is that so? Did I ask you to buy me a drink?' he demanded. 'No, I did not! And do I want you telling me what to do and what not to do? No, I do not! So bugger off and leave me alone.'

The bartender leaned over. 'Now then, David, don't start. Especially when the gent has bought you a drink.'

'Makes no difference. I won't be told what to do. Not by any man.' He glared at Steve. 'You're not from round these parts. It sounds like you're from London? Well, I warn you now, if you're looking for trouble, you've met your match.'

Turning his flat cap back to front, he bunched his fists and leaned forward. 'C'mon then, put 'em up! Let's see what you're made of!'

'Not tonight, thanks.' Steve was more amused than annoyed, especially as the little man was at least twenty-five years older than he was. 'I've an important business meeting in the morning. It wouldn't do to turn up with a black eye.'

The bartender couldn't help but smile. 'Oh, here we go again!' Reaching over the bar, he took the old man by the lapels of his jacket. 'You had a few drinks before you got here, didn't you?'

'Who told you that?' Raising his voice, the Scot announced to one and all, 'I never had a drink before I came in here, and even if I did have a little tipple, it's nobody's business but mine.'

The bartender had dealt with him before. 'No, David! It's my business when you intend fighting every stranger that walks through that door. Last week you caused a riot over a bag o' crisps, and the week before that you caused a row between a man and his woman; with you claiming she was your long-lost wife and kissing her face off.' He shook his head. 'The trouble with you is, you can't handle the booze. One sniff of ale and you're after fighting the world.'

He glanced at Steve, who was lazily drinking his pint and refusing to get drawn in. 'This man is a stranger in our midst, and so far as I know, he's the only one who's ever bought you a pint. And here you are, you ungrateful sod, wanting to knock his lights out!'

Letting go of the lapels, he let the old man settle. 'Are you gonna behave yourself, or what?'

'I always behave myself.'

'I mean it, David. You either behave yourself, or you leave now.'

'I'm not going anywhere, at least not till I've finished my drink.'

'All right then. Finish your drink, and go home.'

'I can't do that!' Setting his shoulders, he gave Steve a sinister glance. 'I have properly challenged this man to a fight,' he declared, 'and being a man of my word, I have every intention of teaching him a lesson he will not forget.' Pretending to throw a punch, he lost his balance and fell against the bar, where he remained. 'I'm not done yet,' he grumbled. 'Let me get my breath, then you'll be sorry. You see if I'm not right!' He glared at Steve.

Seeing how the argument might be brought to an end, Steve picked up the double whisky. 'Right then, David! Being as you don't want the rest of your drink, I might as well enjoy it . . . cheers!' He pretended to tip the glass up to his mouth.

'Gimme my whisky, you thieving Sassenach!' Stretching his small frame to full height, he again put up his clenched fists. 'Taking a man's drink deserves a smacking!'

'Oh, so you do want your drink then?'

'Course I do! It's my drink. Bought and paid for. You'd best give it back, unless you want your arse kicking twice over!'

Taking the drink along with his own, Steve started walking away. 'I don't know about you, but I've had enough of all this fighting talk. I've also had a long day travelling. So if you've anything else to say to me, I suggest you make your way to that far table, where I'll be enjoying my drink in peace.' He added casually, 'Besides, it's the only way you'll get your whisky back.'

'What? You come back wi' my drink, you thieving bugger! Stumbling and cursing, with the bartender smiling behind him, he rushed after Steve. 'Don't think 'cause I'm old and a bit rusty I can't knock seven bells outta you, because I'll have you know I used to be a prize fighter in my time.'

From somewhere amongst the drinkers a cry went up, 'He did, an' all! David McGreggor was a name to be reckoned with. In his time.'

'Sit down, David.' Steve gestured to the chair beside him, 'Let's you and me call a truce, eh?'

'Never!' The old Scotsman ran a discerning eye over this quiet stranger, the only man who had ever dipped his hand in his pocket to buy him a drink. 'All right then, but don't you mess with me. I can be lethal when I'm roused.'

'I wouldn't dream of it.'

So, they sat together in silence, drinking their drinks, with David occasionally giving him sideways glances, while Steve pretended not to notice.

Some musicians arrived and the customers cheered. A few minutes later, the four young men set up on a make-shift stage beside the bar, and began tuning up.

'That takes me back,' Steve said. 'When I was their age,

me and the boys would travel from Land's End to John o'Groats, just to make a few bob.'

After taking a long sip of his drink, David replaced the glass on the table. 'What? You mean you were a musician?'

'We were a group of four . . . two guitarists – one of whom could even throw a song together – and a pianist and a drummer.'

'Which one were you?'

Steve gave a modest little smile. 'I was the guitarist who could throw a song together.'

'Huh!' David was beginning to warm to this stranger. 'I once had a yen to play the drums, but I soon got over it,' he chuckled. 'I went bus driving instead. Did it for twenty-five years and never once regretted it.'

'Good for you. That's what life is all about, doing what you enjoy.'

'What kind o' songs d'you sing?'

'Oh, let me see . . . easy ballads, country stuff, all that. But at that time the music scene was beginning to change. The songs took on a different mood. The new entertainers were getting braver, looking for new challenges; attracting a new, younger and very different kind of audience. Musicians were more adventurous, more show business-like.' He smiled ruefully. 'And now it's all changed again, with a whole spectrum of different tastes. Even so, I don't think I'd be too out of step in the current market . . . if I was younger, that is.'

'Did you enjoy it while it lasted?'

'Sure.' Steve gave a quiet little smile. 'They were good times.'

'I expect the girls were all over you, eh?'

'You could say that, but we were always moving on. There one minute and gone the next . . . ships that pass in the night, as they say.'

'So . . .' the older man gave a drunken little hiccup, '. . . there was never anyone special, then?'

Inevitably, Steve thought of Ruth. 'There was one.'

'What was her name?'

'Ruth. Funny, though, I never did learn her surname.'

'So, it never went anywhere then . . . you and her, making it permanent, like?'

Steve turned to him with a smile. 'You want to know a lot, don't you? Are you usually this nosy?'

'You're right, I am a nosy bugger. I'll tell you what, though.'

'What?'

'All this talking's got me parched.'

'Me too.' Discreetly digging into his pocket Steve handed the other man a crisp note. 'If you get them, I'll pay.' After talking about Ruth, he felt melancholy, wanting to keep her in his mind, if only for a short time.

'Done!' Taking the note, the little fella went off towards the bar.

Just then the music struck up, and halfway across the room, David started dancing, making everyone clap and shout. 'I hope you don't think you're getting paid for that?' somebody yelled. Then a woman's voice rang out, 'I'll give him a bob or two, but only if he strips off.'

'You might regret saying that!' Winking at her, David pulled up his shirt and showed his bare belly, then he swung his hips and gyrated his way to the bar. When everyone clapped and whistled, he gave an exaggerated bow.

'If you want paying, we'll need to see more than your bare belly!' the woman teased.

He gave her a wink but, with her husband sitting beside her, he thought it wise to leave the merriment there.

Juggling a pint and a glass of whisky, he made his way back to Steve. 'There's not much change,' he told him. 'I reckon I should keep it for my troubles.'

Steve agreed and was rewarded with a handshake and a question.

'What did you say your name was?'

'Steve.'

'OK, Steve, so who was this bonny woman – Ruth, wasn't it? One of them "ships that passed in the night", was she?'

'Sort of, I suppose.'

'You liked her, I can tell.' Leaning towards Steve, he asked quietly, 'Fell for her hook, line and sinker, did you?'

'You ask too many questions, old man. Give it a rest, eh?'

'Aha!' David chuckled. 'I knew it. You fell for her, then she walked out on you, and now you're kicking yourself because she's the one that got away. Am I right?'

'I'll have you know, I'm a married man.'

'You're not happy, though, are you?'

'Is anyone?'

'I am! 'Cause I haven't got a harlot nagging at me from morning to night.' He nudged Steve with his arm. 'You know what?'

'What?'

'If I were you, I'd dump that wife o' yours, and find the one that got away.'

'Why would I do that?'

'Because you're unhappy. Don't waste your life with one woman, when it's the other one you're after. We only ever get one life, as far as we know, so grab it with both hands before it's too late.'

A moment later, David had nipped back to the bar for a refill when a cry went up. 'Is there a Steve in the house?'

When his name rang out, Steve was startled. 'What have you done, you old bugger?' He suspected the old man was up to mischief.

'Over here!' The little fella stood up. 'Here he is, ready and waiting!' He tugged Steve by the arm. 'Go on! Here's your chance to show these people what you've got.' He yelled out, 'He's on his way!' And Steve was left with no choice but to accept the challenge.

Secretly, though, he was excited as he climbed onto the makeshift stage, and when he was given the guitar, he felt like a young man again.

'What's the song?' the keyboard player asked.

'Do you know "Are you Lonesome Tonight"?' Steve had not played or sung on stage for many years, but he knew what an audience liked and the song suited his mood.

Returning to his keyboard, the young man briefly consulted with the other players who, like him, were not sure what they'd let themselves in for.

A moment later, they were ready. Steve was introduced, and the silence in the room was palpable. Bowing his head, Steve momentarily closed his eyes and got into the mood. Leaning into the microphone, he struck the first chord and started to sing, his voice strong and sure; trembling with emotion as he sang from the heart. The silence thickened as people put down their drinks to listen and enjoy. As his low, velvet voice wended its way through those memorable words, they felt the emotion. They knew the loneliness of that particular song, and hearts were heavy.

Behind him, the other players looked at each other in astonishment. When the old fellow had asked the favour, they were concerned they might be lumbered with a drunk who just wanted a singalong. But they were amazed at this talented man who had got the audience in the palm of his hand.

When the song ended, people were on their feet, clapping and shouting for more. Deeply moved, Steve thanked both them and the players, and graciously stepped down.

'Jeez! You really can play the guitar, and that voice of

yours could earn you a fortune . . . even now!' David had originally doubted this man's sincerity, but now he was impressed. 'You should take it up again. You're not a bad-looker, and you had this lot eating outta your hands.'

'I've moved on,' Steve told him. 'I was part of the up-front scene once,' he said, 'but I'm older and wiser now, with a whole new dream.'

'Oh, and what's that then?'

'Just a dream,' he answered. 'A dream that hopefully might soon become a reality.'

'Oh, well, I reckon we should drink to that.'

'You sit still. I'll get them in.'

Surprised that he was leaving so soon, the bartender promised, 'I'll make sure he gets home all right, don't you worry.' He kept safe the taxi fare Steve had given him for David.

Steve fished a couple of notes out of his wallet. 'Don't let him use this up too fast. String it out as best you can, for his sake.'

'You've obviously taken to David, as we all have. But you don't really know him, do you?' the bartender asked.

'I know he's a good man, and a rascal,' Steve chuckled. 'That's enough for me. Look after him, eh?'

'I always do.' The bartender watched him walk away. Seems like you're a good man too, he thought. A bit sad . . . a bit private. But a good man all the same.

Turning away, he poured out the whisky then made his way towards David, who was busy chatting to the man on the next table.

Having collected his coat, Steve looked back. He saw the little fella, obviously enjoying the conversation with the man on the next table, and when he heard David's raucous laugh, he smiled and shook his head. Then he saw the bartender leaning forward to speak to David. Just then, the little fellow turned his head, and looked straight at Steve. When Steve raised a hand in farewell, David did the same, albeit with some reluctance.

As Steve went out the door, he heard the racking cough, which concerned him; then the raucous laughter, which did his heart good. 'Give up the smokes, David,' he chuckled, 'and you won't go far wrong.'

One thing was for sure, he would not forget the lively little Scotsman in a hurry. If there had been more time, he might well have frequented the bar again tomorrow.

But for now, he had things to do, places to go, and people to see.

But as he walked away, it was the young girl he had loved and left years ago who occupied his thoughts.

~

Outside on the pavement, Steve stood a moment; so many thoughts racing through his mind. Thoughts of regrets and happiness, and of dreams not yet fulfilled. Thoughts of his younger days and the years in between, and the realisation of how quickly the years had flown by. One minute you were in your twenties, wild and carefree, playing the field and enjoying life, the next, you're a married man with responsibilities.

His heart was laden with regrets as he thought of his life with the woman he'd married. Did he love her? No. Did he respect her. No. They had drifted into a kind of understanding. Sometimes over the years there had been special, tender moments, although, looking back, there was nothing very memorable.

Although he'd had many chances, he had never been unfaithful and, as far as he knew, Connie had not been unfaithful to him. She understood him better than anyone, and while she had no interest in his music, and would never accompany him on his trips, she had always encouraged him to pursue his dreams. For that, at least, he owed her a degree of loyalty.

He looked up and down the street, to see couples arm in arm, chatting and laughing, and his heart was heavy. How long had it been since he and his wife had laughed together like that? He shook his head. Too long.

He suddenly realised that, even though he was often surrounded by people, his life had been somewhat lonely. He felt a surge of regret: 'What I wouldn't give, just to turn back the clock.'

When the night air bit into him, he shivered, quickly buttoned up his overcoat, thrust his hands into his pockets, and walked on.

He had little idea where he was headed, or how long he might walk. For now, it was enough for him to be alone and quiet, to clear his thoughts and draw the shutters against the past. Soon he must get back to the hotel. Not least because his dear sister-in-law was sure to be waiting there with a barrage of questions.

After a while, he turned off the backstreet and found himself on a wide open street with shops on either side. There was a pretty little bridge, which he now crossed. On the other side stood a grand old cinema. Its lights were on but there was no sign of people. In truth, there were very few people about in this part of town.

Following the path right up to the top, he saw it was busier here, with traffic and people, and the sound of music emanating from the pub on the corner. He smiled. It seemed every street had a lamp-post on one corner and a pub on the other.

Drawn to the pub, he crossed the road. He wondered if he should go inside and drown his worries, but his mood was not in keeping with the loud, merry laughter he could hear. He decided just to keep walking until he felt so tired all he wanted to do was fall into bed and sleep.

After walking on for a few minutes more, he paused to admire a church in the square he was passing through. The strong, meticulously sculpted lines gave it such proud character. Appreciating things fine and beautiful, he could not help but wonder about the mind and hand that had designed such a magnificent structure.

A cutting sense of disappointment made him question his own feeble endeavours. What had he actually done with his life? What great feat had he achieved that would leave his mark on the world? Where was he headed? What were his true ambitions? Also, when and if he ever achieved those ambitions, would they even be worthy of his time and effort?

Compared to the person who had created strength and beauty in that wonderful church, he thought himself unworthy, and undeserving.

He walked on into a much busier area of town, with people milling about. There were sweethearts strolling arm in arm, laughing together; and revellers, chattering and singing as they spilled out of the pubs and clubs, onto the streets.

A number of people headed for the boulevard where they climbed aboard the buses, while others hurried towards the grand Victorian railway station beyond.

Within minutes, the spill of people had diminished, the chatter and the singing died down. Soon the streets appeared almost deserted except for a few merry young folk, unsteady on their feet and unsure which direction they should go.

Steve went in search of a taxi. Disappointed to see a long queue at the taxi rank, he thought his best chance of acquiring a lift to his hotel was to carry on walking, and board a taxi further down the street.

Wondering down a narrow side street, away from the brightly lit boulevard, his thoughts turned to the viewings tomorrow, and the possibility that, at long last, he might be on the verge of achieving his cherished ambition.

Sadly, even if his long-held dream was finally realised, his wife would show little interest. He had no children either, and who knew, they might have followed him into the music industry. Not having children was a real thorn in his side, and even if they hadn't followed the music profession, it would not have mattered. Only now did he realise how truly lonely he was.

~

Some distance away from where Steve had first sought a taxi, Ruth stopped to rest. She found herself on a street that was softly lit, and quiet. Hopefully she might find a deep doorway, where she could maybe catch a wink or two, before moving on.

She soon located a suitable place. It was a large Victorian house, with a wooden sign fixed to the wall.

Marilyn's Place
BED AND BREAKFAST
ALSO LONG-TERM BOARDERS
(Professional only)
Suitable terms – Enquire inside

Ruth was relieved to see that the porch was unlit, though there was a soft light above the sign, and another light shining from a bedroom window on the upper level.

Leaning forward, she could see that the big wood-panelled front door was closed. The street was empty, though from somewhere nearby there was music and voices raised in song. But that was usual round these backstreets; especially on a late evening. She was not concerned. It was just some pub turning out reluctant boozers who had overstayed their welcome. More importantly and for her own safety, there was no pub on this particular street.

Reminding herself that it was the kind of quiet night that carried music and voices from a way off, she believed she was safe enough here, for the time being.

Bone-tired and longing to lay down her head, she promised herself that here, in that dark, deep porch, she would be comfortable, at least till daybreak. So she crept into the dark recess of the porch and settled herself down.

When the cold, hard flagstones beneath her struck bitterly cold, she drew her arms inward, out of the long sleeves of her jumper. That done, she clumsily wrapped the loosely hanging sleeves tight about her neck and shoulders, while pulling down and tucking in the body of the jumper itself, wherever possible. Folding her legs beneath her, she then curled into a ball.

Finding the brick walls cold and hard against her back, she shifted herself further into the corner, with her body resting between the wall and the door, which made for a more comfortable position.

Wary of any danger, she took a moment to listen for approaching strangers. But there was only silence and darkness, both of which eased her mind.

Closing her eyes, she gave herself up to sleep, but, as on every night since she'd left Henry Street, her sleep was neither deep, nor restful.

Instead, it was a shallow, uneasy sleep, in which her dreams constantly reminded of the destructive events that had brought her here, to this.

~

Steve was hopelessly lost. Having strayed from the main streets, he was now anxious, and keeping a sharp lookout for a telephone box from which to call for a taxi.

Eventually he spotted a red telephone box beneath a streetlamp on a corner.

Inside, he fumbled through his jacket pockets for loose change.

The first call was to ask the operator for the number of a taxi firm, which he scribbled down on the back of his hand.

The second call was to Connie at their home in Finchley. He let it ring for a long time until it was irritatingly clear that there was no one there to answer it.

'So, where the devil is she?' Muttering impatiently, he dropped the receiver into its cradle. He was used to her gadding about with her chums.

Digging into his jacket pocket, he withdrew the hotel card and carefully dialled the number. When the receptionist answered, he asked to be put through to Mrs Alice Bates.

'Who shall I say is calling, sir?'

'Steve Bates. She's expecting my call.' Some hour or two ago, he reminded himself wryly.

In no time at all, his sister-in-law was on the line. 'Steve, where are you? You should have been back ages ago. Susie refuses to go to bed until she knows you're back safe and well.'

'Sorry, Alice, I got sidetracked. I was talking to this bloke and we ended up in a pub, and then before I knew it, I was up on stage, playing the guitar . . .'

She laughed at that. 'I might have known it. Anyway, I'm glad you called. I was getting worried.'

'Alice, have you heard from Connie? When I tried a few minutes ago, there was no reply. I just wondered if she'd been in touch with you?'

'Nope.' Alice was all too aware of Steve's wife's disinterest in his plans. It saddened her to see that they were increasingly living separate lives. 'After I got back here this afternoon, I actually asked at the desk if she'd left a message for either of us, but they said there was nothing. I shouldn't worry, though, Steve. You know what she's like . . . gone off to some club with her mates, I dare say.' She gave a good-natured chuckle. 'A bit like you, going into some pub with a stranger and showing off on stage.'

He laughed. 'I don't know about "showing off". I was bamboozled into it. Mind you, I must confess I really enjoyed it.'

'Well, there you go then. If you ask me, you and Connie are as bad as each other.'

'Hmm! Well, at least she can't say I didn't try to get in touch.'

'I wouldn't worry about her. You know what they say: "while the cat's away, the mice will play".' The moment she spoke the words, she regretted them.

'What's that supposed to mean?'

'It doesn't mean anything . . . only that she's probably been out shopping all day, spending a fortune on glad rags and make-up. Anyway, Susie's here and she wants to talk to you.'

There was a short span of silence before Susie's excited voice came on the phone. 'Uncle Steve? I've been waiting for you to come back.'

Steve smiled at the sound of her voice. 'You're a little minx! You should be fast asleep in your bed by now.'

'I'm not going to sleep until you come back!'

'I see. All right, I'm on my way.'

'Hurry up then.'

'Oh, I will, don't you worry. See you soon then.'

'See you soon, Uncle Steve. Bye.'

'Bye, sweetheart.'

Replacing the receiver, he stood for a moment reflecting on his conversation with that sweet little girl. "*What I wouldn't give to have a child of my own.*" Thrusting the idea from his mind, he concentrated on ringing the number for a taxi.

'. . . And where are you exactly, sir?'

'Hang on a minute.' Peering outside, along the wall, Steve caught sight of the street name. 'Montague Street. How quickly can you get here?'

He waited for the man to check. 'Twenty minutes at the outside.'

'Good . . . thank you. I need to get to the King's Hotel.'

'Right! We'll collect you from Montague Street in fifteen minutes or so.'

Replacing the receiver, Steve went out onto the street, where he began walking up and down, eagerly watching for the sight of the taxi.

~

Ruth's sleep was haunted by what Tom had done, to himself and to the boy he idolised.

Her subconscious mind was alive with images of his last few minutes. In her fractured dreams, she could see him on the bridge; he was looking down, his face racked with sadness. Now he was silently falling, arms out and eyes closed as he spun down towards the tracks.

And now, she was at the churchyard, watching from the back while the priest talked of 'this fine young man . . . who was in such turmoil that he took his own life'.

She had wondered since what the priest knew that she was unaware of. Did he know that not long before Tom's fatal jump, she had taunted him with the confession that the boy he believed to be his own flesh and blood was not his at all?

Did the priest know of the resentment she harboured towards Tom, and the boy, her own son?

And now, because of her damning confession, Casey and the good man he believed to be his daddy had each paid an impossible price.

The priest could not know that. Neither did he feel her pain, or the unfulfilled longing that never left her: a longing for love and quietness of heart. She had never prayed. She would not know how. But she knew wickedness, and she knew how to hurt.

In her wild youth she had willingly given herself, heart and soul, to a young man, and he let her down so badly that she had never got over it. On the day he went away, leaving her with child, she promised herself that, never again, would she love or trust anyone.

Tom had been a good man who loved her in a way she had never been loved before, with tenderness and compassion, asking nothing in return, except that she might love him back. How could he have known that she was incapable of loving anyone? Instead she had used him, taking advantage of his devotion to her.

The truth was, in all the years they were married, she had never felt anything for him except a sense of disgust that he should be so gullible. He'd accepted her lies without question; lies about her feelings for him; lies about the child she claimed was his, and even lies about the timing of its conception. When she'd raised her little finger, Tom had come running. He'd married her straight away. He'd been in love with her for years and was the happiest, proudest man alive, while she was quietly content that her secret was safe.

From the moment the child was born, she shrank away from him, hardly able to look at him. Whenever Tom cradled the child in his arms, she hated one as much as the other.

She wanted to hurt them and, as the years went on, there was no end to her wickedness.

Even now, with Tom lying in the cold ground, and the boy gone from her, she felt no guilt because her own suffering had swallowed all that was good in her.

And yet, she wished things had been different. But what did she really wish for? Was it peace, and contentment? A kinder heart? To find the love of a mother for her child? No, it was none of these precious things.

What she truly wished for was deeply embedded in the past. It was the time when life was worth living. She wished for the girl she had been, and who, for the one and only time in her life, had fallen in love with every part of her being. She wished for the young man who, in those fleeting hours, had shown her such great joy. They had laughed and played, and their love was very precious dream.

But the dream ended when he went away. He crept into her life like a thief in the night. He stole her heart and soul and went away for ever.

If only she could turn back the clock, to that amazing time before he left her behind, without any explanation.

She wanted him back. She wanted the laughter back. She wanted to hear him sing love songs to her, and make her laugh as he chased her across Blackpool beach. Many times she had been drawn back to Blackpool through these memories.

She thought of him now, strumming his guitar and looking at her while he melted her heart with his tender songs.

Her heart darkened as she thought of the boy. Like Tom, he had a great love for music. Yet there was a difference, because where Tom had been taught it by his father, Casey had picked it up almost naturally, with little instruction or help. As he grew older, his musical talent simply grew as he grew, almost as though it had always been a part of him. And even though she had discouraged it, she was reluctantly drawn by the beauty of his music and the way he held the guitar, close to his heart. It was as though making music was as natural to him as breathing.

Listening to him was almost unbearable, because whenever she heard the boy sing and play, she was transported back, to when she first met his father. They met by chance, and spent the day together. The magic of his music drew her to him, but it was the man himself who held her there.

The short time she spent with him was the best time of her life. A time that would always be precious to her; a time she wished she could go back to. She would gladly surrender half her life, if only she could go back over the years and be with him.

But the past was gone, and it was too late for her now. Tom came into her life and changed everything.

On the day Tom took his own life, was it her fault? After she told him the boy was not his, was it too much for him to bear? Was that the real truth? Had he answered her questions in the letter she had so callously thrown away? She wondered if she should go back and search for that letter. But it must be long gone by now, and besides, would she really want to read his last words to her?

No! She would rather not know . . .

~

Deep in a fitful sleep, Ruth was unaware that she was being watched.

'Ooh, look now. 'Ave yer ever seen such a pretty sight?' Drunk and smiling, the pot-bellied man turned to his equally drunken friend. 'Looks like we've found ourselves a little hussy.'

'Yeah! I reckon there's more than enough there for

the two of us, don't you?' Younger, of tighter build and harder features, the other man took stock of the woman in the doorway.

He licked his lips like a dog slavering after a juicy bone, and his eyes rove over her long, dishevelled skirt and the enticing bare thigh where her constant fidgeting had caused the skirt to shift, revealing a measure of enticing pink flesh.

Bending down, he reached out and, pinching together two fingers, carefully lifted the skirt higher. When the lacy leg of her knickers was revealed, he could hardly contain his excitement.

'Gentle now . . . we mustn't wake her. We don't want her to scream out and wake everyone from their beds, do we? The pot-bellied man glanced up and down the lonely street. 'Let's get her somewhere dark and lonely where we can . . . take care of her.' He gave a knowing wink.

The younger man leaned down to straddle his legs over Ruth's sleeping body. Softly wrapping her long hair around one hand, he pressed the other hand tight across her mouth; effectively stifling any screams or unexpected movements.

In her disturbed sleep, Ruth felt a sense of unease.

Now, when she tried to move her head, it was held fast, and there was something pressing down on her face. She tried to scream, but she couldn't, and panic set in. Someone was hurting her. They were holding her down, and when she managed to blink open her eyes, she saw two men leaning over her; grinning at her, their evil expressions striking fear in her heart.

Left in no doubt as to their lecherous intentions, she fought them with every ounce of strength in her body.

~

A street away, Steve paced up and down, desperately impatient for the taxi to arrive.

Thinking he'd heard a muffled cry, he waited and listened, but all was quiet again, and he casually dismissed it as his imagination. 'I could have *walked* back to the hotel by now,' he muttered angrily, 'if only I knew which way to go.'

As he anxiously paced up and down, the only living creature he encountered was a ginger tomcat, which quickly scurried away at the sight of him.

Now, as he got to the top of the street, he thought he heard that noise again . . . like a muffled squeal, and now the sound of scuffling, and people talking to each other.

Curious, he stopped to listen. There it was again . . . an odd kind of squeal. He couldn't make it out. He knew the sound of cats fighting, and this was different.

Growing ever curious, he took a few steps forward. As he ventured round the corner, the noise got louder and more urgent. Now he thought it sounded like someone in trouble.

'Bloody hell, she's a bit of a firecracker, this one!'

The pot-bellied man had his thick fists locked around Ruth's legs, while the younger man had one hand grasping the roots of her hair, and his other hand pressed hard and tight across her mouth.

'I don't mind her being a firecracker,' he chuckled softly as they staggered drunkenly towards the alley. 'The harder they fight, the more the fun, eh?'

'Shut up, you bloody fool!' the other man hissed angrily. 'Quick! Get her off the street, before somebody sees us.'

'Ouch, you damned bitch!' As Ruth sank her teeth into his flesh, the younger man winced; though she only increased his excitement.

On rounding the corner, Steve saw the two men. As he got closer, he realised they were carrying a woman.

Violently struggling, she was making the muffled noises he'd heard earlier.

Realising their intention, he ran at them. 'Hey! What the hell d'you think you're doing?'

The force of his attack sent the big man sprawling to the ground. Dazed and drunk, he tried to stagger up, but when Steve floored him again with a hard blow to the chin, he scrambled up and fled through the alley, like the coward he was.

His partner didn't even stay to fight. Instead he hot-footed it after the big man, the two of them shouting threats behind them as they scarpered. 'You'd best watch yer back, mate, 'cause we'll have yer! One dark night when yer least expecting it, we'll be there!'

Ruth was lying on the ground, quietly sobbing, Steve helped her to stand. 'Are you all right?' In the gloom of the alley, he could see little of her face, especially with her long, matted hair partly covering her features.

'Yes . . . I'm all right.' She was distressed, but thankfully not badly hurt. Ashamed, she kept her face averted, hardly daring to look at him. She felt dirty and unkempt, but lucky to be safe. 'I need to get back,' she muttered. 'I'll be all right now.' She had no idea where she might go 'back' to.

'Snatched you off the street, did they?' Steve kept an image of the men in his mind. 'Don't you worry, they'll get their comeuppance,' he promised.

Looking down at the ground, Ruth nodded. 'Thank you for helping me.' Deeply shaken and painfully conscious of how this incident must all look to him, she continued to keep her face averted.

'Are you sure you're OK?' Steve wondered why she would not look him in the face. Maybe she was nervous of him, understandable after her shocking ordeal with those two thugs.

'Yes, really. I'm OK now. I can manage. You don't need to stay with me. I can make my own way home.' There was a time when she might have been glad to entertain such a hero, but not tonight, because tonight she had seen a side to life she never wanted to see again.

The odd thing was that now, for the first time, she could see herself through the eyes of others, like those two dregs who thought she was theirs for the taking; and this gentle, caring man, a stranger who had come to her rescue. Seeing herself as they must have seen her was shocking.

The shame and disgust she felt was a whole new experience, and it shook her deeply.

'I insist on taking you home.' Steve could see she was still trembling. 'It's not a problem for me,' he told her reassuringly. 'So, where do you live?' When he noticed she appeared to have no belongings with her, he assumed her assailants must have also robbed her into the bargain. 'Did they take your bag and coat?' he asked.

Ruth nodded. 'I think they must have. I can't remember.' She wondered what he would think of her if he knew she had neither handbag nor coat. In fact, she was homeless and penniless, and that was only half the truth.

'Cowardly scum!' Steve was enraged. 'Once I give the police a description of sorts, I'm sure they'll waste no time in tracking them down.'

'No, please, don't call the police. I can't face it. I can't talk to them. I can't talk to anyone about it. I feel so ashamed. I need to put the experience behind me now. Please . . . I'm grateful for your help, but . . . don't tell the police.' When he caught a glimpse of her upturned face, she quickly turned away. 'I'm just glad to be safe. Let's leave it at that.'

Steve tried to understand. 'I'm not happy with the idea of them getting away scot-free,' he said, 'but if that's what you want, I don't have a choice. All right then, we'll do it your way! The main thing for now is to get you home. Look, I've got a taxi on the way . . .' he looked up and down the street, '. . . that is, if he hasn't already given up on me.'

'I'm able to get myself home,' she graciously refused his offer of help. 'Really! You've done enough. I don't want to bother you any more.' She was desperate to be rid of him, and yet she was suddenly afraid of the night and every chilling sound that echoed through those dark streets.

Steve would not even hear of it. 'I'm sorry, but I would never forgive myself if they came after you again. Let me at least see you into the house.'

He was so insistent, and Ruth was hurting in every corner of her body, so she offered no resistance. 'All right.' She could always pretend to go inside that house with the porch. Then he would surely go away, and leave her be.

From inside that very house, the landlady had also heard the squeals and scuffles. She was still at the window and looking down on the street when she saw a man and a woman come into view. She saw how the man was helping the woman along, and as they passed the streetlamp, she noticed how dishevelled and slow-walking the woman was. She recalled the noises earlier and couldn't help but wonder if there had been a skirmish of sorts.

Throwing on her frilly dressing gown, she ran down the stairs and flung open the front door, just as they arrived at the porch.

'Who the devil are you? What's going on? I heard all the yelling and carrying-on, and I couldn't help but wonder if some poor soul was under attack.' She took a quick look along the street from the direction they'd come. 'Thieves and criminals inhabit these streets of a night,' she revealed cautiously. 'They get drunk and violent, and many a time I've seen them fighting each other. It's not on. I've told the police time and again, the buggers want locking up!'

She added warily, 'To give 'em their due, the police did root them all out some time ago, but I've an idea they're beginning to filter back of late. It's not good for business. No, it is not, and I can see I'll have to have another word.'

Being of staunch character and afraid of nothing and no one, she bore the carriage and confidence of a woman who knew her way about. Looking to be in her mid-fifties, she would never admit her real age.

She made a striking figure, with her masses of wild red hair and plump but shapely figure. Vaguely visible in the flickering light of the streetlamp, she looked a handsome woman, though some would say she made herself up like a tart, with her thick eye-liner and luminous pink lipstick, and her long fingernails coated in vivid purple polish.

Yet she was a kindly soul, if a little brutish of manner.

Steve thanked her for being concerned. 'Two ruffians tried to carry this poor woman into the alley,' he explained. 'I was all for calling the police, but the young lady insisted I shouldn't. She just wanted to get home, and so here she is. I hope you can persuade her to inform the police,' he added worriedly. 'Those scoundrels should not be allowed to get away with what they did.'

'Good-for-nothing cowards, that's what they are!' Concerned, she took a closer look at Ruth. 'You look a bit ruffled, I must say, but at least you had a lucky escape. Come on, luv, let's get you inside.'

Questions played on her mind. How and why did the man come to bring her here? And why should he think this was her home? Also, whatever was she doing, alone in the backstreets at this godforsaken hour. She seemed an attractive young woman despite her lowly appearance.

Relieved when the woman took charge, Ruth was only too willing to let her lead her up the steps and through the front door. 'I'm worried they might come after me again,' she said nervously. 'I've never been so frightened in my life.'

'If they come anywhere near us, it'll be the biggest mistake they've ever made!' the landlady promised. 'Let them try it, and they'll be off down the alley like a pair o' scalded cats. I know how to look after myself. Me and my yard broom are a match for them cowards any day!'

Never one to turn away the needy, she opened her arms to Ruth. 'You look all shaken up, lass. Come on, I'll make us a hot drink, while you call the police.' She noticed that Ruth was not carrying any belongings. 'Took your things as well, did they? Thieving swines! Careful now, I've got you.'

Immensely grateful for their help, Ruth was thankful that this larger-than-life character had unintentionally given Steve the impression that she was actually living here, exactly as she had wanted him to believe.

Turning to Steve, she thanked him again. 'I'll be fine now.' Discreetly blocking the doorway, she made it difficult for Steve to follow, and even now, she did not look up at him. Instead, she kept her face averted. All she wanted was for him to go away because if he looked at her through honest eyes, he might see what she really was: a woman from the streets; a woman without home, or pride.

Even now, though plagued with guilt, she was not yet ready to fully admit being the instigator of her own downfall, along with a good man's untimely end, and the abandoning of an innocent boy.

All these years she'd believed herself to be strong, only to discover now that she was pitifully weak and astonishingly gullible. What she had once seen as her strength she now saw as blatant arrogance.

Those two low-lifes had obviously seen her for what she was, curled up in that doorway. They had seen a tramp, a hussy, a woman of the streets to be used for men's pleasure. And it was true. She was all of those things, and more.

Even when she'd had a good and decent man looking after her, she couldn't help but behave like a hussy; bedding one man after another; often strangers, and all the time trying to recover something special, something she had lost long ago.

For years, she had expected everything and given nothing back. And now, she was amazed at the kindness she had received this night, from complete strangers.

This man had put his own life in danger to rescue her from what would certainly have been a terrible ordeal. And this big-hearted woman had rushed out to help her, opening her arms and her house to her. Ruth had never known such kindness; except from Tom, and all he'd got for his troubles was pain and rejection.

'Are you sure you'll be all right now?' Steve was relieved that at least he had got her home and safe. 'Would you like me to come in and call the police . . . tell them what happened? I really don't mind staying with you till they arrive. After all, I believe I was the only witness, and I can describe the ruffians to them.'

'No!' Panic set in. 'No . . . thank you. You've done enough. Please, leave it to me now.'

'OK. If that's what you really want.'

'I do, yes.'

Steve addressed the older woman. 'Make sure she calls them, will you? She'll listen to you. This was a terrible business, and they must not be allowed to get away with what they did.'

Though surprised that he should think she had more influence over the victim than he did, the woman assured him, 'Don't you worry. I'll make sure she calls them. And you're right, they need to be caught.'

She turned her attention to Ruth. 'Come on then, lady. Let's get you settled.'

Ruth smiled at the idea of herself as a 'lady'.

'Good night then . . .' Bending his head down, Steve tried to see her face, but she drew away. '. . . I didn't get your name.' He suspected she was still in shock after the ordeal.

'Good night. And thank you again.' Ever evasive, she kept the exchange to a minimum. 'I dread to think what might have happened if you hadn't helped me.'

'Ah, well, I'm just glad to have been there at the time.' Respecting her nervousness, and the reluctance to give out her name, Steve did not ask again, and anyway, now that she was safely home, he was anxious to get back to the hotel. 'I'd best be away and find my taxi. Don't forget to tell the police they took your belongings. You never know, it might help track them down.'

He turned away and went quickly down the street, while the landlady closed the door.

Back on Montague Street, Steve was relieved to see a taxi cruising up and down, as though looking for his fare. 'Hey . . . taxi!' Running after it, he caught the attention of the driver. 'I think you must be looking for me. King's Hotel, yes?'

'That's right, lad. You're lucky to find me still here. I was beginning to think I'd got the wrong street.'

When the taxi pulled up to the kerb, Steve jumped in. 'I'm sorry if I kept you waiting. Only . . .'

The driver was shocked as Steve explained what had happened.

'She's lucky you were around.'

'And I'm glad I was.'

Steve thought of the woman. There was something about her that made him curious. He hadn't noticed so much at the time, but when he now thought back, he recalled how she never once looked up at him. She seemed reluctant to talk, and she certainly did not want him going inside the house.

But then he reminded himself how she must have suffered at the hands of those men. He imagined she would be haunted by the ordeal for a long time to come.

Also, it was understandable that she had not invited him into her home. After all, and in spite of his timely intervention, he was just another stranger.

'Let's just hope you don't find any more damsels in distress, eh?' the driver interrupted his thoughts.

'That's right. I reckon I've done my knight in shining armour bit for now.'

Conversation over, the driver said no more, and after the night he'd experienced, Steve was thankful to sit quiet and enjoy the ride.

He hoped by now, that his niece, Susie, was fast and hard asleep.

～

Inside the boarding house, the buxom landlady duly tended to the deep bruises on Ruth's ankles. 'Wicked swines! They should be locked up.' She had plenty to say on the matter.

Ruth had to smile; not only was this woman colourful in character and appearance, she also had an endearing attitude.

While the landlady worked on her bruises, Ruth found her thoughts returning to the man who had rescued her and brought her back here. 'I never even got his name.'

'Whose name is that, then?'

'The man who chased them away and saved me from something I daren't even think about . . .' She envisaged her attackers fleeing. 'No one else has ever done anything like that for me . . . except you.' She added, 'And I do appreciate your help, I really do.'

'Where do you live?'

The landlady was concerned that the young woman should be with her family. 'We'll get you cleaned up, then I'd best call the police. After you've told them what happened, I'm sure they'll be only too pleased to take you home.'

Having bathed and cleaned and finally applied a soothing ointment to Ruth's ankles, she gathered the flannel and bowl, and scrambled clumsily to her feet. 'There! How are your ankles now?'

Having seen the torn skin on Ruth's ankles and lower legs, she could only imagine the rough treatment she'd received; and it made her sick to her stomach.

'I feel much better now, thank you.' The two men had not only hurt her, but they had taken pleasure in it. The big man had gripped her ankles so tightly, she had hardly been able to move them, and when for that split second she managed to wriggle them from his tight grip, he dug his nails into her flesh, causing more pain.

Also, her mouth and jaw were still hurting where the other culprit had clamped his fist over her face to keep her from screaming out.

Even now, although she was safe enough here, her sense of terror lingered.

'I'll make us each a mug of cocoa,' the older woman said. 'It might help you relax.' She could see how upset the young woman was, by the haunted look in her eyes, and by the way she constantly clenched and unclenched her fists. On passing, she brushed her hand against Ruth's shoulder. 'It's all over now,' she told her. 'You should try and relax.'

Smiling over her shoulder, Ruth nodded; and her hostess went away to make the cocoa, a satisfied little smile on her face.

In no time at all, she was back again, carrying two steaming mugs. 'I never asked . . . what's your name?'

'Ruth.'

'And I'm Marilyn Parker.' She sniggered proudly. 'Marilyn after Marilyn Monroe and Parker after the bloke I married.

'He works away most o' the time. He's a lorry driver. One time, he went away for a week . . . got home in the early hours and climbed into bed alongside me.' Grinning, she rolled her eyes to heaven. 'I'm telling you, we were at it for hours. He'd missed me . . . or that was what he said; until I found out later he'd given me the dreaded clap. Got it from some woman who climbed on his running board when he was asleep in the lorry. She offered to "keep him company" and he couldn't say no, and that's how he got the clap and passed it on to me. It goes without saying, I banned him from my bed for a month, only I missed him more than he missed me, so I let him back in after two nights.'

She made a painful grimace. 'The pair of us went to the doctor together. Embarrassing, it was, but I made sure the doctor knew who was to blame. I swear, if he ever goes with another woman again, I'll chop his dufer clean off!'

When Marilyn laughed a raucous laugh, Ruth couldn't help but laugh with her. Truth was, she had taken a real liking to this wonderful, outrageous woman.

In more serious mood, Marilyn placed a mug of cocoa into Ruth's open hands, before sitting opposite with her own. 'If you're determined not to call the police, we really ought to let your family know where you are,' she advised.

'There's a phone in the hallway. I can call them, if you'd rather not.'

'NO!' Ruth began to panic. 'No! You can't! I don't want them worried. I'll be all right. There's no need for them to know.'

The older woman nodded knowingly. 'You don't want me to call them, so I won't. But I'd like you to tell me the real reason why you don't want to call anyone, not even the police.' She was more concerned than curious.

Ruth's heart sank. 'I don't know what you mean.'

'Oh, I think you do.' Watching Ruth closely, she chided, 'I haven't got to this age without learning to recognise a downright lie when I hear it.' She gave Ruth an encouraging smile. 'But if you'd rather not be honest with me, that's up to you.'

Sensing her suspicions, Ruth said, 'I'm sorry, but I'm grateful to you, really I am.'

'But you don't feel you can trust me, is that it?'

Ruth slowly nodded. 'Yes . . . I mean, I don't know.'

'Tell me, Ruth, why did that man bring you to my door, rather than take you home?'

'Because I led him to believe that this is where I live.'

'I see. But why did you do that? I'm sure he would have taken you home, wherever you lived.'

Sipping her cocoa, she gave Ruth time to think about her answer.

'I brought him here because I was sleeping in your porch when those men found me. And because . . . well, because . . . I don't have a home. Or a family.' Afraid of what the future held, a sense of loss and desolation swamped her.

When the tears ran down her face, they were not because of her own predicament, or her son being abandoned, or even the terrifying ordeal she had just gone through.

Her tears were for Tom. The man who had carried her through all the lonely years; the man who had provided a home, and protection from the harsh world. The man who had raised another man's child without knowing it; raised him with love and pride, and a sense of achievement, and even when he was told that the boy was not his, he still loved and protected him. He removed him from her wickedness, and kept him safe, in the only way he knew how.

In her vicious spite to hurt them both, she had destroyed everything Tom and the boy held dear.

The images of Tom's last moments haunted her. She saw him clearly in her mind, standing on the bridge, crippled with all manner of torment, before throwing himself under that train. And however anyone tried to tell her different, she knew that, deep down, it was she and she alone who had driven him to do such a frightening thing.

Suddenly it all became too much and the tears became an uncontrollable flood. When she felt the woman's arms round her shoulders, she had a desperate need to tell her things; private things that she had never told anyone.

'Don't feel sorry for me,' she told her. 'If you only knew the terrible things I've said and done . . . oh . . .' Overwhelmed with grief, she held her head in shame.

'Talk to me,' the other woman urged her. 'Tell me what troubles you.' She patted Ruth's hand. 'You know what they say: a trouble shared is a trouble halved.'

So Ruth told her, and once she started, it was as though she had opened a dam and, even if she had wanted to, she could not stop.

She confessed everything: about the handsome young musician she'd met and fallen in love with all those years back. They were such precious memories, and she could see it all as though it were only yesterday.

'It was the most wonderful night of my life,' she murmured. 'I remember, it had been a beautiful, warm day . . . and the evening was magical. There was a beach party. I went with my friend Connie. Steve and I danced to the music, we were so happy, so right for each other. After the music stopped and the crowds vanished and Connie went back to our boarding house, it was unbelievably quiet except for the sound of the sea lapping against the shore. And the stars! Oh, they were so amazing! Bright and twinkly, shining down . . . lighting our way as we strolled along the beach.' She paused a moment, remembering, and wishing; and regretting what was gone for ever.

As she listened, Marilyn saw a transformation in Ruth. She saw how her eyes lit up, and her whole body relaxed. She saw how her smile softened. More than that, she saw the love in Ruth's face, in her voice, and in her whole demeanour. And she felt her incredible loneliness.

It was obvious to Marilyn that the young man called Steve had been Ruth's first, and possibly her only love. He had been her soulmate; that much was obvious.

Unaware of the older woman's intense interest in her, Ruth lost herself in the memories, talking in a whisper, as though to herself. 'We walked along the beach, and it was like we'd known each other for all our lives. We talked about everything; what we liked and what we didn't like. We swapped dreams and wishes. We talked a lot about music, and Steve told me how, since he was a small boy, he had always wanted it to be his life.'

At this point, Ruth looked up into Marilyn's eyes. 'That's where Casey gets his love of music,' she said wistfully.

'Who's Casey?'

'He's my son . . . and Steve is his father. He plays the guitar just like his daddy . . . like he's part of the guitar . . . like the music is inside him . . . and when he plays it's almost as though his life depends on it.'

Her thoughts strayed back to the past and the day she and Steve met. 'I'll never forget that night with Steve,' she said wistfully. 'We seemed to walk for ages without seeing a single person. It was almost as though we were all alone in the world.'

'It sounds idyllic.'

'Oh, it was; it really was! After a time, we found a quiet corner of the beach, where we lay down together. At first, we were just looking up at the stars . . . saying how magical they were. Then he was holding me, and oh, Marilyn, I felt such love for him.'

'I can believe that.' Slightly envious because she had never known love of an honest kind, Marilyn was deeply moved by Ruth's powerful emotions. 'You obviously loved him then; and you love him still, I see that.'

'You're right, I do love him, with all my heart. But I shouldn't love him. I should hate him! He said he loved me, and then he was gone, and I never saw him again.'

She explained how Steve left Blackpool suddenly. 'I found out I was carrying his child, and managed to get a message to him, but he never returned, and left me to face it all by myself.'

She had never truly got over him. 'He went without even saying goodbye,' she faltered. 'After he'd gone, I tried to forget him, but I couldn't.'

'Was there anyone you could turn to?'

'Only my friend, Connie.'

'What about your family?'

'I have no brothers or sisters, and my parents had more than enough troubles of their own, without me adding to them. Ours was a deeply unhappy home. Most of the time, it was like my parents didn't even notice I was there. They were always at each other's throats, and half the time I had to take care of myself. They made promises they never kept, and many a time they didn't even come home, so I was left on my own. In the end, I stopped trusting them, but I had a good friend in Connie. She was always there for me. I owe her a lot.'

She was made to think of the uncomfortable atmosphere at home, and was shocked to realise how she had created that very same, destructive atmosphere in her own home, with Tom and Casey.

'So, you told Connie that you were with child?'

'I told her everything. She was my best friend. We grew up in the same street and we went to school together; we were always best mates. As soon as I found out, I went straight to her. She said I ought to get rid of it before I was too far on. I was surprised she told me to do such a thing, especially when I still hoped I might be able to contact Steve somehow. Though I knew it would have been difficult, because we never swapped addresses, or anything like that.'

'But how exactly did you tell him that you were carrying his child?'

Ruth smiled sadly. 'It was thanks to my friend, Connie. She wouldn't give up, you see. She said Steve had to face up to his responsibilities. Eventually, she discovered where he was booked to play next, but the tickets were all sold. Connie said we would have to wait at the side door, and hope to catch him when the band came out after the show.

'The day we were due to go, I'd been really bad with morning sickness. I felt tired and washed out, but I still wanted to face him with the truth. Connie wouldn't have it. She said I was too ill; that I should stay at home and get some rest. And, to be honest, I was in no fit state to argue. So I wrote a long letter to Steve, telling him about the baby, and Connie took it to him for me. Connie promised that if she got to speak with Steve on his own, she wouldn't leave until he'd read my letter.'

Ruth went on, 'Connie didn't get back until really late, but she told me the next morning what had happened. Apparently, she did manage to talk with Steve as he came out of the stage door. She took him aside and gave him the letter, which he read under a streetlamp. Then she explained how I was, and that I needed to see him; that things had to be sorted out.'

She took a deep breath. 'Apparently, he went crazy. He said he did not want to know. He claimed he could not possibly be the father, because he and his mates had played cards all night long after their Blackpool show, and that he had witnesses to prove it. He said he didn't remember Connie, and he didn't remember me; and that if she or I ever tried to get in touch with him again, or make such scandalous accusations, we would pay for it dearly.'

In a broken voice, she explained, 'Connie told him he was a liar and that we would not let him get away with it. She was really angry. She said to me that he was nothing like the friendly man we'd met, and that the threats he made were very real. She wanted me to go after him and take it through the courts, but I said no. I knew I could never challenge him like that; especially when Connie told me that he had some very powerful people behind him. In the end, when I decided to leave well alone, Connie agreed. She said I was well shot of him, and I should try and get rid of the kid if it wasn't too late. That way, there would be no responsibility for anyone, and I could get on with my life.'

The older woman kept silent for a while, thinking. When she now spoke it was in a quiet, measured voice. 'Well! If you ask me, she's right in one respect; you *are* well shot of a man like that. But, what about the baby? You didn't take her advice on that, did you?'

'To tell the truth, when I first found out I was pregnant,

I did try to get rid of the baby, but I didn't feel right about it, and anyway it didn't work. I never told Connie or anyone.'

In reluctant tones, she admitted, 'All this time, Tom had been in love with me – admiring me from afar, so to speak. I needed a husband, and quickly, and he was ready and willing. Besides, he was a good catch, with a well-paid job. In no time at all we were married and when Casey was born it was easy to pretend he was a premature baby. Tom never suspected a thing.'

Marilyn made no comment. She was shaken by Ruth's deliberate trickery, though it offered a glimpse of the desperation she must have felt at the time.

Ruth's manner softened. 'I know it was only one night with Steve, but I had fallen so head over heels in love with him, I knew I could never love any other man. It really hurt when he sent Connie away with anger and threats.'

'It's a pity you were not able to go and see him your-self.'

'I know, and I think Connie was more upset about the way he treated me than she let on. I wondered if she was tired of helping me with my troubles, because after Steve sent her packing, she was different; as though she blamed me for him threatening her . . . though she never said that.'

She distinctly remembered Connie's mood changes. 'Whenever we talked about Steve, she would change the subject, and later I suspected why she'd been so distant with me. Apparently, she was not all that settled in her own life, though she never mentioned it to me.'

'Really?'

'It all came to a head some time later. I went round on the Saturday as usual – we used to go to the market and look for cheap bargains, but her mam said she wasn't in; that she'd come home upset the night before. When

Connie told them she'd been sacked from her job at Woolworths, her parents blamed her for losing too much time off work. It seems there was a big row. Then, the next thing I know, she's packed her bags and gone to London, "looking for something better", she told her parents.'

'Were you surprised at that?'

'I'm not really sure, though I was surprised she didn't tell me. We used to tell each other everything, but not this time. I know now I was wrong to let her take my letter to Steve. It wasn't fair on her to have him threaten her because of me. I should have gone myself, no matter how ill I felt.'

'But you said she offered because she was worried about you feeling poorly. You didn't force her to go, remember that.'

'But it was after her encounter with Steve that she seemed to change towards me. It was like she blamed me when he loosed his temper on her. After that, she hardly spoke to me. She didn't even want to go out anywhere with me, and when, at first, I told her I had not given up on contacting Steve, she said that I should accept what had happened; that he'd made it clear enough that he didn't want to know, and how if I persisted on going after him, it would only bring me grief.'

'Well, maybe she was worried for you . . . especially, as you say, he had already made some very nasty threats.' In spite of Ruth's obvious affection for this particular 'friend', Marilyn was not altogether convinced of Connie's loyalty.

Ruth went on, 'I think she really was worried about me, but I don't suppose I'll ever know for sure, because she's never contacted me.'

'You miss her, don't you?' She could see it in Ruth's face and in her voice, whenever she talked about Connie.

'Oh, yes, I miss her a lot, but I wasn't altogether

surprised at her going. Connie was always ambitious, always sure that one day she would snag herself a millionaire and live the high life.'

Ruth recalled the last time she'd heard anything about Connie. 'She didn't write home for ages. Then her mam had a letter saying she was all right, and that she was doing well for herself. There was no return address, and she never contacted me, and, according to her mam, she never even mentioned me. I was really sorry about that, especially as we had known each other all our lives.'

'You must have been really hurt, when she cut you out of her life like that?' Marilyn already suspected that Ruth was no angel, but she couldn't help but feel a stirring of compassion for her predicament.

Ruth fell silent; her mind heavy with hurtful memories, and bitter betrayals. Ashamed and afraid, she covered her face with her hands.

Believing that Ruth's tears had been a long time coming, Marilyn made no comment. Instead, she lay a comforting hand on Ruth's shoulders, and for a time, that was how they remained; each with her own thoughts. Each needing a measure of companionship.

After a while, Ruth looked up, the pain deeply etched in her tear-smudged eyes. In a shaky whisper she confessed, 'When Steve denied me, and then Connie left like that, as though I meant nothing to her . . . that was when the badness took hold of me. I lost my trust in people, and I told myself never to care for anyone ever again, because they would always hurt me.'

'That's a very sad thing to say, Ruth.'

'Yes, I know that now. But the thing is, I made myself be harder inside. I never let anyone get close to me again. And now, I've been wicked for so long, I don't know how to be any different. I don't know which way to turn, or what to do any more.'

Anxious for this troubled young woman who had come into her life, Marilyn began to suspect that few people had ever noticed Ruth as a child growing up; few people had ever truly listened to her, or advised her, or even chastised her. Even worse, one by one, the people who might have cared for her most had callously abandoned her.

Consequently, she had been left without boundaries, without guidance or values, and because she had never experienced real affection, she had none to give out. She had never been able to love Tom, but with Steve it was different, because in the painfully short space of time she knew him, she had given herself to him heart and soul; in a way she had never before experienced. Steve had awakened something in her, and through the love they shared, the fragile beginnings of a life was created inside her.

Yet cruelly, for whatever reason, Steve had also abandoned her. As had her parents, and even her best friend and only confidante. So, one by one, in her heart she abandoned them in turn, and never again did she allow herself to love; not her devoted husband, nor her only child.

It was a sad thing. Easily done, but not so easily undone.

Marilyn had been deeply shocked at the devious and calculating manner in which Ruth had snared a fine man, and she now felt the need to remark on it. 'I understand what you must have felt like, after being let down by everyone you trusted. But from what I understand, you had a good husband in Tom, and your boy had a good father. So, why could you not love them?'

'Because I had no love to give.' Even now, though she blamed herself for Tom having taken his own life, Ruth could find no warmth in her heart either for him, or the boy; except maybe just a tinge of regret. 'The night we had that awful row, I said shameful things. I told Tom that he was not Casey's father. Casey heard, and I didn't even care because I wanted him to hear! I needed to hurt them both. To make them suffer, like I've suffered all these years.

'I never thought Tom would take his own life,' she cried brokenly. 'He made sure the boy was safe with his granddad, and then he . . . he . . .' She just couldn't say it, and her heart was breaking at the way she had driven that good man to his death. 'I never wanted that. I'm sorry. I'm so sorry . . .'

The weight of her guilt at what Tom had done was crippling, yet even so, she felt no stirrings of love for him.

'Ssh, child.' Marilyn cried with her. 'What's done is done, and it can never be undone.'

Ruth lost herself in the memories of Tom and his endless patience with her; of the boy, who had the looks and soul of his true father, the man who had callously turned his back on them both.

While Ruth sobbed, the older woman held her close, her own heart heavy with what she had learned.

'Be strong,' she whispered softly in Ruth's ear. 'I'll help you, if I can,' she promised. 'I won't abandon you.'

She held Ruth until all the sorrow was spent, and then she spoke her thoughts. 'I think you've bottled up all your emotions for too long, and now, maybe, just maybe, you can make a fresh start.'

She had a proposition to help Ruth get back on her feet again. 'As you've no doubt realised, I run a boarding house; though just now it's a quiet time. But my helper left a while back, and I do have need of someone. So, if you want the work, you're welcome to make this your home, for as long as you need.'

She now made a confession of her own. 'We all have something we would change, if we could. I mean, look at me. I was a bit wild myself as a young girl. I was independent and wilful, and by the age of thirty, my parents were gone, and my only sister had moved abroad. I was still single. I thought life was for having fun and doing the things you liked, without someone telling you what you should and shouldn't do. I thought I'd rather be free, to do as I liked and go where I wanted. Only it didn't work out the way I planned.'

Ruth gave a whimsical smile. 'Nothing ever does.'

'That's very true. I soon learned that having your independence, a good job and money to buy nice things and travel is all very well. Only, you soon find you're working doubly hard to earn money enough to live your dreams, and when you find them, they aren't really what you'd hoped they might be . . . if you know what I mean?'

'I think I know what you mean,' Ruth said. 'If you don't have anyone to share your dream, then it means nothing.' In that moment, she was not thinking of Tom, a loyal father and husband. Instead, she was thinking of Steve, a man she had spent one night with nine years ago. A man who had turned his back on her when she needed him most.

The older woman was still talking. 'In my case, I left it too late to find a truly good man; a man who might light up my life, bring me love, and share my dreams. That was never going to happen, so, after a while, I was made to settle for second-best, which is OK, but not what I'd planned.' She made a comical grimace. 'They do say we get what we deserve.'

Ruth understood. 'I'm sorry I couldn't love Tom,' she said. 'It was always Steve I wanted, but he didn't want me.'

'Well, like I said, water under the bridge. It's gone, and we can't bring it back, however much we'd like to. So, if you can, you need to put all your heartache and disappointments behind you, and follow a new plan.'

She scrambled out of her chair. 'Right then! It's late now, and you must be shattered. It's time to get you settled for the night.'

'I'd like that.' Ruth felt incredibly weary. 'I think I'd like to take you up on the offer of work and a place to live. Like you said, I need a plan.'

'Good, but you need to sleep on it before making rash decisions.' Marilyn hardly knew anything about this stranger. She didn't know what kind of person she was, and yet, in Ruth she saw a glimpse of her former self.

Chatting all the way, she led Ruth up the stairs and into the front bedroom.

'This was the previous girl's room,' she told her. 'It's a pretty little room, with its own toilet and wash facilities, and you'll find a clean nightgown in the airing cupboard on the landing. It's one of mine, so it'll probably drown you, but it'll do till we go shopping tomorrow. So! If tomorrow you still want to take up my offer of a job, this will be your room, and your wages will be four pounds a week, after board and lodgings. So, you think on it, and let me know in the morning.'

Ruth didn't need time to 'think on it'.

'I want the job,' she said. 'And I promise, I won't let you down.'

So it was agreed, and each went to her room reflecting on the night's events.

For a while, the older woman stood at her bedroom window, looking out at the night. 'Well, Lord, you certainly tried me out when you sent me this poor, lost soul,' she murmured to the skies. 'By her own admittance, she's done some bad things, but I reckon she might be worth the saving. I've done my best to help her, and maybe, just maybe, my offer of work and a roof over her head might soften the hardness in her. Hopefully, it might also restore her faith in human nature.'

She took a moment to think about Ruth, and the sorry confessions she'd made. Between us, we might discover whether she's worth the saving, she thought. Slowly, slowly though, eh? We'll have to wait and see, won't we?'

Having collected the nightgown from the airing cupboard, Ruth undressed, washed at the basin, and laughed out loud when the nightgown fell about her like a tent. But it was clean and it would keep her warm.

Marilyn Parker, you're a big, handsome lady, Ruth thought as, collecting the excess material into her hands, she smiled towards the door. And I'm very glad I found you.

Leaving the curtains open, she turned back the covers and climbed into bed. After sleeping rough, she found this little room to be a haven.

On the mantelpiece a little clock loudly ticked away the minutes, the rhythmic sound soothing her mind and lulling her into a much-needed sleep.

She was so tired. Her whole body hurt, and her heart ached with all manner of emotion. The sense of terror still lingered after her ordeal with those creatures of the night, leaving her feeling dirty, and shamed.

It was like she had been punished for her wickedness, but if that was so, she still had a long way to go before she might feel easier with herself. If ever.

When the men carried her away, like wolves with their prey, she feared she was about to meet her maker. That fear had shaken her to her very roots. Through the horror and the pain and the thought of worse to come, she saw herself as being no better than the creatures who had taken her.

For the first time, she knew the depth of badness in herself. It was a cruel revelation, and one that had her climbing out of bed and pacing the floor. After a while, and calmer now, she returned to the window.

In a whisper, she bared her soul to whoever might be listening up there, hiding behind the clouds. She spoke of her anger. Anger at her own failings. Anger at Steve, for turning her away as though she was nothing, as though the child inside her was nothing.

She was angry with Tom for allowing her to become the monster she was. The questions raged through her. Why didn't Tom hit out earlier? Why didn't he leave me? Why did he stay with me for all those years? Why could he not see how little I thought of him? How did he not realise that the boy was not his son? And how could he not see how much I loathed the boy?

Her thoughts returned to the callous way in which Steve had deserted her. 'And what about Steve? Someone I truly loved? And yet, what he did to me was only what I did to Tom, and the boy . . . causing them pain. Turning them away, as though *they* were nothing.'

Only now did she fully understand.

But it did not change the truth: that even now, seeing how it had been, she still felt no stirring of love for either Tom or the boy.

Curiosity overwhelmed her. I wonder how it might have been, if Steve had accepted me and the child? I wonder if things might have been different. I think I could have loved the boy, because I would have had his father. Isn't that so? Or is it just wishful thinking?

Either way, one thing was certain: it would never happen, because Steve was gone, and Tom was gone, and the boy was lost to her. She had no one, and nothing. Her life as she knew it was over.

'It's too late now,' she said aloud with a nervous little smile. 'So be it!'

Exhausted, she climbed back into bed and for a while her thoughts raced on. Tomorrow, she had decisions to make. More than ever, she must not be rash or take a wrong turn in her life. Yet she had been offered work and a place to lay her head. She had said yes, but was it what she really wanted?

Did she want to stay here, close to where she had suffered such an ordeal? Would she ever dare to venture out, in case those men saw her? Was it possible they might wait their chance to snare the prey they'd been cheated out of?

She had gladly given the landlady her word. Now, though, after giving it more serious thought, she was not sure what to do.

CHAPTER TEN

A T LONG LAST, the day had arrived.

Casey was so excited, he could hardly wait for his granddad Bob to get ready. He ran into the scullery. 'Hurry up, Granddad! We need to go. He might be closing early, or he might think we're not coming. Please, Granddad, hurry up!'

'Hey!' Speaking from the side of his mouth, the old man swirled the shaving brush over his stubbly chin. 'You'll 'ave me slicing a chunk outta me face if yer don't stop nagging! Read your *Beano* and be patient. I'll be done when I'm done, and not afore. So, be off with yer . . . go on! Let me finish shaving an' we'll be on our way.'

He shooed him out of the scullery. 'Yer mekkin' me a nervous wreck, yer impatient little bugger.' He quietly cursed when the razor edge caught him on the cheek.

'Sorry, Granddad.' Casey knew he should not be hounding his granddad, especially when he was shaving, but he was excited, and fearful at the same time, in case something might go wrong before they got there.

When Casey turned away, the old man gave a little grin. 'We'll be on our way soon, lad,' he muttered to himself, 'an' don't think I'm not excited as you are, because I am.'

He knew well enough what today meant for the boy. After all the sadness in Casey's young life, today was a chink of light; and it was a grand and welcome thing, for both the boy and himself.

When Granddad Bob appeared looking smart and tidy, Casey was impressed, but honest. 'You look like a brand-new man. Dolly won't like it, though, 'cause you look different.'

'O' course she will.'

Taking a deep, invigorating breath, the old fella collected his jacket from the door peg, then took out his wallet and checked that he had enough money. Now he was ready.

'Right, lad. It's time to go.'

The two of them went down the passageway and out the door, then Granddad Bob made sure the house was secured before they set off down the street. 'Oh, and don't forget, yer must say nowt. Yer to leave all the talking to me. I know how these people work.'

'How's that, Granddad?'

'Never you mind.' Giving a knowing wink, he tapped the side of his nose. 'He might be able to bamboozle his other customers, but not me, 'cause I've been around too long to be bamboozled by anybody.'

'Why would he want to bam . . . bomzle you, Granddad?'

'Well, 'cause from what I've been told, he's a canny businessman, and canny businessmen like to squeeze out a tidy profit for themselves, sometimes at the expense of unwary customers.'

'Are you an unwary customer?'

'Never!'

'So, that's good then, isn't it?'

'Absolutely!'

A short time later, with Casey skipping ahead, they reached the bus stop. Having watched the bus draw in, they were surprised to see Dolly climbing down off the platform, carrying two shopping bags full to the brim.

'You're back early, lass.'

'That's because I set off early.' Moving in with these two boys had made her happier than she'd been for a very long time. She'd given up her rented house beside the railway, given Bartie to Billy next door – which pleased both man and dog – and then, with Patrick's help and the now empty wagon, Bob had arranged to collect her belongings.

Granddad gave her a peck on the cheek before she stooped to give Casey a cuddle. She couldn't help but note the boy's impatience to be away.

'We're off to collect the guitar,' Granddad reminded her, 'but there's time enough for us to help you home with them heavy bags.'

Dolly would have none of it, especially with Casey dancing on the spot with excitement. 'Thank you for the offer,' she feigned indignation, 'but I'm not so feeble I can't carry a couple of shopping bags on my own.' She ushered Casey onto the bus. 'Be off, the pair of you, and be careful, eh?' Playfully running her hand through the old fella's sleeked-back hair, she helped him onto the bus.

As she waved them off, she laughingly called out, 'Oh, and I prefer my men with a bit o' stubble, so don't scrape it off again, Bob, it doesn't suit yer. And while yer at it, tek that paper off your cheek. Yer look like you've been in a road accident.'

'See! I knew she wouldn't like it.' Casey couldn't help but smile.

Slightly irritated, the old fella shoved the boy into his seat and plopped down beside him. 'OK, OK, so I were wrong and you were right,' he said grudgingly. 'But for the future, you need to remember a little knowledge is a bad thing.'

'That's not what my teacher says. She says knowledge opens many doors.'

'Is that so? And which doors are we talking about?'

'I don't know.'

'Well, you'd best ask 'er, and when you know, you'd best tell me.'

While Casey was thinking, the conductor arrived. 'Town centre is it?' He popped a stick of chewing gum into his mouth.

'That's it, yes . . . oh, and mek 'em returns, will yer?'

'Right.' He threw the chewing gum round his teeth. 'So, it's one senior, and one child for the town centre?'

'Correct. So, how much is that, then?'

'One and fourpence, please.' He waited while the old fella found the right change.

Having heard the exchange between the old man and the woman who got off, he asked, 'Cut yourself shaving, did you?'

'Might 'ave.' Bob had had enough of discussions concerning his stubble.

The mangled chewing gum did acrobatics on the conductor's tongue. 'So, did you, or didn't you?'

'Yes, I did, as it 'appens.'

Casey joined the conversation. 'It were my fault. I kept bothering him. That's why he cut himself.'

'Your fault, eh?' Smiling, the conductor glanced at the old fella. 'That's kids for you,' he groaned. 'Little sods, they are! I've got three, and I should know.'

Without another word, he quickly wound the tickets from the machine round his neck, dropped the fare into his leather satchel, and with his tongue blowing bubbles through the chewing gum, he sauntered off, humming a merry tune.

Behind him, hoping that the bleeding had stopped, Bob peeled the paper from his cheek. 'Damned rude, if yer ask me . . . chewing that gum with his mouth open in front o' folk!' He'd been unnerved by the sight of that chewing gum, 'Jigging about like cement in a mixer, it were!'

'What did you say, Granddad?' Casey was preoccupied, thinking about his guitar.

'Nowt, lad.' He shook his head. 'I said nowt.'

Casey knew his granddad had been surprised at Dolly's response to his flattened hair, so he left him well alone, and thought about where they were headed.

His excitement grew, and he could hardly wait.

~

They arrived at the boulevard some ten minutes later, with the conductor helping the old fella off, and the old fella helping the boy off. 'I thank you for your help,' Bob advised the conductor, '. . . and I know my old legs aren't what they used to be. But I do not tek kindly to being helped off the bus, an' I'd like yer to remember that.'

'Oh, I will, and I'm very sorry I must say.' The conductor was familiar with Granddad Bob, and he'd forgotten how proud and independent he was. 'Just trying to help, that's all.'

The old fella afforded him a tight little smile, but chose not to answer. Instead, Bob took Casey across the road, past the church, and on to King Street. 'It's nobbut a skip an' a stride to the shop from 'ere, lad.'

Taking hold of the boy's hand, he led the way at a smart pace until, coming onto Whalley Banks, he got a bit breathless. 'We'd best slow down now,' he told Casey. 'I need a minute to gather mesel'.'

Breathless and leg-weary, he made a pretence of stopping to look into a shop window, but when Casey asked if he was all right, he stood up straight and marched on.

'Let me do all the talking when we get there,' he warned. 'Y'see, I'm not too familiar with this partic'lar fella. It were our old friend Frank as told us about him, so you just watch and listen, while I do the business. All right?'

'Yes, Granddad.'

'Good . . . oh, hey-up, we're almost there!' After passing the tripe shop, they were at their destination, their attention drawn to the fascinating bric-a-brac displayed in the windows.

The shelves in both bay windows were a feast for the eyes. Dressed in all manner of beautiful and curious things, they made a fine show. There were ornaments, brass, china and wooden artefacts, bronze and silver medals from the wars, and any amount of heavy, handsome jewellery from a bygone age.

'By!' Granddad Bob took a moment to peruse the display. 'If a fella were looking to buy his lady-friend a present, 'e wouldn't know where to start.'

Like Granddad Bob, Casey was overawed, just as he had been the one and only other time they'd been here when they took the guitar in.

'Are you going to buy Dolly a present?' He saw Granddad Bob eyeing up what looked like a neckerchief.

'Not at these prices I'm not. Unless he's got summat hidden away that fits my pocket.'

'Why don't we ask him then?'

'We'll do no such thing. Once you show an interest, there's no stopping 'em. Like them crafty crabs, they'll catch hold of yer, an' won't let go no how.'

'So, you're not getting Dolly a present then?'

'I'm not saying that exactly, but we didn't come 'ere to buy presents, as well yer know. Then again, I'm not altogether ruling it out. I'm just saying, if I'm of a mind, and if I can afford it after we've paid the bill, I might think about it. But you remember what I said, lad.'

He tapped the side of his nose as a reminder. 'You leave all the talking to me, lad.'

~

Jake Morrison watched them at the window, enjoying their friendly bickering, though, annoyingly, he could not make out what the old man and the boy were bickering about.

Standing behind the counter and watching the goings-on outside his shop was a favourite pastime. Often he would stand there for ages, just watching and listening. Some folks were convinced that he lived, ate and slept behind that counter. Unshaven, unkempt and sloppily attired in a once-fine suit of fading blue check, he presented an image that made this easy to believe.

'Good morning to you.' Leaping from behind his beloved counter, he swung open the door. He swirled his arm in a welcoming gesture. 'Please . . . come inside.' His thick, wayward hair had long since turned grey, and fell round his shoulders like a mantle. But it was the eyes that drew the attention: darkest green and ocean-deep, they took the attention away from his sloppy suit, wild hair and chin bristles.

When he spoke it was with a somewhat refined voice, the legacy of a wealthy childhood. As a boy he was educated in the most expensive schools, where he was taught fine music and good manners; though his privileged experience did not prepare him for the bitter fight that emerged in his early manhood, after the sad loss of his beloved father.

The unhappy event involved his father's will and Jake's wayward brother, the bane of his father's life, but the apple of his mother's eye.

Deeply shaken by the deep and bitter rift that grew

between himself, his sibling and his mother, Jake succumbed to a spiral of wine, women and gambling until, in his late thirties, a near-fatal accident made him realise that life was too short to waste in such a way.

He found a new direction. He threw himself into working every hour he could, for anyone who would employ him, regardless of how difficult or demanding the work might be, and he saved every penny possible.

Disowned by his family, his determination to build up a business was never dimmed, though it took long, hard years to save money enough to take out a lease on the little shop he now owned; and to buy enough small artefacts to tempt the customers. The initial weeks of trading were not a huge success, but with the sale of one artefact, he would buy two more, and so his stock grew in number and quality.

He was a businessman at last, and on the side he would teach music for one afternoon a week, thus increasing his income until he had a cosy little home, a shop window bursting with beautiful things, and the pleasure of knowing that he was his own boss.

Over these past years, he often wondered what his mother and brother would say about him having been successful; not in a huge way, but in a way that meant he was the architect of his own life, at last.

Sadly, though, success came at a price. By the age of forty, he got out of bed in the morning and there was no one to talk with. He went to bed at night with no one to hold. He might laugh at a thought, and there was no one to ask what he was laughing at. Or he might be low, and there was no one to lift his spirits, except maybe the odd customer now and then. His bank account was now quite respectable, but there was no one to share it, and so he remained a lonely man, hungry for the company of someone who might love and cherish him.

At night he would retire to his lonely bed and wish with all his heart that one day, some sweet person might walk into his shop and he would know that this was the day when his life would truly begin. So far, it had not happened, but he held onto the possibility because the idea of him being alone for evermore was too daunting to contemplate.

'I see you've got Casey with you.' Reaching out with a grubby hand, he ruffled Casey's hair. 'It's good to see you, young man. Excited, are you?'

'Yes, thank you.' As on the previous occasion when he'd met Jake Morrison, Casey was overawed; by Jake's eccentric appearance and his voice, which was nothing like his granddad's voice, being sort of posh, and kind of musical.

As for Jake, he had met Granddad Bob and Casey just the once, but he had taken a strong liking to them both. He was aware of the tragic manner in which this good man had lost his son, and then the aftermath of the boy's mother taking off, leaving the child in the care of his granddad. He knew all about family break-ups, and he knew it must have been a very difficult time for these two.

Bob greeted Jake warmly. 'All right, are you?'

'I am, thank you, yes.'

The old fella moved the conversation on. 'So is it ready, then?'

'It is, and though I say it myself, I've done a first-class job on it. I must say, it was a broken mess and no mistake. I've tuned it, played it and polished it, and now all it needs is tenderness.'

'You've played it, you say?'

'Of course. I wouldn't be doing my work properly if I didn't play it. How else would I know if its character was intact?'

Casey had been bursting to speak, and now he could hold himself back no longer. 'Please, Mr Morrison, can I see it . . . please?' It seemed such an age since he'd held his daddy's guitar.

Jake nodded. 'Of course, young man. After all, I understand it's your guitar.' He turned on his heel and went smartly into the back room.

'By! It's been a long time coming, eh, lad?' Granddad Bob knew how concerned the boy was. 'Don't worry, I'm told this man knows everything there is to know about guitars and such, and I'm sure he's done a grand job.' His voice hardened. 'If he hasn't, then he'll be in for a rough ride, you mark my words.'

After what seemed an aching few minutes, Jake returned.

'When you brought the guitar in, it was in an old nylon case, and wrapped in a paper bag, so I took the liberty of searching out an old leather case of mine. It will offer more protection, and it's more fitting for such a splendid instrument. I'm sorry to have taken such liberties, but I'd like you to have it, and I hope you're not offended?'

'Not at all.' The old fella was grateful. 'We never did have a proper case for it, but I hope you're not about to charge us the earth, because if you are—'

'No!' Jake stopped him. 'It's a present, from me to your grandson . . . if he wants it, that is?'

'Oh, yes, please.' Casey thought it was a wonderful present. 'My daddy could never afford a leather one.'

He thought about his father, and his heart was heavy. 'I'm so glad you mended the guitar, Mr Morrison.'

'So am I, Casey. It's an extremely good guitar, with beautiful tone and presence.'

'That's what Granddad says.'

Jake and the old fella exchanged smiles. 'Right then. So now, it's the moment of truth.'

Tenderly laying it onto the counter, Jake carefully removed the instrument from the case.

'Oh, look, Granddad . . . look!' Jumping up and down on the spot, Casey gasped with excitement. 'Look, Granddad, it's all mended!'

Overwhelmed with emotion, he ran to Jake and locked his arms round his legs. 'Thank you . . . thank you so much.' Partly thinking of what his daddy might have said, and partly because he'd feared the guitar could never be put right, his young heart was full to bursting, and now he could not stop the tears.

'Oh, now, now, Casey. You and your granddad did me a favour. It was a joy to work on your guitar.' Having been alone these many years, Jake was taken aback with the boy's tearful gratitude. 'It should be me thanking you, not the other way round.'

Somewhere deep inside, amongst all the bad memories of the downfall of his earlier life, he felt deeply indebted for the few pleasures he had; and especially just now for the gratitude of this young boy.

Stooping to Casey's level, he held him at arm's length, his voice quiet, and his manner gentle. 'I want you to know that, for me, bringing your guitar back to life really was a labour of love.'

'Was it?' Casey wasn't sure what he meant.

Jake explained, 'Something happened to me many years ago, and it made me turn my back on my love for music. When your granddad brought me the broken guitar, I looked on all the sorry pieces and I wondered if I would ever be able to put it back together, and if I did, would it ever be the same again.'

The painful memories of the bad years flooded back. 'When I left home as a young man, I felt like that – all broken and torn inside. And now, after spending many hours taking apart your guitar and then working on it, bringing it back to life . . .' he took a long, shivering breath, '. . . it was as though I was taking apart all the bad memories. Soon I realised how foolish I'd been to turn my back on the many things that I loved, like playing the piano and the violin, and all the other beautiful instruments I was taught to play as a child.'

He gave a little self-conscious smile. 'D'you know, Casey, I even wrote a song once. Oh, it wasn't much good because I was only twelve, but it was mine, and I felt very proud.'

'I did that, too. With Daddy.'

Jake's heart saddened as he looked into Casey's eyes. 'About your guitar – how can I explain? Well . . . it's a bit like finding an old and valued friend after you thought you would never see them again.'

Glancing reassuringly at the old fella, he then looked down on Casey's upturned face, his voice almost inaudible as he told him, 'A very long time ago – oh, long before you were even born – I was brought up with music all around me. It was in the air, it was part of our everyday conversations, it was in the blood . . . my birthright, almost.'

'That's good, isn't it?' Casey felt the undertow of emotion.

'Well, yes. I was very fortunate. My father was a classical pianist, and my mother sang in concert. When my father played, I used to sit at the stool alongside him, and I would watch the keys go up and down. I would follow my father's nimble fingers as they ran over the keys, and I marvelled at the beautiful sounds that he created.'

The bad memories had crippled Jake, but it was these good memories that kept him warm at night. 'As I grew a little older, my father would let me rest my hand on the back of his, and when he played, I would feel the vibrations from the keys. It was like the music was going right through me.'

Casey was amazed. 'That's how I feel when I play the guitar!'

Jake smiled knowingly. 'Well, there you are, my boy. You have the gift, and the guitar responds. It's a very special guitar, and that's because it's been loved and cherished. The thing is, some people were born to embrace the music, while others will never know, or even want to know. The magic comes from playing or singing, or even simply working on musical instruments, like I worked on your guitar.'

He smiled knowingly. 'I thought I might have lost the touch, but thankfully, it's still there – that special sense of discovery and excitement – and I feel alive again. Working on your guitar made me joyful . . .' he tapped his chest, '. . . in here. It wasn't the music that deserted me, it was I who had deserted the music. Only now do I realise how much I missed it.'

'I'm glad, Mr Morrison.' Casey flung his arms round Jake's neck. 'I'm so glad. 'And I know my daddy will be glad as well.' In that very special moment, he felt truly proud.

Jake now addressed Granddad Bob. 'I've never confided this in anyone before.'

The memories were hurtful. 'I was always close to my father, and after he passed on, there was a family fallout between my mother and my elder brother – all to do with the sizeable amount of money my father left. When the solicitors got involved and the bitter fight began over who had what, I saw a side to my family that sickened me. So I turned my back on everyone and everything. Sadly, that also included the music.'

'It must have been painful for you.' It was clear to the old fella that Jake had paid a high price for his family's greed. 'From what you say, I reckon I'd 'ave done the same. It's a sad thing, but true, that wherever there's a will, greed and jealousy are bound to rear their ugly heads.'

'That's right.' Jake continued in a quiet voice, 'I had a few good artefacts given to me over the years – birthday presents and suchlike – so I took them all and sold them off one by one, as and when needs must. They helped me to survive. When they were gone, I put my musical prowess to good use. I taught children to play. I tuned a piano here and there, and one way or another, I managed to scrape a living. But I never played again.' He took a moment to remember. 'To tell you the truth, I lost heart.'

He smiled on Casey. 'Thankfully, I'm happier and more focused than I've been for all these years because you and your granddad trusted me with your beloved guitar.'

Listening to Jake's story, Casey was shocked and sad. It made him realise how lucky he was to have known his wonderful daddy; to have his granddad, and Dolly, and now his guitar. Every night he cried for his daddy, although he was careful not to let Granddad Bob hear him. Yet there was also a small part of him that cried for his mam.

The old fella, too, had been deeply moved by Jake's confession. 'Did you never contact your family again?' he asked.

'No, and I never will. Too much bitterness was festering. Too much was said that couldn't be unsaid, and besides, I've found my place in life, and I'm happy.' He smiled. 'I'm sorry for chatting on. I've never spoken to anyone about my past before.'

'Me and the boy . . . we're glad to have been here for you. Rest assured, what you've said here today will go no further.'

'Thank you, both.'

Collecting the guitar, he held it out to Bob. 'So now, you need to satisfy yourself that the guitar plays as it should play.'

Taking the guitar from him, the old fella turned it over in his hands and after strumming a few chords, he smiled.

'It's good, yes.' He was pleased. 'It's well tuned and the pitch is just right.'

Jake was pleased. 'You need to play it,' he urged.

Without a word, Granddad Bob brought his gaze to the boy, and it was as though a kind of understanding passed between them. 'You know what, Jake,' he kept his gaze on the boy, while addressing the other man, 'I reckon there's only one person who can tell you whether you've managed to keep the character of this very special guitar.'

'I see.' Jake followed Bob's loving gaze, and he felt that he was part of something deep and beautiful between the old man and the boy.

With a proud and aching heart for his lost son, Granddad Bob gave the guitar into the boy's uplifted arms. 'Make it sing, lad,' he whispered shakily. 'And remember,' he gave a reassuring wink, 'your daddy's listening.'

Handing the guitar to the boy, he glanced at Jake, while brushing aside the solitary tear that trickled down his weathered old face.

Cradling the guitar, Casey thought he had never been happier in the whole of his life than he was right now; except for when his daddy first let him play his guitar.

He took a moment to think of his daddy, then, sitting on the edge of the chair, he settled himself comfortably. With the guitar in place and his heart fluttering like a bird, he smiled up at the two men.

'Are you ready, Granddad?'

'Oh, yes, lad . . . we're ready.'

The two men did not know what to expect and Jake in particular, was nervous. First, even though it had been restored and tuned to perfection, it was possible that the instrument might not be exactly the same as before. Like a person, a guitar had a heart, and that heart was created by years of playing it and caring for it. During that very special bonding period, the player and the instrument became almost as one. The player would bring the instrument to life, and the guitar would echo the mood of its master.

In that low-lit, cluttered room, the two men waited. Granddad Bob sent up a silent prayer, asking that the boy would play from the heart, and that holding the guitar that his daddy had held might bring him a measure of comfort.

He knew what a bittersweet trial it would be for Casey to sing and to play like his daddy had taught him. Now, though, as Casey prepared himself, he felt the boy's determination, and his old heart swelled with pride.

Jake Morrison, however, simply crossed his fingers behind his back, hoping his delicate workmanship would meet with their approval.

'What shall I play, Granddad?'

'Whatever you like, lad. Mebbe for now you could just play the lovely melody that you and your daddy wrote together?' The old fella recalled the very day. It had been his sixtieth birthday. Tom and Casey came to his house to sing the song they'd written just for him, and to this day it remained one of his most precious memories.

Closing his eyes, Casey did what he had seen his father do; he slowly ran his hands over the instrument, in his heart and mind renewing his relationship with the guitar, and allowing the memories to gentle through him.

Because of what Granddad had just told him, and because of the way he felt inside, Casey truly believed that his daddy would hear every note he played and, more than anything else, he did not want to disappoint him.

So, with his eyes downcast, he began to play, and the words fell from his lips naturally, even though it had been a long time since he and his daddy had sung them together.

When you have . . . someone to love,
The world . . . is a beautiful place . . .
When the wind blows cold . . . and the skies grow dark,
Love holds the sunshine . . . strong in your heart.

There were three verses, and Granddad Bob knew them by heart. Each line added to the story of a man's love for his family. They revealed the joy he felt, and showed the wonder of having someone to lift your heart, even on the darkest day.

As Casey sang, the two men in his audience were made to think on what they had each lost through the years.

Granddad Bob thought of his late beloved wife, Anne, and the son, Tom, who had been taken from him too soon, though he felt blessed that he had a wonderful grandson who was both caring and talented. Also, he was extra blessed, because he had been given a second chance at love, with the lovely Dolly.

Jake was reminded of the special relationship he had had with his dear father, and the awful bickering that had torn his family apart. Already he had been made to realise how lonely his life had become. Now, though, on hearing Casey's song, he fleetingly entertained the idea of a reconciliation with his family.

In a low, emotionally charged voice, Casey continued the song. He felt the guitar come alive in his hands, and his tears were not far away. In his mind his daddy's image was wonderfully clear, and at one point the boy gave a little smile, as though to his daddy.

As he played, he recalled the very day when he and his daddy had sung the song to Granddad Bob. He even remembered the old man having a tear in his eyes, like now.

He could even recall what his daddy had told him before they set off for Granddad Bob's house: 'It's not a proper song, nor is it perfect, but then nothing is. Anyway, m'boy, your granddad will love it because he'll know we wrote the words to tell him how much we cherish him. Oh, and best of all, nobody else will ever have a present like it. So there we are!'

Now, in that most curious place, the touching words and gentle music carried through the room. The music was joyous, and the boy's melodic voice, though familiar to the old fella, was most surprising to Jake.

When the last note reverberated through the shop, everyone clapped.

In a shaky voice Granddad Bob told Casey, 'By! Your daddy would be so proud of yer, lad . . . as I am.'

Jake said he had not been moved like that in a very long time. 'It was wonderful.'

'That were really lovely!' Having listened from outside, Patrick Riley had crept in so quietly, the others were unaware that he was there. 'I never heard anything so sweet in all me life. You've a voice like an angel, so ye have!' He apologised to Bob. 'I'm sorry to have interrupted, but I'm not here to buy anything . . . as if I could, with no money in me pockets. And even if I had, I wouldn't be so flippant as to waste it on fancy things, as you well know, Bob.' He nodded to the old fella.

'So why have you come in then?' Knowing his old friend, Bob was ready for a long, outlandish tale.

'Why do ye tink I came in?' Paddy was insulted.

'Well, I don't know, do I? That's why I'm asking.'

'For your information, I came in because I got a fright. I don't mind telling ye, I heard the music, and the loveliest voice, and I thought the angels had come to fetch me, so I did!'

Granddad Bob chuckled. 'That tells me you had a few pints too many last night. Am I right?'

'I'm saying nothing.' Patrick made a comical face.

'You don't need to.'

'I will say one thing though, Bob.' Patrick's gaze softened as it fell on Casey. 'That wee boy is too talented to be one o' yours.'

'You're right, Patrick. When I sing, the dogs howl in the street.'

When Granddad Bob looked on Casey, he saw a small, lost boy, who pined for his daddy, and his heart ached. Without a word, he opened his arms and the boy ran to him.

'I wish Daddy was here.' Casey's voice cracked with emotion. 'Do you really think he was listening, Granddad?'

'Aye, lad, I do. An' I reckon he's celebrating up there, telling everyone how proud he is.' Placing his finger beneath the boy's chin, he lifted his face to look at him. 'We're all proud of you, lad.' He smiled at his old friend. 'And look there, you even brought Patrick in off the streets. What d'yer think to that, eh?'

'I think it's really good.' With a shaky smile, he looked at Patrick. 'Thank you, Patrick. I'm glad you came in to listen.'

'I couldn't help it,' Patrick confessed. 'Sure, the minute I heard you play the guitar, oh, and then the singing . . .' he threw his arms out in a gesture of amazement, '. . . well now, I'm telling ye straight, me feet had a mind o' their own. Before I knew it, I was inside the shop, an' me feet were glued to the floor, so they were.'

Delighted with the Irishman's involvement, Casey asked, 'Did *your* feet get glued to the floor, Mr Morrison?'

'Well, young man, like your friend here,' he gestured to Patrick, 'I think I also must have been glued to the floor, because even if the shop caught fire, I would have had to stay until you'd finished your song. In all my life, I have never heard anything more beautiful.'

'Thank you, Mr Morrison, and I think your shop is beautiful too, so I hope it doesn't catch fire.'

Granddad Bob had listened to these two men – so different in taste and background, yet brought together by the talents of his grandson – and he was so proud he could burst. 'He's right, lad!' he told Casey. 'They're both right. And we mustn't forget we owe Mr Morrison a debt of gratitude, for bringing your guitar back to life.'

When Casey thanked Jake again, he replied solemnly, 'With great respect, your granddad is wrong, Casey. It wasn't me who brought your guitar back to life, it was you. All I did was to put the pieces back together again.'

Patrick had an idea. 'I'm wondering if you'd like to earn a bob or two playing your guitar, lad – if your granddad will allow it, I mean?' He gave a wary glance at the old fella. 'As you know, Bob, I keep a market stall of a Saturday, an' I were wondering if the lad might want to play beside my stall? Folks would be so delighted, they're sure to drop a coin or two into his hat. What d'you say?'

Casey began jumping up and down with excitement. 'Please, Granddad, can I? Oh, I'd like to play for people . . . please?'

'Mmm.' Granddad Bob needed to think. He pursed his lips, then he sucked his bottom lip, and now he was staring down at the boy. 'You'll still need to do your schoolwork, and be in bed by eight-thirty . . . every night, mind!'

'I will, Granddad, I promise.'

'And if the folks like you so much that they drop coins into your hat, like Patrick said, what would you do with 'em?'

'I'd give them to you.'

'Think again, lad.'

'All right, if you don't want them, I'd give them to Dolly.'

'Nope.'

'I'd save them in a jar then.'

'No, you won't, lad.'

For a moment, Casey was confused as to what he should do if the people gave him coins. And then it dawned on him. 'I'll give them to Patrick.'

'Well said, lad. And why would you do that?'

'Because if it wasn't for him letting me play at his stall, the people would never hear me, and so the coins would be a thank you to Patrick for being our friend.'

'Hey! You'll do no such thing.' Patrick protested. 'The coins would be yours and yours alone. I'm not in the habit of taking coins from a lad. What next, eh?'

Casey was disappointed 'I just want to say thank you.'

'All right then,' Patrick had an idea, 'I'll tell you what, lad . . .' he gave a sly wink at Bob, '. . . if you're really set on saying a little thank you, I've got a suggestion.'

'What's that then?' Casey brightened up.

'Well . . . you know how the flowerseller lets the flowers go for a few pennies at the end of the day?'

'Yes, I know that, Patrick.'

'Right, well then, what if you spend a few of your pennies on buying a little bunch o' flowers for my wife?' He groaned. 'It might stop her nagging at me. She never stops nagging at me. If it's not about the birds who've been pecking at the milk bottle top, she's nagging about the lavvie leaking in the cellar.' He adopted a hangdog expression. 'The woman drives me mad, so she does. I keep telling her, if it affects her that badly, I'll fetch the wash bucket up of a morning, and we can leave a plate out for the milkman to cover the bottle tops. But as for the lavvie, I've got that in hand. John Lassiter owes me a favour, and from what I've heard, he's a dab hand at mending leaks. I'm seeing him next week to see if we can cobble a deal together. So now, lad, if you're in agreement about the flowers, we'll both be satisfied. Mind you, I want you to have enough pennies left over, to treat yourself OK?'

Casey gazed up. Waiting nervously for an answer, he kept his sorry gaze on Patrick's weathered old face.

'OK, yes. And this has to be the last time you spend any of your hard-earned pennies on me, or the missus, so you remember that, lad. And remember also that you will always be free to play your guitar beside my stall.'

Bob clapped his hands. 'You've got a deal, yes! It's no different from what we've allus done. You help us and we help you. It doesn't really matter what we barter, as long as we're helping each other.'

'Right, so make sure you get the boy to my stall on Saturday, round about one o'clock. Folks are always in a good mood by then, 'cause they've had their bite to eat and they're in a mood to spend their hard-earned brass, so they are.'

Patrick was tickled pink at the prospect of his woman getting a little bunch of flowers. 'I've never been one for soppy gestures like that,' he muttered as he went away down the street, '. . . but you never know. If she gets a bunch o' flowers, I might get a thank you of the like I've not had for many a month.'

He chuckled at the naughty thought, and went away with a renewed spring in his step.

CHAPTER ELEVEN

A FEW DAYS AFTER rescuing the woman from her attackers, Steve was still in Blackpool. All was not going to plan with his site purchase, and he was having to stay longer in the North to see it through. Luckily it was the school holidays and so Alice and Susie were able to stay on too, with the little girl enjoying the seaside.

After reluctantly agreeing to read her a story at the end of a long day, Steve tucked Susie into bed. 'Now then, Little Miss Know-all, you'd best remind me which page we were on, because I've forgotten.'

'It's all right, Uncle Steve, I remember.' Collecting the book from under her pillow, she handed it to him. 'We got to page fifteen.'

'Oh, yes, I remember now. Wasn't it where Mandy fell out with her best friend, and now she's unhappy?' Since reading to Susie, he should have discovered a great deal about female relationships, but all he'd learned was to keep his nose out wherever possible.

'I want them to make up and be good friends again, don't you, Uncle Steve?'

Steve assured her in a solemn voice, 'There is nothing I want more,' thinking the sooner the characters made up with each other, the sooner he would be let off the hook. 'Why didn't you let Mummy read it to you? Then you'd be fast asleep by now.'

'Mummy doesn't read it like you do,' Susie told him. 'You make the characters seem alive, and you change your voice, and it's really funny.'

Flattered but weary, he took a deep breath and commenced, '*Mandy did not know what to do. Her friend Jenny had really upset her, because she had told lies, and that was a bad thing . . .*'

'Was it?' Susie interrupted.

Steve glanced up. 'Absolutely! Always remember, lies will get you nowhere.'

'I know that.'

'So why did you ask?'

'Stop talking, Uncle Steve. I want to know what Mandy does.'

He read on, '*At school on Tuesday, Mandy saw her friend Jenny talking to the other girls, and they were all staring at her. It made her feel very uncomfortable . . .*'

'That's awful! Jenny shouldn't do that, should she, Uncle Steve?'

Exasperated with the interruptions, Steve asked, 'Susie, do you want us to talk, or do you want me to read?'

'I want you to answer my question, please. After that, I want you to read.'

'Well, I'm reading now . . . and please don't interrupt, because it puts me right off my stride. You can ask your questions when I stop. All right?'

'You said I put you "off your stride". What does that mean?'

'Well, I'm just getting into the characters and then you blurt out a question, and then I don't know where I am.'

'Are you angry with me?'

'Not yet, but I'm getting there.'

'OK, I'll stop interrupting.'

'Good!' Fixing his gaze on the page, he searched for the line. 'See that! I've lost my place now.'

'Well, you should concentrate. Don't you know anything?'

Beaten as always, Steve had to agree. 'You're right, but I'm very tired and I've had a setback with the property, and your mummy and I haven't had time to speak with each other today.'

'Please, Uncle Steve, read the story.'

'I will, if you stop chattering.'

Susie crossed her chest. 'I won't chatter. Hand on heart, promise.'

Steve took a deep breath, and resumed the story.

For the next few minutes it flowed beautifully, though he twice looked up from the reading, eager to assure himself that she was paying attention.

The first time he glanced up, Susie was so tired she was struggling to keep her eyes open; then a few moments later, he was relieved to find that she'd slithered down between the sheets and was fast asleep.

Gently, so as not to wake her, he drew the bedcover up to her shoulders, then he placed the book inside the drawer and crept out on tiptoe, softly closing the door behind him.

Once outside, he gave a sigh of relief. I thought tonight we might actually get to the end of the story, he told himself as he ran down the main stairs two at a time.

A moment later, he was relieved to find Alice in the bar, perched on a stool and looking pretty as always.

'I thought you might have gone up already,' he remarked. 'The reading took longer than I expected, what with Miss Chatterbox interrupting every other word.'

'Huh! If you think her interrupting the story is hard, you wouldn't have wanted to be with us today.' Alice rolled her eyes in frustration. 'Susie marched me all over the place as if she intended seeing and doing everything before we have to go home.'

'That's our Susie for you. When her mind is set, she won't take no for an answer.' Steve gestured to a small table by the window. 'How about we sit over there?'

'Fine by me,' Alice smiled. 'So, you managed to get her off to sleep, did you?'

'Eventually, after a little banter or two, and always when I'm in the flow of the story.'

'She does that to me, then it takes a while to find the place where I left off.'

'Really?' Steve laughed out loud. 'Well, it's time you learned to concentrate. Don't you know anything?'

'Cheek!' She gave him a playful slap on the arm. 'That sounded like something Susie might have said.'

They both laughed, recognising Susie and her old-fashioned ways.

Steve gave the bartender the order, and signed for the drinks. 'It's quiet in here tonight.' He was surprised to see just one other couple in the bar.

'It's a quiet time of year,' the bartender answered. 'It's been mostly businessmen this week, and they've moved on.'

'Which is what I had planned to do.' Steve had been disappointed in the need to stay another week, to discuss his plans in greater detail. 'I should have known it was too ambitious a plan.'

Making the drinks, the bartender was thinking he had his own problems. 'Shall I bring your drinks over, sir?'

Thanking him, Steve joined Alice at the other end of the room. 'You look tired,' he told her kindly. 'So, our Susie's been giving you the run-around, has she?'

'You could say that. We went to Blackburn today and we must have been in every shop in the town centre. Then she wanted to walk along King Street, and she heard some boy playing the guitar in one of the shops. She wouldn't even budge until he'd finished.'

Alice, too, had been amazed by the boy's talent. 'I'm telling you, Steve, she had her nose pressed tight to the window for ages. Then all the way back to the bus stop, she kept talking about him, saying how the boy had been on the bus the other day, and he was really nice, and she wanted to go inside the shop to listen, but she was too shy.'

'Shy? Our Susie? I don't think so.' Steve recalled the boy on the bus. 'More like she was too embarrassed to go inside, in case he recognised her. The boy on the bus didn't know where to put himself when she kept smiling at him. So, if he was the same lad, he wouldn't have thanked her for going into the shop to watch him play the guitar.'

Alice made a serious face. 'It's no good,' she said mournfully, 'my daughter is out of control. If she doesn't pull herself together, I'll have no choice but to put her in a nunnery.'

Steve laughed out loud. 'Have a heart for the nuns. Our Susie would run rings round them. I reckon you should get her a job on a building site. That'll teach 'em.'

Now it was Alice's turn to laugh. 'Honestly, Steve, she had me worn out today. But it was good to see her so interested in everything. She loved every minute of it, while, by the end, all I wanted to do was get back and soak my aching feet in cold water.'

She had to admit, 'I did enjoy the day, though. I never dreamed that Corporation Park was so magnificent, with pretty, meandering walkways and lots of majestic old trees at every turn. Standing proud right at the very top of the park are a pair of old cannons from the Boer War. Susie and I sat astride the cannons, and we were so high up, we could see right across the rooftops of Blackburn and far into the distance towards the countryside. It's the most amazing sight!'

'Sound like somewhere I should see.'

'It is, and you must.'

Steve reflected on what Alice had said earlier. 'This boy she saw through the shop window – he was playing the guitar, you say?'

'That's right, and it took all my powers of persuasion to drag Susie away.'

'Was the boy good . . . at the guitar?'

'Yes, according to Susie. I didn't hear too much, but what I did hear was impressive, I have to admit. But as you're fond of telling me, I don't have any musical inclinations. Added to which, I was too busy trying to shift Susie, so I could get back and soak my poor feet.'

'Mmm.' Steve's thoughts were on the boy.

Alice, however, was thinking ahead. 'When's your meeting with the planners?'

'First thing tomorrow. And look, Alice, I'm sorry about all this. You and Susie really should have gone back last week. Don't get me wrong, I'm glad you stayed, but I didn't want you to put your own plans on hold.'

'I couldn't desert you, especially when Susie got herself all upset. She didn't want to leave without you, what with her daddy away and everything.'

'Yes, I know, and you must be home for Mike's return very soon. The good news is, I've already secured the site and providing I can accommodate the Planning Department's requirements, I should be home and dry. I'm told the architect is working late into the night in order to deliver the amended drawings first thing.'

Leaning back into his chair, he drew a deep sigh of relief. 'If luck is on my side, by the time the meeting starts, the planning committee should have studied the new plans, and made a decision.'

'I hope for your sake, it all goes well,' Alice told him.

'Well, all we can do now is to keep our fingers crossed. Hopefully, once this meeting is over, I'll have the green light and can go home, though I'll need to travel back and forth for some time yet, which I don't mind in the least. In fact, if needs be, I'd travel to the moon and back if it would get me what I want.'

'You know Mike and I are behind you all the way, don't you?' Alice reassured him.

'I do know that,' Steve answered, 'and I'm very grateful. I only wish Connie would show a bit more interest in what I'm doing, but she doesn't, and probably never will.'

'I can't understand it, Steve. She should be encouraging you all the way; especially as it's to her benefit as well.'

Steve's face darkened. 'I wish I could fire her interest in it, but I can't. Whenever I talk about having the studio up and running, she just nods her head, and makes pleasant noises, but there's no real interest. No passion. No excitement.' He shrugged. 'Maybe I'm asking too much of her. Connie's interested in other things. I guess I'll have to accept that.'

'She's a lucky woman to have the love of a man like you.'

When Steve made no comment, Alice grew curious. 'You do love her, don't you, Steve?' The moment she'd spoken, Alice could have bitten off her tongue.

Steve laughed it off without giving a direct answer. 'I married her, didn't I? So I must love her.'

Feeling uncomfortable, he changed the subject. 'I expect you'll be glad to get back, won't you, Alice?'

'Well, yes, I can't deny I'm ready for home. Also, your wandering brother will be back shortly, so I expect we'll all be where we should be.' She smiled graciously. 'Mind you, Susie and I have really enjoyed tagging along with you. So, thanks for having us, and I hope we haven't got in the way . . . even if you were roped in to read her bedtime stories.'

Steve made a face. 'That's my punishment for not tying up the business quicker, though in the time we've had, I reckon the team and I have done wonders.'

Alice agreed. 'By the way, the woman in the café today told us there's a market on in Blackburn tomorrow, under the lovely old clock. When she mentioned that there were all manner of toy stalls, Susie wouldn't let it drop. She's been wanting to get a present for her daddy, and so far she hasn't seen anything that excites her.'

'Hmm! That's because she's a right little fusspot, and far too picky for her own good. But it might not be a bad idea to let her have a little walkabout, and who knows, she might find something.'

'That's what she said. So, I promised I'd take her over there.'

Steve felt anxious about the meeting. 'After wanting it for so long, I actually think that it might all be coming together. It's been a hard business, but at long last I can almost see my vision actually edging towards reality.'

'I hope so, Steve, but if it does happen, it'll be your own determination and hard work that's carried you through.'

She felt no guilt in reminding him, 'I know Connie hasn't got the same appetite for the studios as you have. But you still pushed on regardless, and all credit to you for that.'

She was only too aware of how long and hard he'd pursued this business venture; in fact she'd been greatly impressed by the speed in which he'd secured the site outside Blackpool.

Unlike Steve, with his talent and passion for music, Steve's brother, Mike, was a hard-and-fast practical man. Never a musician, his talent was buying and selling property, which he had done very well with.

Like Steve, Mike was a kind and generous man, but where business was concerned, he was hard-headed, with no time for dreams.

When Steve turned to see if the drinks were on their way, Alice quietly regarded him for a moment. She saw a fine man with a fine dream. A kind man. A man who had quietly tolerated his wife's selfish ways, while providing her with the best of everything; even though Connie showed little interest in what he was doing.

She was a selfish woman with a high opinion of herself and a low opinion of everyone else. From the day they were married, she had learned how to manipulate her new husband, until over the years she had managed to elevate herself to where she was today. She lived a pampered life, with a cleaner and a gardener, and money to spare. She demanded the best of everything, and got it, and the more she got, the more she wanted.

Alice and the family first had their doubts about Connie when she came home with Steve from one of his long tours. Steve called her his 'rough diamond', and at the time she seemed devoted to him. She accompanied him on every tour, and rarely let him out of her sight.

Then, on returning from another tour, Steve announced that they were married. At the time, family and friends thought he had made a mistake and as the years rolled on, their fears were proved right.

Locked in a marriage without love, Steve confided to his brother that his marriage had brought him little joy. Connie increasingly treated him more as a trophy than a husband. There were also rumours about her seeing other men. And though he respected Connie's decision not to have children, it was a deep wound to him, because he would dearly have loved to complete their marriage with children.

While touring, Steve had many chances to stray with

other women, but he remained loyal to his marriage vows.

'Alice?' Steve shattered Alice's thoughts.

'Oh, I'm sorry, Steve.' Alice had been caught off guard. 'I was miles away there for a minute.'

'Yes, I could see that.' He felt guilty. 'Thinking about Mike, were you?'

'Sort of, yes.' She spoke quietly. 'I miss him.'

'I know you do, but soon you'll be home and when he returns you'll both be waiting there for him.'

He turned his thoughts to Connie, wondering if she'd be glad to see him. She always made a show of affection when he returned from a trip, but he could never tell if her feelings were genuine or not.

'What will you do when the studios are up and running?' Alice asked.

'What do you mean?'

'Well, I mean, will you stay with the group, or will you disband altogether? You can't possibly manage to rehearse and perform and at the same time hope to manage the recording studios as well. It's not possible.'

'You're right,' Steve admitted. 'To tell the truth, I've been thinking about that a lot. But don't forget, since Lennie left, we've hardly played. Jim and Pete are more interested in their growing management businesses, scouting for new talent and such, and I'm developing the recording studios, partly financed by Jim. So it looks like we have disbanded and gone our separate ways already. Mind you, one way or another, we'll all be in the music business,' he crossed his fingers, 'so if and when it happens, I'm sure they'll be taking advantage of the new studio, which means we'll still be working together at different times. It's like I said to Mike, since Lennie went it was never the same as it used to be.'

Alice could hear the regret in his voice. 'You miss it, don't you . . . the way it was?'

'Yeah, I do miss it, but we all need to move on.' Steve shrugged. 'Besides, let's face it. We're not the bright young things we were, and it's only the die-hard fans that follow us now.'

Alice nodded. 'Well, at least you've got some fantastic memories to keep you warm in your old age.'

'Hey!' Steve wagged a finger. 'Not so much of the old, if you don't mind.' He grinned cheekily. 'I've still got all my own teeth.' He grew serious. 'More importantly, I'm on the verge of realising my big dream.'

There was a moment of quiet, while each reflected on his or her achivements in life.

'Steve?' Alice looked up. 'Can I ask you something?'

'Of course.'

'Don't be angry, will you, only I've always wondered . . .'

'Come on, then! Out with it.'

'Well, to be honest, I could never see why you married Connie. You're so different in many ways. You're a grafter, and she's . . . she's . . .' She struggled to find a word that would not offend.

Steve smiled. 'She's lazy and selfish. That's what you're trying to say, isn't it? And you'd be right.'

Alice was embarrassed. 'No, I didn't mean . . . but, well, to be honest, I would never have put you two together in a million years. Oh, look, Steve, I'm sorry. I should never have said that.' Taking up her glass, she drained it to its last drop. 'One of these days I'll learn to keep my mouth shut and mind my own business.'

'Look, it's already forgotten. Tell you what, I reckon we've got time for another drink. What d'you say?'

Alice gave a sheepish grin. 'I think I might have had enough wine for tonight.'

'Are you sure?'

'Yes . . . no!' She groaned. 'Oh, go on then, I'll have the same again. A small white wine, please.'

'Coming up.' Steve went away to collect the drinks.

A few minutes later, taking a long sip of his beer, Steve admitted, 'I'd best make this the last one, especially as I've got a big day ahead of me tomorrow.'

Alice detected a slight slur in his voice. 'Quite right, too. You don't need a hangover when you meet up with the planners.'

She had never known Steve to drink over his limit. Mike said Steve was always the sensible one, even when they were younger.

Curious, she now dared to ask him something that she and Mike had often wondered about. 'You never did say what actually drew you to Connie? How did you latch onto her?'

Steve took a moment to answer, and when he did it was with a sense of surprise. 'To tell you the truth, I'm not altogether sure. In fact, come to think of it, you could say it was Connie who latched onto me!'

'How come?'

'We'd just finished the last gig in the Northern tour. It had been a long, hard tour. Me and the boys were shattered; looking forward to a break. These two girls appeared next day, full of fun and wanting to chat. One of them was outspoken and a bit brash. That turned out to be Connie. And the other . . .'

He fell silent before going on in a softer voice, 'She was a lovely little thing. In the end, I left Connie talking to Jim while I went to chat with her friend.' He could see Ruth in his mind. 'She had the deepest eyes, and such pretty hair. We had a wonderful day together.'

'Sounds to me as though you took to her more than you took to Connie.'

'You're right, I did. In the evening there was a party on the beach. So, while Jim took off with Connie, I invited the prettier one to go for a walk along the beach. After a time we found ourselves alone, under the pier. There was no sign of the others.'

He paused; the memories were clearer now. 'As I recall, we were soon lying on the sand, in each other's arms, listening to the waves lapping against the pier struts . . . and thinking how wonderful it all was.'

'What was her name?'

'Ruth. She was called Ruth.' Embarrassed, he shrugged. 'It was such a beautiful evening, what with the stars above and the sand and sea and all that, it was kinda romantic. I was weary from the tour. I was young and bold back then and . . . things happened.' He gave a secret little smile. 'She was very special. Over the years, I've often thought about her.'

Alice was shaken by the tenderness in his voice as he spoke of this girl. 'By the sound of it, you took advantage of her, but it's what you men do, isn't it? Meet a nice girl, "get it together" and she's another little tick on your calendar.'

Steve gave a wry little smile. 'To tell you the truth, it wasn't like that. I would have liked to really get to know her, only Connie came and hurried her away . . . she said they had to get back, or there would be Hell to pay.'

'You say you've often thought about her over the years?'

'I have, and that's the truth.'

'So, you regret letting her get away, do you?' Alice took another sip of wine.

'Mebbe. The thing is, there are times when Connie gets ratty and makes life difficult, and that's when I think back to that night, and wonder how different it might have been.'

He looked up, and Alice detected much regret in his voice as he confided, 'All right yes, I admit it, there are times when I wish it hadn't been so fleeting; when I wish

I'd taken Ruth's address, but I didn't, so that's the end of that. So now, I'm married to Connie, and her friend is probably happily married to the old boyfriend she took up with, so that's an end to it.'

Alice wondered, 'If you didn't know anything about her, how come you know about the boyfriend?'

'Because Connie told me.'

Alice was confused. 'When?'

Steve fell back in the chair, 'God! You don't leave any stone unturned, do you?'

'You gave me the impression that you never saw or heard from her again, and now you say she took up with a boyfriend. So, when did you find all this out?'

'When me and Connie got together. Connie turned up at the Birmingham concert hall where we were playing a gig.'

'On her own, was she?'

'Well, yes. At first, I thought she'd come to see Jim, but he wasn't playing that night. So, she singled me out. We got talking, then we went back to the hotel for a drink, and that's when she told me about her friend . . . that she'd got together with an old boyfriend, and that I hadn't meant anything to her . . . that I was just "a bit of a laugh".'

He frowned. 'That surprised me, because I wouldn't have called our time together "a bit of a laugh". It was sensual, and beautiful, and I will never forget it.'

Alice was curious. 'If you felt like that, why did you let her go so easily?'

'We'd got a great new opportunity to extend the tour and suddenly we were moving on. It was a chance we couldn't pass up and we had to leave immediately.' He paused. 'She was different, though . . . kind of . . . real. Maybe if things hadn't turned out the way they did, I'd have found her again, one way or another. But, like I said, I chose my career, I didn't know where she lived and I just left.'

'So when Connie turned up shortly afterwards, you went to bed with her as a consolation prize!'

'Course not! I took her for a drink, because I needed to know where Ruth was, and if there might be a chance that she and I could get together. But then, before I could even ask the question, she said she hadn't seen her friend lately, because she was so wrapped up in her relationship with her old sweetheart. She said she felt really let down, that they'd been friends since school and now she'd been dropped just like that . . . no phone call, no word of any kind.' His voice fell. 'Believe it or not, Alice, I really would have liked to have seen her friend again.'

Alice gave a naughty smile. 'God, you really took to her, didn't you?'

Steve nodded. 'More than I realised at the time, yes. But like I say, water under the bridge and all that.'

'But it still doesn't explain how you and Connie became an item.'

She waited for an answer, but Steve wasn't listening. Instead he was back there, Connie telling him how her friend had reunited with her first love, and that she was incredibly happy.

He had not realised until then how deeply he'd been drawn to Ruth. Oh, yes, they'd made love and it was wonderful, but that was not unusual with the girls he met on tour, and when it was over that was it. And yet, there had been something about Ruth that had stayed with him.

'Steve?'

Steve looked up. 'I'm sorry . . . what did you say?'

'I asked how you and Connie got together.'

'To tell the truth, I'm not altogether sure. I mean, one minute we were talking about her friend finding happiness with her old love, then suddenly she was talking about herself, and her own love life. She'd been dumped, and she started sobbing . . . in a shocking state she was.

I didn't know how to deal with it. She said she was too upset to travel back home, so I booked her a room in the hotel, and she begged me to stay with her. I didn't know what to do. The other blokes had gone off with their dates, and there she was, needing me, so I took her to her room and she wouldn't stop crying, so I stayed and comforted her, and . . . well . . . you're right. We ended up in bed together, and I'm not proud of that. In all honesty, that was the last thing I wanted.'

'But you couldn't resist the opportunity, could you?'

'It wasn't like that!'

'Ah, well, you would say that, wouldn't you?'

'No! Really . . . she was in a bit of a state . . . sobbing, and vulnerable, and for some stupid reason I felt responsible, so one thing led to another, and before I had time to turn round, she was hanging around on the tour with us. Next thing, we were married.' He shrugged. 'The rest you already know.'

Before she could comment, he pushed back his chair and stood up. 'I could do with a nightcap. How about you?'

'No, I think I've had more than enough.'

He chuckled. 'You haven't got Connie's constitution.'

'Oh, you reckon, d'you?' After draining her glass, she handed it to him. 'I'll have the same again, thank you.'

'Right!' Surprised, he went to collect another round of drinks.

While he was gone, Alice couldn't help but wonder if he had ever really loved the cold and extravagant woman who, in her opinion, had bamboozled him into marriage. She suspected that Steve was more unhappy than he would ever admit, and that Connie was only along for the ride. But, as Mike had reminded her, there was nothing they could do unless they were asked. It was best to let married people sort out their own problems.

When Steve returned with the drinks, she took a great gulp of the wine, before asking nervously, 'Can I ask you something, Steve?'

'As long as it's not too near the bone, yes.'

'OK . . . a straightforward question requires a straightforward answer. Do you agree?'

'Now you're making me nervous. Just ask the question.'

'OK. Do you love Connie?'

There was a long, tense moment while he recalled the early days. 'I thought I loved her . . . at the time,' He answered thoughtfully.

'And now?' Alice was not about to let it go.

'I'm not really sure.' He was torn in so many directions. Deep down, he knew how he felt towards Connie, but it was another thing to confess it to someone else; especially to Alice, who had a canny knack of cutting into his thoughts.

Carefully placing her glass on the table, Alice leaned forward. 'You're a lovely man, Steve, but . . . shall I tell you what I think?'

'If I say no, I expect you'll tell me anyway.' Steve wasn't concerned; except for the amount of wine she had downed, when usually she didn't drink at all. None the less, he had always thought his brother was a very lucky man to have such an honest and loving woman in his life.

'Right! Well, this is the way I see it, and stop me if you think I'm out of order.'

'Huh! It sounds like I'm about to get a lecture.' He didn't mind, though. Alice's honest and straightforward manner was a welcome change from Connie's guarded and devious way. In fact, come to think of it, he and Connie hardly ever had an in-depth conversation these days.

'Right then!' Alice drained her glass before unleashing her thoughts. 'First, you have a wife who never supports you in your work; she's never seen to fuss over you . . .

342

kiss you or hold your hand. She never laughs with you, never travels with you, or does anything that includes just the two of you. Instead, she flies off to sunny climates on her own, whenever the fancy takes her. She seems to care more about shopping and holidays than she ever cares about you. Moreover, she hasn't done a day's work since you put a ring on her finger. She's selfish, lazy and demanding. She has a habit of looking down on you, and whenever we all go out to dinner, it's plain to see she's not comfortable with your friends and family, and she's even been seen to flirt with the men at the table.' She wagged a finger at him. 'There! I've said it now.'

In the deafening silence that followed, Alice was horrified at her torrent of honesty. She slunk down into the chair. 'Oh my God, Steve, I'm sorry. I wasn't meant to get so angry. It came out all wrong.'

Steve was shocked to his roots. He had never known Alice to be so condemning of anyone, and he felt the need and duty to defend his wife. 'Look, I know she's got her faults, Alice, but you're being too harsh on her. You've made her out to be a monster, and that's not fair.'

And yet, in between the bitchy bits about the shopping and such, Steve recognised the truth about his wife's character. He knew how difficult she could be at times, but to hear it being spelled out – especially by the normally placid Alice – was hard to take.

Mortified by what she had said, Alice apologised again. 'I'm truly sorry, Steve. I shouldn't have said those things.' Even so, she felt the need to qualify her words. 'The thing is . . . I'm not the only one who thinks she's wrong for you.'

Steve had heard more than enough. 'All right, Alice.' Scraping his chair back, he went to her side and tucked his hand under her arm to help her up. 'Let's talk tomorrow, eh? Tonight you've had a bit too much of the wine. Come on now. Let's get you to your room.'

Alice was devastated. 'Oh, Steve, what will you think of me? I didn't mean to say all those dreadful things. They just fell out before I could stop them.' Though she had meant every word.

In the lift, she leaned heavily on him, apologising again. 'Don't be angry with me. It's the wine. I'm not used to it. I need to see Susie . . . she shouldn't be alone in the room without me.'

'She's not alone, Alice. We organised a hotel babysitter . . . that nice lady who's got children and grandchildren of her own, remember?'

In fact, the hotel babyitter met them at the door. A kindly woman with a sunny smile, she quickly took charge of Alice.

'Don't you worry, sir. You can leave her to me now, sir. I'll make sure everything's all right before I leave.'

'I'm her brother-in-law,' he explained. 'Is my niece in bed? I'd like to take a peek at her, if possible?'

'Oh, yes, it's Mr Bates, isn't it?' She now recognised him as being the occupant of number fourteen, a few strides down the hall. 'The little darling is fast asleep. She's been no trouble at all.' She glanced at Alice, who was having trouble standing up straight, 'I can see to her mammy if you want to get off. I'll make sure everything is all right before I leave.'

Steve thanked her. 'But if you could just keep an eye on my sister-in-law for one moment, I'd like to take a peek at my niece.'

'Of course, sir.'

Taking a sleepy Alice across the room, Steve helped her onto the bed. He gently removed her jacket and shoes before placing them on the chair, beside her handbag. When he covered her with the eiderdown, she promptly closed her eyes and fell asleep.

'She's not used to the drink,' Steve explained. 'She had a couple of glasses of wine, which seem to have gone straight to her head.'

'It does the very same to me, sir.' She smiled over at Alice. 'I'll watch her while you take a look at the child, then I'd best be off . . . if there's nothing else you need?'

She lingered, as though waiting for new instructions; or maybe a small gesture of gratitude.

Steve understood. 'Thank you for keeping an eye on the child.' Digging into his jacket pocket, he drew out some coins, which he handed to her.

'Oh, thank you sir.' She rammed the money into her apron pocket.

While Steve went into the adjoining bedroom to see the child, she went over to the bed and shifted Alice into a more comfortable position. Then she sat herself in the chair to wait for Steve's return.

Susie was fast asleep. 'Rest well, sweetheart,' he murmured. 'It sounds like you've a busy day ahead of you tomorrow, and then it's home again.'

Stooping down, he placed a gossamer kiss on Susie's forehead, tucked her arm under the clothes and drew the bedcover up to her neck. 'Good night, God bless.' He stood a moment watching her, thinking how dearly he would have loved to be a father. But since there was no changing Connie's mind, he had abandoned the possibility of fatherhood.

Disillusioned, he returned to the other room, where Alice was flaked out. 'Thank you.' He could see the older woman was eager to be off. 'I'm sure she'll sleep right through till morning.'

'I'm sure she will.' From her curt statement and the expression on her face as she glanced at Alice's now prostrate body, she did not approve of anyone drinking themselves into such a state. 'I'll be leaving now, but if you want anything at all, just dial zero.'

'Thank you.' He opened the door and saw her out, then, having checked again on Susie and Alice, he headed off to his own room.

Once there, he placed his shoes on top of his suitcase and flung his jacket over the sofa. A short time later, he fell into the welcome softness of his bed, where, bone-tired and weary, he was ready for a good night's sleep, but sleep was elusive. He was haunted by his deep longing for children of his own. He could not understand why Connie had no wish to be a mother.

~

At 7.30 a.m., the ringing of the bedside telephone shocked him awake.

Bleary-eyed and disorientated, he took a minute to focus before inching across the bed to grab the receiver. 'Yes, who is it?'

'Steve? You're a wicked man. You left me lying on top of the bed,' Alice playfully chided him. 'I woke up freezing in the early hours.'

'Sorry, but I didn't want to wake you. I covered you with the eiderdown, so you must have kicked it off in the night.' He stifled a yawn.

'Susie is dressed and ready to go down to breakfast, and I'm almost ready. Shall we meet down there?'

'What? Yes, all right, give me fifteen minutes.'

'You sound rough.'

'I feel it.'

'I don't feel too great myself.'

'Serves you right, knocking back the wine like an old soak.'

'Hmm! You were the one who brought it to me.'

'Ah, yes, but you asked for it. So don't throw the responsibility on me. If you're feeling thick-headed, you've only yourself to blame. Yes, you go ahead and grab a table, and I'll see you down there.'

'OK.' Alice replaced the receiver.

'Oh, jeez!' Realising he had a busy day ahead, he quickly washed and shaved, before collecting a cream-coloured shirt and dark-grey suit from the wardrobe.

A short time later, looking smart and businesslike, he flicked a comb through his thick mop of hair before hurrying out to the lift.

Alice and Susie were in the dining room.

'Where've you been, Uncle Steve?' Susie greeted him, hands on hips and a look of disapproval on her face. 'Naughty Uncle Steve. It's rude to be late.'

Steve made a sorry face. 'You're absolutely right, so now I don't get a hug, is that it?'

In an instance she was up and running round the table, and he swung her into his arms, asking sheepishly, 'Am I forgiven then?'

Her face broke into a bright smile as she flung her arms round his neck. 'All right then, but please don't be late again.'

He made a smart salute. 'Yes, ma'am, I'll make sure I'm on time in future, but right now I'm starving hungry, so can we eat?'

Susie nodded. 'Yes, and then while you're at the meeting, me and Mummy are going to the market. Afterwards, you're going to meet up with us . . . if the men will let you go in time.'

'Huh! Let them try and stop me, and there'll be big trouble.' He gently squashed her nose with the end of his finger. 'I'll be there for you and Mummy, come rain or shine.'

'Good!'

He reached out and gave Alice a peck on the cheek. 'Oh, dear me,' he feigned a look of horror, 'shadows under the eyes; not good!'

'Well, thank you.' Smiling, she reminded him, 'You're not supposed to tell a woman that she's got shadows under her eyes. Where's your sense of chivalry?'

'Only joking.'

'It's a good job I know you.' She was used to his sense of humour.

As they walked to the breakfast room, she watched him with Susie. It hurt her to know that if Connie had her way, Steve would never know the joy of being a father.

Alice took Susie to choose her juices and cereals, while Steve ordered egg, bacon and sausages.

'Would you like toast, sir?' The waitress was a pretty, auburn-haired girl with a tendency to blink nervously whenever she asked a question, as she did now. 'Brown bread or white, sir?'

'Well, I'd like brown bread, but I've no idea what the others want so maybe we could have a selection?'

She wrote it all down. 'Tea or coffee, sir?'

'Again, a pot of each, and a jug of hot milk, please.'

'Thank you, sir.' Blinking furiously, she hurried off to collect the order.

Alice saw her leave. 'Did you remember to order both tea and coffee?' she asked Steve.

'I did, yes. I also ordered a selection of toast, brown and white.' He gave a cheeky wink. 'See! I did remember.'

'I like brown toast, too, Uncle Steve, so can I have one of yours?' Susie asked politely.

'No, you can't.'

'Why not?' She stared at him with big, surprised eyes.

'Because you don't get anything, unless you use the magic word.'

Susie tightly closed her eyes to pretend to concentrate.

'Oh, I remember!' Opening her eyes, she laughed out loud. '*Please*, Uncle Steve, may I have some of your brown toast?'

'I'll think about it.'

'Aw!' She noticed the naughty twinkle in his eye. 'Uncle Steve, you're teasing, aren't you?'

'I'm sorry. You can have as much brown toast as you like. How's that?'

'Thank you, but I only want two pieces. First, I have to eat my cereals.' She began tucking into them straight away, leaving Alice and Steve to chat.

For a while it was Alice who did most of the talking, telling Steve how much she'd enjoyed the trip, and that she was almost certain the outcome of the meeting would be in his favour.

When Susie headed for the juice table again, Steve recalled the sordid events of when that poor woman was snatched from the streets.

'I'm finding it difficult to put it all out of my mind,' he told Alice now. 'I hope she's all right after her ordeal.'

Alice, too, had been shocked and horrified at the incident. 'Well, from what you told me about the woman you believed to be her mother, it sounds to me she's in safe hands now.'

Steve nodded. 'I hope so, because she was in a poor state when I gave her up to the woman.'

Alice wanted to know, 'Can you make time to go back and see if she's OK?'

Steve had already considered the possibility. 'I'm not sure. It all depends on what time there is to thrash it out; and don't forget this is the one and only Saturday meeting ever. According to Edward Mull, the agent, they've called this one because of the huge backlog in applications. So, if it goes badly for me today, it could be months before I get another hearing.'

'Don't even think like that, Steve. Be positive.'

'You know me, I'm always positive, but it's out of my hands. Either way, I intend keeping my promise to Susie, so I'll meet you at the market café. Keep your fingers crossed that I bring good news with me.'

'We will.'

Steve nodded. 'Anyway, we'll have a bite to eat or something, then I'll need to get you both back here to collect your luggage and catch your train home.'

Alice asked him, 'Wouldn't you rather we stayed here with you, until you're finished with all the red tape and such, and then we could all go back in the car together?'

'That's a nice idea, Alice, but I can't let you do that, especially not with Mike on his way home. He's expecting you to be there, and besides, I can't really be sure if I'll be going back myself, just yet.'

'Why do you say that?'

'Well, if the worst happens and the meeting falls through, I'll need to consider the other sites on offer; arrange more viewings, talk to people I haven't already talked to. And even if the meeting goes well, I still have to follow up, what with revisiting the site with the surveyor, and checking with the architect; then tying up all the loose ends.'

'But, either way, you will be at the café today, won't you? Susie would be so disappointed if you're not.'

Susie was horrified, 'Yes, Uncle Steve,' she said. 'I'm going home later, but first, we have to go to the market. That little boy is playing his guitar and Mummy said we can go and see him. You have to come too . . . say you will, please?'

Steve promised her, 'As soon as the meeting is over, I'll make my way to the café, like I've arranged with Mummy. After that, I promise I'll go with you to see this boy, and I hope he's worth the effort.'

A short time later, breakfast eaten, they returned to their respective rooms to prepare for the day ahead.

Susie was cleaning her teeth when Steve knocked on the door. When Alice called him inside, he popped his head round. 'Is there anything you want before I go – money, or anything?'

Alice told him, 'No, thanks all the same. I haven't even spent the money you forced on us earlier.' She glanced at her watch. 'You'd best be on your way,' she reminded him. 'You have to see the agent before the meeting, don't you?'

'Yes, and then we'll make our way to the council offices together.' He paused, a sense of anxiety creeping over him. 'To tell you the truth, Alice, I've never been so nervous in all my life.'

'Ah, go on with you!' Alice sought to reassure him. 'You've thought about this for too long to let nerves get in the way at this late stage. You've done your homework, Steve. You've chased every loophole, and now it's up to them. But it will be all right. I've got a good feeling about it, and even if it doesn't go in your favour, you won't give up, I know you too well for that.'

Coming into the room, he gave her a hug. 'You're the best sister-in-law in the world,' he told her, and when Susie poked her head round the bathroom door, her mouth frothing with toothpaste, he gave a little scream. 'Oh my God! A monster . . . HELP!'

Susie fell about laughing, until Alice reminded her, 'Time's flying by, sweetheart. Hurry up . . . that is, if you want to spend time wandering about the market.' Susie quickly disappeared, calling back in muffled tones, 'Good luck, Uncle Steve. We'll wait at the café for you.'

Susie's comment reminded Steve. 'What with so much to think about, I'm not altogether sure exactly where this café is that you spoke about . . . Can you just run it by me again?'

351

'It's opposite the market. Betty's Place, it's called. Susie and I will be waiting there at twelve o'clock. Look, Steve, just ask anybody to direct you to the market clock. You can't really miss it, because it stands head and shoulders above the stalls, oh, and it's the most wonderful thing. I'm told that people have their photographs taken against it. Sweethearts meet under it, and the stall-holders set their watches by it. You can see the café from there.'

Steve was impressed. 'Well, even if I don't see anything else, I must take a look at this clock.'

'You won't be sorry, I promise,' Alice told him.

With the arrangements clarified, Steve was quickly on his way, leaving Alice and Susie to sort out their clothes and pack them into the suitcases.

They then took the suitcases down to the concierge desk, where Alice arranged for them to be picked up later.

After checking out at the desk, they walked the short distance to the bus stop and caught the bus to Blackburn.

'I'm glad we're going to see the boy again.' Susie was excited as they climbed onto the bus.

After sitting Susie on the inside seat, Alice sat down next to her and lapsed into deep thought about Steve's situation at home. It didn't look too good, she thought sadly.

Beside her, Susie chattered on, with Alice only half aware of what she was saying until Susie's anxious voice penetrated her thoughts: 'Mummy, you're not listening.'

'Sorry, sweetheart?' She was used to switching on and off as Susie chattered about this and that; all of which she had heard before. 'What's on your mind?'

'Do you think the boy really is going to play his guitar, Mummy?'

'Well, I don't know for sure. It wasn't me who overheard

the conversation between the old man and the boy. I only know what you told me,' she smiled, 'before I managed to drag you away.'

'I know, and I already told you,' Susie rolled her eyes, 'the man said he wanted the boy to come to his stall on the market and play his guitar. He said Saturday, and it's Saturday now, isn't it?'

'Yes, well, it was when I got up this morning.'

'So, that means the boy will play his guitar today, doesn't it, Mummy?' She needed reassurance.

'Well, that's right, but to be honest, sweetheart, I wouldn't count on it. Sometimes, people say things and they don't always mean them, or something happens and they can't do what they said they would.'

'But the boy was really excited.'

'I'm sure he was.' Reaching out, Alice stroked a stray hair from the child's forehead. 'Look, I know how much you want to hear the boy play his guitar, but I don't want you to be disappointed, that's all.'

'I won't be disappointed, Mummy.' There was the slightest tremor in her voice. 'Because he told the old man he would, and I know he will. I just know it!'

When Alice turned to look at her, she saw how Susie had turned her face to the window, gazing out with a solemn face.

Instead of talking to her again, she tenderly slid her fingers over the girl's hand. Susie smiled up at her, and they continued their journey in silence, each occupied with her own thoughts.

Alice gave a satisfied little smile as she thought of Mike and how she would be seeing him very soon.

Mike was the love of her life. Every time he went away, she felt so incredibly lonely, which was why she and Susie had accompanied Steve on this trip.

As the bus bumbled along and Susie was lost in the

sights and sounds, Alice turned her own thoughts to Steve's impossible situation.

How much longer would he be able to put up with Connie's extravagant and selfish ways? Also, if Connie was adamant about not having children, why hadn't she told him before he put a ring on her finger?

To Alice's mind, that would have been the right thing to do.

But, having learned a thing or two about Connie over the past few years, she could easily believe that Connie had her own personal agenda in marrying Steve.

After all, he was a good catch; with a successful career; money in the bank, and ambitions that, if realised, could bring him security for life.

PART FIVE

~

Suspicions

CHAPTER TWELVE

'FOR PITY'S SAKE, yer like a cat on hot bricks, Casey. Come away from that window. Patrick won't turn up any quicker with you looking out the window every two minutes!' Though Bob, also, was impatient for the familiar sound of Patrick's wagon rolling over the cobbles.

'What if he doesn't come, Granddad?' Casey took another peek out the window. 'What if he doesn't have a market stall today? What if I don't get to play my guitar for the people?'

Granddad Bob gave a huge sigh. 'You'll get to play your guitar for the people, even if I've to sit yer on me shoulders!'

'It won't be the same, though, will it? Not without Patrick there.'

'Don't worry, Patrick will be 'ere soon enough. Meantime, be a good lad an' fetch yer granddad's baccy from the sideboard.'

Casey ran off to fetch his baccy. 'Are you sure Patrick will turn up, Granddad?' He gave him the roll of baccy.

'Yes, lad. He'll not let us down, believe me.'

'Huh! Never trust a man who sleeps in his socks!' That was Dolly, bringing refreshments.

'Hey!' The old fella wagged a finger at her. 'Yer not supposed to broadcast my personal habits like that.'

'Why not?' Resting the tray on the arm of the settee, she slid the two cups of tea onto the side table. 'It's true, isn't it, you do sleep with your socks on, or you did, until I told you it weren't the civilised thing to do. At least, not for a particular man like yourself.'

She handed Casey a glass of fresh orange juice, while rolling her eyes in frustration as the old fella complained, 'It might be civilised, an' it might not, but it's certainly not the sort o' thing to bandy about, is it?' Feeling shame-faced in front of a woman was a whole new experience for him.

'Why not?' Dolly had learned how to tease him. 'If you reckon it's perfectly acceptable to sleep with your socks on, where's the harm in admitting it?'

'Well, I don't know for sure, but it doesn't feel right, that's what I'm saying. I mean . . . a thing like that is one's own personal business, not for broadcasting to all an' sundry.'

'It's all right, Granddad,' Casey assured him, 'I already knew.' He glanced up at Dolly. 'He never used to take his socks off *ever*. Until you came to live with us.'

He now relayed a certain scene that he'd overheard between his father and his granddad. 'When Granddad's socks got really smelly, Dad used to tell him off. One day they had a little argument, and Daddy told him if he didn't wash his socks, his feet would rot . . .' he had to think hard to recall the exact words, '. . . right through to the bone. That's what he said.'

'Well, thank you, Casey.' Blushing a bright shade of pink, Granddad Bob pretended to read his newspaper. 'I'm sure Dolly needed to know that.'

Feeling a little sorry for him, Dolly still could not resist making the comment, 'Ah! So, now we have the sordid truth. Out of the mouths of babes, as they say.'

Impatient, the old fella tried to explain the incident. 'It were not an argument, as such, 'cause me an' our Tom never argued. It were a little exchange of words, that's all. Anyway, the pair of 'em turned up an hour earlier than they should 'ave. I were late outta me bed, and just tekking off my socks when in they came, large as life . . .' Before Casey could open his mouth, he gave him a warning glance. 'Like I say, it were summat and nowt,' he grumbled. 'It were never an argument.'

In his own defence, Casey concluded the tale. 'Granddad were just taking his socks off when we came in. Daddy told him they stank the house out, and Granddad pulled a face. Then on the way home, Daddy said he was sorry he'd said anything, because Granddad got all uppity.' He thought for a minute, then: 'Granddad, what does "uppity" mean?'

Granddad Bob stuck to his own version. 'Listen to me, lad! You've got it all wrong. Yer daddy were just winding me up. Yer know very well, 'e were allus one for winding me up.' He lowered his voice until it was barely audible. 'If I could turn back the clock right now, I'd let him wind me up till the cows came 'ome.' Tom was never far from his thoughts.

The mood in the room changed. Granddad Bob was horrified when he saw Casey's sorry little face. 'Aw, I'm sorry, lad. Come 'ere to yer granddad, eh?' He opened his arms for the boy to come to him, and when he ran into his fierce embrace, the two of them clung together.

Across the room, Dolly was deeply saddened at the sight of these two dear people, whom she had come to love like her very own.

A moment or so later, the atmosphere was charged with excitement when Casey glanced up at the window. 'He's here, Granddad!' He started leaping up and down. 'Look! Patrick's here!'

And sure enough, the battered old wagon was rolling up to the front door, clanging and banging, and sounding for all the world like it would fall apart at any minute. 'Looks like it's about to conk out,' the old fella moaned. 'I expect the silly old devil's overloaded it.'

'I heard that!' Having parked the wagon half on the pavement and half on the cobbled street, Patrick came lolloping up the path.

Granddad Bob started yelling at him from the door, 'If yer expect me to unload a pile o' junk when we get to market, you've another thought coming. I've been conned once too often to fall for that little trick. And that's that!'

'Ah, will ye shurrup, yer silly ol' divil!' Patrick was not in the best of moods. 'Whether ye loike it or not, this wagon has to be unloaded, an' so far as I can see, you an' me are the only two men 'ere. Am I roight . . . or am I roight?'

When Granddad Bob made no comment, Patrick tried another way. 'I'm sorry, lad,' He gave Casey a helpless look. 'If your granddad won't help me, there'll be no market stall today, an' if there's no market stall, there'll be no guitar-playing and no singing. Don't blame me, boy. The thing is, I've got a bad back, an' there's no way I can unload that wagon by myself.'

'Oh, 'ere we go again!' The old fella had to smile at the other one's antics. 'All right, we can't have you being carted off to hospital with a bad back, can we now?'

'So you'll help me?'

Granddad Bob was well aware that Patrick was putting it on. In fact, they had the same rigmorole every time they went to market; Patrick would assume that his old friend might not want to help unload, and so he'd pretend he had a bad back. 'You're a wily old bugger, Patrick, and for the life o' me, I don't know why you start up with this bad back soonever we arrive at market. I've always helped you unload, and yet you keep up this pretence. Shame on yer.'

He started back into the house. 'I'll not be a minute. Oh, an' don't start without me.' As if Patrick ever would.

Still chuckling, he took the boy back inside to say cheerio to Dolly, who intended meeting up with them later. He tutted while he was putting on his jacket, and he tutted as he marched out with the boy in one hand, and the guitar in the other. 'That Patrick . . . what will I do with him, eh?' He laughed out loud. 'He likes the attention, that's what it is.

''Ere, lad. You'd best hold on tight to this.' Handing the guitar to Casey, Bob settled him into the passenger seat before climbing up beside him. 'This old wagon is about to shiver an' shake all over the place,' he warned the boy, ''cause Patrick is sure to be driving through every pothole that was ever created.'

Casey hugged his precious guitar close, and when Patrick returned from checking his load, Casey asked him worriedly, 'You won't, will you, Patrick?'

'What's that, m'boy?' When he was expecting trouble, Patrick had a habit of tucking his chin into his neck, and looking up through the top of his eyes; and that's exactly what he did now. 'Is the old idjet making trouble again?'

Casey related his granddad's warning, 'I'm frightened my daddy's guitar might get broken.'

Patrick leaned towards the boy, a smile on his artful old face. 'You tell your granddad from me, I do not drive through potholes, nor do I make the wagon shiver and shake. Trust me, I'd cut off my right arm, before I would ever put your daddy's guitar at risk. You have my word on it.'

Casey was greatly relieved. 'Thank you, Patrick.'

Leaning forward, Patrick gave his friend a shrivelling glance, while addressing his comments to the boy. 'Ye must not listen to this rambling ol' divil. Sure he's only jealous, 'cause unlike me, he's not got a grand wagon, nor a market stall. An' that's what niggles him.'

His comment set the old fella chortling; making the other two laugh along with him, and though the teasing went on, the mood remained very jolly.

'D'yer know what we are?' the old fella asked proudly.

'No,' Patrick was ready for the off, 'though I'm sure you'll tell me.'

Bob stuck out a proud chest. 'The Three Musketeers, that's what we are! We're on a very important mission, with a special guitar that was in pieces, and now it's like new again. Moreover, I'm here with my grandson and my best friend in the whole world; even though he can be a crotchety old bugger when he likes. So, when push comes to shove and the whole world seems agin' us, we've still got each other.' Sliding an arm round Casey's shoulders, he felt good. 'What else could a man ask for, eh?' As always, Tom was strong in his mind.

For a while, the mood in the wagon was a merry one; until out of nowhere, a stray football came smashing into the windscreen, 'What the divil . . . !' Patrick shook his fist at the young culprits in the street. 'Ye little monsters, clear off . . . unless ye want yer arses kicking, the lot o' ye!'

'It's you that wants his arse kicking, old man!' came the insolent reply. 'And if you ask me, that rattling old bag o' bones wants dumping in the scrapyard!'

'Hey, mind your tongue!' Trying hard to keep a straight face, Patrick wagged a finger. 'Don't you dare insult my friend Bob like that!'

'Enough o' that!' Bob was not amused. 'The lad didn't mean me. They meant this rusty ol' wagon. And besides, *my* bones don't rattle.'

'I don't suppose they do,' Patrick winked at the boy. 'There's too much fat round 'em, that's why.'

The boys ran off with their football, while the two men continued their light-hearted bickering.

Until Casey felt obliged to warn his granddad Bob, 'If you don't stop arguing, I'll tell Dolly. She'll give you what for.'

His childish warning shocked them into silence, but it didn't last long. 'Sounds to me like she has your granddad well under control,' Patrick said. 'Huh! And this is the man who swore he would never be tamed.'

'Hark at the kettle calling the pan black.' Addressing his grandson, Bob had a twinkle in his eye. 'I'll have you know, young man, there's not a woman on this earth that can tell me and Patrick what to do.' In a whisper, and with a sly little wink to the boy, he added cautiously, 'Mind you, it might not be wise to tell her I said that.'

Along the journey, the two old fellas teased and tormented each other, until Patrick decided to entertain them with tales of his many hilarious escapades.

Consequently, the cab was soon rocking with laughter, all the way to market.

~

'Uncle Steve's not coming, is he, Mummy?' Having eaten two home-made chocolate fancies, and downed a glass of sarsaparilla, Susie was growing increasingly anxious.

'Stop fidgeting, Susie, he'll be here soon.' Alice was also wondering how much longer Steve might be.

'Can I go outside and look?'

'You've been in and out like a yo-yo,' Alice reminded her. 'It won't make him get here any quicker.'

'Aw, please, Mummy?'

'Go on then, but promise you'll stay where I can see you.'

'I promise.'

Susie then went outside to continue pacing up and down. She walked along the street as far as she was allowed, constantly stretching her neck, hoping to catch sight of her uncle's familiar figure.

A few minutes later, while Alice was on her third cup of tea, Susie slouched back inside. 'He's not coming. He's forgotten.' She was close to tears.

'Aw, my little Susie, would I ever do that to you?' From behind her, Steve's voice rang out.

'Uncle Steve!' Laughing excitedly, she ran to him. 'Where've you been? I've been waiting ages for you.'

Swinging her into his arms, he gave her a kiss, then he sat her down. 'I promise you, I got here as soon as I could.'

Wearied by the long morning and the many frustrating discussions, he drew out a chair and dropped himself in it with a sigh of relief.

Alice could see how weary he was, so she didn't ask any questions, but one: 'Fancy a cuppa?'

'After the ordeal I've just had, I certainly wouldn't say no, that's for sure.'

'Are you hungry?'

'No, thanks all the same. I did manage to grab a sand-wich.'

'OK.' Alice went over to the counter and ordered two fresh pots of tea.

She glanced over her shoulder to see Steve and Susie deep in conversation, then Susie was laughing, and Steve was making funny faces.

'The girl obviously loves her daddy.' The woman behind the counter had also seen how the other two were having fun together.

Alice smiled. 'Oh, he's not her daddy, he's her uncle, but you're right, Susie does love him – almost as much as she loves his brother, Mike, my husband and Susie's father.'

'Oh, I'm sorry.' The girl liked to chat. 'So does your brother-in-law have children of his own?'

'Sadly, no.'

'Oh, that's such a shame. He looks like he'd make a wonderful dad.' She handed Alice her change.

Walking back to the table, Alice thought of the girl's comments. She was right; Steve really would make a wonderful father. She and Mike had always known that.

It wasn't long before the waitress arrived with the tea. 'I've brought a lollipop for the child.' She smiled at Susie and then she told Alice, 'It's on the house.'

Steve took a great gulp of his tea. 'This morning has been a real tussle,' he told her, 'but I'm sure you don't want to know all the tiresome details.'

'Of course I do!' Alice gently kicked him under the table. 'I want to know every little detail, so out with it,' she said. 'How did it go?'

Deliberately aggravating her, he took another gulp of his tea, then winked at Susie, who tried to wink back, but ended up squinting cross-eyed.

'On the whole, it went very well,' Steve said. 'It was an uphill struggle, but we got there in the end.'

Delighted, Alice leaned over to give him a kiss. 'Well done, I knew you could do it.'

Not to be left out, Susie climbed onto his lap, looking up at him like he was a real hero.

Steve went on to outline the situation. 'They gave it the thumbs-up, but with some conditions; which I won't go into now, because it's all a bit complicated. What it means is, I'll need to stay here another day. As I suspected, I'll need to speak to a number of people involved, like the lawyer, and the builders, together with the architect, who will need to amend his plans. Then it's back to the authorities, when hopefully they'll agree with the changes and rubber-stamp it, so I can start putting my plans into action.'

Jubilant, he clenched his fists in the air. 'I can hardly believe we're almost there,' he said. 'At least, they didn't turn it down out of hand.'

Susie was excited too. First, because Uncle Steve and her mummy were excited, but mostly because, now that they were altogether, she could go to the market and see the boy play his guitar.

Just now, though, her mummy and Uncle Steve were drinking and talking, and she was growing more and more impatient.

When she could control her impatience no longer, she shouted, 'WHEN ARE WE GOING TO SEE THE BOY?'

Alice quietly shushed her. 'It's rude to raise your voice like that. Uncle Steve and I are having a conversation. As soon as we've finished our tea, we'll take you to see the boy; if you could just be patient for a minute or so longer.' Reaching out, she stroked Susie's hair. 'All right, sweetheart?'

Fed up with waiting, Susie took a moment to answer, but eventually she replied sulkily, 'All right then.'

She cheered up when Steve told her, 'I'm sorry, but I'm still catching my breath. I promise we'll get you to the market in no time at all.'

So, while the adults talked a little longer, Susie glued her nose to the window, taking intermittent licks of her bright yellow lollipop, and watching the world go by.

Every now and then, she would impatiently glance up to see her mummy and Uncle Steve in serious conversation, then she would sigh and groan and take another lick of her lollipop, her gaze constantly wandering towards the market clock.

'I hope we've not missed him, because we're going home today, and I'll never see him again,' she muttered to herself.

She remembered the boy's shy smile from the bus, and it lifted her spirits.

The idea of never seeing him again, though, made her feel miserable.

~

When they'd first arrived at the market early that morning, Patrick had explained to Casey why the stall must be set out as it was now.

'You need the taller stuff at the back of the stall, with the smaller items laid out in front. That way people can see everything, without shifting stuff about and causing a jumble, and you must remember to keep the really small pieces in the bric-a-brac box.'

Casey was fascinated. 'What's a bric-a-brac box?'

'It's for keeping things in like hairpins an' coins, an' bits o' fancy jewellery an' such. Some of it can be worth a bob or two, an' that's why it needs to be at the side, where I can keep an eye on it.'

'Why?'

'Well, 'cause there are too many folks wi' nimble fingers, who would think nothing of dipping into the box and helping themselves.'

Casey was learning by the minute. Earlier, he'd watched with interest as the merchandise had been brought out of the wagon, and he was fascinated by the seemingly endless stream of articles that emerged. There were many items of furniture; a great number of china vases and ornaments; various household stuff; and all manner of tools, some working and others, so Granddad Bob told him, needing repairs.

There were toys of every description, including teddy bears, and a big selection of dolls, some wearing frocks and others totally naked, and even one wearing baggy trousers and a sailor's hat.

There was a rusty old doll's pram, and a long iron

rack filled to bursting with second-hand clothes of all sizes and descriptions. The stall was alive with miscellaneous items, every one painstakingly laid out to display its best angle.

'Patrick?'

'Yes?'

'What's a rag-tatter?'

Patrick was surprised by Casey's question. 'What makes you ask that?'

'Because the man on the food stall said you were a rag-tatter.'

'Oh, did he now?'

'Are you . . . a rag-tatter?'

'Well, yes, I suppose I am.'

'Why?'

'Well now, let me see.' He scratched his nose and gave a little cough, then he tried to explain. 'A rag-tatter is somebody who tatts round the streets, asking folks if they've any old rags or anything else they don't want any more. If the man or woman of the house wants rid of something – like the grandma's rusting old mangle in the back yard, or a suit that's too small and been hanging in a wardrobe since the day of the wedding forty years back – they might give it to the rag-tatter, just to be rid of it. Or they might be moving house and don't have room for all the furniture any more, so they'll sort out what to keep and what to let go. The rag-tatter doesn't mind, as long as he gets to sell it on for a bob or two.'

He gave a great sigh of relief to have achieved his explanation. 'So, does that answer your question?'

'Yes, but . . .'

Patrick wasn't listening. He was watching a child lift something from the stall but was relieved when the mother put the item back. 'What's on your mind, son?' He returned his attention to the boy.

Casey was curious. 'Why don't people sell their own stuff, and make "a bob or two" for themselves?'

Patrick was horrified. 'Heaven forbid! If they did that, how do you suppose poor old folk like me would make a living?'

'But it's their stuff.'

Patrick explained, 'They don't mind, and anyway I'm doing them a favour. I'm taking away their rubbish, which they're glad to be rid of it. What's more, I'm equipped to deal with it, while they wouldn't even know where to start. First of all, they don't have a wagon to carry the stuff, and secondly, they don't have the salesmanship to sell it. And that's where I come in. As you know, I have a fine wagon. I am also a very good salesman, as your granddad Bob will tell you.' Feeling important, he drew himself to his full height. 'If I say so myself, I'm the best man for the job. I've been at it most of my life and my father before me. So there you have it, and that's that!'

Casey began to realise over the course of the morning that what came out of the back of that wagon might seem like a load of old rubbish to some, but to a fine, self-made businessman like Patrick, it was money in his pocket.

'Right! Here we are.' Puffing and panting, Granddad Bob returned with three glasses of sarsaparilla, most of it running down his arm where he'd been jostled by the people. 'By! Yer should see the folks arriving now,' he said excitedly. 'It's getting really busy out there.'

He knew how a market attracted all manner of people. Everyone loved the excitement of the coloured awnings and noisy traders; and the countless choices from a vast array of merchandise.

These would-be customers came from all walks of life. Some were professional buyers. These were easy enough to spot, with their notepads and pencils, and often discreet little eye-glasses in their top pockets, useful for examining the marks on the bases of vases.

Others, with far slimmer wallets, might be on the lookout for second-hand items to suit their own personal requirements.

'Hey! These glasses are only half filled!' Patrick glowered at his old friend. 'What did you do, have a sly drink or two on your way back?'

'Don't be daft. They've spilled over 'cause folks kept bumping into me. I never wanted to fetch the drinks in the first place, as well you know. But I'll tell yer what, next time, yer can fetch 'em yerself.'

'I'll do no such thing!' As usual, Patrick gave as good as he got. 'My job is to do the selling and yours is to fetch the drinks. That's the way it's allus been!'

'I never said I minded fetching the drinks, did I? But I do mind being moaned at, through no fault of my own.'

'You're right,' Patrick apologised. 'I'm a miserable old sod, aren't I?'

'Hmm! Yer can say that again.'

'So, are we still friends?'

'Go on then.' Bob raised his glass. 'Here's to us.'

Chinking glasses with his old friend, Patrick drank the entire lot in one go. 'Phaw!' He wiped his mouth with the back of his hand. 'Sure, ye can't beat a glass of sarsaparilla . . . or half a glass, if you see what I mean?'

'Don't you start again!'

'I'm not. It's just that I've a favour to ask.' Holding up his empty glass, he gestured towards the drinks table. 'I don't suppose there's any chance you might—'

'No, there isn't.' The old fella was adamant. 'If yer want another drink, yer can fetch it yersel'. I'm not fighting my way back through that lot, not even for a gold clock.' And Patrick was left in no doubt that he meant it.

'When can I play the guitar, Patrick?' Casey had helped

set up the stall, and waited around all morning, so now he was eager to play for the crowds.

Patrick understood. 'You've been very patient, so ye have.' He drew out an old orange box. 'Here. Sit yerself on that, and start playing whenever ye like.'

In truth, Patrick was a little nervous. He couldn't be sure whether the customers would appreciate the boy's considerable musical talents, or be put off from buying. Some people were funny like that. They came to market for a bargain. As a rule, they had little time to stand and listen.

Granddad Bob, though, had no doubts whatsoever. 'Don't be nervous, lad,' he quietly encouraged his grandson. 'All you need to do is play from the heart, like always.' He paused before adding quietly, 'I taught yer daddy to play the guitar when he were about your age. Mind you, neither me nor yer daddy could ever put the heart and soul into a tune the same way you do. It's like . . . well, it's like you were born with a natural instinct for the music.'

'That's what Daddy told me. "You bring the guitar to life", he told me, "and when you sing, it's like there's only you and the guitar in the whole wide world".'

'Well, there yer go, lad. That's what I've been trying to say.'

'Granddad?'

'Yes, lad?'

With big, soulful eyes, the boy looked up at him, and each knew what the other was thinking.

In a small, broken voice, Casey said, 'I wish my daddy was here.'

'I know, lad.' The old fella shared his pain. 'He can't be here and, hard as it is, you and me both . . . well, lad we'll just have to try and get used to it.'

'Do you think he might be listening?'

With tears clouding his old eyes, Granddad Bob put on a smile and ruffled the boy's hair. 'I'm sure he's up there right now, looking down on the pair of us, an' I know he'll be giving you all the strength you need. So, go to it, lad. Just play the music, an' mek' the people smile.'

He winked encouragingly. 'Remember what yer daddy taught yer, and play the music like he's right there standing beside yer. Oh, but he'll be that proud, he'll have a smile on him wide as the River Mersey.' He glanced at the people mooching about the stalls. 'They're all here, waiting for you to start. So bring 'em in, lad,' he murmured. 'Bring 'em in.' Taking out his big hanky, he wrapped it round his nose and blew hard, then slyly dabbed away his tears.

When Casey began to play, the people inched nearer, enthralled by the boy and his music. When he started softly singing, they stayed to look and listen, and to enjoy.

Casey was nervous, until he remembered what his granddad had said – that his daddy would give him strength – and believing that, his heart grew quiet.

Lured by Casey's voice and the accompanying music, young Susie broke away from Steve and Alice to run ahead, pushing through the growing crowd, until she was so close, she could have reached out and touched him.

Lost in the song, Casey did not see her. His sensitive young fingers moved softly against the guitar strings, the rhythmic sound mingling with the purity of his voice. The voice was still immature, yet passionate and emotional, in perfect harmony with the music, and the silent crowd were mesmerised.

Just an arm's reach away, the two old men watched.

In Casey, they found Tom. They saw the teachings of the father living on in the boy, and in the pride and wonder of this boy's natural talent was a great well of sorrow for the loss of his daddy.

And yet, in a way, the music and the emotion somehow transcended the sorrow. All was well.

Concerned that Susie could get lost in the crowd, Alice and Steve also pushed their way to the front.

'He's got the most beautiful voice,' Alice remarked softly, 'soft and easy, as though he's talking just to you, and you can believe every word he sings.'

Steve made no comment, being too engrossed in the boy's performance.

Deeply moved and quietly excited, he believed he may have stumbled on a unique talent. True, the voice was not yet honed to perfection, but it was there, like an uncut diamond waiting to be shaped and polished.

In all his professional years, he had never witnessed such raw talent. 'He has a haunting kind of voice,' he said softly to Alice. 'He doesn't just sing the song, he lives it. He feels it, every word, every note.'

Alice had never seen Steve like this; it was as though he was alone here, and all he could see and hear was the talent within that small boy.

So thrilled he could hardly contain himself, Steve knew without a doubt that he was witnessing a star in the making. And he couldn't wait to call his colleagues.

Suddenly it was over, and the crowd went crazy. 'More!' they shouted, and more they got. Even the stallholders came to listen.

Two of the stallholders came up behind Steve, and he couldn't help but overhear their conversation. Like all the locals, these men knew of the recent tragedy that had affected the family, and their hearts went out to the boy.

'What the Good Lord takes away in one hand, he gives back in the other,' one man said, while the other replied earnestly, 'True, but it's not the ones who are gone that suffer. It's them as are left behind. And that little lad there . . . well, to give a performance like that, after the tragedy and all. It's unbelievable, when the poor little devil must be hurting so bad.'

Steve was curious. 'What do you mean?' he asked the stocky fellow with the most to say. 'What tragedy?'

Wary of strangers, the man backed away. 'I'm not one for gossip,' he said, 'but the boy's granddad is stood over there.' He pointed to Bob. 'If you really want to know, you should ask him. I doubt if he'll want to talk about it, though; especially with young Casey being here.'

With the crowd moving forward to congratulate the boy and throw coins into his hat, Steve went to speak with the old man, while Alice and Susie went to speak with the child.

'I told you he was wonderful!' Holding onto Alice's hand, Susie pressed forward. 'I said he was good. I told you, didn't I? Do you think he'll remember me from the bus? Will he talk to me, do you think?' She tugged at Alice's skirt. 'Hurry up, Mummy, before we lose him again!'

Alice had to run to keep up with her.

'LOOK OUT! THE BUGGERS ARE ROBBING JACK'S STALL!'

When the cry went up, Jack and the other stallholders ran off to nab the thieves, who were already fleeing with their haul. This left the way clear for Susie to approach the boy.

Casey recognised Susie straight away. 'You were on the bus,' he said shyly. 'I remember.'

Alice made the introductions. 'This is Susie, and I'm her mother, Alice.'

'Hello, I'm Casey.' He was at a loss as to what he should do or say, though he thought Susie was very pretty, and had a nice smile.

'Your music was lovely,' Susie told him, 'and I like your singing.' She also was a bit embarrassed. It was one thing smiling at a boy on the bus, but here and now, face to face, she felt awkward.

'Who taught you to play like that?' Secretly amused, Alice sensed the awkwardness between these two youngsters.

'My daddy taught me to play the guitar.' Somehow, talking of his daddy to strangers gave Casey a sense of comfort. When he and his granddad talked about his daddy, they both got very sad, but it didn't feel like that when he talked to this nice woman. Instead, he felt proud, and happy.

He invited them to sit down on an upturned orange box, while he entertained them with lively descriptions of his daddy. He told them how the guitar had been handed down from his granddad Bob, though he was careful not to mention how his mummy had deliberately broken the guitar in a temper.

As the three of them contentedly chatted, Casey felt more happy and relaxed than he had done in a very long time.

Not too far away from where Casey and his visitors were chatting, Steve was deep in conversation with Granddad Bob.

'I'm glad you think he could be a real star.' The old fella was excited that Casey had been noticed by a man who seemed important in the music business. 'Though to me and them as knows him, Casey has always been a little star,' he finished proudly.

'I'm sure he has.' Steve sensed the resistance. 'I know I'm a stranger to you, and I know I'm asking a lot, but it's very rare to find such a gift, like the one your grandson possesses. OK, it will need work, and it will take time, but he has it in him to be a major talent.'

Awkward as ever, the old fella reminded the visitor, 'Happen he'll not want to be a "major talent".'

'You're right. Maybe he won't, but have you ever asked him? Has he told you what he would like to do with his life?' He suspected the boy would leap at the chance to make music his life.

'And if he does say he wants to make a career out of his talents, what would happen next?' Granddad Bob fully intended to tread carefully.

'Well, first off I would talk to a colleague of mine. He's ex-band; now a respected manager. He's a man who knows his stuff. If you let me call him with my opinion of the boy's exceptional talent, he'll want to hear your grandson perform. No doubt he'll make his way north, so he can hear young Casey for himself.'

'And if he wants to tek him on, what then?'

'Well, that will be up to Casey's immediate family – his parents perhaps.'

'That can't be.' The old fella put him right straight away. 'Casey's an orphan. I'm his family now, his only family!' Memories of Ruth darkened his manner.

Steve was shocked. 'Oh, I'm so sorry. I didn't realise, though I did overhear someone say there had been a tragedy . . .'

'Listen to me, young man! All you need to know is that I'm the boy's family – me, an' nobody else. Casey is my only grandchild. He lives with me and, like I say, the lad's got nobody else. So, I look after him. I provide for him, and I take good care of him. An' that's an end to it.'

'I understand, and of course in that situation everything will be channelled through you, Mr . . . ?'

'It's Bob!' He was beginning to warm towards this young man; especially as he seemed genuine in his claim to help Casey.

'And I'm Steve.' He shook the old fella's hand. 'I want

you to know, I've been in the music business for some time, and I'm really impressed by your grandson's performance just now. I'm particularly impressed by the confident manner in which he plays the guitar, and his voice is unique. It has that easy, emotional quality that many singers spend a lifetime trying to perfect.' A thought occurred to him. 'Was he ever tutored by a professional?'

'No, he's never been to anyone of that nature. Mind you, I taught myself to play the guitar when I were young. Then I taught my son, Tom, and he taught the boy. It were a family pastime, so to speak.'

'And he's had no singing lessons at all?'

'Never.'

The old fella recalled one particular time Casey sang for them. 'It were a Christmas Day, as I remember. Casey were just six year old. We'd finished our Christmas dinner and I played a tune on the guitar – "White Christmas" – it were one of his late grandma's favourite songs and that day, me and his mammy and daddy sang it to him. Afterwards, we were sitting chatting, the three of us together, when suddenly the lad started singing. I don't mind tellin' yer, it were a real eye-opener. We couldn't believe it. He sang all the way through, every word, all in perfect tune, and his voice . . . well, it were like that of a little angel. Since then, you can often hear him singing, especially when he plays the guitar.' His face beamed with pride. 'He sang at the school concert last year, and everyone got up and clapped.'

Bob shook his head as though in disbelief. 'Where he got his musical talent from, Lord only knows. It certainly weren't from me, nor really from his daddy, although Tom was quite good. As for his mammy, soon ever the lad opened his mouth to sing, or even speak, she'd be down his throat like a mad dog . . . telling him to be quiet . . . that nobody wanted to hear him sing . . .' the old fella's voice tailed off.

'I'm sorry.' Steve felt the need to apologise.

'No need. It's me that should be sorry, for 'avin' brought it up. Sadly, things were not all that good between his parents. But that's not for me to say, and nor for you to worry about, 'cause they're not here; neither of 'em, more's the pity.'

There were many occasions of late – much like today with Casey performing for the crowds – when Bob wondered about Ruth, and his heart was heavy.

Steve was fascinated by the lad's background. 'Well, it's obvious that somewhere along the way, one of your past relatives had an instinct for the music, and it's found its way down to the boy. It's a gift, and it needs nurturing.'

'Hey! Don't get ahead of yersel', fella. Nothing's been decided yet.'

Steve quickly curbed his enthusiasm. 'I'm sorry, but look, Bob, if you want me to go away, I'll go away. But I promise you, I don't want to do anything that will in any way upset you, or Casey.'

'Hmm.' Bob had a good feeling about this fella. 'All right, I reckon I believe yer. I might even be tempted to trust yer, but I need to be sure.'

Steve was encouraged. 'So, can I call my colleague? Can I run it by him and see what he thinks?'

'I expect so, but afore yer do that, you and me had better get to grips with what you have in mind, 'cause whatever the man might think, and whatever me and you talk about, you need to understand, it's Casey who has the last word.'

'Of course. That goes without saying.'

'Good. So go ahead, make your call, and if you come to my house when you're all sorted, we'll all three of us discuss what's on offer.'

Collecting a pen from the stall he scribbled his address on a piece of wrapping paper and handed it to Steve. 'Meantime, I'll talk to the lad an' see what he has to say.'

Steve thanked him. Then they shook hands and went their separate ways.

The old fella hurried off, eager to relay the news to Patrick; though he had decided that it would be unwise to tell Casey anything until he had received certain reassurances from Steve. And even then, he would be guarding the boy's wellbeing every step of the way.

Meanwhile, Steve went in search of Susie and Alice. He found them at a cockle stall. 'We saw you talking to the boy's grandfather,' Alice said, 'so we thought we'd have a quick look round.'

'Look, Uncle Steve,' Susie held up a piece of paper, '. . . me and Casey are friends now. He gave me his address, and Mummy let me give him ours, and now we're going to write to each other.'

'Really?' Steve held out the piece of paper with the scribble on. 'Snap! I've got an address too, and as soon as I can get hold of Jim, I'll be discussing Casey's musical future. Tomorrow, I'll be reporting to Casey's grandfather.'

While Susie was greatly excited about his news, Alice was cautious. 'I can see the boy is talented, Steve, but he's also very young. I know it's none of my business and what I know about the world of music isn't even worth knowing, but I hope you've thought this through. If you don't mind me saying, there are many other issues here, besides music.'

'Yes, I'm aware of all the issues, like home and family, and his schooling. Other than his granddad, I'm told that Casey has no family, and before you ask, I haven't been made aware of the reasons why, although I did overhear someone talking about a tragedy concerning the boy. His home is with his grandfather. If, after hearing him perform, Jim leaps at the chance to nurture young Casey towards a successful career, we must then abide by what both the boy and his grandfather have to say. If it works out in favour of a career in music, we'll need to discuss important things, such as his schooling.'

Alice was satisfied that Steve had the boy's welfare at heart. 'He certainly has something very special,' she said, as they headed away from the market. 'Let's hope everything works out.'

Steve was thinking ahead. 'Like you say, there's a lot to think about, and while I'm convinced that the boy's future lies in music, I'm determined that his childhood must not be disrupted.'

'I know you'll do right by him.'

'I will, but first I'm anxious to know what Jim might say. I do know that when he hears Casey, he won't be able to resist taking him on.' He chuckled. 'First, though, he's got to get past the old man.'

'I think it's sad that Casey only has his granddad.' Susie had an idea. 'Maybe you two can love him, like you love me?'

That made them smile. 'You're a special little girl, Susie,' Steve was deeply touched, 'and I'm very glad we've got you.'

Alice glanced at her watch. 'Come on, you two. We'd best get a move on. There's the luggage to collect, and a train to catch.'

'Don't worry,' Steve assured her. 'If there's time at the hotel before we leave for the station, I'll make that call to Jim then.'

When they arrived at the hotel, Alice went straight to the desk and ordered the luggage.

While the porter loaded the luggage into the boot of the car, Alice and Susie found a table by the window, and Steve made his call to Jim.

'I've to get Alice and Susie to the train station,' Steve began, 'so I'll talk and you listen.'

'OK, I'm listening . . . what's the news?' Jim was a laid-back, canny man with the Midas touch where musical talent was concerned.

Steve told him only as much as he needed to know for now. 'The boy is a real gem,' he said. 'Not only does he possess a warm and engaging voice, he also plays a guitar with heart and soul. He's a natural, Jim. He's never been professionally taught. He's just an ordinary kid, with extraordinary talent, and from what I can gather, he's an orphan into the bargain. He's also got a granddad who would guard him with his life, so you can't just go barging in heavy-footed.'

'I understand that, and I wouldn't dream of being "heavy-footed".' Jim was wounded. 'The thing is, I'm up to my eyeballs with this new group, so if you want me to go up there, I hope the boy is as good as you claim.'

'Oh, he is, I promise you. I wouldn't be singing his praises if I didn't believe in his talent. Like I say, though, he'll need coaxing along for a few years. You'll need to treat him tenderly for his talent to grow and mature. Oh, but what a talent to have on your books for the future. If you don't sign him up, somebody else will. Especially now that he's taken to busking in public.'

'You're really fired up about this boy's talent, aren't you?'

'Yes, but only because I believe he's got something truly special. You can't *not* watch him when he performs. He plays the guitar like someone years older, and when he sings, he has a voice that taps into the emotions. The number of artists who can do that you could count on one hand, and well you know it. If you don't come and see him, you'll regret it.'

Jim was persuaded. 'Trouble is, I'm up to my neck at

the minute with tight schedules and such. I've also got a shop-window gig to organise for that new group. It's taken me weeks to get the powers that be to hear them, but at last I've got a date in the diary. You'll need to give me time to sort it all out.'

'I understand, and how's it all going?' No regrets, eh?' There was a brief silence, before the answer came back, 'I tell you what, Steve, I don't regret being off the road and in a secure situation. I reckon we should have followed our grown-up dreams long before now. Going into the management side for me was the right thing to do; and after talking about your iconic studio for more years than I care to remember, you're now seeing your vision slowly but surely take shape right before your eyes. I'm proud of you. We all are.'

'Thanks, Jim. It's been a long time coming, and we're not there yet.'

'About the boy, Steve, I won't let you down,' Jim promised him. 'We always need new blood, new talent to nurture, and from what you tell me, it sounds like you've stumbled on something special.'

'Well, I think so. Anyway, Jim, I'll be on my way home soon, so if you haven't managed to get hold of me in the meantime, I'll call you when I get back. Soon as I can, I'll relay your thoughts to the grandfather, just so he doesn't think we're messing him about.'

'Good idea, Steve. Got to go now . . . we'll talk later.'

Steve relayed the good news to Alice and Susie, who were waiting in the lounge. 'He's really interested; enough to try and clear his schedules so he can find time to come up here.'

'That's marvellous, but when does he think he'll be coming up?' Alice still had her reservations.

'He couldn't say, but I'll see him when I get back, and we'll sort something out.'

A few minutes later, on the way to the station, both Alice and Susie could not stop talking about Casey and what was happening.

'He's my new friend,' Susie announced proudly. 'Did you tell Jim it was me who found him?'

Both Alice and Steve laughed out loud. 'Casey is a lucky young man to have a friend like you.' Alice gave her a cuddle. 'And he's lucky to have Uncle Steve looking out for him.'

'He'll be treated with kid gloves.' Steve was every bit as determined as the old man to ensure that Jim was kept in line. Even now, he was considering a number of clauses in a possible contract in order to ensure Casey's wellbeing.

To do that, though, he would need authority to represent both the boy and his grandfather, and that would require him earning their trust.

Driving towards the station, it pleased him to hear Alice and her daughter deep in conversation. What he wouldn't give to have children, the thought was never far from his mind.

He grew melancholy.

On the whole, he had been more fortunate than most men, enjoying good health, an attractive wife who brought him many compliments, and being able to fulfil his great love for his music. Yet he felt as though his life was unfulfilled; that somehow, somewhere along the way, he had missed out.

He let his thoughts wander back over the years. Deep down, he knew what was missing; he had always known, although he would never openly admit it.

What he needed was someone special in his lonely life. Someone who would love him for himself, and not for the material things he might provide. Someone who could make him whole, and bring his spirit alive.

A certain someone crept into his mind: Ruth, who had

stolen his heart. Shy and loving . . . her upturned face waiting for a kiss. Ruth was someone he had never been able to forget.

His heart turned over. He could see her now, a passionate young woman, with strong, warm eyes and flowing hair, and a smile that could light up the night skies.

He felt a rush of sadness. He wondered where she was now, that special person who had stolen his heart one wonderful night, lying on a quiet, moonlit beach; with a twinkling sky overhead, and the sound of music in the distance.

His heart sank when he recalled what Connie had told him the night she'd come to see him at the stage door. She was charming and kind, and sorry that he'd 'been used', as Connie put it. She said that she was uncomfortable at having to deliver such a 'cruel' message, but she'd been asked to pass on Ruth's words, that he had been 'nothing more to her than just a bit of fun; a one-night stand that she already regretted.'

Connie delivered the message word for word, revealing how Ruth had made up with her ex, and they were planning to get married . . .

'Steve?' Alice's voice interrupted his thoughts. 'You're very quiet.'

'Am I?'

'Well, yes, you've hardly said two words in the past ten minutes. Are you all right?'

'Oh, I'm fine, Alice, thanks. I was just thinking, that's all.'

'I wondered if you were worried about something to do with the site and all that. I know it's been playing on your mind a lot lately.'

'Well, let's hope it won't be too long before we see the buildings up and standing proud in all their glory. I've known for some time that there's a real need for a studio complex that can accommodate musicians and performers who want the best.'

He confided his wider vision. 'I've already had long, encouraging talks with both the architect and the authorities. I've asked to extend the accommodation wing, and so far, there doesn't seem to be much serious opposition; though I'm counting on nothing yet; especially as the planning permission is still in limbo. Mind you, the fact that the site is huge, and also that at one time it was a holiday complex, is well and truly in my favour. Or at least that's what the agent says.'

Alice never ceased to be impressed by his determination. 'Mike says you told him you could be up to your eyes in debt for the next forty years.'

'That's very true.'

'So, why do you want to build such a big complex? Why don't you just build a block of studios, like you first intended? The people who use the studios can stay in local hotels.'

'Think about it, Alice. I'm aiming at every musician who works at his music twenty-four hours a day, seven days a week. They tour not just this country, but the wide world. When they're on the road, they require a base to call their own, where everything they require is right there at their fingertips. They can eat, sleep, practise and write their music with no worries about upsetting anybody. These musicians want a place to lay their heads. I know. I've been there, and so has Jim; who, incidentally, is one of my backers.'

Alice could see the sense of it all. 'Wow! You've got it all worked out, haven't you?'

'That's because it's been years in the making, but now, at long last I've found the perfect site. And I'll be creating work for the locals which is a good thing.'

'So, *was* Mike right? Will it take you into debt for the next forty years?'

'I'll be honest. Yes, it could break me if it was all on my back, but I do have two genuine backers. Jim can see this project bringing in serious money. I also have the bank behind me, and they would never back such a project unless they could see a healthy return. So, Alice, you're not to worry. You can see I've done my homework and I know that once it's up and running, the word will spread and the money will come pouring in. Then I can pay my debts. Until then, we'll climb the mountains as we get to them.'

'You're a brave man, Steve, I'll give you that.'

'Not brave exactly.' He winked at her. 'I'm just pig-headed, and now that I've started it, I can't let go.'

Alice laughed. 'Do you think we don't know that?'

'Are you gonna be famous, Uncle Steve?' Susie woke from a short nap.

Steve smiled. 'I think I've had my small share of fame, sweetheart, but, great as it is, I've discovered there's far more to life than that.

'What then?'

'Let me see . . . you for a start, and your mummy. If it hadn't been for you two coming up here with me, I'd have had a lonely trip, wouldn't I?'

'Well, Uncle Steve, whenever you're going away, just tell us and we'll come with you every time.'

Both Alice and Steve exchanged little smiles at that. 'Well, now, that's very kind of you, I must say, but we all have busy lives, and I'm just happy you came with me this time.'

'Daddy's coming home, did you know that?'

'I know, sweetheart, and I'm sure he's looking forward to seeing his little girl.'

'I'm excited too.'

'I'm sure you are.'

Steve wished he felt the same excitement at the prospect of seeing Connie, but sadly there was not the same closeness between them. There never really had been.

He thought about his lonely life, and that amazing night on the beach, when he and Ruth had made love, wrapped in each other's arms as they lay on the sand and counted the twinkling stars in the night skies.

And now, he had come to realise that in life if you missed that one chance, that one magical moment, it may be lost for all time.

Where Ruth was concerned, his moment in time had gone, and he deeply regretted that.

CHAPTER THIRTEEN

AFTER WAVING OFF Alice and Susie at the station, Steve felt obliged to make one more errand. He turned from the road he would have taken to his hotel, and headed instead for the backstreets of Blackpool.

He cut across by the amusement arcade and wound his way through a complex of narrow streets until he saw the house where he'd left the victim of the nasty attack.

Realising there was nowhere to park without blocking other cars in, he drove on, keeping a lookout for a space.

As he slowly cruised past, he noticed a woman walking towards the house. He slowed the car, wondering if she might be the very woman he was here to ask about. He couldn't be sure, because that night he'd never really got a proper look at her face.

Now, though, he stopped the car and turned to get a look at the woman as she climbed the steps to the front door, and his heart flipped over. There was something vaguely familiar about her, stirring a memory from long ago of a certain night; a certain young woman.

She had the same flowing hair, the same pert figure and a proud way of holding herself as she moved. The memories flooded back, taking him to the past when he truly believed he had fallen in love.

The woman had stirred his senses.

Suddenly she turned, as though looking right at him, and he tried so hard to convince himself that it was her.

Then he was convincing himself that it was not her at all, that it was only wishful thinking, and besides, after all this time, how would he know her anyway? There must be many young women with flowing hair and a strikingly attractive face.

'Calm yourself, man!' he whispered, forcing a small laugh. 'Ruth has been on your mind for so long, you're looking for her in every woman you meet. It's been years! You don't even know what she looks like now. She might be big as a house with half a dozen kids, or she might have dyed her hair a different colour. She could have even gone abroad.'

Even so, there was something about that woman climbing those steps. Something about the way her hair settled on her shoulders when she turned round. Something. Nothing. His mind was in turmoil.

When the driver of a car behind angrily sounded his horn, Steve almost leaped out of his skin. 'All right! All right!' Being forced to move on, he went down the side road and into the street beyond, where he finally managed to park.

Scrambling out of the car, he turned the key in the door lock and ran back up the street, and on to the boarding house where, breathless and excited, he impatiently banged on the door.

'Who the devil's that?' When the banging started, Marilyn was in the act of pouring two cups of tea; one for her and the other for Ruth, who had just arrived back from the shops.

'Don't worry, I'll go and see.' Turning from the cupboard where she was packing away the groceries, Ruth went to the front window and peeped out. She was slightly shaken by the sight of the man outside.

'Who is it?' Marilyn put the milk in the cups. When Ruth gave no answer, she asked again, 'Ruth, who's at the door?' She came through to the front. On seeing Ruth's worried expression, she made her way over. 'It's not that salesman again, is it? I can see I'll have to give him a piece of my mind!'

Ruth was frantic. 'No! Don't go to the door. I can't be sure, but . . . I think it might be him . . .'

'Who?'

In trembling voice, Ruth reminded her, 'Remember when I told you about the man I slept with on the beach that night . . . the one that made me pregnant?'

Marilyn scowled. 'What? You mean the cowardly bugger who ran off and wanted nothing to do with it? Are you saying that's him, outside my door?' Angered, she took a step towards the door. 'It's time he were told a thing or two about responsibility!'

Before she could open the door, Ruth took hold of her arm. 'No! I'm not altogether sure it's him. It's been a long time and besides, even if it is him, I want to put the past behind me. I've got a new life now. Don't go out, please. Whoever he is, he'll go away in a minute.'

For what seemed an age, the two women stood there, close to the window, but far enough away that Steve could neither see them nor hear them.

Opening the letter box, he called out, 'Hello!' When there was no reply, he called again, 'Hello?'

'It's no good. I'll have to get rid of him. I'll not say anything, and I won't let him in,' the landlady promised Ruth. 'You have my word on it.' She gave Ruth a gentle push. 'Get upstairs . . . go on, hurry.'

On soft footsteps, Ruth went up to her room, while Marilyn opened the front door.

'What the devil d'you think you're playing at?' she demanded. 'It's just as well my boarders are out and about, or you'd have frightened the life outta them. What is it? What d'you want?'

With a shock, she recognised the man who had brought Ruth home that awful night of the attack. 'Oh . . . it's you . . . you're the one who brought her home, aren't you?' Now she didn't know what to think.

If he really was the same man who had made Ruth with child some nine years ago, and if he was also the man who had brought her here that night, why didn't either of them recognise the other?

Huddled on the landing, Ruth was shocked by the older woman's words. Filled with shame, she did not want to believe that this was really the man who brought her home that night. At the time, hurt and ashamed, she was in no fit state to worry about who was helping her.

Now, though, having watched him from the window and listened to his voice, all her doubt as to his identity was gone.

It was him. Casey's real father was really here. Standing just a short distance from her.

Her shame was tenfold. What would he have thought of her, looking the way she had, all dirty and dishevelled, being dragged away by those men like a piece of meat for the taking?

Going softly from the landing to her bedroom, she huddled on the bed, devastated. After all this time he was here and her guilt was crippling.

Since leaving Casey behind, she had lost all respect for herself. These had been dark days, but Marilyn had pulled her through. Now, looking back on her life as a mother, she had come to believe that Casey was better off without her.

She hoped that the man outside would never know

that the woman he slept with that one night was also the down-and-out woman he recently rescued. Back then, when they met up she was younger, without responsibility, she had been footloose and carefree, just out for a bit of fun; but from that fateful, wonderful night, her whole life had been changed for ever.

The stranger didn't love her – why would he? She was just one of many girls who threw themselves at him. Nor did he want to know when Connie took him the letter telling him that she was pregnant with his child, and that she needed to meet with him.

When Connie had got back and told her he was angry and that he wanted nothing to do with her, Ruth had not forgotten the devastation she felt.

As she had recently confessed to Marilyn, if it hadn't been for him abandoning her and the child, she would never have been so bitter. And she would never have fooled Tom into raising the boy he believed was his.

Sometimes, life was so cruel, it created cruelty in others. And once you were set along a certain path, it seemed there was no way back.

It was only since gaining Marilyn's friendship, and being able to confide in her, that Ruth had come to realise how wicked she had been to Tom, and Casey.

Seeing Casey's father again had shaken her deeply. It had also made her realise how much she still loved him.

She heard his voice, and her heart ached for what might have been.

'I've been in the area concluding some important business, but I'm away home soon,' he was telling Marilyn. 'I thought I'd just call by before I go, to see if the young woman is all right after her ordeal.'

'Yes, like I said, she's fine now, thanks to you.'

'Can I see her, d'you think?'

Marilyn had to think quickly. 'Oh, but she's not here

any more. In fact, she's gone back home . . . to be with her relatives.'

Steve was confused. 'I thought she was your daughter . . . or a relative, at least?'

'No. She was no relative; just a friend.'

'And the woman I saw coming into your house just now, that wasn't her?'

'No. She's my cleaner . . . late, as usual. Busy little thing, she is. Got three kids and an old relative who runs her ragged.'

Steve apologised. 'Only, I had an idea she might be someone I met about nine years ago.' He gave a rueful smile. 'She was the one that got away, as they say.' He felt he could confide in this woman. 'We had one night together, and then she was gone. I've not see her from that day to this, and I don't suppose I'll ever see her again.'

His heartfelt comment had Marilyn wondering. 'Why did you let her go if you were that smitten?'

'To be honest, I don't know; except it was only afterwards that I found out how much I cared for her.'

'And so you still care for her, after all this time . . . nine years or more, you say?'

'Something like that,' he answered quietly. 'I loved her, then I let her go. Isn't that a sad tale, eh? But there you are.' He gave a sorry shrug. 'Sometimes life just gets in the way.'

'It does, you're absolutely right there.' She should know.

'Well, thank you for your time, and if you ever see that young woman again, tell her I was glad to be of help.'

'I will.'

He gave a smile. 'Well, I'd best be off. I'm sorry to have disturbed you.'

'Cheerio then, and thank you again for what you did.'

'No need for thanks,' he said. 'Any decent person would have done the same.'

He waved as he went, muttering to himself. *I was wrong. It wasn't her.* He felt incredibly sad. *I suppose it's time to close that chapter in my life.*

Judging by the way she had haunted him these past years, he knew it would not be easy; if possible at all.

Marilyn went upstairs to tell Ruth he was gone. She found her lying across the bed, breaking her heart.

'Hey! That's enough of that, my girl.' Taking her by the shoulders, she sat her on the edge of the bed. 'If you wanted to renew your relationship with him, you could have come downstairs. Though you'd have had to be sure it really was the man who left you pregnant.'

'I'm sure. I heard him talking to you . . . in that same soft, warm voice I remember. I watched him walk away, and for one brief minute he turned round, and he almost caught me looking. He didn't see me, but I saw him. He's older, and looking more like a businessman than the member of a singing group, but it's him all right . . . Casey's real father. I would gamble my life on it.'

'You still have strong feelings for him, don't you?'

'Yes. Since that night we made love, I've never stopped thinking about him. He was all I ever wanted. I know I should hate him for what he did, but I don't. However hard I try, I can't stop wanting to be with him, but I know it will never happen.

'When I found out I was carrying his child, Connie was the only one I told. She was so angry that she found where the group was playing next, and we planned to go and see him. I asked her to take a letter to him, and she promised to make sure he got it.

'In the letter, I told him how much I cared for him, and that I wanted to keep the baby. I said I was sorry not to have spent more time with him, but that I understood how busy he was. I asked that we should meet and talk about what to do.

394

'Connie told me that he did read the letter, and then he got really nasty.'

Marilyn saw how upset she was getting. 'Enough now, dear,' she urged gently. 'You're only punishing yourself all over again.'

Ruth looked up with tear-stained eyes. 'How could he do that?' she asked. 'How could he turn away from me and his child like that?'

In the light of more recent events, Marilyn herself wondered the very same. 'I really don't know, dear. That's why I wondered if you were sure about the man who just left: the man who fought those bullies in the alley. To my mind, he doesn't sound like a man who would have deserted you way back then, when you desperately needed him. Any more than he deserted you in the alley.'

'That's true,' Ruth agreed, 'and I could be wrong about the man who came to the door just now, only there was something about him, I'm almost certain he's Casey's father.'

Burying her head in her arms, she began to sob, and once she started, she couldn't stop. 'I'm a wicked woman,' she confided brokenly. 'I've done terrible things, and now they're coming back to haunt me. Why could I not have loved Casey like a mother should? What happened was not his fault, but I still blamed him, then I learned to hate him.'

Turning to Marilyn, she asked, 'What's wrong with me? How could I have been so wicked? What made me use Tom in such a cowardly way? He didn't deserve it. He was a good man . . .'

Collapsing into the older woman's arms, she blamed herself for Tom's suicide, and the boy's dislike of her. She wanted to go back, to try and put things right, but it was too late.

'It's all too late,' she cried bitterly. 'Because of me,

Tom's dead and my own son hates me. I don't blame them. I should be burned in Hell for what I've done. I should be punished, like I punished them.'

Deeply moved by this young woman's heartfelt plight, Marilyn cupped her two hands about Ruth's face. 'Look at me, child.'

She looked into Ruth's haggard eyes, and in the gentlest voice she told her, 'Don't ever think you're the only woman who has ever palmed a child off on some poor unsuspecting man. From what you told me before about Tom and the great love he had for you, I believe he would have found it in his heart to forgive you anything.'

'Do you really think so?' Feeling lost, Ruth laid her head on the older woman's shoulder. 'Do you really think he's forgiven me?'

'Yes, child, I really do. After all, you gave him a son he adored. A son who brought him untold joy; of a kind he might never have known, if it hadn't been for you.'

'But when I told him he wasn't Casey's father, I destroyed him.'

In her tortured mind, she could see the pain on Tom's face now, and she could hardly bear it. 'Oh, if only you'd been there. He was torn apart, and I did that to him. *Me!* I broke his heart . . . the only man who had ever treated me like a princess. A man who had loved me without condition. I saw the awful shock on his face, and I felt his loathing for me. It should have been me who jumped off that bridge. I should have been the one to die. Not Tom.'

Marilyn grew fearful for her sanity. 'Stop it now, child!' she said sternly. 'I know . . . I do know.'

'You don't! Nobody does, except me . . . and the boy. He was there. He knew that Tom could never find it in his heart to forgive me, and neither could he. But I was so out of my mind, I didn't care.'

When the burden of what she had done cut too deep,

she sat up and, frantically running her hands through her hair, she raised her voice for the world to hear. 'I KNEW WHAT I WAS DOING TO THEM, AND I DIDN'T EVEN CARE!'

She was in turmoil, suffering like she had never suffered before. Because now she could see herself for what she was . . . what she had been. 'That good, kind man took his own life because of me . . . because of what I did to him.'

'Ssh, child . . . ssh now.' The older woman held her close as Ruth's body shuddered with sobs.

Marilyn held her until finally she grew quiet. Then she gently laid her down on the bed to sleep.

Placing a cover over her, she was able to let her own tears fall for this sorry, broken young woman. We all make mistakes, she thought, feverishly dabbing at the tears as they tumbled down her face. Some of us more than others. In the end, though, our sins will always find us out.

At the door, she turned a moment, gazing on Ruth's crumpled body. 'Sometimes, when we're in the grip of a terrible rage, we cause pain and suffering,' she murmured. 'It's the saddest thing, but true. One way or another, we all have to pay the price, when that pain comes back to haunt us.'

Years ago, she too had learned the harshness of blaming others for her own ill fortunes.

She stood awhile at the door, her gaze lingering on Ruth. 'Be strong, child,' she told her softly. 'For too long, you've locked it all away. Now that you've managed to inch open the door, it's just a matter of having the courage to walk through it.'

She turned away, deeply shaken by the ordeal she had just experienced. Taking a hanky from her pinny pocket, she dabbed at her tearful eyes, and took a deep, invigorating breath. Oh! There's a half-bottle o' that brandy you tucked away at Christmas. That's what you need, my dear, she thought, a cup o' tea warmed with a generous nip o' brandy.

The thought of licking her tongue round that brandy brought a little smile to her face.

~

Steve despaired when the meeting next morning with Edward Mull brought more revelations regarding the site.

'We've had a bit of a setback,' Edward informed Steve. 'The surveyors have discovered a network of old water-pipes running through an area that they were assured was clear. Initially, because the area is well away from where the actual buildings will be, it didn't seem to be a threat to the project.'

'So, why is it a threat now?' Steve was frustrated.

'Well, unfortunately, it's been suggested by one of the locals that, many years ago, long before the holiday camp was set up, the back end of the site had been a petrol station. So now, because, for some reason, this garage was never shown on the site plan, it has to be checked and cleared.'

The agent was just as angry as Steve. 'Somebody along the way did not do their job properly, and now we're looking at a hold-up of at least a fortnight . . . if not longer.'

'So, is it likely to affect the permission in the long run, or can it be dealt with?'

'It can be dealt with. I've already had assurances from the council. The trouble is, they have to be seen to be doing their duty, and that means ruling out any possible danger or health threats to the local community. Mind you, it's in our favour that the holiday site was there for many years and, so far as they could find out, the pipes never caused any problem. In fact it wasn't even known that they were there.'

There was little Steve could do, but leave it in the hands of Edward. 'Ring me daily,' he directed the agent. 'Keep me posted at every stage.'

'You can rely on it. So now, go home and take a breather; book a table for dinner with your wife tomorrow night. Just relax. I'll keep this moving here. You'll know any news as soon as I do.'

'All right, but meantime, keep shifting things along. The last thing I need is for the project to be held up for any length of time. Don't forget, I have backers to answer to.'

'I understand, and I'm on it. You have my word.'

With nothing at present for him to do, Steve left; disheartened but not altogether defeated. As far as he was concerned, they'd hit a stumbling block, not a brick wall. With luck, his dream was still intact.

It was just unfortunate that he had no one to share it with.

~

He was eager to get home, he started out straight away.

He recalled the agent's well-intentioned words: 'book a table for dinner with your wife'.

If I never came home again, I dare say Connie wouldn't even notice, he thought.

Glancing at the petrol gauge, he saw he needed fuel, so he pulled off the main route and found a garage.

After he'd filled the tank, he called home to let Connie know he was on his way.

'What time will you be here?' she wanted to know.

'I'm not sure. The traffic is getting heavier, so let's say another hour or thereabouts, to be on the safe side. Oh, and if you like, we can book a table at Forresters for tomorrow night. In fact, you can book it now, if you like?'

'We'll talk about it when you get back. I have a hairdresser's appointment, so I might not be back by the time you arrive home. I'll see you later, though.'

'OK, not a problem. Bye then.' He replaced the receiver. 'Looking forward to seeing you, Steve,' he mimicked her voice. 'Drive safely now, darling.' He grunted. 'Hmm! I can't even recall the last time she worried herself about me.'

After stealing a few minutes to enjoy a sandwich and a coffee, he headed off again.

His mind remained heavy with thoughts of the young woman who had been Connie's friend. It was strange how Connie never spoke about her.

Now, though, with the memory of a certain young woman ever strong in his mind, he found himself curious as to Connie's true nature.

Come to think of it, he hardly knew her. She was barely at home most days.

Pampered and lazy, she had hired people to run the house and gardens. He had never seen her pick up a duster or a frying pan. She even had the groceries delivered.

Their sex life was almost non-existent. From day one she assured him that she had no intention of having children: 'ruining my figure and puking up in the mornings with a belly the size of an elephant' was her view of having a baby.

It was like his eyes were suddenly wide open and he could see her for what she was: a wanton spender who never liked to get her hands dirty, and flatly refused even to discuss the possibility of a family. She was content enough to live life to the full while he was out, earning the money.

And for what? She didn't share his dream, or even his life. They merely shared a house, and the very thought of that house resounding to the noise of children absolutely horrified her. She had that choice, he understood that. But he also had a choice, didn't he? So, what about what *he* wanted, and why hadn't she admitted that she never wanted children before they rushed into getting married?

I am fond of her, though, he told himself. At times she can be funny and interesting. All right, we don't run into each other's arms after I've been away, and we don't have fiery passion, but how many married couples do?

When it came right down to it, he and Connie had rubbed along OK these past years.

Yet again, his thoughts swung back to Connie's friend, Ruth, and he felt sad.

Determined to clear his mind of past memories, he concentrated on the road ahead.

PART SIX

~

*Your Sins
Will Find You Out*

CHAPTER FOURTEEN

IT WAS GROWING dusk as Steve drove into Finchley High Road.

From there it was merely a five-minute drive to the tree-lined lane where he and Connie lived together.

As he turned into the lane, he saw the rear of Connie's BMW as it went up the drive. Slowed down by a taxi cutting in front of him, he turned into the drive just as Connie was closing the front door behind her. She didn't see him as he parked his car behind hers.

'Hi, there, Steve. Back from your travels again, are you?' That was James Walters next door, poking his head over the fence. 'Another concert, was it?'

'Not this time, James, no. In fact, I haven't performed in a concert for some time now.'

'Oh, I see. So, was it business of another nature then?'

'Sort of, yes.' Retired and regimental, the bloke was a bit of a nosy parker, but he meant no harm.

'Oh, I see. Good man! So, might I be curious, and ask what you've got yourself into these days?'

'Oh, this and that . . . but look, James, I'm sorry I've got to go. Catch up with my wife and all that. I'm sure you understand.'

'Oh, I do, I certainly do.' Giving a sly little wink, he tapped the side of his nose suggestively. 'A gorgeous wife like yours, who could blame you?'

When a shrill voice called out for him to, 'Come inside, James!' he went away at the double.

Thankful to be rid of him, Steve let himself into the house, where he went from room to room, searching for Connie.

He was just about to call out her name when he heard the telephone make an odd little ring. Curious, he picked it up, and was shocked to his roots at the conversation he heard.

He instantly recognised the voice of the man talking to Connie.

Don Mills was his new accountant, recently signed up on the retirement of a senior accountant who had previously taken care of Steve's fnancial affairs.

Astonished by what was being discussed, Steve continued to eavesdrop on their conversation, something he would never have done before. This time though, as the conversation deepened, he felt compelled to hear every word.

'Be careful, Don. We need to be sure we've covered every angle.' Connie was both excited and nervous. 'I don't relish the prospect of ending up in prison.'

'Don't worry, that won't happen. I know what I'm doing, and I've been extra careful. The fact that the bank would only forward money for Steve's big venture if both your signatures were on the document was in our favour. Added to which, the new house is officially jointly owned, thanks to your powers of persuasion.'

'Oh, I know how to get what I want.' Connie congratulated herself.

'And don't I know it!' Don went on, 'As you know, these past months, I've worked very closely with Steve. I've gained his confidence, I've made some suggestions, and I've managed to persuade him that they are in his best interests.'

He issued a word of warning. 'Steve is nobody's fool, and up to now, we've been fortunate, because he's been so tied up with this big project of his that I've discreetly managed to manoeuvre him in the right direction.'

Connie laughed. 'I always said you were too clever for your own good.'

'Don't let's get complacent, though. Steve is a sharp businessman. Normally he's ahead of the game, especially where finances are concerned. But juggling time, energy and finances is difficult at the best of times, and Steve has had a rough ride with all the travelling and meetings and worries about the project falling apart. Lucky for us, he has temporarily taken his eye off the ball, but it won't be too long before he smells a rat.'

'OK, I see what you're getting at, and I'll be careful. I'll be ready to move when you are.'

'Good! There are still a few tweaks here and there before it's all tied up, but on the whole we're nearly there. He'll be stitched up so tight, he won't even know what's hit him until it's too late.'

'Can he come after us?'

'He can try, but it won't do him any good, not when I've done covering up the trail.'

Connie was jubilant. 'We're a good team, you and me. I told you I could twist him round my little finger, didn't I?'

Don sniggered. 'You're a witch! You're planning to strip your husband to the bone, and you don't feel even the slightest twinge of guilt.'

'Why should I?' She felt a surge of loathing. 'I cheated to get him, and I cheated to use him for my own ends. I've never loved him. In fact, I hate it when he's even in the house. At this very moment he's headed home, and

I can't wait to get out. I'm only ever happy when he's away and I can meet up with you.' She gave a girly giggle. 'I can't wait to see you at the Markham Hotel this evening. I hope you've booked us a nice room?'

'Of course. The best room for the best girl.'

'I expect I'll have to be patient,' she reminded him. 'Don't leave any stone unturned. I need to make sure I take what's mine. I'm not going without what I'm owed. So, check everything twice over, because I don't want any comeback. I want it tied up so neatly, he hasn't got a leg to stand on. Stitch him up, Don, and I'll show you a life you never even dreamed of. All that . . . and me into the bargain.'

They laughed at that, before she reminded him again, 'Eight o'clock at the Markham. Be discreet. We don't want anything to go wrong at this late stage. It won't be long before we're spending his money in some beautiful, hidden corner of the world, while he's back here, starting all over again.' The thought gave her a great deal of pleasure.

Not for the first time, Don realised he must never underestimate her. 'I hear you loud and clear,' he said. 'And, by the way, remind me never to get on the wrong side of you. Remember, just play your part right up to the end. When it's time, make doubly sure you leave nothng whatsoever that can be traced back to you.'

'Oh, wait a minute!' His timely reminder jolted her memory. 'There is just one thing. It's a little parcel that's been tucked away for so long I'd forgotten I still had it. Don't worry, I'll sort it. It's always a mistake to keep trophies, don't you think?'

'For pity's sake, whatever it is, get rid of it now!'

'Don't worry, I'll do it straight away.'

Angry with herself for having forgotten that vital piece from her past, she replaced the telephone; so intent on her errand, she did not notice the small click as the downstairs phone was also replaced.

Horrified and deeply shaken at her betrayal, Steve climbed the stairs to confront Connie. He could hardly believe what he had overheard. It was painfully obvious that his wife and the trusted accountant were planning to pauper him, and had been planning it for some time. How could he have been so gullible? How could he not have seen what was happening right under his nose? His anger knew no bounds.

As he got to the top of the stairs, he could see partly into the bedroom and there was Connie, standing on a chair, reaching into the back of the wardrobe.

Intrigued, he crept closer, his instincts warning him not to show himself just yet.

Remaining just out of sight, he watched her as she drew a grubby envelope from the top of the wardrobe. Getting down from the chair, she opened the envelope and peeped inside. 'Time to get rid of you,' she said harshly. 'Time to wipe out the past for ever.'

When she made for the door, Steve dodged back.

Keeping her in sight, he watched her go down the stairs. He was nervous when she collected her car keys, coat and handbag from the hallway table, realising that if she went out now, she would see his car and know that he was inside the house. He stayed back and held his breath, reluctant to show his hand just yet.

A moment later, he breathed a sigh of relief when, carrying her belongings, she made for the kitchen. He then heard her go out of the back door.

Quickly, he followed, but he didn't go outside. Instead, he looked out of the window and there she was, walking down the long, winding path that led to the orchard. It seemed as if she was approaching the gardener, who was up the ladder, pruning back the top branches in an old apple tree.

After assuring himself that his house and car keys were in his pocket, Steve hurried out, closing the door behind him. Then he quickly started the car, taking a minute or so to take it round the cul-de-sac and park it where she would not see it.

That done, he ran back to the house, where he went inside and watched from the kitchen window. He saw her waiting impatiently while the old gardener painstakingly climbed down the ladder.

When the two of them walked away towards the spare land at the back of the orchard, Steve saw how they went straight to the pile of twigs and shrub cuttings, which were ready to burn for fertiliser. When Connie pointed to the pyre and was apparently issuing instructions to the old gardener, Steve realised with a sinking heart that her intention was to burn the envelope.

Too late! The old gardener struck a match and, throwing it onto the pyre, he set it alight. Connie threw the envelope into the flames, and then she turned and went out of the side gate, round to her car at the front, and was soon away.

Frantic, Steve ran down the garden, shouting and yelling for the old gardener to douse the fire.

'It's all right, sir,' the old man said, 'it's not catching hold properly. Some o' the branches are still wet from yesterday's downpour.'

Greatly relieved, Steve grabbed a branch from the pile and hooked out the smouldering envelope.

While the old gardener tried to get the fire burning, Steve took the envelope back to the house, where he opened it up.

He found a letter inside. It was addressed to him.

It was an emotional and beautiful letter, with the writer

telling Steve that she was carrying his child, and that she so needed to meet up with him, so they could talk about it . . . that though she would be sad and concerned if he didn't want to see her, she would try not to blame him. But that she really hoped he would want to see her.

The letter was signed 'Ruth'.

Shaken by what he read, he saw the name and his heart turned somersaults. He then dipped into the envelope again and found a photograph. What he saw took his breath away. It was her! Linking arms with Connie was the girl he had fallen in love with on the beach that night. He now realised that she was the same woman he had rescued from those alley thugs, and the woman he had seen going into the boarding house only yesterday.

He turned the photograph over. Written on the back were the words 'Me and Ruth at Blackpool Pleasure Beach'.

Dazed and excited, he read the letter again. Over and over, he read those precious words: 'I'm carrying your child.'

Slumping to the floor, he laughed out loud, then he sobbed as though his heart would break.

Saying her name over and over, he prayed she had not got rid of the child. 'Ruth,' he whispered lovingly, 'I have to find you.'

Clambering to his feet, he washed his face in the kitchen sink, then he went to the phone and called three companies. In the first two conversations, he arranged for the house locks to be changed, and the security system to be recoded.

He then rang the bank and authorised his accounts to be frozen, together with all or any transactions already going through. Also, he blocked any attempt to remortgage the house.

Being well known to the manager, Steve confided, 'You need to know that my finances are being compromised by my wife, and my accountant.' He made arrangements to go straight in and sign any relevant document or authority needed to change all his account numbers.

His phone calls finished, he turned again to Ruth's letter. Connie must have deliberately kept the letter back, so she could worm her way into his life and push Ruth aside. She was a cold, calculating woman, capable of stealing from him everything he had worked all his life to achieve.

Thankfully he had discovered the extent of her treachery in time, and he meant for both Connie and her accomplice to get their comeuppance.

Overriding all of that was his immense joy and excitement. On reading that letter though, his joy was tempered with regret and anger. He hardly dare even think about the possibility that he had a child somewhere.

Suddenly, his hopes were dashed.

When he'd taken Ruth back to the boarding house that night of her attack, there was neither sight nor mention of a child.

For now, though, it was enough that after all this time he had found his Ruth.

CHAPTER FIFTEEN

MARILYN WAS CONCERNED. 'Are you sure you want to go and see them?'

'Yes.' Ruth had thought long and hard about her decision, and it was only now that she felt strong enough in herself to face Tom's father and Casey. 'It's time to make my peace,' she said, 'if only they will let me.' She was nervous but excited at the same time.

'Do you want me to come with you?'

'Yes . . . and no. The thing is, I have to try and make amends for what I did, and it's best if I go on my own. But, I'm grateful for your offer, I really am.'

The older woman wished her well and saw her to the door. 'God bless.' Choked with emotion, she gave Ruth a hug, then she watched her go down the street.

It's taken a lot of agonising for her to go and see them, she prayed. Don't punish her any more, Lord.

She remained long enough to see Ruth out of sight, before turning around and going back inside.

~

Arriving in Blackburn, Ruth got off the bus and walked along Preston New Road until she came to Addison Street, where Tom's father lived.

The walk down to his house seemed never-ending. Eventually, she knocked on Bob Denton's door.

She could hear footsteps coming along the passageway. Then a large and friendly-looking woman, her pinny covered in flour, opened the door.

Ruth was nervous. 'I'm Ruth, Bob's daughter-in-law. I'd like to speak with him . . . if that's all right?'

'That's fine by me,' the woman said, '. . . only he's not here just now. He and the boy have gone to the churchyard. Being Sunday, they allus tek flowers up to . . .' Feeling uncomfortable, she paused. 'They'll not be long, I don't suppose.'

Ruth thanked her. 'I'm sorry to have disturbed you.' She glanced down at the floured apron. 'Seems I caught you in the middle of cooking.'

Sensing her discomfort, Dolly asked politely, 'Would you like to come in and wait for them?'

'Best not,' Ruth graciously declined. 'I just needed to talk with Bob . . . and Casey, my son.'

'Will I tell them you were here?' Dolly was at a loss as to what she should do.

'No, it's all right. I'll come back another time. Thank you all the same.' Disappointed after plucking up the courage to come here, Ruth reluctantly turned away.

As she started off up the street, Dolly called after her, 'I've got fresh crumpets and a lardy cake. You're welcome to share.'

'No, thank you all the same,' Ruth shook her head, smiled at her, and carried on walking.

At the top of the street she waited for the bus and quickly climbed aboard when it arrived. When no one was looking, she shed a few tears. She didn't know if she would ever find the courage to come back here again.

~

In the churchyard, Casey sat on the ground beside his daddy's little garden. 'If I talk out loud, will he hear me, Granddad?'

'I dare say he might.' Bent over the vase, the old fella was arranging the fresh flowers. 'Where's that bottle o' water, lad?' He held out his hand and the boy put the bottle of water into his fist.

Reaching out, Casey tenderly stroked the small marble headstone that marked the spot where his daddy lay. 'I love you, Daddy,' he whispered. 'I love you every day, and I say a prayer for you at night. Dolly says I might not see you on earth again, but one day I'll see you, only we don't know when.'

When his voice broke and he started crying, Granddad Bob took him in his arms. 'There, there . . .' He rocked him back and forth.

'I'm sorry, Granddad.' Sniffling, Casey wiped his eyes with the cuff of his sleeve. 'Only, I can't help it.'

'I know that. There's no shame in crying, lad,' he told him. 'They say it helps to heal the heart.'

'I'm all right now, Granddad.'

'Are yer sure?'

'Course I am!' He had to be brave.

After Granddad Bob had finished with the flowers, they went inside to put their pennies in the box and light a candle.

From her hiding place, Ruth watched them, heartbroken as she remembered that good man lying there.

'I'm sorry, Tom can you forgive me?'

Coming forward, she knelt by his side and told of her pain and regret, and the guilt at what she had done; how if she could turn back the clock, she would treat him right.

'I was wicked, and I know it now. I don't ask forgiveness for that because I don't deserve it. I don't deserve the boy's love either but, oh God! What I would give to have it all back again, with you and Casey.'

Surprising her, the old man's voice boomed out. 'Yer right! You don't deserve forgiveness. It don't matter what yer do now, yer can't ever make it right. You took my son, and you took this lad's daddy, and may you never in your miserable life be forgiven!'

Ruth stood up to face him. 'Every word you say is true. I know that now, and I'm ashamed of what I did. I'm ashamed that I hurt Tom. He didn't deserve that.'

When she now reached out to the boy, he slunk away behind his granddad's back. 'I'm so sorry, Casey, I truly am. I was bad, and I don't know why. But I do love you so very much.'

When her words were greeted with downcast eyes, she told Bob and her son, 'It's too late, I understand that, and I will always be sorry . . . for everything.'

She looked at Casey, who was nervously peering up at her. 'Even though neither of you wants me, I'll always watch from a distance. You're my son – I know you'd rather it wasn't true, but it is – and I want you back. But I have to abide by what you want, and if you send me away, I'll be unhappy, but I will understand, I promise.'

When he didn't answer, and she turned to walk away, the softest breeze got up to ruffle the boy's hair, and in that moment, in the turmoil of his young heart, he could hear his daddy's tender words, written in the saddest letter:

When you're worried . . . you might hear the softest rush of sound about you. It will be me, come to encourage and help you.

Suddenly he was running to Ruth, his arms wide open for her to pick him up. The old man watched in wonder as Ruth swung the boy up to her and gave him a mother's loving kiss, while tears ran freely down her face.

Looking over the boy's shoulder, she smiled at Bob, and when he nodded, she hoped she might be forgiven.

The old man gazed on the headstone. He spoke in clear, warm tones. 'It seems you've forgiven her, son,' he said, 'so it's only right that we should do the same.'

And in that precious moment, to their amazement, a strange and wonderful thing happened.

The breeze strengthened and, within the gnarled branches of an old beech tree, something fluttered and danced until, floating down, it landed at Ruth's feet.

The old man looked at it, and though the paper was mangled and dirty, there was something about it that turned his heart over; something that sent him back to when he opened his own letter from Tom.

'Look there, lass. Look down at your feet!' he urged Ruth.

Carefully placing Casey on the ground, Ruth picked up the fluttering object, her eyes open in amazement as she recognised it as the letter Tom had written to her . . . the letter she had discarded. 'It's Tom's letter. The day he was laid to rest, I threw it away.' The guilt was crippling.

Taking out her hanky, she tenderly dabbed away the dirt and damp, then folding the letter inside the hanky, she slid it into her pocket. She needed to be alone when she opened the letter.

Recalling how wicked she had been, she was tempted to bury it with Tom, right there and then, but that would have been wrong, 'It seems Tom wanted me to have it,' she said. 'He wanted me to keep it.'

'You will keep it, won't you?' Casey asked.

She assured him she would. Then she asked, 'Can I please come back to Addison Street tomorrow? We can talk things over, and I'll tell you where I've been.' Just now, she was overwhelmed with it all, and the need to clear her mind was pressing.

Casey slid his hand into hers. 'D'you promise you'll come back tomorrow?' It was easier to forgive her than he had thought.

Ruth nodded. 'Yes, I promise. I have so much time to make up with you all, and so much I need to tell you.'

Bob insisted on accompanying her into town, where she caught the bus to Blackpool. 'See yer tomorrow then?' he called as she climbed aboard.

Casey waved until she was out of sight.

~

Later that evening, after they'd had their tea, Marilyn and Ruth were working on a difficult jigsaw puzzle, while Marilyn listened to all that Ruth had to tell her. When there came a knock on the door, they were surprised.

'Who can that be?' Marilyn got up to answer it. 'I'm not expecting anybody, are you? Unless o' course Miss Partridge has forgotten her key again.'

'No, I'm not expecting anybody,' Ruth said.

She was bent over the puzzle when Marilyn returned some time later with Steve in tow.

'There's someone to see you.'

When Ruth looked up and realised who it was, she didn't know what to do. 'What do you want from me?' Remembering how he had deserted her, she felt desperately insecure.

When he stepped forward, the older woman made herself scarce. 'I've got things to do upstairs,' she lied. 'And you need to mind your manners, lady.' She winked at Ruth. 'We have a visitor. He's come a long way to see you. I wouldn't be at all surprised if he was ready for a cuppa tea.'

Having spoken her mind, she disappeared upstairs, leaving Ruth flummoxed as to how she should deal with Steve. 'I don't want you coming here reminding me of those awful men who attacked me.' She told him bluntly. 'Why are you here?' She knew well enough, though, why he was there.

Steve ignored her questions and walked towards her. 'You know why I'm here, don't you, Ruth? And now, thanks to your landlady, I know who you are and I'm so glad I found you.'

Taking the envelope out of his pocket he deliberately placed it over the puzzle. 'Connie had this. She deceived you. She deceived both of us, because I never got your letter. She lied to you and she lied to me. She told me you were back with an old boyfriend and were about to get married.'

Ruth was shocked. 'She told me you called me names and said I meant nothing to you . . . that I was trying to put some other man's child on you. I wasn't, though. Casey is your son. There are other things you should know too, about the good man who raised him.'

'I do know . . . all of it,' Steve revealed. 'And I understand.'

'That night we spent together on the beach . . .' His voice trembled '. . . I loved you then, only I didn't even know it. I've loved you every minute of every day since. I would have tried to look for you, but I thought you were happily married to that boyfriend and had forgotten all about me.'

'So, did you never marry?'

'I did, yes.'

Unwillingly, he told her how Connie had wormed her way into his life. 'That's why she didn't want me to know about you and the baby,' he explained. 'She had her sights set on the good life, and we sort of rushed into marriage, though it was a huge mistake . . . at least for me. Now it's well and truly over.'

Taking her by surprise, he cupped her face in his hands, and kissed her, long and hard. 'We were meant to be together, Ruth,' he whispered, 'We both know that.'

Ruth was lost. She didn't know how to deal with this moment, a moment she had waited for since they'd first met. 'There's a lot you need to know,' she warned him. 'There are many things to be taken into consideration . . . mainly for Casey's sake.'

'I know, and I'm ready to listen.'

Ruth looked into his eyes, and saw the truth shining there. She felt his arms around her, and she knew this was where she belonged. Where she had always belonged.

Having watched from the bottom of the stairs, Marilyn swept in. 'I reckon I might go out and leave you two to talk, would you mind?'

And no, they didn't mind at all.

CHAPTER SIXTEEN

Two months later, Connie and her accomplice were arrested.

They were fortunate to escape gaol sentences; but only because Steve had found out their intentions in time to stop any actual funds from being tampered with. As it was, the accountant lost his job and his credibility, and each of them received a crippling fine.

~

By the following summer, Steve's divorce had come through.

Two weeks later, he and Ruth were married, with Casey as pageboy and Granddad Bob as best man. Proud and upright, he carried out his duties like a true soldier.

Both Marilyn and Dolly were maids of honour.

'I feel like a princess in my pink dress,' Dolly said.

Marilyn told her not to be so vain. 'We're just two old birds dressed up like candy floss . . . but don't tell Ruth I said that.' Although, just like Dolly, she was thrilled to be maid of honour.

Eight months after the wedding, Steve and Ruth became

the proud parents of a daughter, whom they named Mary.

'We don't waste much time waiting for paper approval, do we, eh?' Steve laughed.

'It must be that beach,' Ruth said. 'It's magic.'

'Well, whatever it is, it'll do for me.' Steve was now a happy man. He had the family he'd always wished for. But he was even happier when little Mary was followed by a son, who was named after Steve's late father, Edward.

Steve had been thrilled and amazed when Ruth had introduced him to Casey, his son – the child genius he had heard so memorably playing in Blackburn market. It was now evident that Casey had inherited his astonishing talent from his natural father and the two of them grew ever closer. The boy Casey never forgot Tom, the man who raised him. That wonderful man, who had nurtured Casey's gift of music and who had taught him how to respect and appreciate the good and worthwhile things in life.

In the following year, Steve recruited the best music tutor in the North-West to hone Casey's natural talents.

Granddad Bob went along to the lessons 'to keep the lad on his toes', as he informed anyone who would listen.

For Steve, the road had been long and arduous in pursuit of his dream, but now, three years on, the studio project was a reality, and the opening celebrations were planned with great enthusiasm.

Casey was the star turn on the official opening night, and he gave the solo performance of his life. Hundreds of people got to their feet and cheered, clapped and called for more.

Proud and tearful, Ruth uttered a little word for Tom. 'He's playing for you,' she said tearfully. 'Whenever he plays, or sings, he'll be doing it for you. I'm sorry for what I did.' Hurting that good man was the biggest regret of her life. 'Rest easy, Tom, and forgive me . . . if you can.'

Later, when the excitement had died down, Steve took Casey aside and told him that his future as a recording artist was assured.

'I wish my dad could have been here,' Casey said tearfully. 'He would have been so proud.'

'Oh, but he's watching you from somewhere up there,' Steve put an arm about his son. 'He's proud of you. We're all proud of you.'

Long ago, when Steve had first re-entered her life, Ruth had asked him, 'How do you feel about Casey not wanting to call you Dad?' Casey had expressed his feelings on that.

'I'm not hurt, if that's what you mean.' Steve had thought long and hard about it. 'Casey and I have talked it through, and I'm happy to go along with his wishes. The way I see it is this: there is no way we can take away what he had with Tom. I am his biological father, but Tom was the man who raised him; who shaped his good values, and taught him everything he knows. I'm proud of Casey, my first-born son, and he knows I'm here if ever he needs me.'

Now, grabbing hold of her, and full of excitement over the success of the opening, he kissed her long and hard. 'The thing is, my beautiful woman, I am a very lucky man. I have a daughter, two sons, and my heart is at peace. I'm proud of Casey, and I'm proud of my whole wonderful family. A family man – that's what I am now. Whatever happens with the studio, I'll have what I've always wanted right here.'

The following year, they threw a big family party to celebrate Casey's rising star in the world of music. They held the event in their new home at Lytham St Annes, where from their bedroom window they could follow the curve of the beach that stretched to neighbouring Blackpool.

After the party, when little ones were sleeping and the family were chatting with friends in the garden, Steve and Ruth strolled along the beach, hand in hand.

'It's been a long and winding journey, hasn't it?' Ruth asked.

'You could say that, but we found our pot of gold at the end of it, didn't we?'

'We did, my darling, we did.'

When Steve ran on, teasing and urging her to catch him, Ruth looked up at the night skies, and for a moment she felt the strength of Tom's presence. Then, in the blink of an eye, he was gone.

'Good night, Tom,' she whispered, 'and thank you.' She hoped he would understand.

So in love, and with so much still to look forward to, Ruth and Steve lay down, right there on the beach, with the stars twinkling overhead. Two lovers, snuggled together on this magnificent, lonely beach.

Just a heartbeat away from where the story first began.

Q&A

With Josephine Cox

1) When you write your books, do you draw from real life?

I am definitely a people person. When writing my stories, I always draw from real life. All my characters are based on real people, who I've grown up with or met over the years. I've been known to include characters I don't know, but might overhear talking on a train or bus. If I find them interesting, I have to take them home and write them into my story.

2) You write really emotional storylines – do you feel connected to your characters?

In order for a story to touch the reader, it has to reflect real life, and real life has real emotions. I put my characters in real-life situations, so the emotions are paramount. When I write, I write the story with them. If they cry, I cry, and if they're laughing, I'm happy too. You cannot write emotion into a character and not feel it yourself. If you don't feel what they feel, the story will not have a heart.

3) Lots of your books are about extraordinary moments in people's lives – do you have any extraordinary moments that inspire you?

It would fill a hundred books if I was to write about the extraordinary moments I have experienced in my life. Each and every book I write has some element of my own experience at certain points in my life, be they good, bad, terrifying or amazing.

4) What do you love reading for pleasure?

I read anything on any subject that interests me. My all-time favourite story-teller is Charles Dickens – he brings his stories alive, and his characters are timeless, which is why he is still revered today.

5) Do you have a routine when you are writing, or is every day different?

I write seven days a week. I always start my writing round six am. I stop around nine am to have my cornflakes, and work on for another four hours. Then I take a half-hour break and work on, until late evening.

That is my planned routine, but if I'm lost in the story and racing along it often changes. Sometimes I work without a break for several hours. If after that I'm in a scene which excites and draws me on, I can work until my eyes are closing and I have to stop.

Often, when the story is character-driven and has me in its grip, I can't let go. When that happens, I have been known to work through the night.

I absolutely love writing. I love being with my characters, and when I finish that last page, I feel a great sense of loneliness, because all my new friends are gone. But then I'm starting a new story, and all is well again.

Thanks to all of you for loving my stories as much as I do, I consider myself to be a very lucky person.

(I'm off now, to bring in a new character who has kept me awake all night.)

Much love,

Jo x

Jo Cox

Midnight

**All his life, Jack has been crippled by
nightmares he does not understand.**

Jack's relationship with his girlfriend Molly is being
torn apart by the bad dreams that haunt him, drawing
him back to a place where it is always midnight.
Realising that Jack is being driven close to the edge,
Molly urges him to seek help. And, with their
relationship faltering, Jack decides to hunt for answers.

Returning to the streets of his troubled childhood, Jack
finds himself among the people he had known and
trusted as a child, including the one person he could
always turn to. As events unfold, Jack learns the secret
he has spent a lifetime trying to forget. When the truth
is laid bare, neither Jack nor Molly could have
envisaged the shocking event behind the dark images
that have haunted him all these years...

ebook • audio

THE LONER

Home is where the heart is – but it's also
where the pain lies…

Young Davie Adams is all alone. Devastated, he flees his
hometown of Blackburn to escape the memories of the
worst night of his life. With little more than the shirt on
his back he sets off on a lonely, friendless road,
determined to find his father.

Two people are stricken by his departure – Judy, his
childhood friend who is desperate to reveal a secret
she has kept close to her heart for so long, and Joseph,
his grandfather, who is racked with guilt
about that fateful night.

Exhausted and afraid, Davie finds friendship and
a place to stay but when fate deals him another
disastrous blow, he must decide whether to keep
running or return to face his demons…

SONGBIRD

Madeleine Delaney, holds a dark and dangerous secret, one that she has carried with her for over twenty years …

Madeleine is the star of the show at the Pink Lady Cabaret Bar. Her angelic voice and striking looks capture the hearts of many. But she only has eyes for club owner, Steve Drayton, a devastatingly handsome but terrifying man.

Then one night, she witnesses a horrific crime and her life is irrevocably changed forever. The kindness and friendship of one girl, Ellen, rescues Madeleine. But in order to survive, they must flee London, leaving those they dearly love behind, and danger is following them wherever they go …

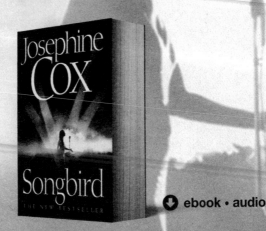

JOSEPHINE COX

Songbird

THE NEW BESTSELLER

ebook • audio

BORN BAD

Harry always knew he would go back one day …

Eighteen years ago he made a decision that drove him from the place he knew and loved. In those early years he carved out a life for himself, and somehow, he had found a semblance of peace.

Every waking moment during those long aching years he was haunted by what happened when he was a boy. He had never forgotten that warm, carefree girl with the laughing eyes.

For Judy Saunders, the pain of her past has left her deeply scarred. Cut off from her family and stuck in a stormy marriage to a man she doesn't love, the distant memories of her first love are her only source of comfort.

Now for the first time in all those years, Harry is heading back and he needs to know the outcome of what happened all those years ago.

And most importantly, he needs to find forgiveness.

ebook • audio

THE BEACHCOMBER

In the summer of 1952 two people arrive in
the pretty seaside hamlet of West Bay,
Dorset to start a new life.

Kathy Wilson dreams of turning the derelict Barden House into
a home free of the pain she suffered back in London. As the
summer stretches before her, she watches her cherished dream
take glorious shape – though she grows curious about the lonely
wanderer who strolls the beach below her window day and night.

His name is Tom Arnold. He also seeks refuge in West Bay,
needing a place to hide when the life he knew was brutally
destroyed by tragedy. Drawn to this aloof loner, Kathy feels a
bond forming that will radically change them both.

But the shadows and secrets that haunt Tom and Kathy will
not easily be dismissed. And as two wounded people try to find
the courage to open their hearts to love, the past threatens
their fragile new beginning …

JOSEPHINE
COX

THE
Beachcomber

THE NUMBER ONE BESTSELLER

LOVERS AND LIARS

In the sleepy Lancashire village of Salmesbury, childhood sweethearts Emily and John are secretly planning a life together when they are cruelly forced apart.

Already abandoned by her father, and unhappy at home, Emily is heartbroken when John leaves the village. Her life takes a devastating turn for the worse when she gives birth to a child. She dare not reveal the identity of the child's father or there will be a terrible price to pay.

Many miles away, John is trying to forget Emily and forge a new life. Having carried her in his heart for years, a chance encounter leads him to believe she has forgotten him.

Emily has never been able to banish thoughts of John. But when it looks as though history is about to repeat itself, Emily must put the past – and John – behind her and safeguard her daughter. But can she forget him?

ebook • audio

LIVE THE DREAM

Luke Hammond: handsome, rich, charismatic, cursed by private tragedy. Amy Atkinson: humble and kind with a good – but wounded – heart. When they meet by chance in a café run by Amy's best friend Daisy, a spark of love takes hold of their hearts.

But neither are sure that they can dare to love again. And what of Luke's public life, hidden from Amy? The owner of a large factory, he is a pillar of the community, married – though in name only. But Luke is also a sensitive and emotional man, whose greatest joy is retreating to his woodland cabin, nestled deep in the Ribble Valley, where he creates powerful paintings. Amy is torn between her head and her heart, but her sense of honour is paramount – and when she discovers his true identity, she is thrown into even greater turmoil.

Then disaster strikes the factory – and with it Daisy. Suddenly, the future looks troubled indeed …

THE JOURNEY

Three strangers are thrown together by chance. It's an encounter which is destined to change all of their lives for ever.

When Ben Morris comes to the aid of Lucy Baker and her daughter Mary, he is intrigued by the story behind their frequent visits to the local graveyard. Later, invited into their home, an old Edwardian place suffused with secrets of the past, Ben hears Lucy's remarkable tale – one she must tell before it's too late.

The story of Barney Davidson, his family and the part Lucy played in his extraordinary life, is one of a deep, abiding love and an incredible sacrifice, spellbinding in its tragedy and passion. And it still exerts a powerful influence in the present day …

The first in a two book story, *The Journey* is Josephine Cox at her mesmerising best. Spanning decades, generations and continents, it will stay with you for ever.

ebook • audio